HELL FOR HIRE

Tear Down Heaven: Book 1

Rachel Aaron

Series Info
Hell For Hire

Look for the rest of the series in 2024-2025.

Publishing and Copyright Info
Hell For Hire

Aaron Bach LLC
"Writing to Entertain and Inform."
Copyright © 2024 Rachel Aaron

ISBN Paperback: 978-19-523-67328

Cover Illustration by *Luisa Preissler*
Cover Design by *Rachel Aaron*
Editing provided by *Red Adept Editing*

Chapter 1

The massive black cat crouched inside his plastic carry crate, fluffy tail lashing with indignity.

"I can't believe you stuck me in the middle seat."

"Would you rather I carried you in my lap?" asked the black-dressed man sitting in the window seat beside him. "And keep it down. Normal cats don't talk, remember?"

The cat lowered his voice to an angry hiss, which wasn't much of an improvement. "I'd *rather* not be on this flying death contraption in the first place. There's no anti-falling ward, no safety charms, no magic of any sort! We're just hurtling through the air in a metal cylinder powered by explosions." He turned his green-eyed glare on the happy family sitting across the aisle. "I'm amazed there are any scalies left if this is how they travel."

"Don't be rude, Boston," the man scolded, though he was secretly wondering the same thing as he stared through the window at the summer clouds drifting far, *far* below. He'd lost his fear of heights ages ago, but soaring through the sky on a broom you controlled was a very different experience from being strapped into a much-smaller-than-advertised chair while scale-eyed humans he'd never met decided his fate.

That was the part that bothered him most, actually. Some of his sisters hated the magic-blind portion of humanity, but he'd always tried to be open-minded. It wasn't the scalies' fault they'd been born with blinders over their eyes, and the things they came up with to compensate for their lack of magic were ingenious. He'd been legitimately excited for his first airplane ride—at least until they'd left the ground and he'd been thrust face-to-face with the reality that his life would be in the hands of someone who couldn't see for the next six and a half hours.

"I'm sure it's perfectly safe," he said, as much for himself as for his cat.

"You could have at least sprung for first class," Boston grumbled, settling onto the plastic floor of his carrier with his paws tucked under his chest. "It's bad enough that we're having to travel this way in the first place, but what sort of self-respecting witch flies coach?"

"The kind who doesn't want to be noticed," the man replied, tightening his grip on the pointed black hat resting in his lap. "Now pipe down before you crack my Nevermind spell."

The people across the aisle were already starting to give him odd looks. The scales in their eyes kept them from seeing the delicate soap bubble of artificial unimportance that surrounded the man and his cat, but the witch could see the magic—and the cracks that were starting to spider across its rainbow surface—just fine. Fortunately, the captain chose that moment to announce they were beginning their descent.

The Nevermind spell seized on the interruption just as he'd crafted it to do, redirecting all the curious human minds toward checking their luggage, finishing their drinks, buckling their seatbelts, and anything else that wasn't the man and his talking cat carrier. Satisfied that he wouldn't have to fight a kick demon in the air today, the witch leaned back in his seat and gazed eagerly out the window for his first look at the city he'd gambled everything to reach—only to discover he couldn't see it yet.

Apparently, mechanical planes didn't go straight down like brooms did. Their descent was a long, slow coast, forcing the witch to endure thirty more minutes of white-knuckled anxiety before the winged tin can finally touched down, its wheels bumping so hard against the pavement that his cat carrier would have slid off the seat if it hadn't been buckled in.

"I am *never* doing this again," said the miserable voice inside.

The witch wanted to assure him this was the last time, but he didn't dare. Now that they'd landed, the scalies were everywhere, grabbing their carry-ons and hunching their bodies like sprinters at the starting line as they waited for the plane to finish its taxi. The moment the contraption stopped moving, they shot out of their seats, pushing one another out for a spot in the aisle despite the fact that the door wasn't even open yet.

It was clear foolishness, but the witch had to restrain himself from joining in. Now that the plane was finally on the ground, he wanted out of his cramped seat in the worst way. But patience was a core principle of witchcraft, so he blew out a breath and bided his time, waiting until the plane was nearly empty before he dismissed his Nevermind spell, tucked his pointed hat under his arm, and began unbuckling Boston's carrier.

"*Finally,*" the cat huffed as they stepped off the plane into the strange, collapsible hallway that connected it to the airport. "We were so close to death up there, I practically saw the Holy City."

"Pray to the Old Wives that you never see that," the witch replied, slipping his hand into the left side of his long black coat. The right concealed over a hundred pockets, each of which was spelled to jump to his fingers with a thought, but the left was for quick use items—wallet, phone, that sort of thing. It was quite full at the moment with all the documentation required for commercial air travel, but a little digging turned up the small, flat object the witch was searching for.

It looked like an old-fashioned flip phone made of solid gold. He'd determined it wasn't *actually* gold when the kobold-courier had delivered it last week, which was a bit of a disappointment considering how much the goblins had charged him for the privilege of carrying the thing. The phone wasn't what he was paying for, though. *That* came next, making him tremble with anticipation as he flipped the gaudy phone open and raised it to his ear to trigger the only call it was designed to make.

The phone rang twice, and then a voice as buttery and expensive as the metal the goblins treasured more than their souls whispered over the speaker.

"Hello again, Mr. Client. I take it you've arrived at your destination successfully?"

The witch glanced at the colorful "Welcome to Seattle!" advertisements covering the connector hallway's flexible beige walls.

"I'm here."

"Wonderful," the goblin on the other end purred. "Your purchase is already waiting for you at ground transport. Be sure to have your payment ready."

"Payment ready, *pah*," Boston scoffed from his carrier as the golden phone snapped itself shut, nearly taking the witch's ear off in the process. "You've already paid that green gouger a king's ransom."

"That was just the goblin's fee for setting up the deal," the witch reminded him as he slid the golden phone back into his pocket. "We still have to pay for our actual purchase. Now be quiet. I can't do a Nevermind while walking, and this place is packed."

The cat grumbled but didn't say another recognizable word as the witch began marching down the disembarkation tunnel toward the sunny, crowded airport terminal.

The next step was the riskiest part of their entire journey. Even deep inside their hidden forest, all witches had heard the chilling tales of lost luggage. The man followed the signs to baggage claim with growing dread, but his fears turned out to be for nothing. Since he'd taken so long to get off the plane, his luggage was waiting for him on the carousel when he arrived: an ancient-looking black steamer trunk with wheels screwed into the bottom, a metal security briefcase with a nasty curse etched into the locks, and, most importantly, his broom.

Despite the humans crowding all around him, the witch couldn't help a sigh of relief as his fingers curled around the smooth, familiar wood. Even by his high standards, the broom was a work of art: an arrow-straight piece of lightning-struck oak with a raven carved into the top of the handle and a fine cone of broom grass bound to the bottom. It was also extremely angry with him.

"I'm sorry," the witch whispered at the fury pouring into him through the carved wood. "You were too big for the overhead bins. I *had* to check you."

The broom's anger intensified as the image of a crowded, depressurized cargo hold forced its way into the witch's mind. The baggage handlers had thrown the broom in there like so much trash. It had nearly been crushed.

"Stop being dramatic," the witch scolded, pulling a leather carrying strap out of one of his spelled pockets and threading the broom's handle through the loops at the ends.

"You were crafted by the Witch of the Bones herself. Surely you can take a bit of rough handling."

The broom responded with a stab of ire so intense, the witch had to check his palm to make sure he wasn't bleeding.

"I know this process has been a trial for all of us," he said patiently as he slid the strap over his shoulders to secure the broom to his back. "But we *made it*. This is what we've been working toward for all these years! If we can't handle the airport, we might as well turn around and go home."

"We could, you know," Boston said, looking up at him through the holes in his cat carrier. "They sell tickets back to Massachusetts."

The witch's answer to that was to retrieve his pointed hat from where he'd stowed it under his arm and place it purposefully on his head. This plus the black coat and the broom drew some strange looks, but the witch didn't spare them a glance. He simply grabbed his wheeled trunk and secured the metal briefcase atop it. When he was sure the luggage stack wouldn't topple over, he picked up Boston's carrier as carefully as he could. Then, broom on his back, luggage in one hand, and cat carrier in the other, the witch turned on his bootheel and strode away, his long black coat swirling behind him like a cape as he marched through the crowds toward the sign that read Ground Transportation.

In an effort to streamline traffic and promote public transportation, the private car pickup zone for Seattle-Tacoma International Airport had been squished down to a mere thirty feet of sidewalk. Since it was eight a.m. on a

Monday, prime business travel time, the place was packed. Ten limos were crammed in along the yellow-painted curb, and their drivers had it even worse. They were huddled together like miserable penguins, desperately waving their paper signs with names written on them at every traveler who walked through the automated doors in hope of escape.

It was ridiculous. The cars might have been packed together like shingles, but there was plenty of room on the sidewalk. They should have been able to spread out as much as they liked, but none of the uniformed drivers would set foot on the other half of the pickup zone's yellow-striped waiting area, where two very different figures were standing: a towering man in a ripped-up jean jacket that barely fit over his massive shoulders, and a short woman wearing a gigantic pair of black sunglasses.

If anyone had asked the humans why they'd given the pair so much room, they wouldn't have been able to explain it. The scales over their eyes prevented them from seeing the foot-tall pair of black horns that rose from the woman's forehead like spires, but they still knew. Blinded or not, there wasn't a human in the world that would willingly stand next to a demon. A fact Bex was grateful for given how stuffy the summer morning was already becoming.

"I can't believe we finally landed a good job," said the giant man beside her, reaching up to polish his own horns, which were the same glossy black as Bex's but shorter, thicker, and with a more pronounced curve, like the horns of a bull. "A witch! And not just any witch, a *Blackwood* witch!"

"Not here, Iggs," Bex said quietly, adjusting the paper sign in her hands, which did indeed say *Blackwood*.

"Scalies barely tolerate us on a good day, and this batch is already looking jumpy." She flashed the huddled knot of drivers what was meant to be a reassuring smile, but they just shuddered and shuffled closer together, making her sigh. "I swear to Ishtar, if your hormones get a kick demon dropped on our heads, I am leaving you to get eaten."

"Relax," Iggs said, waving his giant hand at the crowds streaming across the access road to the towering parking deck on the other side. "We're at an airport. There're always weirdos at airports. No one's going to look twice at us, and I've got good reason to be excited. I mean, just *look* at this!"

He pointed at the back of Bex's sign where her thumb was holding the informational card the goblins had sent over when she'd agreed to this job.

Adrian Blackwood, it read, *Witch of the Flesh.*

"Of. The. Flesh," Iggs repeated, wiggling his eyebrows behind his own sunglasses, which were the same size as Bex's but looked much smaller on his enormous face. "Those are the *sexy* witches. The ones that are all about fertility rites and Beltane fires." His sharp-toothed grin grew almost giddy. "I hope she has a cat!"

"*Iggs!*" Bex snarled, swatting him with the sign. "This is a job, not a blind date. I don't care if the client shows up in a bikini. You will conduct yourself professionally, or I am never taking you on a pickup again."

"Okay, okay, geez," he said, shoving his hands into the pockets of his nearly worn-out jeans. "I was just having a little fun. Don't get your horns in a twist."

Bex rolled her eyes behind her sunglasses and turned back to the automatic doors, scanning the crowd behind the smudged glass for any sign of their witch. Felix, the goblin prince who'd arranged this job, was usually very punctual. The gold phone in her pocket had already chimed to let her know the client had arrived, so she didn't think it'd be long. Then again, Blackwood witches were famous for being technophobic hermits who never left their forest. It'd be just Bex's luck if their client had gotten herself detained by security for trying to slay the luggage carousel. She was pulling out her actual phone to check the port authority office's location just in case they needed to start this job with a jailbreak when she felt Iggs stiffen beside her.

"Oh, come *on*," he groaned in a despairing voice. "You've got to be kidding me!"

Bex looked up in confusion, and then a smile spread across her pale face.

A man was walking through the automated doors directly in front of them. He was tall and lithe with olive skin and thick, dark, curling hair that was barely visible beneath the wide brim of his pointed black hat. He was dressed entirely in black, actually, with a long, cape-like coat that swirled dramatically around his legs, a billowing black linen shirt, and perfectly cut black trousers that tucked into tall black boots, all of which looked custom-made just for him. He was strikingly handsome with his strong, dark brows, cut jaw, and quick, bright eyes that couldn't seem to decide if they were blue or gray, but that was to be expected. As Iggs had just said, Witches of the Flesh were the sensual ones. Bex hadn't realized they came in the male variety, but she'd worked too many jobs to let the surprise show on her face as she pulled herself up to what was left of her full height and waved her sign over her head.

"Adrian Blackwood?"

The man didn't reply, which raised Bex's opinion of him enormously. She couldn't believe how many of her clients gleefully answered to their names before they'd even confirmed that she was their contact. Maybe this *was* going to be a good job, because the witch didn't move any closer to her. He just set down his luggage and reached into his pocket to pull out a golden flip phone.

Bex did the same, handing her sign to a now very grumpy-looking Iggs as she held out her own golden phone.

The witch's eyes lit up when he saw it, and a dazzling smile spread across his face as he finally stepped across the sidewalk to tap his phone against hers. Both devices shivered when they made contact, and then the gold melted together, shifting and stretching until they were each holding one end of an old-fashioned paper contract.

"Identity confirmed," Bex said, giving the witch what was supposed to be a confident, professional smile. It was hard to tell with humans, but this one must have dealt with demons before, because he smiled back with genuine relief.

"Pleasure to meet you."

Bex jerked at his voice. Not because of the power lurking inside it—she'd expected nothing less from a Blackwood witch—but because of how different it sounded. Most of the clear-eyed humans she dealt with were either sorcerers or warlocks who got their magic from chugging quintessence. Consuming all that raw power left their voices ragged and sharp, but this man's voice was as warm and rich as a summer evening. It was so unexpectedly pleasant, she actually got lost in it for a moment. Fortunately, the witch didn't seem to notice.

"I'm Adrian Blackwood," he said, putting down his cat carrier so he could shake her hand without letting go of his end of the contract. "This is Boston, my familiar." He nodded down at the carrier, which growled. "Are you my security?"

"We are," Bex replied, snapping herself into business mode. "I'm Bex, and this is Iggs." She pointed at the giant demon beside her, who was still glaring at Adrian as if his being a male witch was a personal insult. "The rest of my team is waiting off-site. I'll take you to meet them as soon as we finalize the agreement."

"Of course," Adrian said, leaning in to read the golden parchment they were both holding, which boosted Bex's opinion of him yet again. *Finally*, someone who actually read the damn contract before they signed it. Felix was her most reliable fixer, but he was still a goblin, which meant he was as trustworthy as a false-bottomed box. Bex had already read the contract twice when he'd sent it over, but this copy was the one that would actually become binding, so she read it again, tracing her black-nailed finger along the lines of tiny text to make sure she didn't miss a word.

The contract had a lot of them considering how simple the job was. Adrian Blackwood was hiring Bex and her team to provide security for one month. Bex had no idea why a witch of his caliber needed security. Even the Eternal King Gilgamesh didn't mess with the Blackwood, and he'd stomped out practically every branch of independent magic left in the world. If Adrian wanted extra muscle badly enough to go through the goblins, he must be either very rich or *very* in trouble.

Both possibilities were fine with her. Bex needed rich, and her crew needed trouble. Demons got destructive when bored.

Fortunately, it looked like Felix had decided not to screw them over this time. Every word of the contract was exactly as she remembered. The witch must have also been satisfied, because he pressed his thumb to the signature line the moment his eyes reached the bottom of the page, not even wincing when the contract bit him for the blood that would seal the deal. When he turned to watch Bex do the same, though, she kept her free hand firmly at her side.

"Payment first."

He arched one of those dark eyebrows but didn't complain. Just reached down to unhook the metal briefcase from the top of his luggage, which appeared to be an old steamer trunk someone had screwed wheels onto. That struck Bex as an odd choice, but when he undid the locking curses and opened the briefcase to show her what was inside, all other thoughts fell away.

The case was filled with packing cotton, and nestled inside the white tufts like robins' eggs were four glass bottles of the bluest, most beautiful water Bex had ever seen. Even in the glaring light of the summer morning, they glowed like blue fireflies. She already knew they were the real thing, but she reached down to touch one anyway, closing her eyes as the soothing cool seeped through the thin glass into her skin.

"Those were very hard to come by."

The witch's voice made her jump, and she looked up to see him peering down at her.

"Water from the rivers of death is a powerful reagent, but I've never heard of anyone using so much at one time." He tilted his head like a curious cat. "What are you going to do with it all? Is it for a spell?"

"Demons don't cast those," Bex said, pulling her hand back.

When it was clear that was all she was going to say, the witch's smile turned sheepish. "Sorry," he said, closing the metal briefcase and offering her the handle. "Didn't mean to pry."

Bex took the case and handed it to Iggs. When the deathly water was securely in their possession, she turned and pressed her own thumb to the contract. The goblin magic bit her instantly, staining the golden page with her black blood. The moment both agreements were in place, the golden contract split back into two halves that instantly faded over their now empty hands, locking them into the hard golden manacles of goblin contract magic.

"That's that," Bex said, pushing her sunglasses farther up her nose as she smiled at her new employer. "For the next thirty days, my crew and I are at your disposal. Would you like us to take your bags, Mr. Blackwood?"

"I'll handle my own bags, thank you," the witch replied, leaning down to pick up his cat carrier. "And just Adrian is fine."

"Adrian it is, then," she said, motioning for him to follow her across the street toward the massive parking deck that housed all of the airport's non-limo transportation options. "Lys should already have our exit secured. Let's get out of here."

The witch nodded and fell into step behind her, looking over his shoulder at Iggs, who was sullenly bringing up the rear.

Chapter 2

Years of training kept the wonder off his face, but inside, Adrian Blackwood was falling over himself with curiosity. He'd assumed that, since he was working through the goblin princes, he'd have a goblin security team. He'd even brushed up on his card counting in preparation since goblins didn't respect anyone who didn't cheat at least as hard as they did, but demons were a total surprise.

He'd almost turned around and walked back into the airport when he'd spotted them. The only reason he hadn't was because both demons were wearing T-shirts that clearly showed the absence of any slave bands around their necks. Demons were famously good shapeshifters, but nothing could hide a slave mark. Since both their necks were clean, Adrian knew these must be free individuals not bound to any warlock. But while that was the only sort of demon he'd agree to work with, Adrian had no idea how they'd managed it.

King Gilgamesh had taken all demons as slaves when he'd conquered the Nine Hells five thousand years ago, and while the Eternal King's reach was more limited here in the living world, he didn't surrender his property lightly. Free demons were hunted on sight. Adrian would have been shocked to see one out in public, much less two taking freelance security work from goblins, but what really got him was that he didn't know what *kind* of demons they were.

Thanks to parts of his life that he didn't like to dwell on, Adrian was very good at recognizing demons. Even in their human disguises, the tells always showed through if you knew what to look for. Given his enormous size, Adrian was pretty sure Iggs was a war demon, but he had no idea what Bex was.

Since he was walking directly behind her, Adrian took the opportunity to gawk. She was very small for a demon, barely over five feet. With her pale skin and long, straight black hair, she looked more like a witch than he did, but her horns were like nothing he'd ever seen.

Demon horns varied wildly, but Bex's were enormous. They rose a good foot above her head, starting at her temples before curving up and out in two graceful arcs, like the horns of a gazelle. Their glossy black surface was slightly ridged but still looked smooth to the touch. The long length made them appear delicate, but both horns were an inch wide at the base, and the points at the ends looked sharp enough to stab.

How she kept horns like those out in front of normal, scale-eyed humans without getting kicked, Adrian had no idea. He was dying to ask, but after her quick shutdown over the deathly water, he didn't think that was a good idea. There was always the chance he'd find out later, but Adrian wasn't holding his breath. Four weeks was already a *very* tight deadline for what he was planning. If he was going to have a prayer of pulling this off, he needed to stay on target, so he pushed his meddlesome curiosity away and focused on not falling behind as Bex set a breakneck pace through the parking deck and up the escalators to the level where the taxis were waiting.

"Which one's ours?" Iggs asked, which struck Adrian as strange. Shouldn't he already know which car was theirs? But Bex was also scanning the cab line, her brows furrowing behind her sunglasses, which she still hadn't taken off even though they were deep inside the shady garage. He was about to ask if it mattered, since all the cabs were the same, when Bex's face split into a smirk.

"That one," she said, pointing at a yellow passenger van toward the back of the cab line.

That particular vehicle didn't look different from all the other vans waiting for customers, but as Bex led them down the walkway, Adrian noticed their target was rocking on its tires in a very... *suggestive* motion. He would have taken that as a sign to stay away—as a Witch of the Flesh, Adrian was magically and morally opposed to ruining anyone's good time—but Bex walked right up to the van and rapped her knuckles against the tinted window.

The cab stopped rocking the moment she brought her hand down. There was a short, awkward silence, and then Bex stepped out of the way just in time as a middle-aged man in a cab driver's uniform tumbled out of the front passenger door to land sprawling at Adrian's feet.

He looked like a perfectly normal human. Adrian could see the faint outline of the scales in the man's dazed eyes, but he didn't appear injured. Quite the opposite. He looked euphoric, his amazed face frozen in the biggest smile Adrian had ever seen. He was wondering what could have happened to put the driver in such a state when a second figure slid out of the front of the cab like a snake.

"Is this our little witch?"

Adrian shivered as the voice washed over him. He might not be sure what Bex was, but he knew this demon before he'd even looked at them. Sure enough, when he raised his eyes, a lust demon was leaning on the cab's open door, smiling at Adrian like the witch was the newest dish at a buffet.

"Geez, Lys," Iggs said, nudging the euphoric cab driver with his boot. "What did you do to him?"

"Opened his mind to new possibilities," the lust demon purred, running their long-fingered hand suggestively over the muscled chest of the beautiful male body they were currently inhabiting. "Trust me, his life is about to get a *lot* more interesting."

"So long as he stays too addled to care what's happening to his cab," Bex said as she walked around the van to open the sliding side door. It wasn't until she motioned for Adrian to start loading his luggage, though, that he finally realized what was going on.

"Wait," he said, looking from the demons to the pleasure-drunk man and back again. "We're stealing a cab?"

"Never go out the same way you come in," Bex replied in the voice of someone reciting an obvious truth of the universe. "Gilgamesh's lackeys are always watching the ports, especially airports. Doing things this way means we get the benefit of hiding in the human crowd without having to deal with actual humans. It's convenient."

"And it's *not* stealing," added the lust demon, who'd changed into a female body while Adrian wasn't looking and was now smoothing their new curly blond hair over their small horns, which rose out of the front of their skull in two light-colored points, like the horns of a young goat. "We're borrowing. Fairly, because it's not as if our driver hasn't been compensated for his time. I just gave him the best fifteen minutes of his life." The lust demon leaned into Adrian as they finished, gazing up at him with molten amber eyes framed by impossibly long lashes. "Want to see what I can do for you?"

"*Lys*," Bex said sharply, breaking the demon's hold, which Adrian hadn't even felt closing around him until it cracked. "Clients are not food."

17

The lust demon's perfect red lips pulled into a pout. "Spoilsport."

"Sorry about that," Bex said, picking up Adrian's luggage so she could slide it under the van's rear seat. "Lys is a glutton."

"Most lust demons are," Adrian replied, slightly embarrassed that Bex had had to save him. He was normally good at resisting things like that, but he'd been caught off guard, and Lys had been *very* quick on the draw. "Are all your crew demons?"

"Yep," she said as Adrian placed his broom carefully across the far back seat. He'd just finished strapping it in when he looked up to see Bex staring at him with a glare he could feel through her sunglasses. "Is that going to be a problem?"

"Not at all," Adrian told her quickly, opening the carrier to let Boston out. His familiar leaped to freedom at once, scrambling up Adrian's coat to perch on his shoulder. "I'm just surprised. I don't see a lot of free demons on my side of the country."

"You won't see many over here, either," Bex said as she took the metal briefcase containing the deathly water from Iggs and strapped it into the back seat next to Adrian's broom. "That's why we're hustling."

She shoved Adrian's empty cat carrier in next to everything else. When all the luggage was secure, she climbed out of the back of the van to the front and plopped into the driver's seat, which—thanks to her small stature— had enough headroom to accommodate her giant horns. Since this was the long style of passenger van, there were three passenger benches. The rear one was taken up entirely by luggage. Iggs was sprawled across most of the second while Lys had taken up residence on the bench

18

directly behind the driver's seat. Since everywhere else was taken, Adrian stepped over the cab driver, who was still sprawled boneless on the pavement, and got into the front passenger seat.

He was much taller than Bex, so he had to take off his hat to fit. Boston leaped into his lap at once, staying uncharacteristically silent as he watched the demons warily. By the time everyone was strapped in, Bex had the van started and was backing out, avoiding running over the blissed-out driver by inches as she pulled away from the cab line and started down the ramp toward the parking deck's exit.

"So," Iggs said excitedly, leaning over the back of Lys's seat so he could get closer to Adrian. Or, more accurately, to the puffed-up ball of black fur in Adrian's lap. "Is that your cat?"

"I'm his *familiar*," Boston replied in a scornful voice.

The whole van rocked as the Iggs jumped. "He can talk!"

"Of course I can talk," Boston snapped. "I'm a renowned magical expert and fully initiated member of the Blackwood coven. The only reason I didn't say anything earlier was because there were humans around, and I was respecting my witch's wishes not to get us all kicked."

"He's normally very talkative," Adrian agreed.

That comment earned him a set of claws in the thigh, but Iggs didn't look put off in the slightest. "That's amazing!" he said, leaning so far forward he was practically lying across Lys's seat. "Can your cat do magic too?"

"We do magic together," Adrian explained. "Witchcraft is much more complicated than just chugging quintessence and saying some words. Boston helps me manage those complications."

"I'm an invaluable assistant," Boston said, sticking his nose in the air.

"I'd appreciate it if you were a less obvious one," Bex muttered as they rolled past a family loading an entire cart's worth of luggage into their car. "We're still in the airport."

Boston rolled his eyes, but he quieted down, flattening himself onto Adrian's lap without audible complaint. Iggs returned to his seat as well, making room for Lys, who'd changed into a willowy male body tall enough to lean between the van's front seats.

"So," they said, propping their elbow on Adrian's armrest, "what brings a Blackwood to the west coast?"

Adrian was opening his mouth to answer when Bex said, "Not here."

"Come on," Lys chided. "We're in a parking deck. Even Gilgamesh isn't anal enough to spy on traffic."

"Taking a cab lowers our chances of getting spotted. It doesn't erase them," Bex said tersely. "We'll go over the details once we're safe."

Lys fell back into their seat with a huff.

Privately, Adrian agreed with Bex. Her code of silence seemed excessive, but free demons had a lot more to worry about than he did, and he *had* hired these people to be his security. A healthy dose of paranoia was exactly what you wanted from mercenaries being paid to watch your back, so Adrian dutifully kept his mouth shut, though he was surprised when the demons did so as well. He'd expected a lot more back talk, especially since Bex was so much smaller than the other two. In his experience, the biggest demon usually got the final say. Bex must have had something going on that he couldn't see, though, because Iggs and Lys shut right up, leaving them driving in silence

20

as they made their way out of the airport and into the grid of residential streets surrounding it.

Adrian was instantly lost. He'd gotten his driver's license because there were a lot of things he couldn't order off the internet without one, but he'd never done any actual driving beyond what was needed to pass the test. He'd also never been to Seattle. It was just as pretty as he'd hoped, all lush and green with the summer's new growth.

Since Bex hadn't said not to, he rolled down his window to get a lungful of the air he'd be working with. It didn't smell as much like the sea as he'd expected, but all the bays and inlets meant they were still quite far from the actual ocean. It was nicely humid, though, with plenty of sun. He'd arrived during the peak of growing weather, exactly as he'd planned. Adrian was congratulating himself on lining everything up so perfectly when Bex turned them out of the neighborhoods onto an industrial-looking street that ended in a parking lot surrounded by chain-link fence topped with barbed wire.

"Iggs," she said quietly, leaning back in her seat.

The moment she spoke his name, the big demon opened the van's sliding side door and whipped his arm out, almost like he was throwing something. A second later, Adrian realized there was no "almost" about it. Iggs had winged a rock at the security camera on the telephone pole just ahead of them. The stone went through the camera's metal box like a bullet, knocking the whole thing clean off its braces.

He did the same to the camera on the roof of the warehouse across the street, then to the one attached to a floodlight a hundred feet away. By the time Bex turned their "borrowed" cab into the crumbling parking lot, all the cameras that could have possibly seen them were lying broken on the ground, and Adrian had a newfound respect for the demon sitting behind him.

"Nice shots," he said.

Iggs beamed at the compliment, but Lys rolled their eyes. "Don't encourage him. If Iggs's head gets any bigger, it won't fit in the car."

"At least I do something besides cab drivers," Iggs snapped back, but Lys was already out the door.

So was Bex. Adrian hadn't noticed her move, but she was already leaning through the van's side door, hauling out their luggage like they were being hunted. She'd just reached for his broom when Adrian cried, "*Stop!*"

She froze, looking over her shoulder in confusion as Adrian undid his seatbelt and climbed into the back.

"Sorry," he said, reaching over the second seat to unbuckle his broom. "Bran is in a foul mood. I didn't want you to get pecked."

Bex looked skeptically at the wooden raven carved into the top of the broomstick. "A broom can peck?"

"Most definitely," Adrian said, swinging the broom onto his back by its carrying strap to free his hands for his trunk and Boston's empty cat crate. "Mine is usually good-tempered, but he's had a very bad day."

Bex didn't seem to know what to make of that, but she left Adrian to it, grabbing her metal briefcase instead.

"What do we do with the cab?" he asked as he set his wheeled trunk down on the parking lot's crumbling asphalt.

"Leave it," Bex said, slamming the door. "The cab companies have trackers in everything. They'll find it on their own in a few hours, by which point we'll be long gone."

Adrian wanted to ask, "Gone where?" but wasn't sure he'd like the answer. Despite the cameras and the razor wire, the lot they'd pulled into looked abandoned. A faded sign proclaimed it to be *Tacoma RV and Boat Storage*, but the only other vehicle was an ancient Winnebago that looked like it hadn't moved in a decade. He was telling himself this must just be a temporary stop to throw off any would-be pursuers when Bex turned and made a beeline for the RV.

Adrian's eyes widened in horror. *Surely not*, he thought. This *couldn't* be it, but Bex was walking right up to the Winnebago, the one with the peeling paint and the sun-bleached tires. She grabbed the bug-netted aluminum side door as he watched, hitting the plastic button on the handle to unfasten the latch before hauling it open and climbing inside.

"Where's she going?" he asked, slightly panicked.

"Home," Iggs said, giving him a little nudge. "Get the lead out, Mr. Client. Everything will make sense in a moment."

Adrian didn't see how any of this could possibly make sense. He didn't understand how he'd spent a *king's ransom* on a bunch of demons who got around in stolen taxis and lived inside an abandoned RV, but it was too late to complain. Iggs was already escorting him across the pavement like Adrian was a president in danger of being assassinated and the sun-faded Winnebago was Air Force One. Lys scooted ahead to open the screen door, waving Adrian inside with a sweeping bow as if welcoming him to their estate. Clutching his growling cat against his shoulder, Adrian stepped inside...

And wound up somewhere completely different.

"What in the Hells?" Boston cried from his shoulder.

Adrian couldn't have put it better. From the outside, the RV had looked like a relic: a twelve-foot-long beige-and-white box with faded paint, sagging tires, and rusted chrome trim. He'd expected the inside to be even worse, burning hot and rotting from years of neglect. What he got was... not that.

The room he'd just stepped into was twice the size of the entire camper. It still looked like a classic 1980s Winnebago. Everything was beige and built into the walls, the carpet was thick brown shag, and the couches were upholstered in fuzzy, yarn-like burnt-orange fabric, but the place was the size of a house. A *large* house with a full-sized kitchen, dining area, storage closets, and a heavy curtain separating the living space from the driver's seats up front. There was even a staircase in the back that went up and *down*, which shouldn't have been possible in a moving vehicle.

Adrian was still trying to wrap his brain around it all when the curtain hiding the cab was whipped aside by a large, wrinkled arm, and a cheerful voice greeted him in a thick midwestern accent.

"Heya there, Champ!"

Adrian whirled toward the sound, clutching Boston. Up in the RV's cab, an elderly woman was grinning at him from the wooden-bead-covered driver's seat. Her look was pure road-tripping grandma right down to her cargo shorts, "I lost my mule in the Grand Canyon" T-shirt, and red plastic sun visor stuck into her steel-gray curls, but she was most definitely *not* human. Adrian wasn't sure what she was, but he'd already started backing away.

"Don't worry about her," Iggs said, stepping around Adrian to flop onto the U-shaped padded bench that surrounded the RV's faux wood dining table, which was bolted to the floor with a gleaming chrome pole. "That's just Norma. She's our driver."

"It's a hoot and a half," Norma said cheerfully, her blue eyes sparkling like empty glass. "Traffic's a bear, but we keep on keepin' on. You gotta go where life takes ya. My daddy always said it was all about the journey, not the destination. So where're you headed, son?"

Adrian shot a confused look at Iggs, who made a "go on" gesture.

"Um, the Bainbridge Island ferry dock," he replied.

"A ferry!" Norma cried, her weathered face crinkling with what appeared to be real delight. "Now that sounds right pleasant. Here you go, kiddo. This is for you!"

She pulled something out of her pocket and handed it to Adrian. Not wanting to be rude, he took it, looking down to see a handful of hard candies in multicolored plastic wrappers.

"Thank you."

"You stay sweet," Norma ordered, turning back around in the driver's seat to start the RV's ancient engine. "Bainbridge Island ferry dock, coming right up!"

The curtain separating the living area from the cab snapped closed again the moment she announced their destination, leaving Adrian staring at a beige cloth wall as the Winnebago, which hadn't looked like it would ever move again, began to pull smoothly out of the parking lot.

"I'm sorry," he said, pulling off his witch hat to run a hand through his curly hair. "But what is going on?"

"You're inside a sorcerous construct," Bex explained from somewhere behind him.

Adrian turned around just in time to see her walking down the stairs at the back of the RV. The metal briefcase containing the deathly water was no longer in her hands, so he could only assume she'd gone to put it away. Gone *where* in this TARDIS of a recreational vehicle, Adrian had no idea, but he was dying to find out.

"We're in folded space?" he said, trying to look everywhere at once. "*That's* why everything is so big! This whole vehicle is a spell!" He turned to stare at Bex with new wonder. "How did *you* get a mobile sorcerous construct? I thought they were only permitted to loyal servants of Heaven traveling on King Gilgamesh's holy business."

"Usually," Bex said with a smirk. "This one was a bit of an illegal operation. A sorcerer made it in secret so he could road-trip in the style to which he was accustomed. Gilgamesh's cronies would've minced him for it if they'd known, but he was up to a lot of shady shit, including hiring us to steal secrets from one of his rivals. We did the job, but then the sorcerer made the spectacularly bad decision of not paying us, so we 'liberated' his vacation home as compensation."

"And Norma?" Adrian asked, pointing at the curtain cutting off the driver's cab.

"Another part of the construct," Bex explained as she slid into the bench seat next to Iggs. "A great and powerful sorcerer can't be expected to drive himself, can he?"

Adrian supposed not. "Is she intelligent?"

"Not really," Bex admitted with a shrug. "She can follow basic commands and make enough small talk to fool cops and tollbooth operators, but she can't carry an actual conversation or think for herself. The sorcerer loaded her up with all the traffic laws in North America, and so long as we keep buying updated road atlases, she can find her way anywhere. The only downside is she drives like an old lady, but it gets the job done."

Adrian nodded in wonder. On his shoulder, though, Boston was bristling.

"This is ridiculous," the cat declared, glancing up at the RV's twelve-foot ceiling. "How much quintessence does it take to run this monstrosity? And how have you not gotten caught?"

"It *is* expensive," Bex said, pushing her sunglasses higher up the bridge of her small nose. "But we acquire a lot of quintessence in our line of work, and we don't get caught because we're good."

"More like hyper-paranoid," the cat muttered before Adrian could shush him.

"Well, I think it's incredible," Adrian said, sliding his broom off his shoulder so he could take a seat at the table across from Bex. Lys had already made themselves comfortable across the entire back of the U-shaped booth, but this place was so big that he still had plenty of room. Incredibly, Adrian could feel the road vibrations through the cushions even though there had to be dozens of feet of magical construction between his body and the pavement. Truly, sorcery was a marvel. If it hadn't required selling his soul to Gilgamesh, Adrian would've loved to mix some in with his witchcraft.

"Can I have your grandma candy?" Iggs asked. "The strawberry ones are my favorite, but Norma's only programmed to give them to new people."

"Sure," Adrian said, setting the handful of hard candies he'd been clutching on the table.

Iggs reached for them at once, flicking aside the butterscotches and peppermints to pick out the red candies packaged to look like little strawberries. He'd made himself a tidy pile when Bex cleared her throat.

"Now that we're finally safe and on the move, let me introduce you to what you've paid for," she said in the crisp, commanding voice Adrian had started thinking of as her business tone. "Iggs and I are your physical security. One of us will be with you at all times when you're not in the camper. Lys is recon and acquisitions. They'll take care of all our information needs and keep an eye on your enemies. Finally, we have Nemini. She's our base defense and crowd control."

"Sounds good," Adrian said. "When can I meet Nemini?"

Bex arched an eyebrow and nodded at the space to his right. Curious, Adrian followed the motion...and discovered a woman sitting right next to him on the bench.

He jumped a foot off the cushions. Boston jumped even higher, scrambling up the orange curtains that covered the camper's tinted window. If the newcomer was insulted by their reactions, though, it didn't show.

Nothing did. She was very dark-skinned with a face that would have been lovely if it hadn't been so utterly blank. Her eyes were yellow-gold and slitted like a crocodile's, and her shiny black hair was coiled in an elaborate mass of braids on top of her head.

No, Adrian realized, peering closer. Not braids. Her head was covered in a nest of glossy black *snakes.* Each one was no bigger around than a pencil, their little triangular heads turning to look at him with beady black eyes.

He stared back, brain racing. His first thought was gorgon, but that couldn't be true. Even his Aunt Lydia wasn't sure if gorgons had actually existed, and she knew all of history. Also, there was no way he could be looking straight at a sister of Medusa and still be alive. But if she wasn't a gorgon, what was she?

Given the rest of Bex's company, the obvious assumption was demon. But unless they were hidden under her snakes, this Nemini had no horns. She also apparently had no presence. Since he'd blocked her in, she must have already been sitting at the table when he sat down, but Adrian hadn't noticed a thing until Bex pointed her out. Even staring straight at her now, it was hard to keep his eyes focused, but how could that—

Adrian's racing mind stopped with a snap as his face broke into a grin. "You're a void demon."

"Is that what they're calling me?" the yellow-eyed woman replied in a voice just as calm and expressionless as her face. Bex, on the other hand, was regarding Adrian with new wariness.

"How does a witch know so much about demons?"

"The answer to that has to do with why I hired you," he said, motioning for Boston to come down off the curtains. His familiar hopped back onto his shoulder reluctantly, wrapping his fluffy tail around Adrian's neck. When they were both in position, Adrian adjusted his broad-brimmed witch hat to just the right angle and turned to address his audience.

"I'm Adrian Blackwood," he said, looking specifically at Nemini and Lys, who'd been introduced to him only as "the client" so far. "Fully initiated member of the Blackwood Coven and fugitive from Gilgamesh."

That last bit was redundant. All witches were fugitives from Gilgamesh. The Eternal King allowed no magic that was not his own. Unlike the free demons in front of him, though, warlocks and sorcerers tended to look the other way around witches since they were human and made useful tools. Blackwoods especially got a free pass. They were the last major coven that Gilgamesh hadn't

29

crushed. They even had a special vendor permit with the Boston Anchor Market to sell their goods up the chain to the Holy City, Gilgamesh's capital inside Paradise. There were many reasons for this unprecedented leniency, most of which Adrian was violating by being here, hence his need for security.

"I'm going to be starting my own witchwood here in the Pacific Northwest," he told them gravely. "It'll be a fortress once it's established, but until the forest grows in, I'll be vulnerable. Your job is to protect me and my work until I'm far enough along to defend myself."

Bex tilted her head, her face inscrutable behind her dark glasses. "Protect you from what?"

"Warlocks, mostly," Adrian said, spreading his hands apologetically. "That's why I was worried earlier when you told me your team was all demons. I don't know how you feel about fighting warlocks, but—"

"You don't have to worry about us," Iggs said with a bloodcurdling grin. "We *love* beating up warlocks."

"They're slavers and slave catchers," Lys agreed, looking equally eager, and equally bloodthirsty. "It's a shame you already paid. If I'd known this was a warlock-killing job, I'd have done it for free."

"You say that now," Adrian warned, drumming his fingers nervously on the table. "But there might be a *lot* of warlocks."

"Better and better," Lys purred, leaning over the table. They were opening their mouth to keep going when Bex put up her hand.

"It doesn't matter who shows up," she said firmly as the lust demon slid back into their seat. "You paid for security. You'll get security. For the next four weeks, no one will touch you or your work. This is our contract."

She kept her eyes on Adrian until he nodded, and then she turned to Iggs. "I'll take first shift. You go get some food."

The bigger demon's face split into a grin. "Right-o, boss!" he said excitedly, shooting out of the booth the second Bex got out of his way.

Lys exited next, vanishing under the table only to pop up again right next to Bex. They whispered something in her ear, flicking from male to female then to male again as they spoke. When Bex nodded, the lust demon walked away, blowing a kiss to Adrian over their shoulder before disappearing down the stairs.

Nemini stayed right where she was, picking up a giant book from the bench beside her titled *Ley Lines of the Pacific Northwest: An Outsider's Perspective.* She flipped on the light in the console over Adrian's head and settled in to read, her snakes turning their heads in time with hers as she scanned the pages. Adrian was wondering what he should do when Bex touched his shoulder.

"Come on," she said. "I'll give you the tour."

"All right," he replied nervously, looking around at the suddenly empty room. "I'm sorry. Did I say something offensive?"

"Not at all," Bex assured him as she led him through the kitchen. "I cut things off because of them, not you. My team can get pretty zealous when it comes to killing warlocks. I had to break it up before they promised to work for you for free. Someone has to keep the lights on around here."

"I'm sorry you stopped them, then," Adrian said with a laugh. "Honestly, it's going to take a lot more than one month to grow an entire forest by myself, but I could only find four bottles of deathly water."

"Then we'll have to make sure you get your money's worth," Bex told him, leading him down the tiny stairs toward the RV's lower levels.

Chapter 3

Despite his effect on her crew's willingness to work for free, Adrian Blackwood was rapidly shaping up to be Bex's favorite client in years. One of the reasons she didn't take a lot of bodyguard jobs despite the high pay and perfect fit for her small team was because the only clients rich enough to afford their services were usually jaded sorcerers who looked down their noses at her black-market Winnebago, an affront Bex took *very* personally. The stolen construct was the best score she'd landed for her demons this lifetime and the closest thing they had to a home. If the only strangers she invited inside weren't people she was being paid to keep alive, she would have killed them for insulting it, but Adrian seemed delighted.

The RV had four floors in total. The ground level where the doors were contained their sitting area, driver's cab, guest bathroom, and kitchen, which they mostly used for winter gear storage since, Iggs's sweet tooth notwithstanding, demons ate emotions, not human food. The next floor down was the crew level, where Iggs, Lys, and Nemini had their cabins. The client suite was down here as well, and it was the largest by far with a full-sized bed, a private bathroom with the RV's only actual tub, and a fantastic window that looked straight out the front of the Winnebago. But while Adrian seemed appropriately impressed by all of this, he declined to put his luggage in the room, saying instead that he would provide his own accommodation.

"Are you sure?" Bex asked, more sharply than she'd intended. "I mean, we're your security, so you can do whatever you want, but it'll be a lot harder to keep you safe if you're not sleeping inside our defenses."

"I understand that," he said, cracking a delighted smile as he crouched in front of the tinted window to watch the Winnebago navigate the crowded highway. "But the whole point of coming to Seattle was to grow a forest, and I can't do that from inside an RV, even one as wondrous as this."

Bex didn't see how he'd be doing any gardening in his sleep, but the "wondrous" comment convinced her to let it slide. By the time she'd shown him the basement where they kept their bulk storage and the big weapon locker—which she made certain Adrian understood he was *never* to touch for the sake of his own survival—Norma came over the PA to announce they were in the car line for the ferry to Bainbridge.

"That was fast," Adrian said as he and Bex climbed the ladder back to the crew level.

Bex shrugged. "Norma's a slow driver, but she's an ace navigator. She can find shortcuts even locals don't know."

"Does she automatically navigate around traffic?" he asked, sounding genuinely interested. "You said you have to give her maps to keep her road knowledge updated, but do her decision-trees extend to reading traffic reports, or is she just—"

The rest of his question was drowned out by a flood of profanity. They'd reached the crew floor again, and, as usual, Iggs hadn't shut his door. Bex could see right inside to where he was lying on his bunk, his room lit up like a rave from the first-person shooter game he was playing on the 75-inch flatscreen he'd bolted to his ceiling.

"That's what you get, dick tumor!" he screamed, his tanned face bright red as he bellowed into the gaming headset he'd wedged behind his black horns. "Tell your mom to stop calling me, you spawn-camping son of a—"

Bex shut the door before any more could leak out. Iggs's tirade cut off like a switch the moment the door was closed, but not fast enough to stop Adrian's shocked look.

"Is that what you meant when you told him to go eat?" he asked, staring at Bex like she'd just revealed a wonder of the universe. "That's brilliant! War demons feed on conflict and chaos. Normally, they can only get that by fighting. It never occurred to me they could use a video game."

Bex winced when he said "war demon." Fortunately, her sunglasses hid most of it.

"We've learned to get creative," she said, stepping as far around the truth as possible without lying outright. "It's not ideal, but FPS gamers are a bottomless well of volatile emotions, and Iggs isn't a picky eater."

That was supposed to be the end of it, but Adrian still looked so delighted by everything he saw, Bex was starting to wonder how often he got out.

"We'll be on the ferry to Bainbridge in just a minute," she said, changing the subject as they resumed their journey up the stairs. "It's a thirty-five-minute trip across the bay, but there's an observation deck up top with chairs and stuff. Do you want to go out and look around?"

"I'd love to," Adrian said, sounding like he really meant it. "There are no Blackwood groves west of the Mississippi, so I've never seen this part of the country before."

The way he said that made Bex think the Blackwoods moved *only* among their groves. She'd never had a client who appreciated nosiness, though, so she kept her questions to herself. Adrian had already launched into a conversation with his cat in any case. Apparently, Boston needed to wear a harness to go outside with the general public, something he absolutely refused to do. Adrian was still cajoling him when they got back to the kitchen, so Bex left them to it and walked over to Nemini, who was still exactly where she'd left her: sitting at the bolted-down table, reading her book.

"Anyone follow us?" Bex asked quietly.

The snake-haired demon said nothing. Just turned a page. She never said anything unless something was wrong, though, so that was answer enough for Bex.

"Good work," Bex whispered. "I'm taking the client up top for some fresh air. Keep an eye on things."

Nemini didn't nod. She didn't move at all, but there was nothing that happened in the RV that Nemini didn't hear, so Bex left her to it. She stuck her head into the front cab next, looking through the windshield at the cavernous belly of the car-ferry parking deck Norma was pulling them into.

"Get a spot up front," Bex ordered. "I want to be first down the ramp when we dock."

"You got it, sweetheart," Norma said with her usual cheer.

Bex nodded and pulled out her wallet to stuff another twenty into the red plastic cup the construct used for paying tolls, fares, and parking fees. Petty cash topped off, she ducked back through the curtain just in time for Lys to nearly run her over.

"Where are you going?" Bex demanded as the lust demon threw open the camper's side door before Norma had even finished pulling into a parking spot.

"To get something to eat," Lys replied with a grin, transforming their hair into a blowout big enough to hide their short horns. "The tourists are in season!"

"You *just* ate," Bex reminded them, but it was too late. Lys was already bounding across the parking deck, switching to a female body in the gap between cars.

Bex was still watching them go when Adrian's voice spoke practically in her ear.

"Is Lys always so bold?"

She jumped and whirled around to see the witch standing right behind her, his tall body bent over to peer through the screen door.

"Sorry," he said, giving her a sheepish smile.

"It's fine," Bex replied sharply, furious with herself for letting him sneak up on her. How many years would it take before she remembered she had to listen all the time now? Her senses weren't half as sharp as they used to be, especially her hearing. She *had* to stay vigilant, which she did right now by checking Adrian's empty shoulders.

"I take it Boston wouldn't compromise on the harness?"

"Not a hair," he replied, glancing back at his cat, who was sitting on top of Adrian's luggage with a look of disdain so haughty that even Bex was impressed.

"Your loss," Adrian said as he climbed down the steps to the RV's side door.

"*Your* loss," Boston corrected, turning away with a huff to begin complaining loudly to Adrian's broom, which had yet to say a word in Bex's hearing.

"Sorry about him," the witch said as Bex followed him out into the cavernous enclosed parking deck that took up the ferry's lowest level. "Boston doesn't weather indignity."

"I imagine he's had a rough day," Bex said, glancing at the empty cat carrier before she closed the RV's aluminum door.

"He'll be much more civil once we're done traveling," Adrian promised, his gleeful smile returning as he looked around at the crowds of tourists getting out of their cars. "Where to?"

Bex motioned for him to follow her as she led the way to a steep set of rubberized stairs.

"Seattle has a lot of ferries, but they're all basically the same design," she explained as they climbed up toward the middle deck. "Parking on the bottom, observation platform up top, and a big main deck in the middle with an exterior ring for taking in the scenery plus an indoor area with AC and cushy seats. That's also where the café is, if you're hungry. You'll have to let us know when you want to eat. We don't mind being sent for takeout, but we're pretty bad about keeping up with human meal schedules."

"I can feed myself," Adrian assured her, bounding over to the railing to look out at the green water and the bright, sunny city that lined the bay.

Bex stepped beside him nervously. Now that the ferry's parking area was full, the observation decks were quickly filling up with humans. A swarm of people wearing Seattle Kraken jerseys had already crowded in beside Adrian to take selfies with the city skyline. One of them actually asked Bex to take their picture, which she did as silently and quickly as possible.

"Thanks!" the middle-aged lady said when Bex handed her back her phone. Then her made-up eyes went to Bex's tall horns. "Great hair, by the way."

"Thank you," Bex murmured, pressing her back into the railing to make herself as small as possible as the happy lady and the rest of her gaggle bustled away to take more pictures up by the prow.

"I wonder what the scales make them see," said Adrian, who was studying Bex's horns when she turned back around.

"I've never been brave enough to ask," Bex confessed, leaning on the railing beside him. "It always seems to be something different, though. One time, a guy was convinced I had a bird on my head. I nearly got myself kicked when he tried to shoo it off me and couldn't."

Adrian chuckled and returned his attention to the bay, leaning so far over the railing that Bex grabbed his coat to make sure he didn't fall in.

"Are there seals in the water?" he asked excitedly.

"Sometimes," she said, tightening her grip. "You don't normally see them this close to the pier, though."

He looked horribly disappointed as he slid back down to his feet. "You seem to know a lot about this place. Do you live in Seattle full-time?"

Bex let go of his coat as she thought about how to answer that. She wasn't used to clients being so chatty, and she definitely wasn't used to them smiling so much. Adrian had already turned back to the water, so she sneaked another look at him through her dark glasses.

To her surprise, he was worth the look. Bex didn't normally see humans as anything other than threats, but there must have been something to all that stuff Iggs was saying about fertility rites and Beltane fires, because Adrian

Blackwood was undeniably attractive. If she hadn't already burned herself out, she might have been in trouble. Not much could get her worked up these days, though, so Bex let herself enjoy the view, leaning against the railing so she could watch Adrian and their backs at the same time as she finally answered his question.

"We base out of Seattle a lot," she said, moving closer to make sure he was the only one who could hear her over the howling wind. "The local warlock cabal is criminally lazy, and Felix, the goblin prince who set up this job, has a lot of work that matches our skill set."

"He was very quick to answer my request," Adrian said, looking up at the cloudless blue sky. "But I have to say I'm surprised. I'd read that Seattle's famous rains are mostly a winter phenomenon, but I didn't think it'd be so clear. You can see all the way to the Olympic Range."

He pointed behind them at the wall of mountains lining the northern horizon like jagged blue-and-white teeth, but Bex shook her head. "You got lucky," she said. "The humidity and pollution normally hide more of the view, but we get some nice days in early summer."

Adrian was opening his mouth to ask another question when the ferry horn blared, drowning out everything else. The engines rumbled to life a moment later, churning up the green-brown water as the ferry pushed out into the Puget Sound. Tourists were everywhere now, crowding the upstairs observation deck and the railing Bex and Adrian were leaning against. The interior sitting area was empty since the weather was so nice, but Bex didn't think she'd be able to peel Adrian away from the view, so she led him to the back of the boat instead, where the crowds were thinner.

"So," she said, raising her voice over the roar of the turbines, "now that we don't have an overeager audience, I was hoping you could tell me more about what we're in for."

Adrian, who'd pulled out his phone to take pictures of the retreating city, shot her a curious frown.

"You said we might be facing a lot of warlocks," Bex clarified. "It'll be easier to do my job if I know how many and how soon."

"That depends on them," Adrian said, sliding his phone back into his coat.

Bex nodded, waiting for more, but Adrian had fallen silent, his dark brows furrowed beneath the wide brim of his pointed hat, which, though fluttering wildly in the wind, seemed in no danger of being blown away. Bex supposed that made sense for a witch's hat. Couldn't have it flying off when you were riding a broom, after all. She was wondering if he held it on with magic or if the hat was just really well fitted when Adrian finally continued.

"I don't think they'll come immediately," he said in a quiet voice, ducking his head lower so that he was speaking directly next to Bex's ear. "I was careful when I left. The warlocks are always watching our main forest in Massachusetts, but they can't watch everything. That's why I flew commercial, and why I went to the other side of the country." His face grew grim as his voice dipped even lower. "I'm sure you've guessed by now that I'm not exactly a normal witch of the Blackwood."

"I picked that up," Bex murmured, looking hard at his now very close face through her sunglasses. "I've met a few other male witches, but I've never heard of a male Blackwood."

"That's because I'm the only one," Adrian replied. "We had as many men as women up until a few centuries

41

ago, but when the witch hunt craze in Europe forced the Old Wives to move the Blackwood from England to the New World, they had to make a deal with the new warlock cabal."

He looked down at where his tanned hands were curled into fists on the white-painted railing. "King Gilgamesh outlawed all magic other than his own eons ago. That's why he put the scales in humanity's eyes. The blinders kept them from noticing what they'd lost, but children born in the Blackwood are different. Unlike every other human, we come into the world with open eyes. That early awareness means we can handle more magic than anyone not born in the Holy City. Unlike the denizens of Heaven, though, we're born into the *living* magic, which means we can stay on earth."

Bex nodded. All of Gilgamesh's approved magics required quintessence, a glittering substance that could only be made in Paradise and was only accessible through him. Doling out quintessence was how the Eternal King kept his sorcerers and warlocks in check, but as powerful as it was, the magic quintessence granted was unnatural. Using too much for too long made it impossible for humans to stay in the living world, which put a serious damper on how strong sorcerers and the like could become.

That was why Gilgamesh had spent the first two thousand years of his reign crushing every other magical tradition. Couldn't have magic stronger than your own running around loose. The Blackwood witches were the last and most notable exception. Bex had always assumed that was because they lived in an impenetrable magical forest full of monsters. From what Adrian was saying, though, it sounded like there was more to it.

"How did you keep Gilgamesh from crushing you?"

"Bribery," Adrian said in a frustrated voice. "And being too expensive to fight. Our coven invests every bit of magic we get into making sure that any war the Eternal King launches against us will cost him just as dearly. We're also the only producers of potions, magical cosmetics, and other luxury magical goods that are highly prized in the Holy City, which is why we're allowed into the Boston Anchor Market despite being heretics. But while these factors keep Gilgamesh from sending his princes to burn the Blackwood to the ground, they don't protect us when we're outside our forests. For that, we have a complex network of agreements with local officials, one of which requires that every boy born in the Blackwood be apprenticed to the New England warlock cabal."

Bex jerked away like she'd been burned. "You were a warlock?"

"No," he said, baring his teeth. "*Never.* I hate them."

"How did you get out?" she asked, settling back into position next to him. "Were you not born in the Blackwood?"

"I was born in its heart," Adrian said proudly. "My mother is also a Witch of the Flesh. Children of the Blackwood don't have to become witches, but from the moment I saw her magic, it was the only thing I wanted to do. If I'd been born a girl, I would have been apprenticed to her as soon as I could be trusted not to fall into the cauldron, but I was a boy. They still taught me witchcraft because I refused to learn anything else, but the day I turned thirteen, I was handed over to the New England cabal to start my apprenticeship."

Bex frowned. "I thought you said you weren't a warlock?"

"I wasn't," Adrian said vehemently. "I ran away my very first week and every week after that. No matter how many times they punished me or beat me or locked me up, I kept escaping and running back to the Blackwood. This went on for six months before my mother decided she'd had enough and told the warlocks I wasn't going back."

"She could do that?" Bex asked, surprised.

Adrian nodded gravely. "My mother is very powerful. She's the only one who could have done it, but while the warlocks couldn't force me to return without fighting the entire Blackwood, they didn't let it go. They've been harassing my coven ever since, locking down our borders and taking shots at every witch who steps out of the trees. They can't bother us at the Anchor Market because the denizens of Heaven still demand our crafts, but they can and do make our lives miserable everywhere else."

He turned and looked at her with a determined glare. "My decision not to be a warlock made my entire coven's life hell. That's why I'm here. The warlocks' quarrel is with me, not my family, so as soon as I finished my apprenticeship and became a fully initiated witch, I started preparing to make my own grove as far away from the main Blackwood as possible. I would have gone across the ocean if I could, but the roots of all the groves still have to reach each other. Seattle was as far as I could get without breaking the connection, so here I am."

Bex smiled. "You're going to fight them."

"I'm going to try," Adrian said, gazing down at the water. "I embarrassed a lot of powerful men when I chose witchcraft over their cabal, and warlocks don't take blows to their pride lightly. Seattle is a long way from Massachusetts, but the New England cabal is the biggest in the country. They can swing a *lot* of force when they want to, and they're going to swing it all at me as soon as they realize I'm finally outside of the Blackwood's protections." He looked back at Bex with a wince. "I'm sure that's not what you wanted to hear."

"I wouldn't say that," she replied with a shrug. "As you might have noticed earlier, killing warlocks makes my crew pretty happy."

"I could tell," Adrian said, his smile returning. "You must be very good at it. I've never seen so many free demons moving around together in the open, much less running a business."

"There's more of us than you might think," Bex assured him. "My team is just flashy."

She thought he'd roll his eyes at that, but for some reason, his smile got wider. "You freed them, didn't you?" he said excitedly. "That's why they follow you."

"They follow me for a lot of reasons," Bex replied, dropping her eyes even though he had no way of seeing them through her dark lenses. "And I haven't freed nearly as many as I should."

"Any is still a number to be proud of," Adrian argued. "I spent as little time as possible with the warlocks, but I was still there long enough to see what they do. They're Gilgamesh's slave catchers. They bind demons by their true names and use them to hunt down any of their own kind who manage to escape the Hells. They're paid in quintessence for every demon they bring back, which means their magical power is tied to how many fugitives they can catch. I've seen the lengths warlocks will go to in order to recapture even one free demon. I can't imagine what you've had to put up with to keep your demons safe, especially since you all seem to be so old."

"We're not *that* old," Bex said with a nervous laugh.

Adrian gave her a skeptical side-eye. "You have a lust demon who can change their shape in a blink and a void demon, which are supposed to be extinct. Catching either of those would make a warlock's career, and that's not even counting you and Iggs. I'm not going to pry further than that, but you can't tell me you're not at least a thousand."

"I won't, then," Bex said, dropping the subject like a hot coal. "I'm just glad you're so confident in our abilities."

"I have to be," he said, turning his head to look at the green mass of the island the boat was slowly approaching. "This is what I've been training for my entire life. I'm the best I could possibly make myself. If you're the best, too, then we've got a real shot at this, but it's still going to be a *very* high bar. Unlike sorcery and demon binding, witchcraft takes time. There's no amount of skill or magic that can grow a forest overnight. Even with your help, if the warlocks find me before I'm ready, this might be a very short job." He shook his head with a self-deprecating smile. "Good thing I paid you in advance, huh?"

"Don't write us off too soon," Bex told him with a smile of her own. "My team's pretty good at staying alive, and being on an island gives us the advantage." Her smile transformed into a predatory grin. "Warlocks don't like places they can't run away from."

Most humans flinched when she did that, but the Blackwood must have been a terrifying place to grow up, because Adrian just grinned back.

"You've sold me," he said, pushing off the railing. "Let's get back to the RV. I want to be ready to drive out the second we land."

Bex motioned for him to lead the way, jogging to keep up with his long legs as Adrian strode through the swirls of scale-eyed tourists back to the stairs that led to the parking area.

Chapter 4

Given Lys's comment about tourist season, Bex was worried she'd have to go looking for them, but the lust demon was sitting in the passenger seat next to Norma when she and Adrian got back to the RV. The witch immediately started gathering his belongings and talking to Boston, so Bex took her chance to join Lys up front.

"How was your meal?" she asked, squatting in the gap between the cab's throne-like seats.

"Delightful," the lust demon replied, trading out their lanky male body for a petite female one so they could flop their legs over the armrest without kicking Bex in the face. "How was the witch?"

"We're in for a fight," Bex reported. "He pissed off the New England cabal personally, and you know how hard warlocks roll when their pride's on the line."

"That wasn't what I was talking about," Lys said, wiggling their perfect eyebrows. "Surely even you're not immune to a famous Blackwood Witch of the Flesh."

"Quit it, Lys."

"I'm just saying he looks fun," the lust demon went on, turning around in the seat so their head was pillowed on their folded arms right next to Bex's face. "And since you don't eat humans, the 'no eating clients' rule doesn't apply to you."

Bex took off her sunglasses to give the demon a cutting glare, but Lys wasn't Iggs, so it rolled right off.

"This could be a golden opportunity for us," they said quietly, their voice no longer playful. "The Blackwood coven is powerful. Even Gilgamesh doesn't attack them outright. Now we've got one of their witches paying us to kill warlocks while he builds a fortress. That's not a chance that lands in our laps every day."

Bex put her sunglasses back on with a sigh. "You're making a lot of assumptions about a job we've barely started."

"I know we're all tired of acting like we actually enjoy security work," Lys said, tilting their head to the side. To anyone else, the position probably looked relaxed, but Bex had known Lys all her life, and she could see the tension running through the lust demon's body like a coiled cobra.

"I'm only saying that we should consider our options," they murmured in Bex's ear. "A witch's help could do a lot for our cause. It's still not too late to—"

"It's seven years too late," Bex interrupted sharply. "It's burned, Lys. Leave it be."

"But—"

"*Leave it, Lysannae.*"

The command came out like a shot, making Lys jump a foot out of their seat. Bex jumped too. She didn't normally go that hard over something this small, but sometimes, things just came out. Apparently, this was one of those times.

"Okay, okay, it's left," the lust demon said quickly, scrubbing a shaking hand through their hair.

Bex sighed again. "I'm—"

"Don't say sorry," Lys snapped, sitting up in the seat with a glare. "Even if you are, you don't say that."

Bex nodded and reached out, silently squeezing Lys's shoulder. Lys reached up to grab her hand a moment later, squeezing back.

"It's fine," they said, putting their bare feet up on the dash. "Just forgot myself for a moment. You go on. I'll keep an eye out up here."

Bex nodded and slid back through the curtain... and nearly ran into Adrian.

"How long until we dock?" he asked.

Bex had no idea. She'd been too focused on Lys to even look out the windshield. Fortunately, if it involved directions, Norma was on it.

"Pulling in right now," the construct announced happily, whipping open the cab's curtain. "One ferry to Bainbridge, as requested! Now where're we headed next?"

"Here," Adrian said, reaching past Bex to place his phone on the RV's dash so Norma could see the map on its screen.

"That looks like the middle of the woods," Lys said, pulling their feet off the dash to peer Closer at the marker on Adrian's phone.

"It *is* in the middle of the woods," the witch replied proudly. "I bought that whole hill last year in preparation for today."

Bex stared at the giant green swath of prime waterfront real estate. "You bought all of that?"

Adrian nodded as if purchasing several million dollars' worth of undeveloped land on an island only thirty minutes from downtown Seattle was a perfectly normal thing to do.

"You should have asked for more bottles of deathly water," Lys whispered in Bex's ear.

Bex nodded glumly, sinking down to sit on the arm of Lys's seat as the ferry's gangplank swung open, and the cars began trundling off.

Ten minutes later, they'd cleared the ferry dock and the touristy shopping area just beyond. It was well into the morning now, and the summer sun was high and hot, but Bex barely felt it through the bright green canopy of thick, fluffy trees that lined the road. True to his word, Adrian took them straight into the least developed section of the island's southern tip. The road was well maintained by the owners of the big houses on the water farther down, but the forest was so dense with undergrowth that driving through it felt like sailing down a green canyon.

Things got even crazier when they reached the actual property. Norma flat-out refused to drive down the dirt track Adrian told them to turn onto because the spell that formed her didn't recognize it as a road, so Bex had to turn her off and take over. One inch at a time, she eased the RV onto the rutted path, which looked more like a deer trail than a driveway. Fortunately, the RV was high clearance, so at least they didn't get stuck as they bumped through a little valley and then up a long hill.

For all that it looked like little more than a gap in the trees, the dirt track went a surprising distance back into the woods. Bex had no idea why. As Lys had observed earlier, they were in the middle of nowhere. There were no other houses, no sheds or signs of logging, not even a burned-out chimney. It was all just forest. Thick, dense, impossibly green forest everywhere she looked.

"You can't even see the water," muttered Iggs, who'd come upstairs to see what the commotion was about. "How'd you find something like this so close to Seattle?"

"My family has connections with the Department of the Interior," Adrian said, grinning at the trees like he couldn't wait to get started. "This is a protected watershed, but the local government agreed to sell it to me if I promised to keep it as forest."

"You certainly got your money's worth," Bex said, nodding at the wall of branches sliding over the windshield. "What is it, ten acres?"

"Ten and a half," Adrian said as he ducked back through the curtain. "And this is far enough. Stop the RV."

Bex tapped the brakes, rolling the RV to a stop under a giant maple. Adrian was out the door at once, hopping down the rickety steps with his broom in one hand and his trunk in the other with Boston's empty cat crate bouncing on top. Boston himself jumped out a second later, galloping across the leaf litter after his witch.

Bex followed like a shot, vaulting over Lys to thread her body through the half-rolled-down passenger window. It was the sort of move that would never pass as human, but there was no one to fool out here, and she wasn't about to let her client run off alone into an unsecured area, even if it was one he owned. She landed in a crouch right next to the RV's tire, but when she popped up, all she saw, smelled, and heard was forest.

They'd stopped just shy of the hill's crown, though even that much was hard to make out through all the undergrowth. Now that she was outside, Bex was glad Adrian had called a halt. The dirt track had vanished several feet ago, and there were a lot of rocks and stumps ahead that would have screwed up even the RV's magical suspension. Adrian had already set his trunk down in the little clearing at the hill's crest and was now walking through the trees with his broom in his hand and Boston trotting in front of him, sniffing the ground with his cat nose like a bloodhound.

The sight was so different from everything else she'd seen today that it made Bex pause. At the airport and on the ferry, she'd thought Adrian's witch getup looked slightly ridiculous. Out here in the woods, though, he looked like part of the landscape. With his cloak-like coat billowing behind him and his raven-carved broom in his hands, he could have been a druid from a thousand years ago.

"Looks like he'll be busy for a while," Lys said, leaning out the passenger window above Bex's head. "Want me to go have a look around town?"

"Yes, please," Bex said, relieved that the lust demon was acting normal again. "Sorcerers especially." Warlocks might be their main worry, but sorcerers worked for Gilgamesh, too, and they flocked to rich, connected-yet-remote places like Bainbridge.

"I do so love humbling a sorcerer," Lys cooed, switching to a long-legged male runner body as they flung open the door and hopped onto the pine-needle-covered ground. "Don't wait up if I'm not back by midnight!"

Bex waved at Lys's back as they jogged away and walked across the clearing to Adrian, who'd fallen into a crouch in front of a gigantic Douglas fir.

"Do you need us to move the RV?"

"Hmm?" he said, looking up like he'd just remembered she was there. "Oh, no, I can work around it. I was thinking of making this the heart tree, anyway. It's roughly in the middle of my plot, and Douglas firs go deep." He placed his hand against the shaggy, needle-filled branches that drooped all the way to the ground. "It's about my age, too. That helps enormously with the connection."

Bex craned her neck to look up at the towering conifer. She didn't know how you determined the age of a tree without cutting into it to see the rings, but she supposed a Blackwood would know. Adrian certainly seemed committed to his choice. He'd already gone back to his trunk and popped the latches, digging through carefully organized—and unsurprisingly all-black—piles of clothing to pull out a beautifully carved wooden box.

Clutching it reverently to his chest, he came back over and fell to his knees in front of the fir tree. Then, setting the wooden box carefully to the side, he plunged his bare hands into the needle-covered ground and began to dig.

"Um," Bex said, scuffing her combat boots nervously, "do you want to borrow a shovel?"

Adrian shook his head as he moved handfuls of soil with surprising efficiency. "This has to be done by hand. I'm a good digger, though. It won't take me long."

He wasn't kidding. Bex had seen a lot of weird stuff in her life, but she'd never seen anything like Adrian Blackwood digging a three-foot-deep hole through hardpacked, rocky soil using nothing but his fingers. He didn't even rip a nail. There *had* to be some magic behind that, but Adrian didn't say a word the entire time. He just kept going until he had a neat, knee-deep, root-filled pit wide enough to sit in.

"There," he said, brushing the earth off his fingers as he climbed out of the hole. "Now we're ready."

Bex was dying to ask, "Ready for what?" but she didn't dare speak, because Adrian had picked up the wooden box again. The moment his hands touched it, a hush fell over the clearing. Bex had never heard anything like it, but she knew big magic when she felt it, and whatever Adrian was doing had the whole hill's attention.

Silently, reverently, he climbed back into the hole he'd just made and got down on his knees, placing the wooden box into the nest of roots at the bottom. When everything was positioned exactly where he wanted it, he removed the box's carved lid. The wood came off with a delicate scrape, revealing the object inside, which looked exactly like a human heart.

A *live* human heart. It contracted as Bex watched, the dark-red muscles pumping in the deep, regular motion of a heartbeat. It didn't look bloody or wet. It was just a heart beating in Adrian's hands as he removed it from the box and began to bury it in the ground.

The hush got deeper with every handful of dirt he scooped over it, and then a pulse began to run through the soil under Bex's boots. The sound got louder and louder as Adrian filled in the hole he'd just made. By the time he stood up to press the dirt flat with his boots, the whole hill was pounding with the beating of the heart.

It shook the trees and frightened the birds, filling the air with flapping wings and the crushing feeling of something huge and ancient, something larger than human. Even a demon like Bex, who wasn't part of the living world's magic, had to fight to stay on her feet beneath the weight of so much power. Just when she was sure it was going to flatten her to the ground, Adrian brought his hands together in front of him with a clap, and the horrible pressure vanished like it had never been.

"Well done!" Boston called from the branches he'd climbed up into. "That went even better than it did in practice."

Adrian was panting too hard to answer. He'd been perfectly calm the whole time he was filling in the hole. Now that he was finished, he collapsed onto the needle-strewn ground with a gasp, sprawling under the trees with a triumphant smile on his face.

"When you said you were going to make a heart tree, I didn't realize you meant literally," Bex said as she crouched down beside him.

Adrian's smile grew wider. "I'm called a 'Witch of the Flesh' for a reason."

"I see," she said, offering her hand to help him up. "So whose heart was that?"

"Mine," Adrian said as he grabbed her fingers.

Bex nearly dropped him. "You buried your own heart?"

"Of course," he said. "I can't do magic with anyone else's."

She supposed that made sense, but... "Don't you need your heart to live?"

"It's still there," he protested, reaching out to touch the tree he'd just buried his most vital organ beneath. "But now it beats for the forest too." His smile grew softer. "'The heart of a witch is the Blackwood, and the heart of the Blackwood is a witch.'"

That was definitely a quote from someone, but Bex could only shake her head. And here she'd thought eating quintessence was dangerous. Human magic was insane. She was about to ask if all those roots could clog his arteries when she caught a glimpse of the luggage tag on Adrian's trunk, and her own heart skipped a beat.

"Wait," she said, eyes wide. "You had that in your trunk the whole time?" When Adrian nodded, her jaw fell open. "Did you seriously baggage-check your *heart*?"

"It was the easiest way to get it through security," Adrian said with a shrug.

"What if it got lost?" Bex cried in horror. "Your heart could have ended up at an auction warehouse in Tucson!"

"I'm very good at finding lost things," he said, waving her worries away. "And I'd much rather track down a missing trunk than go through the effort of digging my heart out of my chest again."

It sounded obvious when he put it that way, but Bex was watching him with a new wariness. Fortunately, the next wooden box Adrian pulled out of his luggage didn't contain any organs. When this one opened, all that came out was a tiny wooden house. It looked like the sort of thing you saw in hobby shops for model train enthusiasts, but Adrian carried it even more carefully than he'd carried his heart, holding it in front of him like a talisman as he began pacing the clearing again, talking to Boston all the while.

Bex made a serious effort to follow their conversation this time, but it was hopeless, and not for the usual reasons. When she tried to eavesdrop on sorcerers, she was usually tripped up by the fact that all their spells came from stanzas of Ancient Sumerian poetry. Adrian and Boston's conversation was entirely in English, but it was just as incomprehensible because so many of the words were missing.

Clearly, these two had been working together forever. They didn't even seem to use nouns anymore. When Adrian said, "We need the thing for the thing," his black cat just nodded and asked about the other thing. Not knowing what qualified as a "thing" in the first place, Bex couldn't make heads or tails of it, and their actions weren't much help either. They mostly seemed to be running their feet over the ground, stopping occasionally to tap down a root or rock that stuck up out of the soil.

Bex fully expected the obstacles to get up and move themselves after the witch touched them, but now that the heartbeat earthquake was over, the woods seemed to have gone back to being a normal forest. She'd just hopped onto the RV's roof so she could watch the show from a seat that wasn't in the dirt when Adrian strode to the middle of the area he'd been walking around for the past half hour and placed his model house on the ground.

He started running the second after he put it down, sprinting back to where Boston was crouched by the heart tree like he'd just lit a stick of dynamite. Bex was at his side in an instant, but before she could ask what in the Hells was going on, the little wooden house expanded with a *pop*, going from a toy model to an actual wooden cottage in the time it took to blink.

"What the—" Bex stumbled back. "What is *that*?"

"My house," Adrian said, beaming proudly as he pushed out of the branches he'd been hiding behind.

She still couldn't believe it. "You brought your *house* with you to Seattle?"

"I wasn't going to leave it behind," he said as he hurried up the steps of his new front porch. "Do you know how long it took me to build this place?"

"You built this?" Bex asked, more amazed than surprised now.

"We build everything we use," Boston told her smugly as he trotted past. "It is called witch*craft*, after all."

Adrian had a good laugh at that as he opened the intricately carved front door and waved Bex inside. "Come on, I'll show you around."

Bex followed with far more trepidation than usual, placing her combat boot on the first step like she was edging onto thin ice. Despite how suddenly it had popped up, though, the smooth-lathed wood felt solid as a rock. All of it did. There wasn't a creaky board or misaligned hinge to be spotted as she followed Adrian and Boston into the most charming cottage she'd ever seen.

Unlike their RV, the house was not bigger on the inside, but it was very well designed. Most of the space was taken up by a single vaulted room that seemed to be a combination kitchen and workshop. Where they weren't pierced with tall antique-glass windows, the wooden walls were covered with built-in shelves containing every sort of witchy ingredient from rosemary to dried snakes.

One entire corner was dedicated to a fieldstone fireplace with a massive cauldron hanging from an iron chain at its center. The kitchen area beside it had a wood-fired iron stove along with a deep enameled sink and a spice cabinet the size of a wardrobe. Well-used copper pots and pans hung from an iron rack above the wooden island, which had a second cauldron stowed beneath it as well as rows of glass bottles in all different shapes and sizes. For potions, Bex realized dimly.

A small bedroom lay off to one side of the workshop, and a door out the back led to a glassed-in greenhouse patio that was already full of plants. The ceiling was steeply pointed and braced with massive oak beams, one of which supported a ladder-accessed loft that appeared to be Adrian's office. There were several bookcases up there along with a large circular window to let in the light, a comfy-looking pile of cushions for reading, and, oddly, a laptop computer. Other than that, nothing in the house seemed to use electricity, which was probably for the best, since Bex had no idea how they were going to run power up here.

"Nice, isn't it?" Adrian said, pulling his phone out of his pocket and hooking it up to a portable solar charging panel, which he shimmied up the ladder to place under the loft's sunny window. "The greenhouse out back already has full rainwater capture and filtration, which means I won't have to worry about digging a well. I use a combination of aquaponics and compost for waste removal, so that takes care of septic and trash. Food scraps will go to the garden as soon as I start it. I will have to buy some real solar panels for the roof eventually, but this should do for now."

Bex nodded, looking at the tree-dappled sunlight falling like water across the smooth polished wooden floor. "I see now why you didn't want to stay in our guest room."

"It's a very nice suite," he assured her. "I wouldn't have minded being there at all, but I needed my workshop."

All this stuff definitely wouldn't have fit in the RV's client cabin. Bex supposed she should be happy that she wouldn't have to worry about a stranger living in their home, but all she could think about was how easy it would be to break into a place that had so many giant, unguarded windows.

"I'll be putting in security," Adrian promised, reading the worry off her face despite her sunglasses. "This is just the beginning."

Hell of a beginning, but Adrian was already talking to Boston again, something about sunlight alignment. They went back outside at once to check it out. Bex followed right on their heels, partly because it was her job but mostly because she wanted a front-row seat for whatever miracle Adrian pulled out of his trunk next.

Alas, the pop-up house seemed to be the last big show. Adrian spent the rest of the long summer afternoon walking around his property and talking to Boston. Bex followed as a matter of course, but the woods were every bit as green, quiet, and peaceful as they looked. The three of them did eventually make it all the way down to the water, which met Adrian's forest in a long, muddy-sand beach covered in sea birds, but the only things to see were the fancy houses on the other side of the waterway, and they left quickly. Neither Adrian nor his cat seemed to care about the saltwater inlet in any case. All of their attention was consumed by the forest itself, every inch of which they seemed determined to touch.

By the time the sun started to set, Bex had done enough hiking to last her a year. Boston and Adrian had finally returned to the top of the hill and now sat in the shade of the giant fir tree Adrian had buried his heart beneath, having some kind of discussion that involved a lot of diagrams sketched into the dirt with a twig. Bex was about to hop back up to her favorite spot on top of the RV when she felt something wet on her stomach.

She looked down with a curse, slapping her hand against her oversized black T-shirt. It was impossible to see against the dark cotton, which was the whole reason she wore the thing, but her hand was covered in black blood when she lifted it away. She curled her fingers into a fist at once, glancing over her shoulder at Adrian and Boston, who were both bent so far over their latest diagram that their noses were practically in the dirt.

"I have to go inside for a second," she called, careful to keep her bloody front turned away. "Come get me if you need something."

Adrian nodded without looking, and Bex took her chance to bolt. It was incredibly unprofessional, but nothing had happened all afternoon, and Nemini was in her usual position, reading her book at the front table just inside the door, so Bex decided to take the risk.

"Keep an eye on things for a minute," she told the snake-haired demon as she climbed into the RV.

Nemini's yellow eyes didn't glance her way, but her head bobbed a little, which was as good as a thumbs-up. Bex nodded back and jogged toward the rear of the RV, hand pressed hard against her bloody side. Iggs must have forgotten to close his door again, because Bex could hear him shouting all the way up the stairs. She briefly considered going down to tell him to take over but decided against it in the end. She asked too much of her demons as it was, and she could finish her own damn shift. This would only take ten minutes, so Bex padded silently up the spiral stair toward the only part of the RV she hadn't shown Adrian during the tour: her room.

The whole front of Bex's shirt was soaked by this point, the black blood dripping through her fingers. She swore and started moving faster, ripping off her shirt to stanch the blood as she turned the last spiral of the narrow stair into the circular, high-ceilinged room that had been her home for the last six years. She lurched for the bathroom the second she was inside, grabbing the well-worn first aid kit off the built-in shelf that was supposed to be for towels.

Her hands were so bloody by this point that she had to close the bathroom door with her elbow. The moment she'd sealed herself inside, Bex tossed her sunglasses into the sink and started stripping off her clothes. All the bending and moving made the wound leak faster, and by the time Bex was down to just her skin and the large black ring she wore on a leather thong around her neck, black blood was pouring down her body like a waterfall. She sopped the worst of it up with her wadded T-shirt and turned to the mirror to get a look at the damage.

It looked like someone had taken a giant pair of scissors and snipped a hole across the left side of her waist. The cut was as clean as a razor: a perfect ten-inch-long slice that followed the curve of her lowest rib all the way around to her back. A piece of navy string dangled from the cut's upper edge, all that remained of the stitches that were supposed to keep the damn thing closed.

Her demonic regeneration had already filled in the holes left by the unraveled sutures, but it couldn't touch the wound itself. Nothing could. The hole still gaped as fresh as the day she'd gotten it, a perfect window to her black insides, which were going to become her outsides if she didn't get a move on.

Keeping her shirt pressed tight against the wound with one hand, Bex used her other to open the first aid kit and dig out the curved surgeon's needle. The suture thread was right beside it, already cut to the length she needed. She had to let go of the cut briefly to get the needle threaded, which dropped another pint of her black blood onto the bathroom's beige plastic floor, but that was why she had a drain. Bex had the pressure back in place in an instant, gritting her teeth as she pinched the needle between her calloused fingers and began the arduous task of stitching herself back together.

Ten minutes later, every inch of the bathroom floor was black with her blood, and Bex felt like she was going to pass out. But while she looked like a wax statue under the sink's hideous yellow light, her wound was shut again, sealed up tight with fifty perfect little stitches. It wouldn't stay that way, of course. Even if she did nothing but lie in bed, her own regeneration would force the sutures out eventually, but the dam should hold for a week at least, two if she was careful.

Slumping against the sink with a sigh she felt to her toes, Bex tossed her cold, soggy clothes into the hamper and started cleaning up. The blood on the floor was easily taken care of, washed down the drain with water from her flexible shower-head. She washed herself off next, sluicing the warm water over her skin as carefully as possible to avoid hitting her wound, which hurt all the time but was particularly tender after a stitching. She couldn't get the blood out from under her fingernails, but they were naturally black anyway, so it didn't matter.

The first aid kit couldn't go into the shower, but it was already stained beyond redemption, so Bex settled for wiping the plastic parts down with a disposable disinfectant wipe. She cleaned the needle the same way, scrubbing it with disinfectant until its curved length shone clean and silver. She probably should have done that *before* sewing herself up, but Bex had never heard of a demon getting an infection, and she was too tired to care. Big bleeds always took it out of her, but she didn't have time to lie around. She had to get back to work, so Bex staggered into her bedroom and sat down on her bed to dig through the plastic bin that held her clothing.

This turned out to be a very bad idea. The bathroom floor had been cold and hard, but her bed felt lovely. She tried to focus on getting dressed, treating each piece of clothing like a mission, but by the time she was decent again in a fresh black tank top and black jeans, the room was spinning so hard she couldn't stand up.

That wouldn't do. She was on duty. At the very least, she needed to call Iggs and get him to cover for her, but when she went to grab her phone, she realized it was still in the pocket of her bloody jeans. The ones that were in the hamper all the way back in the bathroom.

They might as well have been in China. Bex wasn't sure she could sit up anymore, much less crawl the ten feet to her bathroom door. She fell back onto her bed instead, staring up at the high windows that formed a ring at the top of her ceiling. She'd just rest for a minute. One minute, that was all, and then she'd get back to—

She didn't even get to finish bargaining with herself before her eyes fell shut, dropping her like a stone into a deep, dreamless sleep.

Chapter 5

Meanwhile, outside the RV, Adrian was having a crisis of his own.

"It's not going to work," he told Boston, shaking his head at the fifth diagram they'd drawn in as many minutes. "There's too much saltwater intrusion. If we grow the forest as quickly as we need, we'll suck all the fresh water out of the water table and kill every other plant on the island."

"Which is why *I* keep saying we need to set up a desalination spell," Boston insisted, stabbing his paw at the line he'd drawn with his claws two minutes ago. "Clearing the salt will let us draw water straight from the inlet. We won't even have to touch the water table."

"But that will make the roots grow the wrong way," Adrian argued. "No desalination spell lasts forever. If we create a false water source, all the trees will grow toward that instead of down toward the groundwater."

"Then dig a trench," Boston snapped. "We just need to flood the ground temporarily. The moment you stop accelerating the forest's growth, water needs will fall back to baseline, by which point we'll have other systems in place. One year, max. That's all we'll need."

Adrian pulled off his hat to scrub his hands through his hair. He *hated* relying on magical cheats to shore up what should be a natural process. It went against the core principles of witchcraft, but Boston had a point. If he wanted to grow a forest on an island, he was going to have to deal with the sea. He'd actually brought along a store of materials for precisely this situation, but having never set foot on Bainbridge before today, he'd failed to account for just how *much* saltwater he'd be dealing with. No matter which way he turned the problem, though, there was no other solution, and he slapped his hat back onto his head with a sigh.

"You're right," he admitted as he hauled himself to his feet.

"Of course I'm right," Boston said with a lash of his tail. "It's my job to be right. Fortunately, this is an easy fix. All we need is some Lot's Salt."

"Which we don't have," Adrian reminded him.

"But can easily get," the cat countered. "There's an Anchor Market just across the water in Seattle."

"You mean the one that's going to be crawling with warlocks?"

"That's why you hired security," Boston said. "Make those demons earn their keep."

Adrian blew out a frustrated breath. There was a big difference between hiring someone to guard your back while you grew a forest and expecting them to walk into the lions' den with you, but he didn't see any other way. Ordering something as rare as Lot's Salt through the mail would take weeks. If he was going to have a chance at staying on schedule, he had to get it tonight, which meant the Anchor Market.

"Don't look so sulky," Boston scolded. "Weren't you the one who said it was time to stop hiding and fight back?"

"In my own grove," Adrian snapped, looking around at all the work he hadn't even begun yet. "The Anchors are Gilgamesh's territory. The land there doesn't listen to me. All I'll have is what's in my pockets."

"Then don't let anyone see you," the cat suggested, giving himself a shake before he trotted off into the woods. "I'm going to catch a mouse for supper. Call me when we're leaving."

Adrian waved him away and turned to look for Bex, but he didn't see her anywhere. He dimly remembered her saying something about going inside, but he'd been up to his eyeballs in Boston's diagrams at the time and hadn't paid attention. Now that he thought about it, he hadn't seen her in a while. Not that that was a problem since there was nothing out here, but she'd stuck to him like glue from the moment they'd signed the contract, which made her absence now feel odd.

She was probably just working on something else while he was busy, Adrian reasoned. Witchcraft was fascinating if you were the one doing it, but even he could admit the setup stage was pretty dull from the outside. He *did* remember Bex saying to come get her if he needed anything, and an Anchor Market trip definitely felt like something that should be discussed in advance, so Adrian brushed the fir needles off his clothes and walked over to Nemini, who was reading her book on the RV's steps.

"Excuse me?"

The void demon didn't look up at his voice. She just turned the page, causing the snakes that made up her hair to swivel their heads in unison as all their glossy black eyes jumped to the new text. He was clearing his throat to ask again when she spoke.

"Do you need something?"

Adrian nearly jumped out of his boots. He'd thought her voice sounded expressionless before, but that was back at the table when he'd been surrounded by other demons. Hearing it now when it was just them made Adrian feel like he was standing on the edge of an abyss. He was struggling not to fall into it when Nemini spoke again.

"If you're looking for Bex, she's upstairs," she said without looking up from her book. "Not that it matters, since we'll all become the same dust at the end of time, but that's her current spatial location."

"Right," Adrian whispered, wiping the cold sweat from his brow. "Thank you."

Nemini dipped her head and leaned to the side, making room for him to step past her. Adrian did so with great care, lifting his leg high to put as much space as possible between himself and the terrifying demon as he climbed into the RV.

Bex's tour hadn't included an upstairs, but there was only one staircase, so it was easy enough to find. The spiral going up was smaller than the one going down, but otherwise it looked like everything else in the RV. Same beige plastic walls, same yellow runner lights, though he didn't understand why the carpet here was black. Every other floor in the RV was covered in brown shag, even the closets. He was wondering if the top floor of the Winnebago had a different style when he noticed some brown sticking up in the stairs' corners, and he realized the carpet wasn't black at all. It was *stained*.

The whole staircase was saturated in an inky black substance. Now that he knew what he was looking for, Adrian could see small splatters going up the walls as well. It looked like someone had knocked a bucket full of ink down the stairs, or maybe there'd been a fire? There was a noticeable smoky smell as he climbed higher, but not like something was actively burning. This was like walking through a place where there'd been a forest fire weeks before. He was wondering how the carpet had ended up just black instead of burned to a crisp when he reached the top and froze.

When Nemini had said Bex was upstairs, Adrian had assumed she'd meant in an office or other public space. He'd also assumed there'd be a door. Both of these were incorrect. The spiral staircase he'd been following led straight into a circular room that was clearly the Winnebago's master bedroom. It was much bigger than any others he'd seen inside the RV, and it had by far the best natural light thanks to the ring of windows that lined the edge of the high ceiling. But while the walls up here were paneled in the same pebble-textured beige plastic as everywhere else in the RV, Adrian could hardly see them through all the bottles.

Every inch of wall in the room was covered in narrow wooden slats holding row upon row upon row of hand-sized glass bottles filled with the most beautifully glowing liquid he'd ever seen. Each one shone as blue as a summer afternoon sky, and that was just the first glance. The longer Adrian looked, the more colors he could see dancing inside the glowing bottles like motes of dust. The combined radiance was so lovely, it took him an embarrassingly long time to realize that these were more of the same bottles he'd given Bex this morning. Water from the rivers of death.

Adrian's eyes went wide as he spun in a circle to see even more bottles stacked above the doorway. There had to be a hundred gallons of deathly water in here, a staggering amount for a reagent that was generally used by the drop. He had no idea why Bex had chosen to store such a fortune on the walls, but none of the bottles looked in danger of falling. Now that his eyes had adjusted to the dazzling light, Adrian could see that the shelves were covered in the same black plastic netting he'd seen in the RV's kitchen to keep the glasses from rattling while the vehicle was in motion. He was still boggling at how much work it must have taken to build up such a collection when he finally spotted the bed.

That stopped him hard. He'd been so distracted by the magical treasure trove he'd stumbled into, he hadn't realized this place was still being used as a bedroom. Bex's bedroom, specifically, going by the plastic bin of black women's clothing lying in the middle of the floor. There was a small bookcase with a desk lamp clipped to its side and a guitar stand with an acoustic six-string so old and used that all the frets had been worn off. The light in the bathroom was on, but the tiny room was clearly empty. Adrian was about to go back down and ask Nemini if there was another upstairs where Bex might be when the black lump on the bed, the one he'd thought was a pile of laundry, suddenly sat up.

Adrian jumped so fast that he nearly fell back down the stairs. Bex was sitting up in her bed, looking around with a panicked expression he was actually able to see, because she wasn't wearing her sunglasses. Her face was bare for the first time since he'd met her, and as she turned to look at him, Adrian's breath caught.

The first thing he noticed was how thin she was. He'd thought Bex was just petite, but the girl in front of him looked like she hadn't eaten in a year. He hadn't noticed earlier due to her baggy clothing, but now that she was wearing a tank top, there was no hiding how skeletal her arms were, and she was so *pale*. Not fair pale—deathly pale, which sent his mind reeling back to the black stains on the stairs.

They were in here as well. The thick carpet of Bex's bedroom had swaths of black running from the staircase to her bathroom and her bed. He hadn't connected it at the

71

time since he was human and thus expected blood to be red, but demon blood was black.

That was a terrifying discovery. But as horrible as the blood trails and her unhealthy thinness were, what really caught Adrian were her eyes. Before he'd escaped, his warlock teachers had paraded examples of every known demon variant in front of him. Every one had obviously inhuman eyes when you looked close enough, but he'd never seen any like Bex's.

It looked like someone had built and then banked a fire inside her head. Her irises literally glowed around the black circles of her pupils, the light shifting like real embers as she stared at him in horror. For three long heartbeats, they watched each other, frozen, and then Bex covered her face with a squeak.

"I'm sorry," Adrian said at the same time, stepping forward before he thought better of it and turned around instead. "I didn't mean to. That is, Nemini said you were up here, but I didn't realize it was your—"

"No, no, it's fine," Bex insisted in a voice that sounded both exhausted and furious. "You did nothing wrong. I'm the idiot who fell asleep on the job."

"You look like you needed it," Adrian said, staring determinedly at the black-stained carpet under his feet. "Are you… Are you all right?"

He heard the bed creak, and then Bex heaved a long sigh. "As good as I ever am," she said, sounding just exhausted now. "It's okay. You can turn around."

Adrian did so slowly, wincing when he saw her sitting with her head in her hands.

"I'll give you a refund," she offered in a small, defeated voice.

"That's not necessary," Adrian assured her. "Nothing happened."

"It could have," she snapped, clenching the black ring that hung from a leather string around her neck. "I should have sent Iggs to take over the moment I left. I thought it'd be fine, but clearly, my judgment was wrong." She unclenched her bony hand with a bitter breath, looking at him with those wild, glowing eyes. "My behavior was unprofessional and inexcusable. If you want another security team, I'll call Felix right now and—"

"It's really okay," Adrian insisted. "I absolutely don't want to go through the bother of getting another team when you're already here, and it wasn't as if you left me alone. Nemini was right there, and I *am* a witch. Just because I hired you to help me fend off the hordes doesn't mean I'm incapable of protecting myself."

"It was still wrong."

"Yes, but I'm not going to fire you over it," he said firmly. "Nothing bad actually happened, and if there had been an emergency, I'm sure you would have come running. The only thing I mind is that we're still wasting time discussing it, so if it's all right with you, I'd like to move on."

That final part came out sharper than he'd intended, but Bex had lost her awful defeated look halfway through and was now staring at him like she didn't know what he was.

"Are you sure?" she said at last.

"Positive," Adrian said, striding into the bathroom to grab the sunglasses he'd just spotted lying on the rim of the sink. When he walked over to hand them to her, though, Bex dropped her eyes like she was ashamed.

"I wasn't trying to hide them from you," she said as she took the glasses from his fingers. "They're just too much for the scalies to handle. If I don't cover them, I get kicked."

"I can see why," Adrian said, leaning down to get a better look at her glowing eyes. They bore an even stronger resemblance to embers up close, their light shifting as they smoldered. She smelled like a fire, too. Not sulfurous hellfire, but woodsmoke and ash. It reminded him of the smell of burned-out bonfires the morning after Beltane, and Adrian tilted his head in confusion.

"What kind of demon are you?"

"The bad-employee kind, apparently," Bex grumbled, shoving her sunglasses onto her face. She reached down to snag a leather jacket off the floor next, sliding it over her tank top as she pushed to her feet. "Thank you for being lenient, Mr. Blackwood. It won't happen again."

"It's Adrian, and it really is fine," he insisted. "If you're tired, just tell me and we'll change the schedule so you can rest. I'm not a slave driver."

He regretted his choice of words the moment they were out of his mouth. Fortunately, Bex didn't seem insulted.

"Well, I'm ashamed enough for both of us," she said as she walked into the bathroom to dig her phone out of the pocket of what must have been her previous pair of jeans. She picked up her black combat boots off the floor as well, walking back to her bed to sit down while she put them on.

"Just because you're not willing to come down on me doesn't mean I can let this slide," she told him as she stomped her black-socked feet into her shoes. "If you don't want a refund or a new team, how about I give you another week of security work on the house? It's the least I can do to make up for slacking on the job."

74

"Now that's an offer I can't refuse," Adrian said, breaking into a grin as he stuck out his hand. He'd intended to help her back to her feet, but Bex shook on it instead, squeezing his calloused fingers with her thin, pale ones.

"The deal is made," she said, letting him go to haul herself off the bed on her own. "Now, what was it you came to find me for?"

So much had happened in the last few minutes that Adrian had to pause and think. "The Anchor Market," he said, snapping his fingers. "I need to go to the Anchor Market."

Her expressions were hard to read now that she had her giant sunglasses back on, but it didn't matter. Adrian could *feel* her scowl, and he held up his hands at once.

"I know, I know, it's a terrible idea, but I'm missing a critical reagent, and the Anchor Market's the only place I can get it in a timely fashion."

"Then I guess we're going shopping," Bex said with a sigh, walking over to snag a bottle of glowing water off the wall. Adrian watched with keen interest, but all she did was slide the bottle into her jacket pocket and stomp down the stained staircase, yelling for Iggs as she went.

Chapter 6

Bex was so furious with herself she wanted to scream. The second she was out of Adrian's line of sight, she snatched the bottle of deathly water out of her pocket and chugged it.

As the glowing liquid poured down her throat, strength surged into her body. She knew it was only temporary just like she knew she'd regret drinking so much later, but she had to do *something*. She'd been cutting as hard as possible to conserve every drop, but this was too much. If Adrian hadn't been so understanding, she could have blown the whole job. What was the point of rationing her water if she lost a four-bottle payment because she'd been too cheap to keep herself up?

Shaking her head at the near disaster, Bex stuck the now-empty bottle back into her pocket and hopped down the last curve of the stairs. This put her at head level with Iggs, who was coming up from below. He stopped when he saw her paleness, his mouth pulling into a hard frown, but Bex snapped into action before he could say a word.

"Keep your glasses on," she ordered, snatching the sunglasses off the collar of his shirt and shoving them onto his face before Adrian saw any more of their secrets. "And get your paint kit. We're going to the Anchor Market."

"The Anchor Market?" he repeated, fumbling his glasses into position. "Have you gone nuts? The Market's a death trap. We can't go there, especially not when you're..."

He trailed off with that worried frown again, and Bex sighed. "I'm fine," she insisted, showing him the empty bottle from her pocket before heading to the kitchen to put it in the dishwasher. "Just had a little slip. I'm stocked now, though, which is good, because we need to be on our A-game. The client needs a reagent from the Market tonight. Now go get the paint kit so we can get this over with."

"Right, right," Iggs grumbled, shooting her another worried look as he stomped down the stairs.

Bex was pulling out her phone to check the ferry schedule when she heard Adrian behind her.

"What do you need a paint kit for?"

"Slave bands," she replied, tapping her neck. "The market is Gilgamesh's territory. Going in there as a free demon is the same as serving yourself up on a platter. So, to get around it, we paint fake bands on our necks."

"And that works?" Adrian asked skeptically.

"Most of the time," Bex said, sliding her phone back into her pocket. "Since warlocks are lazy, stuck-up bastards who can't be bothered to do their own shopping, the Anchor Market's always full of bound demons running errands. Iggs is pretty good at drawing fake marks, so we should be able to blend in with the crowd as long as we don't try anything too fancy." She frowned at him. "This thing you need to buy isn't contraband, is it? Because if that's the case, we're going to need a different plan."

"No, it's legal," he assured her, though he looked much less certain than he had back in her room. "But are you *sure* you'll be okay? I don't want to make you go somewhere you'll be in danger."

He sounded so earnest that Bex almost laughed. "Being in danger's the whole point of hiring security," she reminded him. "I'm much more worried about you. Not many people bother looking at demon slaves, but a witch will draw all kinds of attention. Mostly the wrong kinds." She shot a pointed look at his black hat. "I don't suppose you'd be willing to change into something less conspicuous?"

Adrian tensed at the mere suggestion, which wasn't a surprise. Even hiking around the woods with his cat, he wore his witch garb like a uniform. Bex was about to ask if he could just tell her what he needed and let them do the shopping when Adrian reached up and removed his hat with a sigh, proving yet again that he was the most reasonable client she'd ever had.

"Thank you," she said, looking him up and down to assess what was left. "We should probably ditch the coat as well. Not that the all-black look isn't very warlock, but most Anchor Market customers tend toward the designer-suit end of the spectrum rather than the homemade one."

"My coat stays," Adrian said firmly, sliding his hat into the right side of his long jacket, where it vanished far more quickly than Bex had expected. "But there might be something else I can do. Let me check my house."

Bex nodded and followed him out of the RV. When he was safely walking up the steps to his cabin, she pulled out her phone and called Lys.

"Are you busy?" she asked the moment they picked up.

"In a manner of speaking," the lust demon replied in a husky female voice. "You were right. There *was* a sorcerer on the island, but I've got the matter well in hand."

A man gasped in the background, and Bex grinned. "Nice work. How soon will you be done?"

"Not for another hour," Lys said. "Tedious, I know, but you've got to hook them deep the first time or it doesn't stick. Why? Do you need me?"

"Yeah, but it sounds like you're doing something more important." Getting the local sorcerer under control was critical for long-term security, and Bex knew better than to question Lys's judgment on stuff like this. "It's just an Anchor Market trip. We can handle that without you."

"Take Nemini," Lys suggested. "She needs the exercise."

"Exercise is meaningless," Nemini said from the steps, where she was still reading her book. "No matter how much effort we invest or how hard we try, we all still die in the end."

"If it's all equally futile, then you might as well waste your time with us," Bex told her with a smile before returning her attention to the phone. "We'll handle the client. You stay there and get the island secured."

"Don't worry. This one's not going to be reporting anything," Lys promised. "Have fun shopping."

Anchor Markets were the opposite of fun. It was going to be especially obnoxious without a lust demon to distract the guards. But while Nemini's skill set wasn't quite as well suited as Lys's, she was no slouch, and they'd have Adrian with them. Having a human around always lowered the bar. Anchor Guards were happy to harass unescorted demons, but they stayed away from warlocks, and as a human walking around with three demons, a warlock was the only thing Adrian could be.

Bex just hoped he'd be able to play the part. She didn't know the witch well enough yet to say if he was a good actor or not. His hatred of warlocks was a huge check-mark in Bex's book, but he couldn't go making that furious, insulted face every time someone asked him a question.

She drummed her black nails against the RV's plastic paneling. Maybe they *should* wait for Lys. The lust demon was their best shapeshifter, hands down, and they'd pretended to be a warlock before. If Lys played the slaver, that meant Adrian could pretend to be a sorcerer, which made much more sense for someone coming in to buy… whatever it was he was buying. Warlocks didn't even use reagents. They just chugged quintessence and made their demons do all the heavy lifting. But just as Bex was about to convince herself that they should hold off, Adrian came out of his house.

She did a double take when she saw him, and then her mouth curled into a smirk. She should have had more faith. Even if he'd spent most of it escaping, he'd been a warlock's apprentice for six months. It only made sense that he'd still know how to dress like one.

As he got closer, Bex saw it was more than just clothes. The man walking out of Adrian's witch house looked so smarmy, she wanted to punch him. He still had Adrian's tall, lean body and olive skin, but his dark hair was slicked back like an old-style gangster's, and his slim-fit Italian suit was even more atrocious. It was still black, but the faux-velvet fabric had a gaudy *fleur de lis* pattern that she could see from here. Even his raven-topped broom had been transformed into a raven-topped cane, which struck Bex as more sorcerer than warlock, but she wasn't about to nitpick.

"Nice work," she said, stepping out into the clearing to meet him. "How'd you manage all of that so quickly?"

"Mimic potion," he said in an embarrassed voice that was totally at odds with his sleazy new exterior. "I had a bunch left over from back when I used to sneak out of the cabal. Never thought I'd be using them again, though."

Bex blinked. "You're using a potion you created when you were thirteen?"

"It's not as if they have an expiration date," Warlock-Adrian replied with a shrug. "And making potions is a lot of work. I don't waste any of them if I can help it."

"I was more impressed you made something that good when you were a kid," she said, pulling off her sunglasses for a real look since he'd already seen her eyes.

He puffed up with pride. "Potions have always been one of my specialties."

Clearly. Bex was already making a mental note to ask about buying some of those off him when this job was over. It'd be useful to have someone other than Lys who could play a warlock. For now, though, Bex was feeling much more confident about the plan, especially when Iggs came out of the RV with the slave band already painted around his neck.

"Wow," Adrian said when he saw it. "You're really good at that."

"Why is everyone always so surprised that I can paint?" Iggs grumbled. Then he did a double take when he realized who'd said that. "Wow dude, you look like a total asshole."

Bex took a hissing breath. But before she could lay into Iggs for speaking that way to a client, Adrian's face broke into a genuine smile that completely ruined his disguise.

"Thank you!" he said, crouching down to let Boston, who'd just appeared from nowhere, hop onto his shoulder. "I'm quite proud of it."

Since Adrian wasn't mad, Bex let Iggs's comment slide, pulling down her jacket collar so the bigger demon could start painting a slave band on her neck.

"So," she said, trying not to flinch when the cold paintbrush hit her skin, "what are we buying?"

Adrian opened his mouth, but Boston beat him to it.

"Lot's Salt," the cat said in a clipped, professional voice. "It's a key component in desalination spells. Normally quite rare, but I'm betting the Seattle market will have plenty since we're surrounded by saltwater."

"I don't know about that," Bex said, tilting her head down so Iggs could paint her nape. "I've never met a sorcerer who cared about the environment."

"That's precisely why they'll have it in stock," Boston told her authoritatively. "Lot's Salt is used for manipulating ecosystems, not preserving them. It's also a key component for turning people into pillars of salt, which I'm given to understand is a popular pastime among Gilgamesh's faithful."

Adrian was looking less happy by the word, but Bex thought it sounded great. "That's good to hear. Purchasing something that turns people into salt will cause a lot less talk than a warlock buying gardening supplies."

"I would never buy *anything* for my garden from an Anchor Market," Adrian promised.

Bex smiled at his obvious horror and stepped back to check her neck in the RV's side mirror. Her skin still looked pale as chalk, but she didn't feel the blood loss anymore with a whole bottle of deathly water rushing through her, and the mark on her neck looked fantastic.

"Great job as always, Iggs," she said, turning her head from side to side. "I look like a proper bootlicker."

"I just wish I didn't have to do them," Iggs said, bending down behind her to check his own mark. "Is Lys coming?"

Bex shook her head. "Just us and Nemini."

Iggs looked surprisingly happy to hear that. Or not so surprisingly considering how much fun Lys had ordering him around when the lust demon was playing their warlock. When the big demon closed his paint kit, though, Adrian held up his hand.

"Doesn't Nemini need a fake band too?"

"Nah," Iggs said, going back into the RV to wash off his paintbrush in the sink. "She's good."

"Warlocks can't bind void demons," Bex explained at the witch's nervous look. "But it's fine. Unlike the rest of us, Nemini knows how not to stand out."

"You could do it, too," said Nemini, who still hadn't looked up from her book. "All you need is to surrender the illusion of self and embrace the truth that we're all just insignificant specks of organic matter hurtling through an infinite cosmos we can neither affect nor control. It's very freeing."

"I'm good," Bex replied, reaching up to open the RV's passenger door. "Just give me five minutes to get Norma turned back on, and we can drive over to the ferry."

"There's no need to move the entire Winnebago," Adrian said, tapping the illusion off his raven cane to reveal the broom beneath. "I can fly us."

Iggs scoffed. "There's no way we're all fitting on one broom."

Bex had been thinking the same thing, but Adrian's fake face pulled into a very real, and very smug, smile.

"I don't think it'll be a problem."

He let go of his broom as he spoke. The carved wooden handle fell from his fingers like a chopped tree. Then, just before it hit the ground, it stopped. Stopped and *changed*, the carved wood stretching and moving until it wasn't a broom at all. It was a raven. A huge wooden raven the size of a car with broom-grass feathers and carved wooden eyes that Bex swore she saw roll in annoyance when Adrian hopped onto its back.

"Come on," he said, holding out his hand. "It's perfectly safe."

She *definitely* saw the raven roll its eyes that time. Bex gave it an apologetic look as she took Adrian's hand and stepped as lightly as she could onto the broom-grass feathers.

"I see now why you warned me about getting pecked," she said as Adrian turned to help Iggs up. "Did you make this too?"

"I'm afraid I can't take credit for Bran," he said, holding Iggs steady as the huge demon eased his giant foot onto the raven like he was afraid the bird might crack. "He was a gift from my aunt Lydia."

"Must be some aunt," Bex said, taking a seat beside Nemini, who'd already made herself comfortable on the broom-raven's tail.

"She's a great and powerful witch," Boston explained in a reverent voice as he trotted up to perch on the raven's head. "Also a vengeful one, so try not to break anything."

Bex instantly removed her hands from the smooth broom grass she'd been secretly petting.

"Don't listen to Boston's worrying," Adrian said as he braced his feet on the raven's shoulders. "Bran's as tough as the bones that made him."

"I thought he was made of wood?" Iggs said.

Adrian's answer to that was a cryptic smile as the broom shot into the air.

Bex grabbed the broom grass with a jerk. The raven hadn't even flapped its wings. It just shot straight up into the evening sky like a cork. They were high above the trees in an instant, in perfect view of the boaters enjoying the sunset from the island's inlets. The moment Bex saw them, she braced for the kick, because there was no way scalies could handle something like this. To her amazement, though, nothing happened. Even when they zoomed right over the incoming ferry, none of the tourists on the deck looked up, leaving her gaping.

"How are they not seeing us?" she yelled over the wind at Adrian, who was standing confidently at the front of the bobbing wooden bird like he did this every day.

"A whole combination of things," he called back. "Bran was already a raven, so I combined wing feathers from every member of the Corvus genus in North America with all twelve variations of the Nevermind spell and a whole lot of creative license to craft a semipermanent illusion." He pointed down at the tourists on the ferry. "When they look up at us, all they see is a flock of crows. Works on non-scaled humans as well."

Bex stared at him in awe. "Could you make us one?" Because that sounded useful as hell, but Adrian was already shaking his head.

"Not unless you're also looking to hide a broom crafted by a Witch of the Bones," he explained apologetically. "Doesn't mean I can't make you something, but all witchcraft is custom. This piece was particularly tricky, and it's not without its drawbacks. The illusion is only trustworthy between dusk and dawn, and only in areas where crows are found natively. That's most of the world, though, so it's not so bad."

Bex thought it was amazing. The only humans she knew who could do full illusions were high-ranked sorcerers, the lifelong loyalist sort who didn't sell to demons. Even if she could have convinced one to work with her, sorcerous illusions only worked when you fed quintessence into them like coins into an arcade machine. Adrian's bird-broom looked much more convenient, not to mention it *flew*.

That was worth any number of drawbacks in her book. From the magic she could feel flowing off Adrian into the broom like a summer rainstorm, Bex was pretty sure she lacked the right sort of oomph to power one herself, but it was still fun. She was leaning over the raven's wing to watch the water fly by below when Iggs grabbed her arm.

Bex rolled her eyes at him. "I'm not going to fall."

"I wasn't worried about that," he whispered, shooting a suspicious look at Adrian, who was definitely showing off. "I just don't see why you're letting him do the driving. We already have a ride."

"Well, this is faster," she said. "And now we don't have to worry about parking."

Iggs looked supremely unconvinced, so Bex leaned closer to tell him the truth.

"Just let him do what he wants. I needed to grant some concessions since he caught me sleeping on the job, and this is a cheap one."

"*You* fell asleep? In the middle of the afternoon?" Iggs's jaw tightened. "I *knew* you looked pale. How much blood did you lose?"

"Not all of it," Bex hedged, fighting the urge to press her hand against her still-throbbing wound. "But it knocked me for a loop. And before you say anything, I was going to call you, but I passed out before I could get to my phone."

Iggs ground his sharp teeth, and she sighed.

"It's okay," she promised. "*I'm* okay. But I owe Adrian for not firing us, so let's shut up and enjoy the cool broom ride."

He didn't look like he believed her, but it *was* awesome being up in the sky with the birds, and Bex *had* drunk her water like he was always hounding her to, so Iggs let it go pretty fast. Good thing, because at the speed Adrian's broom was flying, it wasn't going to be a long ride. Not ten minutes after they'd left the forest, they were setting down in a pay-by-the-hour parking lot just down the road from Pike Place Market.

Adrian put them down in an empty parking spot hidden between two giant pickup trucks. The broom-raven had to fold its wings to fit, so Bex went ahead and jumped off, clearing the six-foot drop no problem. Iggs came down right behind her, but Nemini stayed on the bird until Adrian turned it back into a broom, dropping her unceremoniously onto the pavement.

"Sorry," he said sheepishly, offering a hand to help her up. "I thought you were going to jump."

Nemini just stared at him, looking with her yellow eyes plus all her snakes until he lowered his hand and stepped back.

"Okay, fun time's over," Bex said, sticking her head around the F-150's giant butt to check the situation. Even out here in the overflow parking, there were still a decent number of cars, but she didn't see any people. Satisfied that the coast was clear, Bex turned back to the others. "What time is it?"

"Time is an illusion," Nemini said.

"Seven-thirty," Iggs replied.

"Perfect," Bex said, turning to Adrian, who was still staring at Nemini like he'd just glimpsed the void waiting at the end of time—which, to be fair, he might have.

"Hey," Bex said, waving her hand in front of his face. When the witch snapped back to reality, she laid out the plan.

"The Seattle Anchor Market is technically open twenty-four hours a day, but all the legitimate merchants pack up around nine. That gives us an hour and a half to get in, get what you need, and get out again without being spotted. Since you're pretending to be a warlock, Iggs and I will have to walk behind you, but if you feel threatened at any point, just tell us to attack like we're your actual bound demons."

"*Can* you attack in an Anchor Market?" Boston asked from his usual perch on Adrian's shoulder. "I thought Gilgamesh's guards prevented such things."

"Depends on how responsible they're feeling," Bex said with a shrug. "The guards are there to preserve the Eternal King's peace. They'll thrash independent vendors at the first opportunity, but warlocks work for Gilgamesh as well, which makes confronting them problematic for both sides. I'm not expecting trouble since we're only here to buy salt, but that doesn't keep it from happening, so let's stick together and do this quick."

"Right," Adrian said, replacing the illusion that made his broom look like a walking stick.

"Can you illusion your cat too?" Iggs asked.

Boston gave him a cutting look, and the big demon put up his hands. "I'm just saying, I've never seen a warlock with a cat before."

"Actually, that's a good point," Adrian said, scowling in thought, which looked more like sneering in thought thanks to his punchable warlock disguise. He considered the issue for several moments, then whispered something to Boston. The cat hissed back, which led to a short argument that Boston must have lost, because when Adrian opened the right side of his jacket, the cat jumped inside, vanishing as quickly as the witch hat had earlier.

"Whoa," Iggs said, looking Adrian up and down. "How big is your coat?"

"Not big enough," Adrian grumbled, smacking the pocket of his costume's garish suit jacket, which seemed to be moving. "But it's better than leaving him behind. Boston knows a lot more about rare reagents than I do. It's one of his specialties."

"A useful familiar, then," Bex said.

"The best," the witch replied with a smile.

This must have appeased Boston's ego, because the shaking inside Adrian's coat calmed down after that, leaving them free to walk through the half-empty parking lot to the sidewalk that would take them into the warren of shops and alleys that was Pike Place Market.

When she'd first come to Seattle, Bex had been shocked to learn that the Anchor—the magical marketplace and center of the Eternal King's power in this part of the Pacific Northwest—was hidden inside a tourist trap. She'd been informed by several people and no few historical plaques that this was because the Seattle Anchor had been built back when Pike Place was an actual public market servicing the thriving shipping lanes that went up the West Coast to the rich new territory of Alaska. That fit King Gilgamesh's typical strategy for Anchor placement, though personally, Bex felt the current cheesy-tourist-money-sponge vibe fit the Market *much* better.

Anchors Markets were the crossroads between Gilgamesh's Holy City and the living world. They were the only places where people could travel between Paradise—land of the dead and home to Heaven and all nine of the

Hells—and the mortal world without having to die first. After five thousand years of rule, Gilgamesh had Anchors in every major population center on the planet, and all of them had a market selling earthly goods to the denizens of Heaven and heavenly goods to the denizens of Earth. They also sold demons, which was why Bex didn't go to Anchor Markets unless forced. She still remembered how to get into this one, though, and by the time they'd wound their way through the empty, closed-up warren of shuttered shops that was Pike Place after six p.m., everyone knew the plan.

The Anchor Market had several entrances distributed throughout the waterfront. Bex had chosen the service door on Post Alley, more colorfully known as the Gum Door due to its location just across from the Gum Wall, an absolutely disgusting tourist attraction where people stuck their chewed-up gum on the side of a building, sometimes in terrifyingly high spots. Bex had no idea how normal humans got chewing gum fifteen feet up a brick wall, and she didn't want to find out. The only reason she set foot in the place was because the lingering smell of fresh mint, saliva, and dirty alley kept everyone else away, leaving only a few scale-eyed tourists to witness her opening the gum-covered metal door in the wall with a napkin so she wouldn't actually have to touch it.

The gum smell mercifully faded once they got inside. Since this was a service door, there was a big loading area where vendors could park their carts as well as two golden-armored Guards of Gilgamesh. Guards of Gilgamesh were normal humans under their suits, but the metal they wore pulsed with so much quintessence that a full career of wearing it left the guards unable to remain in the living world. Because of this, Guards of Gilgamesh were promised a place in Paradise at the end of their service, a reward that made them fanatically loyal and functionally unbribable. They were, however, very distractable, which was where Nemini came in.

She'd never be the life of the party, but Nemini was secretly Bex's favorite demon to work with. Her fundamental nature of nothingness meant most humans and plenty of demons didn't see her unless she wanted them to. It worked particularly well on straightforward men-of-duty types like Anchor Guards, who didn't even notice Nemini walking straight at them until she grabbed their arms.

The moment her hands landed, both guards went stone-stiff inside their suits. When Bex was sure they'd stay that way, she gave the signal, and then she, Iggs, and Adrian walked right past, ducking under Nemini's arms to slip into the tunnel behind the guards. When they were safely inside, Nemini let the guards go and followed, leaving the armored men too busy trying not to cry at their posts to realize what they'd just let sneak by.

"That was terrifying," Adrian whispered, looking over his shoulder at the snake-haired demon with respect bordering on dread. "What did she do to them?"

"Showed them the inherent futility of their efforts," Nemini replied before Bex could say a word. "All hierarchies are false constructs built on the hubris of ego. No matter how hard you work to climb the ladder, you can never change the fact that there *is* no ladder. All our perceived accomplishments are just shadows dancing on the wall of an unfeeling universe that will never know or care that we existed." She held out her hand. "I can show you if you like."

"No thank you," Adrian said, moving closer to Bex, who grabbed his arm and steered him to where he was supposed to be walking: at the front.

"No more talking," she ordered, nodding toward the glittering light at the end of the brick tunnel. "We're on."

The others dutifully shuffled into position. Bex moved into hers as well, walking right next to Iggs and one step behind Adrian as they exited the tunnel and entered the spectacular wonder of Paradise.

Not *actual* Paradise. That was still far away, but the Anchors worked by overlapping the worlds of life and death, which made them the closest to Heaven—or Hell—that you could get on Earth.

Even Bex, who hated everything Gilgamesh made on principle, had to admit the place was beautiful. Despite being inside a building, the Seattle Anchor Market looked like a giant open field under an endless blue sky. Gentle hills rolled as far as the eye could see in all directions like waves in a green-gold ocean. The air smelled of sweet grass and, if Bex breathed deeply enough, water. Beautiful, flowing water, winding slowly through the meadows.

The rivers of Paradise.

Something wet rolled down her cheek, and Bex lowered her face with a silent curse. Her tears weren't as black as her blood, but the ashy streaks would still give her away, so she took a risk and pushed up her glasses to wipe her face on the sleeve of her black jacket. When she was sure the evidence of her weakness was gone, she resettled her sunglasses and lifted her head to see what they were in for.

A crowd seemed to be the answer. From this distance, the Anchor Market looked like an old-fashioned fair. The tunnel for the service entrance let out at the foot of a hill covered in brightly-colored merchant tents divided by paths of freshly-trimmed grass that never got trampled down no matter how many people walked on them. Flags signaling what each tents had for sale waved in the gentle breeze, and above it all soared the golden chain of the Anchor itself, rising into the sky like a glittering path straight to Heaven.

It was a crowded path tonight. Anchor Markets were always busiest in the evening, when the denizens of the Holy City left their pleasure palaces to pick up supplies for the night's festivities. Every night was a party in Heaven, and the demand for new entertainments and novelty was immense. To cater to that endless need—and to sweep up all the quintessence the Heavenly hosts threw around like dirt—the vast majority of the Anchor Market was dedicated to the sale of earthly delights.

Bex had always thought it was an odd fixation for people who *literally* lived in Heaven, but all of Gilgamesh's faithful, including Gilgamesh himself, had once been human. This meant they still coveted the pleasures of mortality. Particularly beer, but also wine, liquor, chocolate, designer handbags, consumer electronics, movies, and pretty much every other comfort of modern life. Local vendors capitalized on this by buying whatever earthly goods were currently trending and reselling them at ludicrous prices.

This month's hot item seemed to be lobsters. Being so close to the big fishing lanes, the Seattle Anchor Market had always tried to differentiate itself by focusing on seafood. Usually salmon, but tonight the merchant tables were packed with lobster tanks. Bex couldn't turn her head without seeing some poor little crustacean looking back, its rubber-banded claws waving futilely.

As depressing as that was, it was safer to look at than anything else. Thanks to the pre-party rush, the grassy paths between the tents were crammed with Heavenly citizens in their dazzling finery. They paraded around like they owned the place, ordering their demon slaves to pack the lobsters into the ice-filled Styrofoam boxes that would keep the animals alive until it was time for them to be boiled to death.

None of the bound demons looked at Bex. She didn't look at them, either, but that didn't keep the black ring she wore around her neck from growing so heavy, it felt like it was going to snap its leather cord.

Iggs looked over when she grabbed the heavy black band, his face as angry as Bex knew her own must be. She shook her head at him, forcing herself to let the ring go and focus on Adrian before she got them all killed.

Luckily, the witch didn't seem to have noticed her strange behavior. He was too busy staring at the chain to Heaven glittering in the sky and the huge golden statue that anchored it to the ground.

"It looks *exactly* like the one in Boston," he whispered excitedly. "I've never been to another Market. Are all the Anchors the same?"

"All the ones I've seen," Bex whispered back, her glowing eyes narrowing as she looked up through the dark film of her glasses.

Rising above the merchant tents like a god above insects was a giant golden statue of Gilgamesh. As always in his public depictions, the Eternal King was in full battle armor with the crown of Anu, god of wisdom, civilization, and kingship, on his head. His bearded face was stern as he stared up at his raised left fist, which clutched the golden chain that connected his two realms. In his lowered right hand, he held the sacred sword of Ishtar, goddess of love and beauty, war and battle, fertility and abundance, and life and death.

As always, the sight left Bex seething. Gilgamesh had no right to that sword. No right to *any* of this. But as angry as the golden propaganda piece made her, it was still better than the sight waiting at the statue's base.

Cut into the Anchor's foundation, positioned directly beneath the statue's giant golden boots, were seven figures. Unlike the king above them, they were not made of gold. Their images had been carved from granite, the gray stone deliberately left unpolished so that their features would appear as coarse and monstrous as possible. Each one was a demon: a horned woman on her knees with her hands lifted up to the Eternal King in surrender.

If the sight of Gilgamesh holding Ishtar's sword had made Bex furious, the kneeling demons made her see red. In all his statues, the king presented himself as a magnanimous conqueror who'd opened the doors of Heaven to all mankind, but that Heaven had never been his. He'd *stolen* Paradise from the people who already lived there, the same demons whose queens he'd depicted kneeling at his feet.

There should have been nine of them, one for each of the Hells he'd forced the demons into. But while seven queens had surrendered to Gilgamesh rather than see their people destroyed, two had not. One, the Queen of Pride, had fought back, and for that, she'd been killed. Her broken figure was still in the statue as a pile of granite rubble under Gilgamesh's golden heel. The other one, though...

Bex dropped her eyes. She didn't want to see the ninth queen, but it'd be hard to avoid. Her figure was the only part of the Anchor that changed from location to

95

location, and her position in Seattle happened to be right where Adrian was heading.

The fancy, lobster-obsessed merchants took up most of the Market's front stalls and all the tents around the Anchor itself where the chain from Heaven let out, but the back half of the Market was dedicated to Gilgamesh's servants in the living world. These tents catered specifically to warlocks and sorcerers. The witch was already headed straight for the reagents section, whispering frantically into his coat as they turned down a grass-covered aisle full of tents that specialized in rare magical ingredients.

"All right," Adrian said, looking over the rows of merchant tables filled with every kind of oddity, powder, and preserved body part Bex could imagine, along with plenty she couldn't. "We need salt."

"Try the table with the rocks," Boston suggested from inside the witch's coat.

Adrian's disguised face pulled into a scowl. "He's a mineral dealer."

"Salt is a mineral."

That logic must have been good enough for Adrian, because he walked right over and started asking questions. The man running the table practically fell over himself to answer, but that was to be expected. With multiple demons and his gaudy suit, Adrian reeked of warlock, and since warlocks got paid wheelbarrows of quintessence for every runaway demon they dragged back, they were always choice customers. Bex was doing her best to focus on Adrian's witchy parts before anger over that thought got the better of her when Iggs bumped her shoulder.

She turned at once, and immediately regretted it. The mineral vendor had set up his tent at an intersection, and down the opposite path from where they were standing was the stage for the slave auctions. No one was selling at the moment—demon auctions were a big deal, held only on weekends and holidays—but the cages beside the stage were full, presenting next weekend's offerings to a sparse crowd of men in flashy suits very much like the one Adrian had whipped up for himself.

The sight made Bex go tense. The demons in the cages were *very* young, so fresh from the Hells that they didn't even have human guises yet. Most were lust demons like Lys, though they hardly looked it without the older demon's skill at hiding their tail. One cage held an entire pack of toad-faced greed demons huddled together like frightened chicks, while another contained a weeping sorrow demon wrapped up like a cocoon inside her dripping wings. They were all heartbreaking to look at, but what really rubbed salt in the wound was the statue perched like a weather vane at the top of the slave-auctioneer's stand.

Appropriately for the location, it was a demon. A granite statue of a female just like the queens at Gilgamesh's feet, only this one wasn't kneeling. She was running, fleeing from the king's golden statue with her back turned on the caged demons below, because this was the ninth queen. The one who'd run away from Gilgamesh and left her people to die. The story was right there, engraved beneath the queen's running feet for every demon to read while they waited to be sold.

Behold the Coward Queen, it said, *who chose her life over yours.*

"We could break it," Iggs whispered, clenching his giant fists. "You, me, and Nemini—we could destroy this whole place. Just tear it all down."

"We could," Bex agreed. "But then we'd die."

Iggs didn't look like he cared at the moment. His skin was already turning red, his denim jacket creaking as his huge body swelled even bigger. His fangs were starting to poke out of his mouth when Bex dug her fingers into his arm.

"We. Will. Die. If we start shit in an Anchor, it won't just be the guards. They'll send down a prince."

"But—"

"But nothing," she snapped, glaring at him over her glasses. "I didn't risk everything so you could get yourself slaughtered."

That shut him down hard. All at once, Iggs's color went back to normal. His body shrank and his teeth pulled back under his lips as he reached up to rub his eyes behind his dark glasses.

Bex released his arm with an apologetic pat. She hated it, too. Hated all of this, but there was nothing to be done right now. She was trying to figure out how to remind Iggs there was still hope in the future without saying something compromising in enemy territory when Adrian suddenly whirled around.

"Got it!"

His cheery expression was so out of place after what had just happened, Bex could only blink at him.

"Got what?"

"The Lot's Salt," he said excitedly, opening the paper bag in his hands to show her what did, indeed, look like a lump of rock salt. "I took his first offer, so I got fantastically ripped off, but I've never been good at haggling, and I figured you'd like to get out of here sooner rather than later."

That was the best thing anyone had said to Bex all night. She happily motioned for Adrian to lead the way, which he did with astonishing speed, striding down the grassy path so fast, Bex had to grab Iggs to make sure he kept up. They'd just fallen into a trot when Adrian asked, "Where's Nemini?"

Bex waited for the void demon to answer for herself. When Nemini didn't, Bex stopped cold, holding herself perfectly still as she opened her senses to the market.

That didn't usually net her much these days, but chugging that bottle of deathly water must have given back more than she'd realized, because Bex could feel the telltale emptiness of Nemini's presence over by the slave-auction cages. That didn't strike her as a good place for one of her demons to be, but unlike Iggs, Nemini knew her limits. Whatever she was doing, it wouldn't get them killed. That was as much as Bex could ask, so she left the demon to it.

"Nemini can take care of herself," she said. "Let's just get out of here."

Adrian nodded and started walking again at a pace that would have been a jog for anyone else. The fast pace drew an uncomfortable amount of attention, but Bex didn't tell him to slow down. The only thing she wanted at this point was out, and they were nearly there. The tunnel back to the gum alley was already in sight: a freestanding doorway framed by waving grass a dozen feet beyond the Market's edge. They'd just cleared the last of the stupid lobster tents when a hand shot out of nowhere to grab Bex's shoulder.

She nearly pulled whoever it was over. That clearly wasn't what the grabber had expected, because she caught a little squawk of surprise that quickly transformed into an inhuman growl. Bex growled back, reaching up to pry the hand off her shoulder only to stop short when she saw the unmistakable shiny bronze skin of a transformed war demon.

If they'd been anywhere but an Anchor Market, that would have been reason enough for Bex to rip his hand off. War demons were traitors, bloodthirsty battle fanatics who'd joined Gilgamesh against their own kind in return for the promise of endless combat. Their betrayal had earned them a privileged position under the Eternal King's boot, but it was their innate need to follow orders that made them the warlocks' favorite pets.

This one wasn't even a choice specimen. Despite being in his true shape rather than a human guise, he was barely taller than Iggs. His skin was literally bronzed, as shiny as polished metal and just as hard, and his flat, bone-colored horns covered his entire skull like a helmet. He had two arms, not four, so he must have been *very* young, but his gleaming neck was ringed only with the same tattooed slave band that Iggs had painted on himself and Bex. There was no sin iron control collar or pain cuffs, which meant this baby war demon was already a trusted bootlicker.

He certainly acted like a loyal dog. The moment his warlock—a sneering, middle-aged man with hair plugs and a suit even gaudier than Adrian's—jerked his head, the war demon let go of Bex and skittered back, making room for his master to step forward.

"Blessed Gilgamesh," the warlock said, looking Bex up and down like he was trying to figure out if she was venomous. "What in the Hells are you?"

Bex didn't answer, both because she didn't owe this scumbag shit and because it would blow their cover. Warlocks spoke for their demons, and since Adrian was currently pretending to be hers, he was the one who had to step up.

He did so after only a few moments' hesitation, looking down on the stranger with an expression that wasn't nearly as haughty as it should have been but was still a good show compared to his usual friendliness.

"Is there a problem?"

The other warlock was too busy staring at Bex to answer. "What did you do to grow her horns so big?" he asked, reaching out to grab Bex's left horn, or at least he tried to. Iggs got there first, smacking the man's hand away so fast, the warlock didn't seem to understand what had happened.

"What kind of stunt are you trying to pull?" he demanded, clutching his hand as he turned his snarl on Adrian. "Control your demons, or I'll control them for you."

"My demons have done nothing wrong in my estimation," Adrian replied, sounding impressively scary now. "Hasn't anyone taught you not to touch other people's property?"

The warlock narrowed his eyes suspiciously. "You're awful high and mighty for someone who's not even in his own territory. What cabal are you from? What are you doing here?"

"Working," Adrian answered crisply. "I'm here on behalf of the New England cabal under the personal direction of the High Warlock."

Bex was impressed by that smooth line of bullshit. She just hoped Adrian could keep it up through the interrogation that was bound to come next. To her surprise, though, the warlock started nodding.

"That explains it," he said. "We just got word this evening that he was on his way. Some kind of priority operation, but I'm not surprised his minions are already swarming. The Spider always did like sticking his pincers where they weren't wanted."

Adrian's sneer faltered, and for a second, Bex was worried they'd just lost it. Then his nose went up again. "I'm sure my master would be flattered to hear your opinion," he said in a voice as sharp as a knife across the neck. "Can we count on the Seattle cabal's support in our endeavors?"

The warlock snorted. "Not on your life. The Spider's climbed high enough as it is. None of us are lifting a finger to help him unless he begs. Tell *that* to your bloated insect when he comes to spin his webs, and teach your demons some manners." He snapped his fingers. "Kirtz!"

The shiny bronze war demon leaped to obey, following his master like a puppy as the warlock stomped away.

"Traitorous filth," Iggs spat.

Adrian didn't say anything. He just turned and started for the exit at slightly less than a panicked run. Bex and Iggs matched his pace easily, jogging one step behind him like the loyal demons they were pretending to be. Bex was making a frantic plan for how they were going to get past the guards without Nemini when the void demon suddenly appeared beside them like she'd never left.

"Where were you?" Iggs hissed. "We could have used a hand back there!"

"You didn't appear to need assistance," Nemini replied with her usual calm. "Not that my help would have changed anything since we're all—"

"Give it a rest, Captain Bringdown," Iggs snapped, waving his hand at the golden-armored elbows that were already visible at the end of the tunnel. "Go get the guards."

If Nemini was ruffled by Iggs's anger, she didn't show it, but she also didn't do anything until Bex nodded her permission. Only then did the void demon pull ahead, reaching out to touch both guards just in time for the other three to run past.

No one said anything else until they were back in the gum alley, and that was only so Bex could order them to go up to the street level. They ran in silence for another three blocks, heading up the hill into downtown Seattle, where the normal humans lived and worked. Only when they were well out of earshot of anything remotely magical did Bex finally call a halt. She tossed a street-cart vendor a twenty and snagged an armful of bottled waters so she and Iggs could clean the hated slave bands off their neck.

"You want to tell me what that was about?" she asked as she washed the paint off.

The question was aimed at Adrian, but it was Nemini who answered.

"I went to the slaves," she said, looking at Bex with her clear golden eyes.

Iggs's brows shot up over his sunglasses. "You didn't do your void thing on them, did you?"

When Nemini didn't deny it, Iggs's face went scarlet. "How could you?" he yelled. "Haven't they suffered enough without—"

His rant cut off like a dropped knife when Nemini turned her gaze on him. "It's because they suffer that I did it," she told him in a calm, quiet voice. "There is freedom in nonexistence. There is no pain in the void."

Iggs took a step back, shaking his head the whole way, but Bex smiled.

"You did a good thing," she said, touching Nemini on the shoulder. The contact filled her mind with terrifying nothingness, but no one else ever voluntarily touched Nemini, so until the demon told her to stop, Bex was determined to keep it up. "I'm just glad you didn't get caught."

"How could I be caught?" Nemini replied in her usual monotone. "You can't cage nothing."

Bex wasn't sure if she was speaking literally or philosophically, but Nemini's snakes were dipping down to touch her hand with their blunt noses, so she decided to count it as a positive outcome.

Once her demons were in order, Bex turned to Adrian, who'd shed his warlock costume and was back in his usual black with his broom tucked under his arm. He hadn't put on his witch hat yet, but Boston was on his shoulder again, and the two of them were glued to Adrian's phone.

"How bad is it?"

They both jumped, and then Adrian lowered his phone with a sigh.

"Not as bad as it could be," he said, clearly grasping for a silver lining. "I didn't think they'd find out I was gone— or where I'd gone—so quickly, but there's no other reason for New England warlocks to be in Seattle. It sounds like the local cabal is determined to be maximally unhelpful, though, so that's a bonus."

Bex wasn't sure about that. "And the Spider?"

"He's the *really* bad part," Boston answered in a doomed voice. "The Spider is the head of the New England cabal, a position that gives him nearly unlimited authority within his territory. Fortunately for us, we're not in his territory. *Un*fortunately for us, the Spider's one of the oldest and most powerful warlocks in the Americas, and he didn't get his name through the usual macho posturing. 'The Spider' isn't just a moniker. It's his title, an honor granted by Gilgamesh himself in return for years of faithful service."

That explained it. Among the Eternal King's cronies, granted titles were effectively the word of God. They replaced your name and anything else that got in the way of making "Tool of Gilgamesh" your sole identity. Bex didn't go east of the Rockies much, so she'd never heard of the Spider specifically, but she had no reason to believe he wasn't an absolute nightmare, especially with the face Adrian was making.

"I suppose I should be flattered he's come after me personally," the witch muttered, staring bleakly at his phone screen. "But on the bright side, if the Spider's doing this himself, that actually gives us more time."

"How do you figure that?" Bex asked.

"Because the Spider is patient," Adrian explained. "He didn't earn his title by being sloppy. He takes his time and weaves his webs until there's no escape, and he won't be in a hurry since he knows I can't abandon my new grove." He flashed her a grim smile. "I'll just have to hope that I can grow a forest faster than he can get ready to tear one down."

Bex sighed. "If that's the situation, our best bet is to make sure no one in Seattle's magical community knows where you are. The more time we can force the Spider to spend looking for you, the longer we'll have to prepare."

Adrian nodded rapidly. "My thoughts exactly. That's actually why I chose Bainbridge. I knew whoever the warlocks sent would expect a Blackwood to run for the rainforests on the mainland, or up into the Olympic mountains. They'd never expect me to stay close to civilization, or try to grow a witchwood an island."

"Good," Bex said. "We can leverage that even harder by going to ground. Is that salt the last thing you needed?"

"The last magical thing," Adrian said, pulling out his phone again. "I still have to buy enough food to tide me over until I get my garden going. I was planning to go to the grocery store on the island tomorrow, but since we're suddenly on a deadline, I'd rather take care of it here."

Bex looked up at the skyscrapers glinting in the last light of the sunset, none of which looked like a grocery store. "*Can* you take care of it here?"

Adrian tapped his phone a few more times before turning the glowing screen around to show her a map. "There's a Korean grocery mart one block away."

Since she wasn't a masticator, that meant nothing to Bex. "Is Korean good?"

"Best produce you can find at a chain store," Adrian told her authoritatively as he started down the sidewalk. "Come on. Let's go stock up before we disappear."

Bex nodded and fell into step beside him, motioning for Iggs and Nemini to watch their rear.

Chapter 7

Forty-five minutes later, Adrian had secured enough food for the week.

"I can't believe you brought your own shopping bags," Iggs said as they walked up the wide staircase connecting the basement-level grocery store to the sidewalk outside. "How much stuff can you fit in your coat, anyway?"

"Fifteen cubic feet," Boston answered authoritatively, hopping off the cement planter he'd been forced to wait on, since cats weren't allowed in grocery stores. "Though he can push it to sixteen in a pinch."

"And yet, somehow, it's still never enough," Adrian lamented, using the city's harsh shadows as cover while he crammed the reusable canvas bags filled with fruits, vegetables, and spicy dried noodles into the largest of his pockets. "It's also still heavy."

The big demon gave him a skeptical look that even his ever-present sunglasses couldn't hide. "It's only four bags."

"Want us to carry them for you?" offered Bex, who'd been keeping watch on the corner.

"I've got it," Adrian assured her. "This way all of our hands are free."

And speaking of free hands, he took the opportunity to pull out his phone and check his list one more time. The forest would be able to provide for all his needs eventually, but his grove was barely started, and his garden wasn't even in the ground. He'd probably need at least one more supply run before he was self-sufficient enough to get by, but he wanted to go ahead and lay in as many nonperishables as possible. He was checking his map for any other stores that might be useful when he noticed an exciting icon not five hundred feet from their current position.

"Can we make one more stop?"

"Sure," Bex said, stepping around Nemini to stand in front of him. "What do you need?"

"It's not a need, exactly," Adrian admitted, showing her his phone. "But there's a boba tea shop I've been wanting to try right around the corner. We don't have any authentic boba places where I live, and this one is supposed to be *really* good."

Bex's mouth pulled into a confused frown. "Can't you make tea at home?"

"Yes, but this tea is cold and has tapioca pearls in it."

She looked unconvinced. "I thought our plan was to lie low."

"We will," Adrian promised. "But you can't work all the time, and the Spider just got into town today. He *definitely* won't be looking for a forest witch in downtown Seattle, which means this might be my only chance." He flashed her his best cajoling smile. "Come on, it'll only take ten minutes."

Bex sighed and motioned for Adrian to lead the way. She fell into step beside him the moment he started moving, while Iggs and Nemini brought up the rear. That was going to take some getting used to, but it was still nice to have people he trusted around him. Aside from those horrible months with the warlocks, this was the first time Adrian had been away from home and apart from his fellow witches. If he'd been by himself in a strange city, he would have felt quite adrift, but it was impossible to be lonely with Bex walking so close that he would have stepped on her if she hadn't been so fast.

Since it was now very dark and she was right there, Adrian took the risk of getting a closer look at her. She'd been acting normal all evening—or at least what he assumed was normal for Bex—but he hadn't forgotten what he'd seen in her bedroom. Now that he knew how thin she was under her baggy clothes, he saw it in her every movement. She was still quick, still efficient and in command, but Adrian had the distinct impression he was seeing a shadow of what she should be. He didn't know if it was starvation or sickness or some other malady unique to demons, but he'd healed enough people to know pain when he saw it, and there was no doubt in his mind that Bex was hurt. Fundamentally, critically injured in some way he didn't yet understand. And while he couldn't do anything about that until she trusted him enough to tell him what was wrong, Adrian was determined to do *something*. He was still racking his brain to figure out what when they reached the shop he'd marked.

It looked just like its photo on the internet, all lit up like a lantern with its bright windows shining onto the gloomy sidewalk in welcome. Even out here on the street, the scent of sugar and high-quality black tea was intoxicating, reminding Adrian that he hadn't eaten since his airplane breakfast this morning. There'd just been too much going on to think about food. Now that he'd remembered, though, nothing could stop him. He burst into motion, pausing only to set down Boston—who wasn't allowed in tea shops any more than he'd been allowed in supermarkets—before yanking open the jingly door and plunging himself into the sweet-smelling heaven inside.

The shop was part of a Taiwanese chain and clearly doing well for itself. The small interior was bright white and spotlessly clean. A huge iron kettle full of jet-black boba pearls bubbling in brown sugar syrup was proudly displayed on the counter, and even with a staff of four flying around the tiny kitchen, the line of customers reached almost to the sidewalk.

Iggs and Nemini bailed the moment they saw it, going back out to the street to wait with Boston. Only Bex stayed with him, standing practically on Adrian's feet in her efforts to get away from the non-magical humans, who were already giving them strange looks.

Adrian wasn't worried about that. He wasn't doing any magic at the moment, and no one got kicked just for carrying a broom and wearing a witch hat. He was very aware of how much he and Bex stuck out, though, which was exactly what they *weren't* supposed to be doing. Bex couldn't do anything about her horns, but he had plenty of options on the table, starting with his hat, which he deftly removed and slid into his pocket.

A few seconds later, he put his broom in as well. There wasn't really enough room, but even when Adrian held him close, Bran was *big*. Far too big for the small shop, which was both rude and dangerous since humans tended to remember things that inconvenienced them. The broom had to go, so Adrian sucked it up, using the long drape of his coat to hide what he was doing as he fed Bran, bristles and all, into the largest of his pockets.

When he'd gotten everything arranged so the carved handle wouldn't poke his ribs too badly, Adrian reached over Bex's shoulder to snag a plastic menu off the tea shop's counter. The descriptions were all in Mandarin, which he didn't read, but there were pictures of every drink along with names written in English. Since he'd obsessively poured over every Seattle food review site before leaving home, Adrian already knew exactly what he wanted, so he passed the menu to Bex instead.

"I don't know why you're handing this to me," she whispered, passing it back. "Demons don't eat physical food on this side."

"But you can still taste it, right?" Adrian asked. "Iggs likes candy."

"Well, yeah, food is delicious," Bex admitted. "But it doesn't do anything for us, so there's no point."

"Being delicious *is* the point," he argued, a smile creeping over his face as he held the menu in front of her. "Go ahead. Pick anything you want. My treat."

She shook her head. "Don't waste your money. I don't need boba tea."

"Need has nothing to do with it," he insisted, "and it's not a waste if you enjoy it."

Bex opened her mouth to keep arguing, but Adrian cut her off, bending over slightly until he was looking right into her sunglasses.

"Blackwood witchcraft is a braid of three parts," he told her quietly. "The bones, the flesh, and the soul. Every witch uses all three, but we dedicate ourselves to just one. Those who bury their bones are witches of the past. Those who bury their souls are witches of the future. I buried my heart. That makes me a witch of the present, and in the present moment, there is no greater gift than joy." He tapped the menu with his finger. "If it makes you happy, I count it well bought. Now, what do you want?"

Bex stared at him for a long moment, and then he saw color steal over her cheeks as she turned her hidden eyes to the menu in his hands. After studying both sides, she pointed at a pink cup decorated with bright red strawberry slices.

"That one."

"Strawberry milk," Adrian read, adding it to his mental list. "And what do you think Iggs and Nemini would like?"

"I have no idea," Bex confessed, shaking her head.

"We'll go with the most popular, then," Adrian said, not bothering to hide his smile as the line shuffled toward the register.

He bought the drinks and then moved back to the front counter to watch them get made. Adrian loved watching other professionals work, especially if food was involved. There was just something so fascinating about how jugs of black tea and scoops of cream came together into a beautiful whole that looked exactly like the pictures on the menu by the time the employees sealed the drinks and handed them over.

"How is it?" Adrian asked, not even taking a sip of his crème brûlée black tea with black sugar boba and added coffee jelly in his excitement to watch Bex taste hers.

She gave him a self-conscious head tilt, but she used the sharp end of her boba straw to spear the drink's flimsy plastic lid with expert force. She put the straw to her lips next, taking a sip only to jump when she actually got the drink into her mouth.

"It pops," she said, putting a hand over her lips in surprise.

"It's got popping boba," Adrian said smugly, finally taking a sip of his own drink, which was every bit as good as the internet had promised. He closed his eyes for a moment to savor the delightful contrast of bitter coffee jelly and burnt sugar with the sweet, cold, milky tea, and then he turned back to Bex with a smile.

"Do you like it?"

"I don't know," she confessed. "I've never had anything like this." She took another sip, and then, at last, Adrian got what he'd been waiting for when her mouth curved into a smile. Not a smirk, not a grin, not a polite turn of the lips, but a real smile that lit up her entire face.

"I do like it," she said. "Thank you."

"You're welcome," he replied, beaming back at her as he collected their other two drinks, which the staff had just placed on the counter. Bex had to help him carry it all, but eventually they got everything together. They'd just made it back to the door when Adrian heard the familiar sound of Boston's yowl.

He burst out onto the sidewalk to see his familiar having a standoff with Iggs in the middle of the street. The black cat's back was arched, and his fur was poofed to twice its normal size. Neither was a good sign, and Adrian stepped in at once.

"What is going on?" he demanded, setting their drinks down on one of the café's outdoor tables so he could deal with this situation properly.

"Don't yell at me," Boston snarled, his green eyes narrowed to furious slits as he bared his pointed teeth at Iggs, who looked even bigger than usual. "Tell it to the idiot war demon who can't keep his paws to himself!"

"I'm not a war demon!" Iggs bellowed. "And I was *trying* to pet you! You're a cat! *I like cats!*"

"Iggs," Bex said.

The warning in her voice cut through the tension like a knife, but while the demon backed down immediately, Boston was having none of it.

"*I will not be treated like a stupid animal!*" he roared, spitting in fury. "I am a familiar of the Blackwood! The

113

product of untold generations of magical pedigree! I am a great and powerful creature! *I am not yours to pet!*"

"*Boston!*" Adrian yelled, but unlike Bex's demons, cats were not obedient, and it did no good. Boston just got bigger, his black body swelling until he was the size of a Doberman.

"How do you like that, horn boy?" he taunted, baring his new, impressive fangs. "Want to try petting me now that I can bite off your—"

"Holy shit."

Everyone froze. Adrian, the demons, even Boston went stone-still as the woman coming out of the café behind them—the *human* woman with scales clearly visible in her wide eyes—dropped her freshly made cup of boba tea.

"It's a giant talking cat!"

Adrian had just enough time to see Boston's ears go flat against his skull before the kick hit him.

Having spent nearly his entire life inside the Blackwood, Adrian had never been kicked before. No one he knew had. Kicks were something that happened to cocky sorcerers and other quintessence-drunk idiots, never to clever, sensible witches like the Blackwoods. But today was a day of many firsts, and Adrian's first kick caught him square in the chest.

Oddly, his very first thought was that the name was far more accurate than he'd expected. It really did feel exactly like a giant metal boot had kicked him in the ribs, knocking out his breath and sending him flying. He landed hard on his back a few seconds later, his lungs seizing as he struggled to breathe. He was still working on it when a pair of hard hands grabbed him by the shoulders.

"You okay?"

Adrian wasn't sure. He'd never been knocked so flat by anything in his life, and his aunts hit *hard*. Nothing felt broken, though, and his lungs started working again a few seconds later, so he bobbed his head. The moment he nodded, the hard hands yanked him to his feet. Just picked him right up off the ground until he was standing nose to nose with a grim-faced Bex.

"First time getting kicked?"

Since he was still panting too hard to speak, Adrian nodded again. He turned to check on Boston next, but what he saw made him freeze.

They were no longer on the dark sidewalk in front of the cheery boba shop. Instead, he, Bex, Iggs, Nemini, and a now much smaller Boston were standing in an empty landscape of pure swirling gray. There were no buildings, no landmarks, no sun or sky. If his feet hadn't been planted on it, Adrian wouldn't have said there was a ground. It was all just gray, like they'd been dropped onto a sheet of unprinted newspaper.

"Where are we?" he whispered, holding out his arms for Boston, who leaped into them at once.

"Limbo," Bex replied, breaking into a jog. "Come on. We have to get moving before they find us."

"Before who finds us?" Boston whispered in a tiny voice as Adrian jogged after her.

"The kick demons," Bex said, her voice all business as she picked up the pace.

Adrian winced. He'd read about kick demons, but that was early in his apprenticeship, and he hadn't bothered with the subject since. He was trying to remember anything that might be useful when Boston's claws dug into his arm.

"I am so sorry," he said, sounding more scared than Adrian had ever heard him. "I'm the reason this happened. I—"

"Don't worry about it," Bex said, motioning for Iggs and Nemini to form a triangle around Adrian. "This is what you paid us for, and Iggs shouldn't have tried to pet you."

"How is this my fault?" Iggs snapped, but Bex must have given him a glare for the ages, because he shut right back up.

"We're going to die," Boston moaned, his ears pressed so flat against his fur that Adrian almost couldn't see them. "No one survives a kick. We're going to be stuck in this horrible place forever and—"

"We've survived plenty of kicks," Bex told him in a calm, practical voice. "It's not fun, but it's totally doable if we keep moving."

Boston made a scared little sound, and Adrian took the opportunity to tuck him into his coat. It was a tight fit with his broom and everything else, but for once, his familiar didn't complain. He dove right inside, curling himself into a terrified little ball.

Adrian gave him one more pat before turning his attention back to Bex. "What are we in for?"

"Hopefully nothing," she said, turning her head from side to side as if she were looking for something. "Kicks are an automatic punishment, not a smart one. When a human sees something they shouldn't, the scales remove the incident from their brains and kick the offenders into Limbo."

She waved her hand at the gray nothing that didn't seem to change no matter how fast they ran, and Adrian's mouth pressed into a tight line. "How do we get out?"

"We don't," Bex said. "Limbo is a disconnected space, neither Paradise nor Earth. Even Gilgamesh can't keep us here for more than five minutes without coming down personally to damn our souls, which he doesn't care enough to bother with. Limbo's just where the kick dumps you to de-escalate the situation and get you away from whatever scaley you spooked." She shot him a bitter smirk over her shoulder. "Can't have the normies realizing magic is real and demanding their share."

"I understand that part," Adrian said, struggling to match her pace. "But what happens after five minutes? Do we just get dumped back out?"

"Pretty much," Bex said. "The tricky bit is making it that long. We might not be damned to Limbo, but the kick demons are, and we're their only source of food."

Adrian looked around the empty gray nothing. "I don't see anything."

"You won't," she said, grabbing his arm to make sure he was keeping up. "But I promise they've seen us. Demons don't normally eat other demons or human flesh, but since Gilgamesh damned them to this emptiness five thousand years ago, the prisoners of Limbo are starved enough to eat anything. Kicks are the only time they get fed, and they never miss a—"

She slid to a halt, stopping so suddenly that Adrian nearly tripped trying not to crash into her. He was still opening his mouth to ask what was wrong when he saw it.

A shape was standing ahead of them. It was as gray as everything else, which made it very hard to see, but the few bits Adrian could make out were enormous. The creature had to be fifteen feet tall, bigger than any war demon he'd ever seen. It was vaguely humanoid in that it was standing upright on two legs, but its body was a mountain of hard, lumpy muscle, and its huge jaws were so packed with teeth that they were practically rectangular. Worst of all, though, were its horns. They were absolutely enormous, two giant curving spears that tapered to stabbing points just like Bex's did. But where hers were gracefully long and thin, this demon's horns were thick like an ox's. Every part of it was the same unrelenting gray as the rest of Limbo, but its mouth was as black as demon blood when it opened its jaws and roared.

"*Shit,*" Bex hissed, shoving Adrian behind her. "We would get a big one."

The small, calm piece of Adrian's mind that still noted such things was happy to hear not all kick demons were this monstrously gigantic. The rest of him, however, was flipping into battle mode.

"How do we fight it?"

"*We* don't do anything," Bex said sternly. "*You* hang back where it's safe and let us do what you paid us for. Nemini!"

Adrian jumped. The void demon was so quiet, he'd forgotten she was there, but she stepped up the moment Bex said her name.

"Lock down Adrian," Bex ordered, taking off her sunglasses and shoving them into her jacket pocket. "Iggs, you're with me."

Iggs stepped forward at once, but when Adrian tried to tell Bex he was not going to hang back and be *locked down* while they fought, Nemini's hand landed on his arm, and the nothingness washed into him.

"Emptied him" would have been more accurate. As soon as Nemini's delicate fingers touched his sleeve, all of Adrian's fears drained away like water into dry sand. He tried to claw them back immediately—not because he wanted to be afraid, but because he couldn't afford not to care right now. Bex and Iggs had already stepped up to face the charging kick demon, but they looked like tiny dolls compared to the horrifying gray monstrosity thundering toward them. Bex especially looked small and frail as she clenched her fists and braced her short legs, ducking her head low like she meant to spear the rampaging demon with her delicate horns.

"It's all right," Nemini said calmly when he began to struggle. "There's nothing you can do. Just let it go."

Adrian shook his head. His mind was emptying like a sieve, but he could still feel the adrenalin surging through his body, and, since he was a Witch of the Flesh, his body was what he listened to. He shoved his hand into his jacket, flicking through the hundreds of pockets for the one he needed. He was still searching when the rampaging demon slammed into Bex.

"*No!*" he shouted, or meant to shout. The cry never actually made it past his lips, because the moment the demon's giant leg landed on Bex, she caught it.

The blankness that filled Adrian's mind then had nothing to do with Nemini. This was good old-fashioned shock as he watched Bex—the same starved, skeletal Bex he'd found passed out from exhaustion just a few hours earlier—grab the gray leg that was bigger than her entire body and twist it sideways. This sent the monster stumbling into Iggs, who grabbed its flailing arm and twisted the same way Bex had, using the momentum she'd started to send the giant demon flying out into the gray nothing of Limbo.

"*Go!*"

Adrian didn't even realize Bex was shouting at him until she grabbed his hand and yanked him forward. Nemini let him go at the same time, sending all the fear she'd drained out rushing back in. If Bex hadn't been hauling him forward like a train, the shock would have knocked Adrian flat on his face. Thanks to her, though, he was able to keep moving, shooting his hand back to his pocket for the curse Boston was already shoving into his fingers. It felt like one of his good ones, but when he yanked back his arm for the throw, Iggs grabbed him.

"Stop that!" the big demon yelled, shoving Adrian's arm back down. "Weren't you listening? You don't fight!"

"I have to do something!" Adrian yelled back—in an admittedly panicked voice since Nemini was no longer keeping down the mortal terror of being chased by a demon the size of a truck. Bex and Iggs's throw didn't even seem to have done damage when he looked over his shoulder. The kick demon was already back on its feet and charging after them again, its huge-toothed jaws flying open in a bellow so loud, Adrian felt in his chest.

"We can't just run away!" he cried frantically, clutching his fist around the curse, which, in its inactive form, looked like a dried stag beetle.

"We can and we have," Bex said, tightening her crushing grip on his other hand. "This is a time trial, remember? We don't have to beat anything. We just have to not get eaten for five minutes."

"I don't think that's a realistic goal," Adrian said, desperately striving to match her calm. "It's faster than us, but it doesn't seem very smart. We could—"

"Kick demons are plenty smart!" Iggs yelled. "Now put that weird witch-bug thing back in your coat of holding. We're not fighting them!"

"Why not?" Adrian demanded.

"Because it's not their fault," Bex said.

The sadness in her voice hit his anger like a bucket of ice water. He'd been so focused on the kick demons' monstrousness, he'd completely forgotten that they were demons just like the ones he was running with. These were their people, damned to Limbo by Gilgamesh. They couldn't help that they were mad with starvation. But while Adrian finally understood why Bex had chosen this path, he still didn't think it was going to work.

"What if I used something nonlethal?" he compromised, putting the beetle curse back into his pocket. "A sticky trap or—"

His suggestions cut off with an *oof* as Bex stopped on a dime, causing Adrian to crash into her back. This, in turn, caused Adrian to *oof* again. She might have looked like a ninety-pound skeleton wearing a too-big leather jacket, but running into Bex felt like running into a cement pole. He was still trying to get his breath back when Iggs said, "Shit."

Adrian's head snapped back up. Limbo's unrelenting grayness made it difficult to see anything in detail, but if he stared into the blankness hard enough, he could just make out a crowd of shapes. Huge, fang-toothed, monstrous shapes. He wasn't sure when it had happened, but at some point during their running, they'd become surrounded, and now, kick demons were all Adrian could see.

"They're fast today," Bex said in an irritated voice, looking over her shoulder, but not at Adrian. Her fiery eyes—clearly visible now that she'd taken off her sunglasses—were locked on Iggs.

"You up for this?"

"Don't have much choice, do I?" the big demon said, taking off his own sunglasses and tossing them at Bex. "Just make sure you're ready to catch me."

Adrian had no idea what that meant, but Bex gave her demon a determined nod.

"I've got you," she promised, placing his sunglasses carefully next to hers. "Roll 'em."

The moment the command left her lips, Iggs changed. Adrian had seen demons revert to their true forms before, but that was years ago, back at the cabal during the training he'd tried very hard to forget. Even if he'd been a jaded expert, though, Adrian had the feeling Iggs's transformation would still have been incredible. There was no stretching, no warping, no ripped clothing. He simply flipped like a switch, going from a large, thick-necked, dark-haired, horned man dressed in worn blue denim to the biggest demon Adrian had ever seen.

Biggest and *strangest*. All this time, Adrian had assumed, like Boston, that Iggs was a war demon. There were simply no other demons whose human guises got that big. Even when he'd flat-out told Boston he wasn't one, Adrian hadn't thought much of it. War demons were famously hated as traitors, so it hadn't struck him as surprising that a free war demon running with Bex's crew would deny the name. Now, though, Adrian saw that Iggs had been speaking literally.

The demon Iggs turned into looked nothing like the bronze-skinned lug from the Anchor Market. His skin was crimson, bright red and slightly pebbly, like the skin of a rhinoceros. He had hair, too, a huge dark crop of it on top of his giant head, which was every bit as fang-filled and square-jawed as the kick demons'. Like them, he was huge and enormously muscled, but what really stole Adrian's breath were his horns. They were black instead of gray because Iggs wasn't damned to Limbo, but his horns were the same curving, ox-like spikes as the monster he and Bex had sent flying earlier.

"He's a kick demon," Adrian whispered, stepping forward in wonder.

"No," Bex said, yanking him back behind her. "He's a wrath demon."

Adrian blinked. He'd never heard of a wrath demon, which struck him as very wrong. Even witches who'd never had to endure a day of warlock training knew there were only seven types of demon. Eight if you counted the supposedly extinct void demons like Nemini, but he'd still heard of them. Adrian had never heard *anyone* talk about wrath demons before, which was a real shame, because Iggs was extraordinary.

Even the mad kick demons saw it. The moment Iggs transformed, they started backing away, cowering like the shadows Adrian could now see they were. All the gray monsters that had seemed so terrifying only seconds before now looked like shriveled husks, literal pale imitations of the giant, healthy, fire-engine-red demon standing in front of them. For a moment, it looked as if that was going to be enough to stop the fight. Then the mad hunger flashed in the kick demons' gray eyes, and the whole mass leaped forward, falling on Iggs like a pack of starving wolves.

He threw them off again with a roar that shook the ground. Adrian ducked as a kick demon flew over their heads, but though it landed right behind them, the gray beast seemed to have forgotten that the rest of them existed. Every kick demon Adrian could see was fixated on Iggs, flying back at him as fast as he could tear them off. But while the damned demons were clearly weaker, there were a *lot* of them, and even more were coming.

Iggs's roar must have been a siren call, because the gray nothing of Limbo, which had looked so empty while they were running, was suddenly boiling over with kick demons. They came from all directions, throwing themselves at Iggs with a mad hunger so intense, Adrian could feel an echo of it inside his own stomach. Their weak gray teeth had trouble penetrating Iggs's tough red hide, but a few must have made it through, because the ground under Iggs's clawed feet was rapidly turning black with his blood. But when Adrian turned to ask Bex how they were going to help, her pale hands locked him in place.

"Don't interfere."

"We have to do something!" Adrian cried. "They're tearing him to shreds! He won't last long like—"

"He doesn't have to last long," Bex reminded him, her burning eyes pinned on Iggs. "How many minutes have we got left?"

"Two," Nemini answered, no comment about time being an illusion this time.

"He can make it," Bex said with a relieved breath, easing her death grip on Adrian slightly. "Iggs is tough."

That was obvious, but it was still harrowing to watch. Iggs was buried in kick demons now, but while they were chomping on him like piranhas, the wrath demon never chomped back. He didn't claw them, didn't punch. Other than throwing them off whenever he got the chance, he didn't fight back at all.

"He doesn't want to hurt them," Boston said, finally sticking his head out of Adrian's coat.

"Of course he doesn't," Bex replied. "They're his people."

"I suppose this explains why there are nine Hells but only eight types of demon," Adrian's familiar said, his green eyes shining with curiosity as he leaned forward for a better look. "The ninth ones got stuck in here."

Adrian had been thinking the same thing, but he still didn't understand. "Why did Gilgamesh damn them to Limbo? Every other sort of demon was enslaved and put to work. Why not Wrath?"

"Because he couldn't make them kneel," Bex said, her fingers tightening on Adrian's arm again as she watched Iggs bleed. "Time?"

"Fifty-nine seconds," Nemini answered.

They were harrowing ones. With all the roars shaking the once-quiet world of Limbo, more kick demons were arriving from far and wide. Many were huge like the first one, but smaller demons were starting to show up as well now. Children, Adrian realized with a wince. Little demons with stumpy baby horns were crawling under the bigger ones' feet, lapping Iggs's black blood off the ground as the final minute ticked down. Then, right after Nemini called the five-second warning, Bex finally released her death grip on Adrian's arm.

Adrian had no idea why. There were so many kick demons piled on top of Iggs now that his giant red body was no longer visible. Getting anywhere near that fight looked like suicide, but Bex ran straight at it, her short legs pumping as she charged the writhing gray pile of flashing eyes and chomping teeth.

"Two seconds," Nemini whispered, grabbing Adrian's hand to keep him from going after her, but Adrian hadn't moved. He couldn't, because the ground was already dissolving under his feet, the gray floor ripping like wet paper to leave him in free fall. The only reason he didn't panic was because panic was impossible while Nemini was touching him. All he could do was keep his eyes on Bex as she elbowed her way deeper into the writhing mass of kick demons. And then, just when Adrian thought they were all going to fall away into nothing, he heard her yell out.

"*Iggerux!*"

Her voice cut through the demons' roars like an arrow, but it was the command inside it that made Adrian stagger. He'd spent as little time around warlocks as possible, but Adrian still recognized what Bex had done. She'd spoken Iggs's name. His true name, and she'd spoken it *hard*, which should have been impossible. So far as Adrian knew, warlocks were the only ones who could true-name demons. It was the root of their magic, the basis for their control. Knowing a demon's name was how you bound it to your will, but demons couldn't command other demons.

At least, that was what he'd been taught. No one seemed to have told Bex, though. She'd shouted Iggs's name like an attack, and the moment she said it, the gray pall of Limbo fell apart.

Adrian fell with it, dropping from what felt like a staggering height. Even with Nemini's void sucking the caring out of him, his arms began to windmill on instinct, frantically trying to slow his descent, but there was nothing to slow. Not a heartbeat after he started to fall, his feet landed on smooth, slightly tilted cement.

Adrian staggered as Nemini finally released him. When he finally caught his balance, he looked around to see that he was right back where he'd started: standing on the sidewalk in front of the brightly lit windows of the boba shop. Even the teas he'd put down when he'd gone for Boston were right where he'd left them, sitting on the metal café table in a puddle of condensation. Adrian was still trying to wrap his brain around it all when Boston clawed his way out of his coat.

"*Look,*" he hissed.

Adrian's head whipped around, though he already had a pretty good idea of what he'd see. Iggs had been buried in kick demons when they'd fallen out of Limbo, but unless he could change back as fast as he'd hulked out, there was no way he wouldn't still be huge. Adrian needed to get a Nevermind spell up quickly before one of the humans on the street spotted the giant red demon and kicked them all again. But as he dug into his pockets for his materials, Adrian actually *looked* at where Boston was pointing and saw there was no need.

There was no giant demon to Nevermind. With the exception of his absent sunglasses, which he'd handed to Bex, Iggs looked exactly the same as when he'd picked Adrian up from the airport this morning. He was normal sized, human colored, even back in his distressed denim. The only difference was that he was now on his knees, crouching in front of Bex with his head bent so low, his black horns touched the pavement at her feet.

The sight filled Adrian with dread. He knew that pose. It was the same one demons were forced into at the end of a warlock summoning, the surrender that made them a slave. But Iggs didn't look defeated. He was grinning when he raised his head, and his eyes—which were as red as Bex's burning ones, though without the fiery glow—were shining with triumph as he grabbed Bex's bony hand in his huge ones and pulled himself back to his feet.

"Nice catch!"

"Nice work," she replied, grinning back at Iggs as she handed him his sunglasses. She put her own on next, pushing them tight against the bridge of her nose before she turned to check on Adrian and Nemini.

"Everyone okay?"

"Nothing about that was okay!" Adrian cried, waving his hands frantically at Iggs, who was still getting his glasses settled over his ears. "What was *that*? How did you do... do *that*?"

"Relax," Iggs said, giving Adrian a cocky smile. "I'm a lot slower coming out of my true shape than going in, so Bex helps me out."

"He can't shrink down while they're gnawing on him or he'll get eaten," Bex explained in a calm voice. "But he can't come out of Limbo all big or we'd just get kicked right back in, so we figured out a solution."

"I understand that part," Adrian said, refusing to be deterred. "But I know what I saw. That was a warlock binding! You true-named him and forced him to kneel just like a—"

"*Hey*," said Iggs, who was suddenly right in his face. "Warlocks didn't invent this shit, and Bex didn't force me to do anything. She just saved my life and yours, so can it with your human-centric bullshit before I—"

"Iggs," Bex said, "leave it."

Her voice was so quiet, Adrian barely heard her over the bigger demon's yelling, but Iggs backed off immediately, stomping back to her side with a glare Adrian could feel through the wrath demon's dark glasses.

"I think that's enough excitement for one night," Bex said, putting her hands into her pockets. "Did you finish all your shopping?"

It took Adrian an embarrassingly long time to realize that question was for him.

"Yes," he said belatedly, shoulders slumping. "Yes, I'm done. We can leave any time."

"Good," Bex said, reaching over to snag one of the plastic-sealed drinks that were still sitting forgotten on the cafe table.

"What's this?" Iggs asked when she handed it to him.

"Boba tea," she answered. "Adrian bought it for you earlier."

That sounded like far too little and *far* too late, but to Adrian's enormous surprise, the big demon's face lit up.

"Sweet!" he cried, grabbing the drink out of Bex's hand. "I've only seen this shit on the internet before." He turned his grin on Adrian. "Thanks, man!"

"You're welcome," Adrian said after a moment's hesitation.

Iggs grabbed a boba straw from the cup by the café's door and stabbed the sharp end into the caramel-colored drink the girl at the register had assured Adrian that everybody liked. Sure enough, Iggs looked delighted. He sucked the whole cup down in seconds, not even complaining that most of the ice had melted during the five minutes they'd been in Limbo. He grabbed the drink Adrian had bought for Nemini next, happily slurping it down while Bex directed everyone up the hill toward a dark alley where Adrian would be able to bring out his broom without getting them kicked again.

"I'm sorry," Adrian said when Bex fell into her usual spot beside him.

"Don't worry about it," she said. "Iggs management is a learned skill."

He rubbed the back of his head. "No, I mean, I'm sorry for what I said. It was wrong of me to accuse you of acting like a warlock. I shouldn't have jumped to conclusions."

He looked at Bex nervously, but she just shrugged off his apology and kept walking, which only made him feel worse.

"You freed him, didn't you?" he asked quietly, looking ahead at where Iggs was attempting to offer Nemini's snakes a taste of his tea. "You saved him from Limbo. That's why he kneels to you, even though the wrath demons didn't kneel before Gilgamesh."

"What Iggs kneels for is his business," Bex said in a voice that, while not actually sharp, warned Adrian loud and clear that this was the place to stop. "Though if you really want to make it up to him, you should let him pet Boston. Iggs loves cats."

Her eyes flicked to his familiar, who was sitting in a sad little ball on Adrian's shoulder.

"I suppose it's the least I can do after the trouble I caused," Boston said, lowering his head to Bex. "I sincerely apologize for my loss of temper. If letting Iggs pet me will make amends, I'll bear it gladly."

"Only if you want to," Bex said, taking a sip from her strawberry milk tea, which Adrian hadn't even seen her pick up. "Like your witch said, we're not slave drivers."

Adrian took a deep breath. Before he could even think of how to reply, though, Bex held out his own barely touched cup of tea. He accepted it with murmured thanks, taking a long drink of watered-down—but still delicious— tea as his brain scrambled to make sense of everything that had just happened.

Chapter 8

After the kick, things got much easier. Boston didn't just let Iggs pet him, he sat in his lap the whole broom ride back, for which Bex was very grateful. Going into Limbo always made Iggs maudlin for perfectly understandable reasons, but between having someone buy him boba tea and getting to pet a magical cat as much as he wanted, her wrath demon was a ray of sunshine for a week afterward. A welcome development, since Lys was being a pill.

"It's just so *boring*," the lust demon moaned for the millionth time, hanging upside down from the tree branch Bex was using to keep an eye on the whole hilltop at once. "I thought witchcraft would be more fires and human sacrifices, but so far all he seems to be doing is yardwork."

Adrian did do a surprising amount of manual labor. He hadn't even gone to bed after they came back from shopping. Instead, he and Boston had gotten right to work digging a trench to bring in seawater from the inlet which would then be desalinated using the spell he'd bought the Lot's Salt for... or something. Bex honestly wasn't entirely sure what was going on. From where she was sitting, it looked like Adrian had spent a week digging a ditch and then filling it back in.

And not a week of normal days either. The witch worked in daylight and in dark. So far as Bex knew, he hadn't slept since he'd arrived.

When she'd asked him about it—because working yourself to exhaustion felt like a liability when you were expecting to be attacked—Adrian explained that he'd been bottling his sleep for the past year in preparation. Apparently, he had enough stored up to stay awake for two months straight if necessary, which struck Bex as insane, considering the amount of work he was doing during all those waking hours.

This morning, for example, Adrian and Iggs were using giant rocks unearthed by the trench project to make a stone circle at the center of the clearing in front of his house. Technically, rock-moving wasn't part of their job, but as the cat-bringer, Adrian was now Iggs's favorite human. It also helped that Adrian had treated him with enormous respect ever since the kick incident, which puffed her wrath demon's head up nicely.

"He's going to be insufferable after this," Lys warned, flipping into a small female body as they hauled themself back onto Bex's branch. "You spoil him rotten."

Bex shrugged. "Iggs has had a hard life."

"We've all had hard lives," Lys reminded her, resting their head on Bex's shoulder. "But at least the view is nice."

It *was* nice. Adrian had been every inch the proper, professional witch when she'd met him, but the moment it came time to get his hands dirty, he seemed to have forgotten clothes existed. He was at it right now, rolling a giant rock in nothing but his perfectly cut black trousers and well-earned sweat, which was making the summer afternoon much hotter than it should have been.

"Witch of the Flesh indeed," Lys purred, tapping their sharp-clawed fingers hungrily. "The constant stream of bare-chested physicality is the only thing that makes this job tolerable."

"If you're that bored, why don't you go into the city?" Bex suggested. "The Spider guy Adrian mentioned should be on the move by now. You could catch some food and see what he's up to."

"I *could* go for a dinner downtown," Lys said. "The spying, not so much."

"Why not? You love spying."

"I do," the lust demon admitted. "But poking the Spider is how you get webbed."

Bex frowned. "You've dealt with the Spider before?"

"*We've* dealt with the Spider before," Lys corrected. "He wasn't called the Spider back then, but he was still nasty enough that you scrapped the whole job and ordered us not to engage."

"*I* did that?" Bex asked, surprised.

Lys nodded. "Why do you think we've been on the West Coast for so long?"

Bex reached up to fiddle with the black ring hanging around her neck. She didn't remember any of that. Not that it was unusual for Lys to remember things Bex didn't, but it felt so strange to hear about decisions she'd made and not know her own reasoning. She must have had a good one to call off an entire mission, but no matter how hard Bex thought about it, the memories weren't there. They were *never* there, but that never stopped her from trying.

"Spying wouldn't make a difference, anyway," Lys went on. "Even if I managed to steal the Spider's day planner, our shirtless hunk of a client is already witching as hard as he can, and it's not as if we don't know where they're going to attack. Honestly, me going out will just put us in *more* danger. Our only defense right now is secrecy, and it's impossible not to get noticed when you're as delicious as I am."

Bex chuckled at the truth of that. Lys was the best shapeshifter Bex had ever met, but their lust-demon nature prevented them from taking forms that weren't desirable. That still left a broad spectrum since people's preferences

133

ranged so widely, but failing to notice attractive things was not a human strength, and Lys was always attractive to somebody.

"I'm going back to my room to work strangers into a froth on dating apps," Lys announced. "It's the lust equivalent of instant ramen, but if Iggs can maintain those huge shoulders on nothing but gamer rage, I suppose I can take one for the team."

"Thank you for your sacrifice," Bex said solemnly.

"Yes, well, desperate times and so forth," Lys said, shimmying down the tree as agilely as a squirrel. "Have fun watching the grass grow."

That was clearly supposed to be a joke, but honestly, Bex *had* been having fun, because it wasn't just the grass that was growing. When they'd first driven the RV up here, the forest had been a pretty but unremarkable woodland full of saplings and undergrowth. Ever since Adrian had gotten his water system working, though, the plants had been getting taller by the hour. The fir tree he'd buried his heart under was now as big around as Iggs, and even the branch she was sitting on was noticeably higher than it'd been this morning.

It was all changing so quickly, and getting so *huge*, Bex didn't know how the island's other residents hadn't noticed. But despite the fact that there were houses just across the inlet, no one seemed to see or care that the woodsy hill at the end of the island was turning into an old-growth forest practically overnight. According to Adrian, this was because most people didn't look at trees as anything other than background. That felt like flimsy cover to Bex, but Adrian was the one who would know, so she'd let it slide.

She was letting a lot of things slide, to be honest. Lys might complain about being bored, but in Bex's secret opinion, this was the best job they'd ever worked. The growing forest was beautiful and peaceful, and Adrian's witchcraft was so interesting to watch.

He hadn't done anything super flashy since the first day, but his magic was still like nothing Bex had ever seen. Even when he was moving rocks and digging ditches, he and Boston were constantly working with the land, moving in patterns that left beautiful markings on the ground wherever they went. He'd grown an entire garden overnight just by touching the plants with his hands. A proper, witchy one full of nightshade and wormwood, but also enormous vegetables twice the size of any Bex had seen before.

And it *smelled* so nice. She hadn't even noticed a smell on the drive in, but Adrian's new forest smelled like leaves and water and wild places. Far, far wilder than a ten-acre plot only a few miles from the ferry dock had any right to be. She'd known it would be magic from the moment he'd buried his heart in the ground, but knowing and experiencing were two wildly different things, and as Bex watched Adrian fit the last of the standing stones into the new circle that already felt ancient, all she could think was that *this* was why Gilgamesh had stomped out all the other witches. This was *real* magic, deep power of the sort that couldn't be copied by chugging quintessence and saying a few lines of poetry, and the Eternal King was right to fear it.

That thought made her happier than anything had in a long time. Adrian was still standing inside the circle of rocks he'd just finished, talking with Boston as they drew spiral patterns in the dirt, so Bex took the opportunity to reach for the worn guitar hanging by its shoulder strap from the branch above her.

She couldn't remember the last time she'd taken her guitar out of the RV. It wasn't really professional to have it out now, but Adrian didn't seem to mind the noise, and it was just so *pleasant*. Sitting up here in the leaves and the dappled sunlight, looking down at the ever-changing forest, letting her fingers do whatever they wanted as they moved over the familiar strings... it was the closest thing to a vacation Bex could remember having.

She was sure the warlocks would be along to ruin that soon enough. For now, though, she let herself enjoy the moment, closing her eyes to focus on the sunlight, the breeze, and the vibration of the guitar strings as she moved her fingers through one of her favorite songs to play.

It wasn't just that the music was fast and complicated. It had a beautiful, wistful energy you really had to pour yourself into to get right. Bex didn't normally have the luxury of sinking so deep, but today, with the calm and the sunlight, she was hitting every note perfectly. She'd just finished her best rendition ever and was about to start over from the top to see if she could do it again when a voice spoke practically in her ear.

"Is that 'Mood for a Day' by Yes?"

Bex jumped with a yelp, nearly falling out of the tree before she caught herself. Since she'd stupidly forgotten to put the strap over her shoulder before she'd started playing, her guitar wasn't so lucky. It tumbled right out of her hands, plummeting through the tree's green leaves. It would have smashed to pieces on the ground if Adrian hadn't swooped down and caught it.

"Sorry," he said, rising up on his broom—which was in actual broom form today, not the giant raven he'd used to fly them into town—to hand the instrument back to her.

"It's my fault," Bex said, furious with herself. "Some guard I am, letting my own client sneak up on me."

"I was being quiet on purpose," he confessed, leaning closer with his elbows on his knees, which struck Bex as a gutsy thing to do when you were sitting sideways on a broomstick thirty feet off the ground. "That was fantastic playing. Are you a Yes fan, or do you just like to challenge yourself with really hard songs?"

Bex slid her guitar strap over her head as she tried to think of a safe answer to that question—and to keep her eyes off Adrian, who was still distractingly shirtless.

"I'm not a fan," she admitted at last. "I didn't actually know who wrote that song or what it was called until you told me just now." She fiddled with her tuning pegs. "Are *you* a fan?"

"Didn't have much of a choice," Adrian said with a laugh. "I grew up in a witch commune. Prog rock was inescapable." He chuckled a bit more, then his smile faded to a curious frown. "How'd you get so good at playing 'Mood for a Day' if you didn't know who it was by? It wasn't exactly a chart-topping hit."

"I just know it," Bex said with a shrug.

Adrian's frown deepened. "What does that mean?"

There was absolutely no safe answer to that one, so she changed the subject.

"What are you working on?"

His face lit up immediately, and Bex took a moment to silently congratulate herself. She might have only known him for a week, but it was impossible to miss how much Adrian Blackwood loved talking about his craft.

"I'm putting in the circles," he told her excitedly, swinging his broom parallel to her branch so they were

137

both looking down at the clearing from the same perspective.

"All magic comes from the great cycles," he explained with a grand sweep of his arm. "Life, death, the seasons, the weather, the phases of the moon, the orbits of the earth and sun—they all turn and spiral through each other, and that movement creates magic. A big part of being a witch is learning how to capture and use that magic in a way that makes your forest greater, which is why I'm putting in the stones. Rocks are much less susceptible to weather than trees. The magic that pools between them will act as both a reservoir and an overflow, keeping the entire forest balanced even when the seasons start to change."

"I guess that makes sense," Bex said, leaning back on her branch. "But why not use rocks for everything if they're so sturdy?"

"Because they're nothing compared to the living forest," Adrian replied, pointing at the waving treetops all around them.

"Everything that is belongs to multiple overlapping natural cycles. The more cycles that run through an object, place, or person, the more magic it can potentially produce, but forests are special. They're closed energy systems that take sunlight, water, and minerals from the outside world and turn them into *more* forest. They do the same thing with magic. Since forests are filled with every sort of life, every conceivable cycle runs through them. But where a rock would just sit on all that magic, forests use it to make *more*. More trees, more life, more power. That's why every forest feels magical whether it's witchmade or not. They're giant living generators! All I'm doing is helping that magic build faster and more evenly."

"Really?" Bex said, genuinely impressed. "I didn't realize there was still that much magic around. I thought Gilgamesh ruined it all when he dammed the rivers of Paradise."

"He ruined *human* magic," Adrian said scornfully. "But we're not just souls waiting around for our chance to go to Heaven. The natural cycles run through humans the same way they do every other animal. That magic might not come in a convenient chewable form like quintessence, but it's as powerful as life itself for those of us who know how to use it. That's why witches bind ourselves to the forest. By braiding our lives into the tapestry of the Blackwood, we become part of its magical engine."

Bex smiled. "Sounds intense."

"You have no idea," he said with a laugh. "I'm actually pretty low-key by Blackwood standards. I've got sisters who refuse to wear shoes and sleep in burrows like rabbits so they never lose connection with the mycorrhizal fungus network that runs through the soil."

"Real sisters or witch ones?"

"Both," Adrian answered, reaching up to touch the bright green oak leaves above them. "All Blackwoods are family through the coven, but my mother also has a lot of actual children. I'm just one of the herd."

"Sounds like fun," Bex said wistfully. "I used to have sisters."

That came out sounding way more pathetic than she'd intended, and Adrian's head whipped back to her.

"What happened to them?"

Bex shrugged, picking a melody on her guitar so she wouldn't have to talk about the subject she'd so stupidly brought up. Maybe this *wasn't* her best job after all. Working for sorcerers might be obnoxious, but at least they never lulled her into confessing personal secrets. She was about to ask Adrian to show her what he was working on next—the nuclear ordinance of subject changes—when her phone buzzed in her pocket.

"One sec," she said, moving her guitar to the side so she could dig her phone out of her jeans without falling off the tree. She'd assumed it was Lys or Iggs calling with a question rather than walking all the way out of the RV to ask in person—Bex wasn't the only one who'd let this job make her lazy—but the number wasn't one of theirs. It was Felix, the local goblin prince and independent fixer who set up all of Bex's jobs, including her deal with Adrian.

"Wonder what he wants," she muttered, shooting Adrian an apologetic look. "I've gotta take this. Can you...?"

He backed off at once, descending so quickly it looked like his broom had fallen out of the sky. When Bex was sure he hadn't actually plummeted to his death, she tapped her finger against the green icon.

"*Bexxy!*" the goblin prince cried the second the call picked up. "Sweetness, darling, horned light of my life, do you have a minute?"

"No," she said flatly, refusing to play along. "I'm still busy working the last job you gave me."

"Come on, baby, don't be like that," Felix cajoled in a voice so smooth, Bex was surprised he wasn't oozing through the phone. "What's the point of keeping all those demons if you can't nip out for a bit of moonlighting now and again? I promise it'll be worth your time. You know I know what you like."

He *tinged* something against the mic, and Bex's mouth went dry. Technically, it could have been anything made of glass, but she already knew it was a bottle of deathly water. A big one, which was absolutely worth putting up with a little bullshit for.

"What time should I be there?"

"How about five?" he purred. "Though you're welcome to come sooner and wait in my office. My door's always open to—"

"Five is good," she said. "See you then."

Bex hung up before the old con artist could wheedle anything else out of her and hopped out of the tree. That wasn't the smartest move since she was still holding her guitar, but Bex kept her knees loose to absorb the impact and managed not to knock the instrument too badly when she stuck the landing.

"Is something wrong?" Adrian asked, clearly alarmed by her quick exit.

"No," Bex said, sliding the guitar strap over her head. "I've just got to head into the city for some business. Iggs and the others will be here if you need anything."

His expression darkened when she mentioned the city. "Is there trouble?"

"Nothing you need to worry about," Bex assured him, pulling up the ferry schedule on her phone. "Getting over there will probably take me longer than the actual meeting, but I should be back by eight."

He still looked worried. "Do you want me to fly you?"

Considering he'd been giving up sleep to work, that was a *very* generous offer, but Bex shook her head. "I'll walk. It's a nice day, and I need the exercise after a week of sitting in trees."

"Okay then," Adrian said, giving her a smile. "Be careful."

"Always am," Bex replied, walking over to the RV to find Iggs.

Not surprisingly, her wrath demon was more than happy to take her shift. Since learning how much Iggs liked food, Adrian had taken to cooking for him, and Bex being out until eight meant that Iggs would be on duty for the dinner hour. He quit his game the moment she told him and ran straight up the stairs to ask Adrian if they could have pasta again.

Satisfied that her client wouldn't be left alone, *ever*, Bex made a quick trip up to her room to drop off her guitar and grab a bottle of water. Because things had been so calm, she'd managed not to have a drink since the bottle she'd chugged after Adrian caught her sleeping. She still felt pretty good thanks to all the sitting around, but going into the city with no fuel when warlocks were on the hunt was asking for trouble.

She almost went ahead and drank it, just to be safe. There was no point working her ass off to collect the stuff if she was going to swill it as fast as it came in, though, so Bex just slid the bottle of deathly water into the pocket of her favorite leather jacket. When it was zipped up tight, she stuck her sunglasses back on her face, retied the knot in the leather thong that kept her ring around her neck, and set off for the ferry.

It was a pleasant walk. Even with the afternoon sun blasting overhead, it was shady and cool under Adrian's newly gigantic trees. Quiet, too. The sort of deep-wilderness silence that made you want to lie down and sleep for a hundred years, though that might have just been Bex. Pushing so long without water always left her exhausted.

At least she didn't have far to go. She'd told Adrian she was going into the city, but Felix's office was actually on the pier not a quarter mile from where the ferry put in. The hardest part would be getting out of Adrian's unoccupied corner of Bainbridge, but even when she was feeling low, Bex was still a demon. She'd taken her time strolling through Adrian's enchanted forest because it felt like a crime not to, but as soon as she left the trees for the road, it took her only forty minutes to run the six miles to the ferry dock.

She was panting by the time she got there, but it wasn't a terrible showing, *and* she'd scored the ferry with the cushy leather chairs. She flopped into one the moment she was on board, leaning her head against the window to watch the water and get her game face back on.

She and Felix had had a good working relationship for nearly five years. He was still a goblin, though, which made him untrustworthy by definition. Goblins didn't go to Paradise when they died, so Gilgamesh had no control over them, but they tended to operate in ways non-goblins found hard to understand. They even had their own system of magic that revolved entirely around treasure. The more treasure goblins collected, the more powerful they became, though what counted as "treasure" was surprisingly flexible. Old-school goblins still went for the classic piles of gold and jewels, but the younger princes preferred more modern metrics, like stocks and real estate.

Felix, being both young and ambitious, had stretched the concept even further. He collected people, leveraging a vast network of informants, spies, and freelance operatives like Bex to move the wheels for the world's rich and influential. Mostly the magical world, but his books included plenty of normal politicians and CEOs. When important people needed something, they went to Felix, and that was what made him powerful.

Unique as his fixer business was, however, Felix was still a traditional goblin in a few crucial ways. Specifically, he was biologically unable to resist easy money, which was why his office was located in a tourist trap just down the pier from the cruise ship docks.

The whole building was done up to look like an old-timey western trading post. There were carnival rides, ice cream counters, souvenir shops, and cheap arcades all boxed together in a polished pinewood maze lined with black-and-white photos of prospectors and a whole endangered species list's worth of taxidermy animals. All his restaurants sold frozen seafood at fresh-caught prices, and bottom-shelf liquor flowed freely in giant plastic souvenir cups.

The operation was cynical capitalism at its finest, and—thanks to the goblins' unique ability to misdirect human attention for the sake of profit—none of the scale-eyed tourists even noticed that the hucksters running the fudge shops and novelty photo booths were three feet tall and green. They all waved at Bex when she walked in, the surest sign yet that whatever this was about, Felix wanted it *bad*. Goblins never noticed you unless you were worth something. If the floor crew was rolling out the smiles, then maybe this job really was legit. Hopes climbing to the sky, Bex waved back and headed down the service ramp toward the part of the building below the tourism crust where the actual work got done.

Since Felix's scam was on the pier, meaning over the water, the business level was down on the seabed. To get there, Bex had to go down a staircase built inside one of the giant wooden posts that held up the building. It wasn't exactly a pleasant trip. The wood was always wet and reeking of tar, especially at low tide, but the view from the bottom was spectacular.

Felix did his main business out of a retrofitted tourism submarine, the kind with a huge glass dome that let passengers look out at the fish and kelp as they cruised by. It had some magic to keep it hidden from the Coast Guard, who occasionally had to come under the piers to fish out swimmers and insane people, but otherwise, it was just a good old piece of human engineering. Felix was at his desk as usual when the guards let Bex inside, but he shot out of his velvet chair the second he saw her, rising to his full height.

Goblin princes were *much* larger than their peons, and the richer they were, the bigger they got. Felix was quite respectable at seven feet tall, not the biggest but definitely no slouch. He towered over Bex's current five foot two, a fact he made sure to show off by sweeping a ridiculously low bow to kiss her hand.

"My ravishing demoness," he crooned, stroking her fingers with his long green ones. "I can't begin to describe how I've suffered pining for your company."

"Save the buttering up for someone who'll fall for it," Bex said, prying her hand away. "I'm here because you said you'd make this worth my while, so go ahead. Start making."

"Always so quick to business." Felix chuckled, settling back into his throne of an office chair. "I knew there was a reason I let you steal my heart."

Bex arched an eyebrow and waited for him to get to the point.

"A proposition just came across my desk that I thought you'd be interested in," he explained at last, steepling his sharp-clawed fingers in front of him. "Small work for big reward, your favorite kind of job."

"A suspicious kind of job," Bex corrected. "What is it?"

"A meeting," he said innocently. "I'm not even aware of the particulars. I'm merely the go-between, but I do think you should hear him out."

"Really?" Bex said flatly, liking this less by the second. "And where is this mystery client?"

"Just in the other room," Felix said, flashing her a wall of gleaming golden teeth. "And before you ask, he's already accepted the pledge of neutral ground. He's even thrown in a tip, to make sure you know he's serious."

The goblin's hand moved as he spoke, and Bex held her breath as a large bottle of glowing blue water—the same bottle he'd tapped against the phone, she was sure of it—appeared in his grasp.

"Do I have your attention now?"

"All I've got to do is go to a meeting?" Bex confirmed. "On neutral ground?"

"Completely peaceful," Felix promised. "Not even Gilgamesh himself can breach a goblin vow of neutrality. So long as you're on my turf, you're as safe as safe can be."

Bex still didn't like it, but that was too good an offer to pass up. She held out her hand, and Felix gave her the deathly water. It much bigger than her usual bottles and heavy with power in her hands. The urge to drink it right now was overwhelming, but Bex forced herself to slide it into her pocket next to the other.

When both of her treasures were safely stowed, she motioned for Felix to lead the way. He did so with great gusto, rising from his chair and holding out his arm like an old-fashioned gallant to lead her across the submarine to the room at the back, which he used for delicate matters.

Unlike Felix's office, which only had windows on the top, the meeting room was located in the former submarine's nose, which meant it was glass all the way around. This had the uncanny effect of making the overly ornate marble conference table Felix had squeezed inside look like it was sitting in the muck at the bottom of the bay. But while Bex normally liked getting to do her business surrounded by fish and the occasional harbor seal, she didn't even look at the water this time. She couldn't, because the moment she stepped through the oval submarine door, the man sitting on the opposite side of the meeting table took up all her attention. The man who was most definitely a warlock, flanked by his demons.

"Hello, Miss Bex," he said in a dry, cold voice. "Won't you have a seat?"

Bex was about to tell him not on his life when Felix thrust her forward, shutting the metal door behind her with a *clang*.

Chapter 9

"Now, now, there's no need to act like a trapped rat," the warlock said as Bex slammed her fists into the door. "We're both bound by the prince's hospitality, which means I can't hurt you any more than you can get away from me. You've already accepted my payment, so you might as well sit down and hear me out."

Bex didn't want to listen to a word this man said. She already felt like a gullible idiot for letting Felix bribe her, but the warlock was right about one thing. She'd accepted the payment, which meant she was bound tight by the goblin's contract magic. She could already feel it sapping her strength, causing her legs to wobble. If she didn't sit down soon, she was going to be hearing this man out on her back, so Bex made a field decision and stomped over to the conference table, dropping her body into the padded chair like she was attacking it.

"All right," she said, resting her elbows on the marble table to put a barrier between the man and her face. "I'm sitting."

The warlock's thin lips curled into a smirk. Now that she was actually looking, Bex saw that all of him was thin. He had thin hair, thin eyes, a thin nose, and a thin, pointed chin that jutted out over his thin chest. He looked like the sort of person who'd never enjoyed a single bite of food he'd ever eaten, but it was his hands that told the real story.

The warlock had only two demons with him at present—an untransformed war demon whose human form was so tall that his head touched the curved glass of the submarine's ceiling, and a greed demon in a yellow sports coat, his slightly too wide-set eyes gleaming like golden coins even in his human guise—but all ten of his long, bony fingers were covered in slave-binding marks up to the top knuckle. Even if they were all suck-up sellouts, that was way too many demons for your average warlock, and Bex rubbed her hands over her face with a sigh.

"Let me guess, you're the Spider."

"And you're well-informed for a stray," the Spider said, his thin mouth pulling into a sneer. "I don't want to be in your presence any more than you want to be in mine, so for both our sakes, I'll make this quick. I understand you've been employed by a certain witch to protect him while he builds his little treehouse."

"That's an interesting story," Bex replied, dropping her hands with a glare. "Who told it to you?"

"I figured it out myself," the warlock assured her. "Not that I didn't see Prince Felix drooling to sell you out when I told him how much I was offering. Alas, he's as bound by his contracts as you are by yours. That protection is the only reason anyone bothers to pay his ridiculous fees, but no contract can stop a man from drawing his own conclusions, and unlike you, I know how Adrian Blackwood thinks. He was my apprentice, after all."

He paused there, waiting. When Bex didn't take the bait, the Spider continued.

"I knew he'd run as far as possible to spare his family from the blowback. I knew the size of team he'd need to hire and how much he'd be able to pay. With those variables, it wasn't hard to winnow down the available freelancers and locations."

"He can't be that easy to corner if you're trying to bribe his location out of me," Bex pointed out.

"That is the incompetent Seattle cabal's fault," the Spider said irritable. "If they'd done their job, I'd already have him. Of course, if they did any work, we wouldn't be having this conversation. If a runaway slave tried to set up a freelance business in *my* territory, I'd have sent her back to the Hells before she finished her first contract. But I'm not here to do another warlock's job for him. All I care about is the boy."

"Why?" Bex asked, tilting her head.

"Because I don't tolerate theft," the warlock growled. "Adrian Blackwood was contracted to me centuries before he was born. He might be a miserable failure right now, but his lineage is impeccable. If he can just get over himself, he has the potential to be the greatest warlock of his generation, capable of consuming enormous quantities of quintessence with no ill effect. *That* is what I was promised, and that is what I shall collect, but there's no reason you have to get crushed in the process, so here's my offer."

He leaned across the table, his eyes so hard and dark they looked like black marbles behind the thin slits of his lids. "I understand you only take payment in deathly water. I can promise you twenty gallons straight from the source. I am in the Eternal King's personal favor and speak with his divine princes often, so such a thing is well within my power. In return for this great gift, you will tell me where Adrian Blackwood is building his grove. Once I have him back in my possession, you and your associates will be free to go."

"And you expect me to believe that?" Bex said, hiding her anger under scorn. "You would just let a runaway demon go free?"

"Yes," the warlock said testily. "In case I was not clear earlier, *you* are not my problem. I am merely seeking to retrieve my property in the most efficient and expedient manner possible, and since I have no intention of killing the brat, you won't even be in violation of your contract. There is no loss in this situation for you, demon, and also no way out. Even if you turn me down, forests can't move. I'll find the Blackwood eventually whatever you decide, so unless you want your little run at freedom to end in an express ticket straight to the lowest of the Hells, I suggest you use the brain I can only assume still exists beneath your ridiculously overgrown horns and take my generous offer."

Bex leaned back in her chair, making a show of thinking it over before she spoke the word she'd been dying to say since the moment she first saw the warlock sitting across the table.

"No."

The Spider's narrow eyes grew narrower. "I'd advise you to reconsider," he said in a calm, deadly voice. "I only ask nicely once."

"And I only say no nicely once," Bex replied, rising from her chair. "But it doesn't matter what you're offering. I don't work for slavers."

The Spider stared at her for a long moment, and then he spread his tattooed hands with a smile that didn't touch his eyes.

"Your loss."

Bex didn't dignify that with a reply. As soon as she'd turned him down, the requirement to hear him out had been satisfied, which meant she was free to go. Bex did so at a slow pace, because there was no way in the Hells she was letting this man see her run. The Spider didn't speak the whole time she was walking away, but just before she opened the door, he said, "See you soon."

She responded with a rude gesture. Not the most professional reaction, but this bastard didn't deserve that from her. Bex was more concerned with getting out of here as fast as possible, because while the pledge of neutral ground protected her within Felix's domain, it didn't do squat to keep the Spider's demons from jumping her the moment she stepped outside.

Given how many slave-binding marks were on the warlock's bony fingers, he could have an army waiting. The only way to beat that trap was to get out before it closed, so the second Bex stepped back into Felix's office—his empty office, the coward—she bolted for the stinking wooden staircase as fast as her legs would carry her.

She yanked her phone out of her pocket the moment she was inside. She was already pulling up Iggs's number to tell him to keep an eye on Adrian while she gave the Spider the slip when she remembered the greed demon.

Bex jerked her phone back down with a string of curses. She'd been so focused on the warlock, she hadn't even looked at his demons. Rookie mistake. Warlocks never brought demons anywhere unless they meant to use them. The war demon's purpose was obvious—he was muscle and intimidation, a show of power to remind Bex just how big a bear she was poking—but greed demons had no combat powers. Their talents lay in contract writing, legal shenanigans, and get-rich-quick schemes. That was a useful combination for doing business with goblins, but with the rise of electronic banking, the ambitious greed demons had developed another skill set Bex had been on the receiving end of too many times to ignore: hacking.

Since the Spider didn't seem like the sort of man who needed help dealing with Felix, Bex would have bet both her bottles of deathly water that her phone had been compromised during that little conversation. It wouldn't even have gone against neutrality since the goblin's magic applied only to Bex herself, not her electronics.

That had probably been the warlock's plan from the start: bribe her to show up and then, if she didn't agree to sell out, wait for her to call her people and trace the signal right to his target. It was what Bex would've done if she'd had a greed demon on her crew. Her phone was probably already feeding them location data, lighting her up like a clay pigeon for the beat squad that was no doubt already waiting on the other side of Felix's doorstep.

Put it that way and the decision was easy. Bex didn't even hesitate as she took her smart phone between her hands and snapped it in half. She broke the halves in half for good measure and dumped the pieces into the deep fryer at one of the oyster stands that ringed Felix's tourist trap. The goblin cooks screamed at her for ruining the fry oil, but Bex had already left the building, breaking into a run the moment her feet landed on the boardwalk.

She didn't waste time looking to see if anyone was chasing her. She didn't stop for anything. She just ran, pulling out the smaller of her two bottles of deathly water and drinking it as she went to give her feet wings as she tore through the city in the opposite direction of Adrian's Blackwood.

By the time Bex finally slowed down, it was full dark. She wasn't sure where she was since no phone meant no map, but she'd been going south whenever she got the choice, so she should be somewhere near the airport. It certainly looked like she was back in the industrial area where they'd stashed the RV before going to pick up Adrian, but the buildings here were much more run-down. There was a train yard to her left with lines of empty, graffiti-covered cars waiting to be picked up but no workers or cameras that Bex could see. Just a fence topped with razor wire, its rusted links rattling in the night wind.

Since no one was watching, Bex ripped a hole in the metal fence and ducked inside, jogging across the dirty gravel to take shelter behind a stack of rusty shipping containers. She barely managed to get her back against the metal before she slid to the ground, lungs heaving as she sucked in the dusty air.

Bex couldn't remember the last time she'd run so fast for so long. Definitely not since before she'd been injured, but, ironically, the bottle of deathly water she'd chugged kept her from feeling dead. Her legs were sore, and her lungs felt like they'd never work right again, but she was reasonably certain she'd given the Spider the slip, which made it all worthwhile. She was scanning the train lot for an office she could break into and call Iggs to let him know she was running late when Bex heard the crunch of footsteps.

Very heavy footsteps.

It was a sign of how far she'd fallen that the war demon had made it all the way to the gravel before she heard him. Seven years ago, Bex could've picked up that distinctive *clomp* from three blocks away. Now, she had no choice but to push herself back to her feet. If he'd already chased her this far, running again was pointless, especially on her aching legs. That left fighting, so Bex pulled her jacket straight and stepped out from behind the shipping container to see what she was in for.

She'd already guessed who it would be, but Bex still cursed when she saw the enormous war demon from her meeting with the Spider striding between the train tracks not fifteen feet away. He stopped moving when she came out, looking her up and down with his glinting black eyes.

Bex glared right back. Unlike the baby war demon who'd grabbed her at the Anchor Market, this one was actually a threat. Even in his human form, he was six-and-a-half feet tall with tanned skin, sandy hair, and two gigantic bone-colored horns that covered the entire top and back of his head like a helmet. He was the biggest war demon Bex could remember seeing, but that made sense, given who he worked for. Quintessence hit war demons like Miracle-Gro, and the Spider had clearly been popping those pills for ages. Size wasn't everything, though, so Bex crossed her arms over her chest and tilted her head back, meeting the war demon's eyes with a bored glare to show this oaf just how unintimidated she was.

"Have a nice run?"

"It was certainly better than yours," he replied in a deep, booming voice, like a drum on the battlefield. "I'm not the one who was panting so loudly, her enemy didn't even have to look."

"Dogs *are* very good at running," Bex agreed, glancing pointedly at his neck, which sported only the slave tattoo, not the heavy sin iron collar needed for demons who actually fought back. "You must be quite the loyal pet if your master let you run this far on your own, but I'd expect nothing less from a war demon traitor."

"What did we betray?" the war demon growled, curling back his lips to show her his pointed teeth. "I wasn't even born when the Eternal King defeated the gods and conquered Paradise, but I could still tell you it was a losing battle. Ishtar was dead, and the demon queens could not stop Gilgamesh's armies on their own. To continue fighting would have been suicide. Surrender was the only tactically viable option."

"But you didn't just surrender, did you?" Bex taunted, showing him her own teeth, which were still human and flat in this form but no less willing to bite. "You didn't merely kneel before your conqueror. You joined his army to help him slaughter and enslave the rest of us, your own people!"

"And won ourselves a place of power in the new order," the war demon replied. "While the rest of you fools suffered for your pride, we were spared and rewarded. Even now, war demons serve as guards at the Holy Palace itself, while the rest of you stubborn filth slave in the Hells."

"*And who made them Hells?*" Bex roared. "There was no Heaven or Hell before Gilgamesh came. All was Paradise! The most beautiful land imaginable, until he *ruined* it."

"What does that matter?" the war demon asked, rolling his huge shoulders. "The war's been over for eons. We live in Gilgamesh's world now. Smart demons do what they must to ensure their continued comfort and survival, which is why you'll be coming with me."

He held out his hand, but Bex stepped back, digging her boots into the gravel as she took her stance.

"You can't be serious," the war demon said with a pitying look. "You are puny, *bony*. The only reason I haven't crushed you already is because my master wants you alive. Now come quietly, or—"

He cut off when Bex kicked a rock at him like a bullet. The war demon bashed it away before it could hit him, but with his arms up to protect his face, there was nothing to stop Bex's fist from slamming into his unguarded stomach.

The blow hurled him backward into a string of empty train cars. The war demon landed hard enough to knock the whole line off the tracks, but Bex didn't wait for them to finish falling. She was already running forward, grabbing a piece of scrap metal off the ground to use as a dagger as she leaped into the falling train cars and came down point first, her makeshift knife positioned to stab through the first and most vital of the war demon's three hearts.

She was almost there when a huge pair of arms snatched her out of the air. As she tried to kick her way free, a *second* pair of arms grabbed her legs and slung her like a whip. They would have slammed her headfirst into the metal train tracks she'd just knocked the cars off, but Bex got her arm out at the last second, hitting the ground with her hand instead to grab the rails and rip her legs free. She finished the flip on her feet several yards away, holding her makeshift dagger in front of her as the war demon punched his way out of the crumpled train cars.

He must have shed his human after she punched him, because the demon who ripped himself out of the wreckage looked nothing like the man who'd mocked her earlier. His skin was true bronze now, metallic and gleaming. His arms, all four of them, hovered ready at his sides, and his feet were giant cloven hooves that tapered to knife-sharp points. Only his eyes were still the same, as black as demon blood and glittering with malice in the harsh white light of the train yard's single halogen floodlamp.

"That was impressive for such a tiny demon," he admitted, staring at Bex like he was seeing her for the first time. "What are you?"

"Your ticket back to the Hells," Bex snarled, switching the scrap metal dagger to her left hand as she ran in low.

The demon's bottom arms grabbed for her the second she got in range, so Bex stabbed her makeshift weapon into the inside of his elbow. War demons were armored all over, but the metal was thinner at the joints. The torn scrap metal point punched through it easily, making the war demon hiss in pain. It was a tiny hesitation, but it bought Bex the opening she needed to shoot past his upper pair of arms and land her fist square in the hollow beneath his massive jaw.

That got a reaction. The war demon bellowed in pain and rage as Bex dented the underside of his jaw. She leaped away again as soon as she heard the crunch, kicking off his gleaming bronze chest to get out of his reach, but he didn't even try to grab her. He was too busy coughing out the tooth he'd inhaled, spitting mouthfuls of black blood onto the dusty gravel as he glared at her.

Bex glared right back, dipping down to grab an even larger piece of scrap metal off the ground. She'd go for a knee this time, she decided. War demons were as armored as tanks and hit like wrecking balls, but they weren't fast or flexible. If she could disable his legs, he'd go down like a turtle on its back. She was still lining up the shot in her mind when the war demon finally stopped choking and charged.

She dodged with room to spare, dancing to the right to get behind him. Her new piece of metal was already flying at the soft spot behind his right knee when the war demon whirled much faster than she'd expected and slammed her with both of his left fists. The upper one clocked her ear, making her head ring like a bell, but the lower one hit her square in the side, right on top of her stitched-up wound.

Pain shot through Bex like a spear. She staggered sideways, coughing up black blood of her own. She was still reeling when the demon's kick caught her in the back, punting her across the train yard.

She flew through the air like a cannonball, barely reacting fast enough to duck her head before she slammed straight through the corrugated steel wall of the warehouse at the end of the tracks. She hit the cement floor next, tumbling over and over before slamming to a halt against a stack of shiny new steel rails. The landing knocked her head again, filling her vision with dancing spots as she gasped for breath and got a lungful of blood instead.

Bex pushed up onto her hands and knees, coughing her lungs clean as she blinked the spots out of her eyes. Her sunglasses must have gotten smashed off her face at some point, because she could see much better than usual, well enough to make out the size of the black pool that was rapidly spreading across the floor beneath her.

Shit.

She burst into motion, not even waiting to get her breath back before she scrambled up the pyramid of steel rails she'd landed against. From there, she jumped onto the web of support struts that held up the roof, leaving a bloody trail behind her as she fled into the darkness. She'd just hauled herself on top of one of the warehouse's banks of fluorescent lights—currently off—when the war demon stepped through the hole she'd left in the wall.

"There's no use hiding!" he bellowed, his huge voice bouncing through the metal warehouse like a ricocheting bullet. "You put up a good fight, little girl, but there's no way you can keep going after losing all that blood. Come out now, and I will spare your life."

Bex rolled her glowing eyes and silently took off her jacket. She peeled off her bloody shirt next, ripping the cotton into strips as quietly as possible. When she had a good pile, she tied the strips tight around her waist to stanch her wound.

Stanching was the best she could do. The war demon's punch had ripped out every one of her careful stitches, leaving the hole in her side bleeding like a faucet. Her black jeans were already saturated, as were her socks from where the blood had dripped into her boots. If the war demon caught her like this, she was done for, so Bex dug into her jacket with a silent curse and pulled out the large bottle of beautifully glowing water Felix had used to bribe her.

She knew she should be thanking Ishtar that the bottle wasn't broken, but cracking the seal on the screw cap felt more painful than getting kicked through a wall. Bex couldn't believe she was wasting *two* bottles of deathly water on this crap, but there was nothing else for it. If she died here—far from her team, in the presence of her enemy—everything she'd suffered for was over, so Bex put the bottle to her lips and drank, sucking the glowing water down in huge gulps.

It'd been years since she'd drunk so much at once. The strength went through her like fire, burning away the exhaustion and pain. Except for the never-healing cut in her side, every bit of damage she'd taken was cast off in an instant, leaving Bex feeling like a live wire as she set the empty bottle down. She put her jacket back on next, zipping it up to hide her wound. Then, black and silent against the dark ceiling, Bex crept along the metal rafters until she was directly above her enemy.

The war demon was still standing by the hole she'd put through the corrugated steel wall, looking around the dark warehouse like he was scared to go farther in. He must not be able to see in the dark as well as she could, Bex realized with a grin. That would be useful, because while the deathly water was making her feel like a god right now, her wound was still dripping under her makeshift bandage. Once she lost enough blood, no amount of water would keep her standing, so Bex positioned herself exactly where she wanted and jumped, falling silently through the dark to land with both feet on the war demon's left shoulder.

He went down with a shriek, collapsing to the ground rather than letting her break his collarbone. The moment he was on his back, Bex shifted her legs to pin his arms—all four of them—and started pummeling his face with her new strength, punching so hard that she cracked the protective helmet of his horns. She cracked the floor as well, driving the bigger demon into the cement with seven years' worth of pent-up rage.

As hard as she was hitting, though, the war demon was harder. His bronze face was a dented mess, but the skull beneath was as hard as steel. Bex was still pounding at it like a jackhammer when the war demon finally got his lower pair of arms out from under her boots and hurled her off him.

Bex righted herself at once, landing neatly outside in the train yard only to stumble again when the dizziness washed over her. She couldn't feel anything but fury when the water was lighting her up, but the big black splats on the gravel beneath her didn't lie. She was running out of time. That beatdown should have been a fight ender, but the giant war demon was already pushing up from the crater she'd pounded him into, his bronze skin dented and warped but still intact. She hadn't won yet, and if she didn't move fast, she never would.

With a slew of curses that would have made even Lys gasp, Bex turned and ran. Not away—there was no hope of that with the blood trail she was leaving—but she got some distance, hopping up on one of the train cars she hadn't knocked over before jumping her way to the top of the crane used for loading shipping containers. The height wouldn't stop the war demon, but the metal lug couldn't jump half as high as she could, so it should slow him down. As safe as she could get for the moment, Bex pressed her back against the rusty box that housed the crane's pulley and reached into the collar of her jacket for her ring.

The heavy black band leaped into her grasp like it had been waiting for the chance. That should have been a warning, but Bex was in too much of a hurry to care. She bit through the leather string and tore the ring free, cramming it onto the third finger of her right hand. The metal loop was far too big for her bony digits, but that had never mattered. The moment it was in position, the ring bit down on her finger like a pair of fangs, and a deep voice—that old, familiar, obnoxious voice—roared into her head.

What do you think you're doing?

"Fighting," Bex muttered, tugging her makeshift bandages tighter before zipping her jacket back up to her throat. "Now get out here and help me."

I will do no such thing, the ring snarled, biting into Bex's finger so hard it drew blood. *Look what you've done to yourself! You're weak as a newborn lamb!*

"I didn't wake you up for a lecture," Bex hissed, shaking her bleeding hand violently. "A war demon the size of a rhino is looking for me right now. If you don't get out here and help, I swear to Ishtar, I am *never* putting you on again."

Any other time, the ring would have laughed that threat off as toothless. It must have heard the fury in Bex's voice, though, because it gave in with a growl. A wave of weakness came next as the ring pulled on the strength she'd gotten from the water, drinking her down as fast as she'd chugged the bottle. For a horrible moment, Bex was sure she was going to pass out. Then her nose filled with the familiar acrid scent of smoke, and a sword appeared in her right hand.

The weapon was as black as the ring it came from, a straight blade longer than Bex's leg with the sturdy hilt and wide guard of the heavy chopping weapon it had been before the eons ground it down. But though time had worn it needle-thin, Bex had yet to find anything the sword's smoking edge couldn't slice, which was why she'd brought it out. This was her chance, dearly bought, and she meant to use it, creeping along the arm of the crane toward the war demon, who was still following her trail of blood on the ground below.

I can't believe you let things get this bad, the sword grumbled in her mind. *You're practically a husk. What have those idiots who care for you been doing?*

Bex shook her head and kept creeping along the crane until she was directly above the war demon yet again. The idiot still hadn't learned to look up, so she took her chance, raising the black sword to her lips.

"Name me."

ABSOLUTELY NOT! the blade roared. *Are you suicidal? You can barely manifest me in your present state! I will burn what's left of you to ash if you make me—*

163

"Name me, Drox," Bex said in an iron voice. "That's an order."

The blade stiffened in her hand. She could feel it trying to fight her, but as mad as he was right now, Drox had always been her sword, and he had no choice but to obey.

So be it, he said in a voice as hard as her own. For a moment there was silence, and then Bex felt power snap down on her brain like fangs as Drox did as she'd commanded.

Burn again, he whispered, his deep voice shaking with effort. *Rebexa.*

At the sound of her true name, all of Bex's pain vanished in a fiery blast. There was no weakness, no fear, nothing at all. Not even gravity could touch her as she launched off the crane like a javelin, her black sword slicing through the war demon before he'd realized she was there.

She took off both of his left arms with that first attack. The moment her feet touched the ground, Bex spun and sliced off the two on the right. The war demon didn't even have time to scream before her sword was at his neck, its smoking edge hovering just above the marks of his slave band.

He froze when he saw it, his sliced-up body going as still as the bronze statue it resembled. Black blood poured from the stumps that had been his arms, but he still didn't move. Neither did Rebexa. She just stood there with her smoking sword pressed against his throat. Her body was smoking, too, smoldering with the last of her dearly bought power until, at last, she let her blade drop.

The war demon dropped with it, falling to his knees in the lake his black blood had made on the ground. Bex could already see his regeneration closing off the stumps to keep him from bleeding to death. That should have been her signal to finish the job. Drox certainly thought so. Her sword was screaming at her to behead their enemy, but following her destructive impulses had hurt Bex enough for one lifetime, so all she did was step back.

"Why?" the war demon gasped as she retreated, his once-booming voice gone hollow from the pain. "Why did you stop?"

"Because I'm *not* a traitor," Bex said, shaking his blood off her sword. "I don't kill my own kind."

This was normally the point where Bex's enemies would express gratitude or relief, but the war demon looked more terrified than ever.

"No," he begged. "I can't go back to him like this. The Spider has no use for failures. He'll damn me to the Hells!"

"You should have thought of that before you agreed to lick his boots," Bex snapped, but the war demon had already started to cry, whimpering pathetically in the blood at her feet until she couldn't take it anymore.

With a sigh she felt to her heels, Bex raised her sword again, using the last of the embers Drox's naming had blown to life inside her to press the tip of her sword against the war demon's slave band. The moment Drox touched them, the black markings flared up like tissue paper in a campfire. When the blaze died down, the slave band was gone, blown away like smoke to leave the demon's bronze neck bloody but clean.

The war demon fell over when it was finished, lying on his back as he gasped for air.

"What did you do?" he asked when he could speak again.

"I set you free," Bex replied, stabbing her sword into the gravel for support as the last of the fire left her. "Your life is your own now. Run back to your master or off into the hills, I don't care. Just don't follow me. I never want to see you again"—her eyes narrowed—"*Trinaeous.*"

Speaking his true name nearly sent Bex to the ground. She'd forgotten how hard it was to name demons who hadn't pledged themselves to her already. Drox always knew them, but even when the sword placed the name in her mind, Bex couldn't speak it unless the demon yielded or she was strong enough to overpower them. She hadn't thought that would be a problem, seeing as Trinaeous was down four arms and crying in a lake of his own blood, but he must have been tougher than she'd given him credit for.

No, you *are weaker,* Drox hissed in Bex's mind. *What were you thinking, naming him in your state? We must get you back to safety* now. *If you do not submerge yourself in the waters of the sacred rivers, you will be—*

Bex opened her hand and dropped her sword on the ground. It turned back into a ring before it hit the gravel, clattering furiously against the bloody rocks before Bex stopped it with her boot. It was a childish way to behave, but she didn't have the patience to deal with Drox's scolding right now. The war demon was still weeping, but his warlock would have felt the slave bond break, which meant it was time to go.

That suited Bex just fine. She was past done with this place, and since she'd bound the war demon by his true name not to follow her, he couldn't even watch to see which way she went. The force of her command had already turned his battered face away, leaving Bex without an audience as she scooped up her ring, shoved it into her jacket pocket, and limped out of the train yard into the quiet street beyond.

Phone, she thought as she stumbled down the sidewalk. She needed to find a phone. Taking off her ring cleared Drox out of her head but also removed the crutch his presence gave her. Now that she was alone again, Bex was crashing hard. All the water she'd drunk was long gone, and her wounded side was throbbing so hard she could feel it in her toes. Black blood dripped from her boots with every step, leaving a shiny, inky trail in the light of the moon that was just now coming out from behind the clouds.

Bex stared at it for a moment before wrapping her arms tight around her middle and limping faster. She needed to find a phone and call Iggs. He'd bring her a bottle of water and her first aid kit, then she'd sew herself back together and everything would be fine. She just needed an office or a house. Even a pedestrian would do. Everyone had cell phones these days. She'd have to club them over the head to avoid the kick when they saw her black blood, but even in this sorry state, Bex was pretty sure she could take a scaley. She'd take anything to get a damn phone so she could call for...

Her thoughts trailed off as her bloody boots stumbled to a stop. She couldn't call Iggs. His number had been in her phone, which she'd broken in half. Their whole team changed phone numbers every three months as a safety precaution. She'd ordered a clean sweep just before the Blackwood job, but she'd never memorized Iggs's new number, or anyone else's.

Bex stood still on the pavement, listening to the soft *drip drip drip* of her blood as the horrible truth sank in. She couldn't call for help. She'd been careless like an idiot, and now she was screwed.

167

The swell of defeat she felt then nearly made her cry. She'd run thinking she was being smart and keeping the Spider away from her team, but all she'd actually managed was to waste two bottles of deathly water getting lost. She was going to die out here in the middle of nowhere where no one could find her, and then she'd have to start all over.

For a horrible moment, Bex almost sat down and let it happen. She'd put it off for a long time, but Bex had always known the wound in her side would kill her eventually. Maybe it was time to let the inevitable happen. She was so tired of the constant pain, and it wasn't as if she hadn't done this before. The others would find her eventually. They always did, but Bex didn't have to be here for it. All she had to do was let go.

The thought was horribly tempting. In the end, though, Bex couldn't do it, and not for the usual reasons. Her demons could manage her death, but she'd promised Adrian she'd guard his forest. He wasn't ready yet, and that horrible man was looking for him. Looking to force him into his service just like he forced his demons. She couldn't let that happen, not to someone as nice as Adrian, so Bex forced herself to take another step.

One foot at a time, she dragged herself down the road toward the first likely target she saw: an ancient Ford pickup someone had parked on the curb. Bex no longer had enough strength to rip the door open, so she settled for smashing the window. She popped the lock next, pausing to brush the glass off the worn bench seat before hauling herself inside.

She almost got stuck then. It just felt so *good* to sit down. But she could already hear the *drip drip* of her blood hitting the floor, so Bex forced herself to lean over. Using her hard black nails, she ripped the plastic panel off the steering wheel column and pulled out the tangled wires inside, sorting them by color as she struggled to remember what Lys had taught her about hot-wiring a car.

Chapter 10

"**F**or the last time," Boston groaned, "she's *fine*. She's certainly doing better than we are, because if you don't start paying attention, this whole pot is going to blow up in our faces."

"I know, I know," Adrian said, stirring the cauldron of bubbling liquid he was supposed to be turning into fertility potions for his fungus population. "But it's almost nine. Bex said she'd be back by eight."

"She's a mercenary," the cat reminded him, hopping up on the cauldron's edge so he could glare at his witch properly. "One *you* hired. She can take care of herself."

"She's also a demon," Adrian snapped, stirring faster. "A free demon with no slave mark in a city where the Spider is hunting for me."

"All the more reason for *you* to stay put and leave this to the professionals. What's the point of paying for security if you're just going to waltz out there and make yourself a target?"

"I didn't say I was going out," Adrian replied sulkily, lifting his giant wooden spoon to taste his concoction. "I just said that I was worried."

Boston gave him a withering look. "Adrian Blackwood, I've been your cat since you were seven and your familiar since you were thirteen. When you say 'I'm worried,' I know what you *actually* mean is 'I'm about to do something colossally stupid,' so don't even try."

Adrian slammed his wooden spoon down on the spoon rest. "I'm starting to see why mother gave you to me. You sound just like her cat."

"Good," Boston said, hopping onto the herb-covered work table behind him. "Someone needs to speak sense around here."

Adrian didn't dignify that with a reply. He just grabbed his metal funnel and started ladling the finished potion into his giant tin garden sprayer.

"You should let that cool down before you use it."

Adrian ignored him and kept ladling, though he did pour the steaming liquid from higher up.

Boston's furry body slumped as he heaved an enormous sigh. "Look," he said. "If you're that concerned, why don't you ask one of her demons? I'm sure they know where she—"

A knock on the front door cut him off. Boston had barely turned to look before Adrian was there, yanking the door open to find Iggs standing on his front porch.

"This is about Bex," he said before the demon could get a word out. "What's wrong?"

"I don't know," Iggs admitted, clenching his huge hands nervously. "It could be nothing, but she's late, and she hasn't called." He took off his sunglasses to give the witch a pleading look. "Bex is *never* late, and she *always* calls."

"I understand," Adrian said, striding back into his workshop to grab his broom. "I'll move the forest so you can get the RV out."

"Thank you," Iggs said. "Lys and I will do the searching, but we'll leave Nemini here so—"

"No need," Adrian told him as he pulled on his coat. "I take it you can't track her phone?"

Iggs shook his head, and Adrian nodded. "Then you should take everyone. You'll be a harder target if you're all

171

together, and my forest is big enough now that I can fend for myself for one night."

"I can't do that," Iggs said, wringing his hands. "Bex would kill me if I left a client alone while—"

"That's not your call," Adrian reminded him. "I'm the client. If I say all of you go, then all of you go. I'll be fine for a few hours, though I do need to get something out of the RV before you leave."

The demon blinked. "What do you need from our RV?"

"A starting point," Adrian said, marching past Iggs into the night, which was *very* dark inside his forest despite the nearly full moon shining overhead. "If I can get something of Bex's, I can use it to work a finding charm. It'll take me a while, but it's a thirty-five-minute ferry ride to the mainland. By the time you get to the city, I should have a location for you."

"Really?" Iggs said excitedly, running up beside him. "You can do that?"

Adrian stopped scowling long enough to flash him a smile. "I *am* a witch."

"Thank you *so* much," the demon said, hurrying ahead to open the RV door. "I'll take you to Bex's room."

Adrian already knew where Bex's room was, but he let Iggs lead him anyway. The stains on the spiral stairs weren't nearly as visible now that it was night, but the sight of all that black on her carpet still made him flinch when Iggs turned on the lights.

"What do you need?"

There was so much blood on the floor that Adrian probably could have used a patch of carpet, but he chose a hair from Bex's pillow instead. He was still wrapping the

172

long, dark strand around his fingers when Iggs grabbed something off the wall.

"Here," he said, shoving a glowing bottle of deathly water into Adrian's hand. "In case she comes back while we're out."

"What do I do with it?" Adrian asked as he slid the bottle into his coat's quick-draw pocket.

"I'm forbidden from saying, but it should be pretty obvious," Iggs replied as he turned and ran down the stairs. "Thank you again, Mr. Blackwood!"

"It's Adrian," Adrian said as he hurried after him. "And it's my pleasure. I'll call you the moment I find something."

Iggs nodded and moved to the RV's front cab. Lys was already sitting in the driver's seat, looking more serious than Adrian had ever seen them. Even Nemini seemed to be on edge, not even glancing at her book on the table as Iggs buckled himself into the passenger seat.

Adrian wished them good luck and hopped out of the RV. He got onto his broom next, rising soundlessly into the night sky to begin moving his trees.

It was a lot easier than he'd worried it would be. Forests grown in a hurry had a bad habit of going brittle, but the trees here were supple and compassionate. All Adrian had to do was let his worry bleed through the connection his beating heart shared with the forest, and the woods parted like a curtain, opening a path for the RV as it roared down the hill.

"I hope you know what you're doing," Boston said when Adrian swooped back to the ground. "This is the Spider we're dealing with. There's a good chance this whole situation is a ploy to trick you into leaving yourself unguarded."

"I know," Adrian said, tapping his foot on the forest floor to signal the trees it was okay to pull back. "But I don't care. If this is a trap, then we'll just have to be better. I'm a witch of the Blackwood, not some sitting duck."

"A witch whose Blackwood is only a week old," Boston reminded him, but he didn't say anything else as Adrian marched back into the house to start gathering materials for a finding charm.

Forty-five minutes later, Adrian had a map of Seattle—the big paper kind that was usually sold as a poster—laid out at the center of a circle of fir boughs cut from his heart tree. Above the map was a tripod made of driftwood (for the lost) and fox bones (very good trackers). From this tripod, he'd suspended a moonstone pendant (because the moon shone on everything) from Bex's long hair and was now on his hands and knees, tracking its movements as the pendant swung wildly across the map.

"Got anything yet?" Iggs's voice asked over the speaker of Adrian's phone, which was lying on the floor by the witch's knee.

"Still searching," Adrian said, fighting the urge to adjust something. Patience had always been the hardest part of witchcraft. "How about you?"

"Lys is interrogating the goblins," Iggs reported. "We traced Bex to Felix's no sweat, but the trail gets fuzzy after that."

There was a muffled conversation on the other end as Iggs put his hand over the phone, and then the demon's voice came back. "Lys says the goblins say Bex ran deeper into the city. Not sure why she'd do that, but according to the fry cook, she did it in a damn hurry. We're going to keep looking that way while you finish your spell."

"It shouldn't take much longer," Adrian promised. "Hair is a strong connector, and the moon is nearly full. If the moonlight's touched her tonight, I'll find her."

"Call us the second you do," Iggs said, and then the speaker clicked as he hung up.

Adrian tapped the red *End Call* button on his phone before turning his attention back to the moonstone pendant, which was still swinging wildly over the blue expanse of the Puget Sound.

"I don't get it," he muttered, pulling off his witch hat to scratch his head. "Why does it keep going back to the water?"

"Maybe you should have used fresh fox bones," Boston suggested from his perch on the table. "Or picked a different locator condition. Moonlight is broad but fickle, and it only works if the target goes outside. If Bex has been locked up in some warlock's penthouse all night, you're not going to find her."

"Bex wouldn't get caught by a warlock," Adrian said. She would die fighting him, he was certain of it, which made the pendant's position over the water all the more alarming. What if they'd already killed her and dumped her body in the bay?

He thought frantically back to the interactions he'd had with his old master, trying to remember if throwing a body into a public waterway was something the Spider would do, or if Adrian had let his sisters talk him into listening to too many true-crime podcasts. He was still working on it when he noticed the pendant wasn't jerking wildly anymore. It was swinging back and forth, rocking like a pendulum over a smaller and smaller portion of water dead in the middle between Bainbridge Island and the Seattle mainland. Right over the dotted line indicating the public transit routes.

A grin spread over his face as he dove for his phone. Iggs picked up on the first ring, but Adrian didn't even let him say hello before blurting, "She's on the ferry."

"For real?" Iggs cried. "But we just got off of—"

The phone erupted in a series of scratchy noises, and then someone new spoke.

"Coming or going?"

It took Adrian several seconds to recognize the cold, deadly voice as Lys's. "Hang on," he said, leaning over the pendant, which had stopped swinging and was now pointed like an arrow at the blue water with its tip moving slowly toward Bainbridge.

"She's on the boat coming toward the island."

"Damn," Lys hissed. "That's the last one of the night."

"At least we know she's moving," Adrian said, trying not to think about what a low bar that was.

"But we can't reach her," the lust demon snarled. "We're stuck on this damned pier on the wrong side of the thrice-damned water."

"I can go get her," Adrian volunteered, standing up to grab his broom, which was on the table beside Boston.

"That's a terrible idea!" his familiar yowled.

"Do it," Lys ordered. "And call me the moment you find her."

Adrian was about to say he didn't have Lys's number when the demon hung up, leaving him staring at a fuming Boston.

"I'm going," Adrian said, turning to march out of the house.

There was a thump followed by the gallop of paws as Boston ran in front of him.

"Adrian, think about this for a moment," the cat said, blocking the way with his body. "You know how seriously Bex takes her work. Sending her demons away was tolerable so long as you were still in your forest, but this is too far. She won't thank you for putting yourself in danger to pick her up from a ferry that's already halfway to the island!"

"What if she's hurt?" Adrian demanded.

"What if she's fine?" Boston countered, sitting back on his haunches with his black tail lashing behind him. "She probably just lost her phone and got delayed. All of this could still be nothing."

"Maybe," Adrian said, grabbing the door handle. "But I'd rather go through trouble for nothing than stay here and leave her alone through something."

"That doesn't even make sense," Boston complained, but it was too late. Adrian was already out the door, rising on his broom through the quiet night.

At least Bran had no objections to a rescue mission. He flew through the moonlit sky as swiftly and silently as the raven on his handle. By the time Adrian looked down, they were high over the dark water, shooting across the Puget Sound toward the giant boat lit up like a lantern at its center.

Since this ferry was the last for the night, there was hardly anyone on board. Adrian was able to land right on top of the crew bridge next to the radar array. He started moving the second his feet hit the metal, shoving his broom into its carry handle before slinging it onto his back to free his hands for the ladder that would take him to the upper observation deck.

He searched each floor of the boat methodically. When he still hadn't found Bex by the time he reached the enclosed passenger deck—the gigantic, chair-filled, yellow-lit lounge area that took up the ferry's interior and was the last stop before the car-ferry at the bottom—Adrian was starting to get a little panicked. He was heading for the stairs to check the parking level when he spotted a pair of black horns sticking up over the back of one of the big, cushy armchairs that looked out through the ferry's rear windows.

Relief hit him like a punch. "Bex!" he called, jogging toward her. When she didn't turn around, he tried again. "*Bex!*"

Still nothing. Adrian was wondering if she'd passed out again when he rounded the empty line of chairs and saw a sight that turned his blood to ice.

Bex was slumped down in the seat with her eyes closed. Her leather jacket was zipped all the way to her chin, and her hands were clenched tight over her stomach, but the real sight was the chair itself. It had looked normal enough from the back, but now that Adrian was standing in front of it, he could see that the whole cushion and the linoleum floor beneath it were drenched in inky black blood.

For one long heartbeat, Adrian stood frozen. Then he burst into action, sticking one hand under Bex's nose while using the other to check her pulse at the neck. He felt her breath faintly, and her heart was still beating, but her skin was the same temperature as the air, and she was so *pale*. He swore he could see her skull through her skin as he unzipped her jacket to find the source of the blood.

His hands were black by the time he got the zipper down. Her entire middle was wrapped in strips of soggy black cloth beneath her bra. Her shirt, Adrian realized. She'd ripped up her T-shirt and tied it around her as a bandage, but the blood-logged cotton was already slipping toward her hips, revealing the wound beneath.

Adrian hissed when he saw it. Bex's too-pale skin was bruised all over, but nothing compared to the laceration that split her side open like a razor slash. He had no idea what kind of weapon could cut flesh that cleanly, but the wound had clearly been bleeding unchecked for a while.

Pinning that as his first priority, Adrian dug into his coat for his medical kit. The version he carried in his pockets had both regular medical supplies and witchcraft. In cases like this, though, simplicity was best, so he chose a large gauze pad and a roll of medical tape. The wound would need stitching, but that could be done later. Right now, he had to stop the bleeding before Bex finished bleeding out.

Moving as fast as he could, Adrian pressed the gauze pad over her wound and started binding it place with the tape. When he'd wrapped her whole stomach up like a mummy, he slid his arms under her to lift her out of the chair. His plan was to carry her back to the house where he would have more options, but as he pulled Bex into his arms, something fell out of her jacket pocket, hitting the linoleum floor with a loud metal *clang*.

He jumped at the sound, looking down to see a large black ring lying in the blood by his boot. It looked important, so Adrian crouched down to scoop it up. He was about to shove it into his pocket and get back to saving Bex's life when the ring slid onto his finger of its own accord, and a voice roared into his head.

Witch of the Blackwood!

Adrian jumped a foot. He looked around next, spinning in a full circle, but no one was there. He and Bex were still alone at the back of the ferry. He was telling himself to forget about it and keep going when the strange ring bit into his finger hard enough to make him gasp, and Adrian looked at his hand to see the black band vibrating in sync with the voice as it spoke again.

There is no time, the ring said, the words stabbing into his mind. *You must make her drink.*

"Drink what?" Adrian asked, setting Bex back down in the bloody chair for a moment while he attempted to pull the painful ring off his finger.

Water from the rivers of death! it roared, refusing to budge. *I can feel you have some on you. Get it out. Quickly, you fool!*

Adrian didn't see how deathly water was supposed to keep someone alive, but Bex did collect the stuff, and Iggs *had* given him a bottle, presumably for emergencies like this. Bex's ring was also the one telling him to do it, and Adrian supposed it would know. So, though it went against every medical instinct he had, he let go of Bex and reached into his pocket for the vial of glowing water.

It shone beautifully as always, as blue as a summer sky even under the ferry's yellow fluorescents. That seemed like a good sign, so Adrian unscrewed the cap and raised the bottle to Bex's lips. He poured the smallest amount possible into her mouth since giving an unconscious person liquid was a sure way to make them choke, but while the glowing water made it in just fine, nothing happened.

You have to make her drink it, the ring insisted, rattling on his finger. *She'll die if she doesn't.*

"How?" Adrian demanded. "I can't pour it down her throat while she's passed out."

Then wake her up, the ring said. *Name her and bid her drink. That'll do the trick.*

Adrian jerked back so fast, the ring almost flew off his finger. "I'm not going to name her!" he cried. "Commanding demons by their names is warlock magic, and I have *never* done that. Also, I don't know Bex's true name."

I will tell you if you swear to save her, the ring said, growing heavy on his hand. *I would do it, but my strength is her strength, and we are too weak. You are a witch, filled with magic. It must be you.*

"I won't," Adrian said stubbornly. "Even if it would save her life, Bex is free. I'm not going to bind her."

Who said anything about binding? the ring snapped. *I'm not asking you to put a slave band on her neck! Just speak her name and order her to drink before that stubborn fool drains us both so dry that we never recover.*

Adrian looked away with a scowl. He wanted nothing to do with this. Even when his cabal tutors had beaten him, he'd never spoken a demon's true name. He especially didn't want to do it to Bex, but he knew nothing about healing demons, and she looked so terrible. He couldn't even see her breaths flickering in her throat anymore. Iggs wouldn't have given him the water without good reason. It *must* be important, so he took a breath and raised his fisted hand until the ring was right in front of him.

"What's her name?"

Rebexa, the ring replied in a hushed voice, as if it were a holy word. *You must speak it strongly. She is almost gone.*

Adrian nodded, placing the hand with the ring over his chest where he could feel his heart beating back in the Blackwood. His forest was young, but it still offered its power freely, handing him the magic he needed as Adrian took a breath.

"Re—"

The word froze in his mouth. His brain knew the syllables he was trying to form, but Adrian couldn't force his body to say them. Speaking her name felt like trying to push a boulder up a mountain with his tongue. He was still struggling when the ring's voice roared through him.

*I said speak it **strongly***! *You think she is some common demon to be ordered about by any oaf with a voice? Fool! You are addressing a daughter of Ishtar! Put your back into it, and hurry up.*

Adrian *had* been putting his back into it. Whatever Bex's name was, it was more than his sapling forest could handle, especially way out here on the water. He needed something stronger and closer, so Adrian reached into his coat, fishing through dozens of pockets until he found what he was looking for.

When his hand came out again, he was holding an acorn the size of a golf ball. It came from his mother's heart tree, and even locked up in a dormant seed, Adrian could feel the magic radiating out of it like sunshine. He'd been saving it in case his forest needed a last-second boost, but preparing for future disasters was never more important than preventing one right now, so Adrian clenched his fingers around the acorn's hard green shell, drawing the strength of the Blackwood's heart into his flesh as he tried again.

"Rebexa."

The name left him like a thunderclap, rattling the ferry's windows. It rattled Adrian as well, shaking his bones and stealing his breath. The air was still leaving his lungs when Bex's body spasmed. Her glowing eyes shot wide as her bandaged stomach arched as far as it would go toward the ferry's drop ceiling, and then she collapsed back into the bloody chair in a coughing fit.

Adrian sprang back to her side, sliding one arm behind her back to help her sit up while his other held the bottle of glowing water to her lips. Bex grabbed it at once, tilting her head back to drink in thirsty swallows. When she'd emptied the whole thing, she slumped against Adrian's arm, rubbing her eyes weakly with her bloody hands.

"Thanks," she whispered.

"You're welcome," Adrian said.

Bex jolted at the sound of his voice, her head whipping up to stare at him with horrified, glowing eyes. "What are you doing here?"

"Helping," Adrian answered, pulling her talkative ring—which had *finally* stopped biting him—off his finger and dropping it back into her jacket pocket. When he'd zipped it up tight, he slid his free arm under Bex's knees to pick her up.

"I bandaged your wound to stem the bleeding, but it's not going to be enough," he explained as he balanced her carefully again his chest. "We need to get you back to my house."

"I'm fine," Bex insisted. "Put me down."

"You can't walk."

She glared at him, but Adrian had a great deal of experience dealing with stubborn patients. He held on tight, looking over his shoulder at Bran, who was still strapped to his back.

"Clean this up, please."

The broom jerked against him. Then it wiggled out of its holding strap and started eagerly sweeping the floor and chair. Everywhere its bristles passed, Bex's blood vanished, and a few seconds later, what had looked like a black-and-white murder scene was sparkling clean.

"How did you do that?" Bex whispered.

"Bran *is* a broom," Adrian reminded her with only the slightest bit of smugness as he carried her toward the door that led to the ferry's exterior deck. "Though he doesn't work for free. I let him eat your blood in exchange for cleaning our trail."

She shrank in his arms. "Your broom *ate* my blood?"

"You weren't using it," he said with a shrug. "And better it go to Bran than some human janitor. Demon blood is a powerful reagent. You might have cursed that poor worker by accident."

Bex's blood could also be used to trace her location by any sorcerer worth the name, but Adrian didn't mention that part. He was too busy carrying her out onto the deck. Bran followed right behind, floating just above the floor. When they were in a good spot with a clear line of takeoff and no witnesses, Adrian stepped onto his broom and rose into the sky, balancing like a bird on a wire as Bran shot through the night toward the dark shape of the island.

"Do you have to stand?" Bex whispered nervously, curling into a ball against him.

"It makes for a faster takeoff," Adrian explained, flashing her a reassuring smile that she probably couldn't see in the dark. "But don't worry. Bran is very happy right now. He won't let us fall."

His broom was ecstatic, actually. Cleaning something as powerful as demon blood was a rare treat, and Bex had dumped a lot of it. She was *still* bleeding, which shouldn't have been possible. He'd taped her up tight, and demons were famous for shaking off damage. Adrian had thought they were in the clear when she regained consciousness, but he could already feel the warm blood pooling inside her jacket.

That couldn't be good. He crouched low Bran's back, urging the broom to fly faster as he shifted Bex in his grip. He was still trying to find the angle that would let him put the most pressure on her wound without risking her falling out of his arms into the bay when Bex started to wiggle.

"Stop that," he ordered.

"I'm getting blood all over your clothes," she said in a miserable voice.

"It's fine," he assured her. "Everything I wear is black."

For some reason, that made Bex laugh. She stopped immediately with a hiss of pain, but it must have still been funny, because her pale face was smiling in the moonlight when Adrian looked down.

"That's why I wear black, too," she explained.

Adrian scowled furiously. Bleeding was *not* why he wore black, and he didn't like the idea that Bex got into these situations so often that they determined her wardrobe choices. Before he could say anything about it, however, Bex's body went slack in his arms. She'd passed out again.

"Blackwood protect us," he muttered, holding Bex tight against him as Bran shot into the forest like a diving falcon.

Chapter 11

Bex woke to the most incredible feeling. It was so pleasant and unusual that it took her a staggeringly long time to realize she wasn't in pain. The eternal ache in her side was gone, replaced by warmth and a feeling of weightlessness, almost as if she were floating in a pool of—

She opened her eyes with a start, splashing water all over herself before she realized she was in a bathtub. A moment later, Bex decided that couldn't be right. Bathtubs were white and filled with water and soap. She was in a basin carved from a single gigantic piece of greenish-gray soapstone. It was long enough to hold a much taller person and deep enough to keep her whole body submerged in something that looked like pond water but smelled like fancy herbal tea.

Whatever it was, it was *stuffed* with plants. The water around her was so thick with leaves and grasses and flower petals, Bex couldn't actually see her body until she sat all the way up, which was when she realized she was naked.

"You're awake!"

Practically half the tub sloshed over the edge as Bex dove back under the water. She pressed her back against the tub's curved bottom, frantically swishing the floating leaves over herself as Adrian suddenly walked into view. His hat and coat were gone, and his shirtsleeves were rolled up to his elbows, but while his face looked exhausted, the expression on it was proud.

"I was starting to worry," he said, reaching down to unhook the loose cloth strap that prevented her unconscious head from actually dipping under the water. He took a seat on the wooden chair beside the tub next, which was when Bex finally realized the dark room wasn't a bathroom. They were inside the glassed-in patio at the back of Adrian's cabin, the one she'd always thought of as a greenhouse because it was crammed with plants.

The foliage looked even thicker in the dark, the trailing leaves and vines catching in Adrian's curling hair when he leaned down to rebuild the fire in the little iron stove that heated the tub, the only source of light in the otherwise pitch-black garden.

"You lost a great deal of blood," he continued when the flames were going strong again. "The wound in your side wouldn't stop bleeding no matter what I did. That's why I had to put you in the tub."

"Did you have to strip me?" Bex snapped. Much more sharply than he deserved, but she was just so embarrassed. She hadn't been naked in front of anyone except Lys since she was a child, and never in her current state. The idea of Adrian seeing her like this—bony, wounded, *weak*—made Bex want to vanish under the floor, but the witch just waved her words away.

"I had to take your clothes off to treat your injuries," he explained in a calm, practical voice. "But I promise I had no ulterior motives. I'm a Witch of the Flesh. My entire magical tradition revolves around life and the body, which means I've seen a *lot* of naked people."

He grinned as if that statement were hilarious, but Bex just sank lower in the tub.

"The rest of your team is on their way back," Adrian continued, dipping his fingers into the water by her feet to check the temperature. "They went out to find you last night and ended up getting stuck on the mainland due to the ferry schedule. They're on the first boat back right now and should be arriving in half an hour or so."

187

He flashed her a reassuring look, but all Bex felt was shame. She was scrubbing her hands over her face to hide it when her fingers brushed against something soft just above her forehead. Braids, she realized a second later. Adrian had braided her hair around her head so it wouldn't get wet, which only made her feel even worse.

"I'm sorry," she whispered, the forbidden words grating through her teeth.

"You have nothing to be sorry about," Adrian said. "I'm the one who told Iggs to take everybody, and I decided to fly out to get you on my own."

"You shouldn't have had to do anything," Bex argued, wrapping her thin arms over her naked chest. "I'm going to have to give you a refund now. Forcing a client to rescue his own security is definitely a breach of contract."

"You didn't force me to do anything, and I don't want a refund," Adrian said, leaning forward in his chair. "Though I would like an explanation."

There was a soft *tack* as he finished, and Bex looked up in horror to see he'd placed Drox's black metal ring on the rim of the tub.

"That ring spoke to me when I found you," he said, watching her face intently. "It called you a daughter of Ishtar."

"Oh, it did, did it?" Bex growled, snatching the ring off the stone. That overgrown fire-poker was *dead* as soon as she got strong enough to pull him out again.

"Is it true?" Adrian pressed, leaning closer.

"Ishtar was the goddess of Paradise," Bex hedged, putting Drox on the lip of the tub behind her since she had no pockets right now and like hell was she sticking him back on her finger. "She's the one who made the demons, so, technically, we're all her children."

188

"Not like this," Adrian said, sliding off his chair. "That ring had me use your true name to wake you up. I know it takes a lot of magic to command demons, which is why warlocks are always popping quintessence, but I had to pull down on the roots of the Blackwood itself just to get yours out of my mouth." He knelt beside her on the floor, gripping the tub's stone edge with his fingers. "Why? What are you?"

Bex looked down at the plant soup she was stewing in. When it was clear she wasn't going to answer, Adrian sat back on his heels with a frustrated sigh.

"At least tell me what put that hole in your side," he muttered. "You're my first demon patient, but I've been sewing cuts back together since I was nine, and I've never seen anything like it. All your other wounds and bruises healed right up when I treated them, but not that one. Why? What happened last night?"

"It's not from last night," Bex admitted. "I did get into a fight, but—"

"A fight with whom?"

"A war demon," she said, happy to move to a safer topic. "I went out last night to meet with Felix, the goblin prince who set up our job. He said he had a lead that I'd be interested in, but when I showed up at his office, the Spider was waiting."

Adrian's olive face turned ashen. "The Spider trapped you?"

"Not trapped," Bex said, smiling at last. "I'm not *that* easy to corner. But he'd guessed that you'd hired me and paid Felix to set up a meeting on neutral ground. I'd already taken the bait by the time I realized who I'd be talking to, so I had to hear him out. He wanted me to tell him where you were."

Adrian's eyes went huge, and Bex scrambled to reassure him. "I didn't tell him anything. Even if we didn't already have a contract, I don't work for warlocks. I was going to come right back here, but the Spider had a greed demon who'd likely tapped my phone, so I chucked it and ran. My plan was to lose any tails and circle back around, but I got caught by one of his overgrown war demons."

If Adrian had looked scared before, he looked horrified now. "You *fought* one of the Spider's war demons? The big ones?"

"Size isn't everything," Bex said, raising her chin. "War demons might be built like tanks, but they're slow and rely too much on their armor. I was spanking him until he hit my wound. I still beat him and got away, but I was pretty far out by that point, and I couldn't stop the bleeding."

"Why didn't you call for help?"

She flushed. "I was going to, but I couldn't remember anyone's number. That was my biggest screwup. Everything would've been fine if I'd just thought to look at my contacts list before cracking my phone in half."

Adrian moved back to his chair with a sigh. "If the Spider's already figured out where I hired my security, it won't be long before he finds this place."

"That's not all," Bex said, sitting up as much as she could without exposing herself. "The warlocks aren't just coming to punish you for running away. The Spider still wants to capture you and make you a warlock."

That was supposed to be the big drop, but Adrian just nodded. "I know."

"You know?" she repeated, blinking at him. "Why didn't you tell me earlier?"

"Because it didn't change the job," he grumbled, resting his head on the back of the chair. "And it's not exactly something I'm proud of. The New England cabal has been taking Blackwood boys for centuries. Nearly all of them are my cousins or closer." He frowned. "I think the Spider might be the only member of their inner circle I'm not related to."

Bex couldn't believe it. "You're being hunted by members of your own family?"

"They're *not* my family," Adrian said hotly. "They share my blood, but no Blackwood would ever do what they do. That's why I came here. The Old Wives of the Blackwood are powerful, but the New England cabal reports directly to Gilgamesh's princes. Defying them is the same as defying the Eternal King. My coven couldn't take a risk that big for my sake. All they could do was hide me in the forest and hope the warlocks stayed too scared to come in after me. That worked for a long time, but I'm not a little kid hiding behind trees anymore. I'm a fully initiated witch with my own grove. If I want to fight, I can do that here without dragging the rest of my coven into it."

"Can you win, though?" Bex asked. "I've talked to the Spider. He's not giving up."

"Then I'll fight him until he has no other choice," Adrian said angrily. "We witches have always been stronger than Gilgamesh's stooges give us credit for. Let's see how the Spider feels about forcing me back into my apprenticeship after my forest eats half his warlocks."

He finished with a defiant lift of his chin, but Bex just sank into the water. It wasn't that she disagreed with what Adrian was trying to do. She was actually proud of him for taking a stand, she just didn't think it was going to work. Warlocks didn't give up and go home just because you killed a few. Bex would know, too. She'd been killing warlocks her entire life, and they still chased her every chance they got.

Unlike Bex and her crew, though, Adrian couldn't stay on the move. He had literal roots holding him in place, and as powerful as Bex knew his witchcraft was, no one defended forever.

She wasn't about to tell him that, though. Adrian looked terrifyingly determined, sitting there with his eyes gleaming like knives in the dark. She'd seen that same expression on her demons' faces countless times. Bex used to get it, too, back before she'd been wounded. Now, though, she just felt tired. Far, far too tired to be the one who stomped on Adrian's hopes.

"We'll fight," she promised, looking up at the dome of leaves hanging over their heads. "I screwed up pretty bad tonight, but I still kept the Spider from learning where you are. He's throwing his money around hard, but that doesn't matter if the information he needs isn't out there. If we keep lying low, we might still be able to get you your month after all. I don't know if that'll be enough time, but—"

"It'll be enough," Adrian said, rising to his feet. "My Blackwood is already strong. We will need to heal your wound before he arrives, though, or this will just happen again. How long has it been like that?"

Bex frowned, doing the math in her head. "Seven years, three months."

Adrian looked down at her with a jerk. "You've had a bleeding wound in your side for seven *years*?"

"It doesn't bleed like this all the time," she assured him. "It's just bad right now because I've been drinking so much deathly water. It'll be much more manageable once I dry out again, and anyway, it can't be healed."

"Every wound can be healed," he told her authoritatively.

"Not this one."

Adrian arched a skeptical eyebrow, and Bex breathed a long sigh. She could already see him gearing up for a fight, and she just didn't have the energy. It wasn't as if Adrian would turn on her at this point, so she decided to take a risk and tell him the truth. Part of it, anyway.

"I was struck by a Blade of Gilgamesh."

The skeptical look fell off his face, replaced by horror. "You fought one of the Celestial Princes?"

When Bex nodded, his eyes bulged. "*How?*"

"It was Iggs," she said quietly, clenching her fists under the water. "You were right before. He *was* a kick demon, and I did free him. What I didn't know was that Limbo has a prince assigned to keep an eye on it at all times. The moment I broke Iggs out, he came down on me like a hammer."

"*How* did you get him out, though?" Adrian pressed, crouching so close to the tub that he was practically in the water with her. "And how did you survive? The Celestial Princes are Gilgamesh's sons, his own flesh and blood. Surely this one didn't let you and Iggs just walk away."

"Of course he didn't," Bex said with a snort. "Have you met a prince? They're the most obnoxious, arrogant, pains-in-the-ass you can imagine. The one that dropped on us didn't even wait for Iggs and me to get dumped back into the real world. He was going to slaughter us right there in Limbo. I couldn't let that happen, so I killed him."

Adrian stared at her as if she'd just claimed to be Ishtar herself. "You *killed* one of the seven princes?"

"It's not as impressive as it sounds," Bex assured him. "Gilgamesh is the king of Paradise, meaning he has total control over the land of the dead. Killing a prince just sends him back to Daddy. The one I beat was patched up and back in the field within days. That still gave me and Iggs time to escape, but I never fully recovered from the battle, and I'm not just talking about the window in my side."

Bex looked down at her rail-thin arms. She'd never talked about this next part with anyone but her demons. She didn't even like to admit it to herself, but if Adrian was going to bet everything on their defense, then he deserved to know.

"Killing that prince burned everything I had," she confessed. "That's why I look like this." She gestured at the collar bones that were clearly visible beneath the tissue-thin layer of her skin. "I was actually pretty normal before it happened, but after..." She trailed off with a shrug. "Let's just say I'm not the Bex I used to be. That's why I've never tried to free another kick demon. If I had to face another prince like this, I wouldn't stand a chance."

"I'm amazed you stood a chance the first time," Adrian said, gazing at her in wonder. "You must have been incredible."

"I was definitely a lot more impressive. I mean, I used to be five six. I was also seventeen and thought I was hot shit, which was how I got into such a stupid mess in the first place."

Adrian did a double take. "Seventeen?" he repeated in a shocked voice. "So if you fought the prince seven years ago... that means you're only twenty-four years old."

Bex frowned. "Do I look older?"

"No," he said quickly. "It's just that demons get stronger with age, and everyone on your team looks up to you so much, it simply didn't occur to me that you wouldn't be ancient."

Bex chuckled. "Sorry to disappoint."

"I'm not disappointed," Adrian said with a smile Bex wasn't sure how to interpret. "But you should still let me have a go at that wound. It's clearly causing you a great deal of suffering, and I'm sure you'd like to get out of that tub at some point."

His insistence was touching, but she shook her head. "Thanks for the offer, but it's really okay. Everyone knows wounds from a Blade of Gilgamesh can't be healed, and we're on the clock hard now. I wouldn't want you to waste your time on a lost cause."

"It's not a lost cause," Adrian argued. "You're the head of my security team. Getting you back into fighting shape is mission-critical, and I've yet to meet an injury I couldn't fix. I might be young, but I was the second-best healer in the Blackwood before I left."

"It's *really* okay," Bex said, sliding a bit farther down in the tub. "Even if you can heal my cut, the rest of my body is still wrecked. I'm never getting back what I lost killing that prince, so please don't trouble yourself on my account."

"Fixing a problem that causes you constant pain is *not* 'troubling myself,'" he said angrily. "Why don't you want me to heal you?"

"Because my life doesn't matter."

Bex knew she'd stepped in it the moment the words came out of her mouth. Adrian's expression was furious, but it wasn't what he thought. Unfortunately, it was impossible to explain that to him without telling Adrian the whole story, which she absolutely couldn't do. She *really* didn't want to keep arguing about this, though, so Bex decided to tell him part of the truth. The safe part.

"I reincarnate," she blurted, cutting Adrian off before he launched into the tirade she could see building behind his eyes. "I'm not twenty-four because I had a mom who gave birth to me twenty-four years ago. That's just when the last version of me died. Whenever I get killed, I come back

195

as a baby in the nearest river. This is actually my hundred-and-ninety-eighth life, and like I said, it's already toast. That's why I've been hoarding deathly water. I knew this wound would kill me eventually, so I've been building up a stockpile for the next Bex so she can have it easier. It's the best I can do with the time I've got left, but there's no point wasting resources trying to heal me. All my injuries are going to vanish when this body dies, and then I'll be reborn whole and strong again, so it's really not important."

Bex was shaking by the time she finished. That was more than she'd ever told any outsider, but while Adrian no longer looked angry, he did look very worried.

"When you're reborn," he said at last, "do you keep the memories from your previous lives?"

"No," Bex admitted. "But I do keep what my muscles learn. That's how I knew that song you heard me playing. What was it called?"

"'Mood for a Day,'" Adrian supplied.

She nodded rapidly. "Yeah, that one. I had no idea what it was, but a previous version of me must have liked it enough to learn the fingering. That's why, even though I don't remember the song, my body still knows how to play it. Honestly, I'm really lucky. If I had to relearn how to fight every time I reincarnated, my lives would be even shorter than they already are."

That was supposed to be a joke, but Adrian didn't laugh. "If you lose all your memories every time you're reborn, how is that any different from being dead?"

"It just is," Bex insisted, rubbing her wet hands over her face. "It's always been like this for me, okay? And it's not as if I'm a unique person. Lys has been with me through four reincarnations, and they say I'm the same every time. It's not like being *dead* dead. I just lose some time."

"You lose your entire *life*," Adrian said angrily, staring at her as if he couldn't believe he had to say that. "If you'd bled to death on that ferry, you wouldn't remember me or my forest or anything that's happened. You wouldn't remember Iggs or Lys or Nemini. You'd be a baby, a fresh new life. Even if it's the same soul, it wouldn't be *you*."

She lowered her head. Adrian wasn't saying anything Bex hadn't secretly thought, but he didn't understand. Reincarnation was the only way to fix the damage her stupid decision to fight the prince had done.

When she'd woken up and seen the ruin she'd made of her body, she'd seriously considered offing herself. The only reason she hadn't was because she didn't want to waste the seventeen years Lys and Nemini—but mostly Lys—had spent raising her back into a functional adult. She'd started taking mercenary jobs a year later. It wasn't what any of them wanted, but Bex figured if she could get a big enough stockpile of deathly water, maybe the next version of her would be strong enough to free a kick demon *without* destroying herself.

It was the only way she could think of to salvage a life that would have been wasted otherwise. Having a goal made Bex feel like she was doing something constructive, which in turn made it easier not to think about how much she'd lost. It really only bothered her at times like this, when she was hurt and weak and scared because of it.

But that was Bex's problem, not Adrian's. He was fighting his own war, and Bex would damn herself before she let her client—the person she was being paid to protect—risk his one and *only* life trying to fix what was ultimately a temporary problem. She was trying to think of a way of explaining this that wouldn't make Adrian balk when the witch rose to his feet.

"I can't force you to let me heal you," he said, staring down with an expression that made Bex wince. "But before you brush me off completely, I would ask that you let me try. Just because you're not as strong as you used to be doesn't mean your current life has no value. I hired you to be my security exactly as you are, and that wound is clearly a giant liability. Therefore, as your client, I'm asking you to at least let me attempt to fix the problem so that we don't have to go through all of this again."

Bex bit her lip. Adrian was clearly still very angry, but his request was so reasonable that she couldn't figure out a way to tell him no.

"I can't pay you," she said instead.

"I wouldn't accept it," he told her, his eyes hard. "I'm doing this on principle, because in *my* Blackwood, when someone comes in with a gaping wound, I fix it. Unless, of course, you enjoy fainting in pools of your own blood."

"I suppose I deserved that one," Bex muttered, rubbing her wet hands over her face. "Okay, we'll try, but don't be disappointed when it doesn't work."

"I'm only disappointed that you have so little faith in me," Adrian said, crossing his arms over his chest. "Have I been such a mediocre witch?"

"Of course not," Bex said quickly. "Everything I've seen you do has been amazing. I just didn't want to waste your time."

"Helping you will *not* be a waste of my time, because everything I've seen *you* do has been amazing." He smiled for the first time since she'd messed up and said her life didn't matter. "If you beat one of the Spider's giant war demons with a gaping hole in your stomach, I can't wait to see how good you'll be when you're well. Think of it as an investment to increase the value of your services."

Bex nodded, not sure what else to say. When he turned to walk back into the house, though, she did manage "Thank you."

"You're welcome," Adrian replied, grabbing his witch hat off the peg by the door. "I'm going to go start my preparations. I'll send the others to you as soon as they arrive."

Bex murmured her thanks again, but Adrian was already gone, leaving her alone in the dark, warm greenhouse full of plants.

"And you just *told* him?" Lys cried.

"Yes," Bex said, floating in the bathtub, which she *still* hadn't managed to get out of.

She'd tried when she'd heard the RV pulling into the clearing. The moment she'd left the water, though, blood had started seeping between the perfect little stitches Adrian had used to close her wound, and she'd had no choice but to go back in. Probably for the best, since she still didn't have any clothes.

Lys slumped into Adrian's wooden chair with a sigh. The lust demon looked neither male nor female this morning. It was what Bex thought of as their "serious business" shape, the one they changed into when they didn't want to worry about performing to expectations. It was the form Lys had worn through most of Bex's childhood, and seeing it now made her nostalgic as she reached for her demon's hand.

"Trust me, this was the safer path," Bex said, squeezing Lys's elegant fingers. "Drox already spilled my name on the ferry, so it could have been *much* worse, but

Adrian didn't recognize me. All he knows is that I reincarnate."

Lys didn't look happy about any of that, but there was hope in their eyes when they bent down to examine the sewed-up wound in Bex's side.

"Do you actually think he can heal it?"

The *no* was already on Bex's lips when she stopped herself. "Adrian thinks he can," she said instead. "And I've agreed to let him try. Worst that happens is he fails and nothing changes."

"I still can't believe Felix set you up," Lys snarled. "The next time I see him, I'm going to skin his green hide and wear it as a coat."

"Don't commit any fashion atrocities on my account," Bex said, getting more comfortable in the warm, leafy water, which still felt quite lovely. "And it wasn't a *total* disaster. My meeting with the Spider netted some useful information. Warlocks usually travel with their strongest hand, but the only reason I had trouble with his war demon was because the bastard punched me in the stitches. If that hulking bronze snail is the best the Spider can throw, we might not be in as much trouble as I thought."

"Unless he calls for help," Lys said, looking pointedly at Drox's ring, which was still sitting on the edge of the tub.

Bex bit her lip. "Are you mad I freed him?"

"No," Lys said with a tired smile. "You've always freed demons, even when it was a terrible idea. That's why I follow you, but it was still a risk. Adrian's young and sheltered, but the Spider is one of Gilgamesh's trusted henchmen. We got a lucky break that he didn't recognize you the moment you walked into Felix's meeting room, but if his war demon runs home with a tale about a sword that can cut slave bands, we could be in a lot more than one witch's worth of trouble."

Bex slumped in the water. "I—"

"That's not a bad thing."

She jerked back up to see Lys grinning.

"Just because we were forced to stop fighting when you got hurt doesn't mean we gave up the war. Adrian's situation has given us a chance to fight one of Gilgamesh's most influential warlocks away from his seat of power. That's an incredible opportunity by itself, but Adrian's a witch of the Blackwood. They're famous for working miracles, and after seeing him in action, I believe it. If he really can heal you, just think of the hell we'll be able to unleash when the Spider finally shows up."

The hope in their voice made Bex want to scream. "No, Lys, we've been through this," she groaned. "You're the one who told me going into Limbo for a kick demon was a stupid risk, and you were right. I've never regretted freeing Iggs, but I'm also not going to sit here hoping for things that won't happen."

"But Adrian—"

"Adrian can't fix me," she said stubbornly. "The only reason I'm letting him try is because he wouldn't take no for an answer."

"You're brushing this off too quickly," Lys argued. "Maybe Adrian can't fix everything, but we don't *need* everything to get you back in the fight. The you that freed me four lives ago looked much worse than you do now, and you still slaughtered my old warlock like a pig."

Bex looked away, wishing for the millionth time that she could remember. The Bex in Lys's stories always sounded like a superhero, smashing warlock cabals and freeing demons left and right. A prince had eventually killed that Bex, but the cocky bastard hadn't stuck around to check the rivers, and Lys had been able to escape with the next infant Rebexa, whose life the current Bex also didn't remember.

"We could do it again," Lys said, their amber eyes gleaming like fire in the morning sunlight that streamed through the greenhouse's steamed-up windows. "The cabals have grown lazy and careless since you stopped raiding. The Spider is one of the last true monsters. If we use the Blackwood to kill him, there'll be nothing stopping us from going on a slave-freeing spree like they haven't seen in eighty years."

"Which will get us attacked by the princes again," Bex said glumly. "And unlike me, the rest of you don't reincarnate."

"Can't fight a rebellion without breaking a few eggs," Lys said, reaching out to pat Bex on the horns as they'd done when she was a child. "But those are bloody plans for later. Right now, I have to go reassure Iggs that you're not dead. Poor baby was scared out of his mind. This is his first ride on the Reincarnation Rodeo, and he still hasn't wrapped his brain around the fact that you're unkillable."

Bex smiled at the old joke, but inside she was cringing, because she didn't feel unkillable. As Adrian had so pointedly reminded her, reincarnation wasn't the same as eternal life. Rebexa would live on. She was the immortal one. Bex was just who was here right now, and right now, she felt very, very mortal.

"Are you okay?" Lys asked, giving her a worried look.

"I'm fine," Bex lied, rolling Drox's ring between her palms. "Tell Iggs thanks for me. If he hadn't given Adrian that bottle of water, you'd be dealing with a newborn right now."

"Fate worse than death," Lys agreed, strolling toward the door to Adrian's house.

"And bring me some clothes!" Bex yelled after them.

The lust demon waved over their shoulder, leaving Bex to stew in her watery prison.

Chapter 12

"**T**his isn't going to work."

"I'm getting very tired of people telling me that," Adrian said through clenched teeth as he dug his bare fingers into the loamy dirt at the center of his new stone circle.

"I'm not talking about repairing a cut from a Blade of Gilgamesh," Boston snapped, sticking his face right in the middle of where Adrian was trying to dig. "I'm talking about doing a healing while you're angry. If you go into this with your mind all jumbled, you might end up transferring Bex's wound to yourself, and *then* where would we be?"

Adrian scooped out a handful of dirt without comment. It wasn't that Boston was wrong—Boston was almost never wrong—but he wasn't entirely right, either. There was always more than one way to cast a spell, and anger was a legitimate emotion.

"What are you so mad about, anyway?" his familiar grumbled, sitting back on his haunches. "It's not like you."

It wasn't. Adrian hated feeling this way, but he couldn't seem to stop. Hearing Bex talk about her life as if it didn't matter—as if saving her was an *inconvenience*—insulted him on every level, and the fact that this was obviously an ongoing problem only made it worse. Bex's bloody carpet was a testament to how bad she'd let things get. Stains like that didn't happen from a one-time bleed. The scene he'd witnessed when he'd found Bex passed out on her bed was clearly a regular occurrence. Her demons had to know it was happening, and yet they'd done nothing to help.

Adrian slammed his hands into the ground like a spear, making Boston jump. How could they do that? How could *she* do that? Treat her unique, wonderful gift of a life like a broken part to be replaced? It was abhorrent.

He felt a breeze against his wrists as Boston lay down in the dirt with a sigh. "Adrian," the cat said patiently, "I realize you're upset, but you have to accept that not everyone sees the world the same way you do. Even in the Blackwood, there are witches who spend their entire lives working on spells that won't be completed for generations. From what you've told me, Bex's situation isn't so different. There's nothing wrong with dedicating your life to a larger purpose."

"Maybe not," Adrian growled, shoving another handful of dirt out of the hole he was making. "But this *is* wrong. She nearly died on that ferry. *Would* have died if her ring hadn't told me what to do, but do you know what she was most worried about? Getting blood on my clothes."

Adrian snatched off his hat to rake a dirty hand through his hair. "I just don't understand what she's thinking. It's obvious she's not a normal demon. I don't know what she is, but her whole team obeys her without question and charges to her side at the first hint of danger. She's clearly beloved and doing something important, but Bex acts like none of that matters. Like *she* doesn't matter."

Boston gave him a pitying look, but Adrian wasn't having it.

"I'm going to heal her," he promised, stabbing his fingers into the earth again. "All of her. The cut, whatever she lost in Limbo—I'm going to put it all back. Maybe then she'll start treating her life like it's worth a damn."

"And how are you going to do that?" Boston demanded, sitting back up. "You had to burn a treasure of the Blackwood just to speak her name. What you're talking about will take far more, assuming it's even possible. I took a look at her while you were getting the bath ready, and her injuries are like nothing I've ever seen. She's completely hollowed out, like the trunk of a burned hardwood after a fire. Forget the sword wound. I don't know if that sort of damage *can* be healed."

"Not with that attitude," Adrian said, reaching his arm down to measure what was now a very large hole at the center of the stone circle. When he was satisfied it was deep enough, he sat back on his heels.

"All right," he said, rubbing his hands together. "Time to do some witchcraft."

Boston glowered, but he didn't argue again, for which Adrian was grateful. Doing magic when he was this upset *was* risky, but it could also be powerful. Emotions were forces of the present, as dear to his witchcraft as the body itself. The bones could be logical and cold, the soul detached and dispassionate, but the flesh demanded conviction. Adrian was at his strongest in moments like this, which was why he didn't hesitate as he pulled a short-bladed, slightly crooked knife out of his pocket and sliced it across the inner flesh of his forearm.

Witchcraft was a very fair magic. The more you offered, the more it gave, so Adrian didn't hold back. He squeezed his hand around the cut, pushing on the flesh to pour his blood into the hole he'd dug. When he started to feel lightheaded, he slid his fingers over the slice to seal it back up and looked down at his knife.

The tool wasn't elegant, but he'd held onto it for years, because it was the first and only piece of metalwork he'd ever made. He'd never taken to blacksmithing like he had to sewing and woodcraft, but he'd always liked his little knife. It was a convenient size, and it reminded him of home. Looking at it now filled him with nostalgia. Good, strong feelings that Adrian leaned into as he dropped the knife into the bloody mud at the hole's base.

He reached into his pocket next and pulled out a piece of scrap paper and a pen. Using his knee as a table, he smoothed out the paper and wrote the name of the scale-eyed man he'd found passed out on the road at the edge of the Blackwood last winter. The old fool had been drunk and dying of frostbite. He would have lost both his feet if Adrian hadn't treated him. He'd been extremely confused when he'd woken up next to a man in a witch hat with a cat on his shoulder, but also profusely grateful, especially when he'd learned that Adrian hadn't called his wife. The man had sworn up and down to repay him, but Adrian had refused his money and sent him on his way. Now, though, the witch was calling in his due, tossing the paper with the man's name into the bloody mud beside his knife.

When it was all there, Adrian grabbed the dirt he'd dug out and began filling the hole back in. He moved in reverent silence, focusing only on the task in front of him. When the ground was even again, he bowed his head until his curling hair touched the packed-down earth.

"The offering has been made," he said, his voice ringing with all the furious magic he could summon. "A keepsake from my past, a pint of my present, and a debt for the future owed to me. By the covenant of my bones, flesh, and soul, I offer three pieces of myself in exchange for a boon from the Blackwood."

The world was absolutely still by the time he finished. The wind didn't blow, the trees didn't rustle, the birds didn't sing. What was left was a far deeper silence than his little forest could ever have managed on its own, because Adrian was no longer addressing only his grove. He was speaking to all Blackwoods, the single, eternal forest whose roots held the world together.

Those same roots rose now, curling up through the dirt he'd piled over his offerings. The trees leaned closer, dropping their branches to brush his hair. Spiders and insects crawled out of the leaf litter. Worms came up from the dirt. Snakes slithered out of the cool darkness under his porch. Squirrels and birds came down from the trees. Deer and foxes emerged from the forest. Within minutes, all of nature was sitting around him, staring at Adrian with the same heavy silence as the forest waited for its witch to speak.

"Yours is the wisdom older than humanity," he told the Blackwood, sitting up again at last. "If you do not know, it cannot be known, so I ask you: how do I heal Rebexa?"

He barely got the last word out. Even when he wasn't using it to command her, speaking Bex's name took everything he had. Adrian would rather not have invoked it at all, but failing to be specific could be disastrous with magic this big. Because he'd never had a grove of his own before, this was Adrian's first time casting such a spell, but he'd heard plenty of stories. You had to be resolute and precise, confident in your power. The Blackwood's heart might be its witches, but it was still a forest, and it was not nature's way to coddle the weak.

Again, his anger came in useful here. He'd never spoken directly to the forest, the *big* forest, before. Any other time, he would have been terrified, but Adrian was too mad right now to feel fear. He held onto that fury like a prize, all but throwing Bex's insistence that going around wounded was fine and her life didn't matter at the forest's feet.

To his delight, the Blackwood shared his anger. In the great cycle of life and death, the will to survive was paramount. Everything that lived did so only because of the tenacity and resourcefulness of the billions of generations that came before it. To treat such a gift as disposable spat in the face of everything the forest was. It would not stand.

"It will not," Adrian agreed, his face splitting into a grin. "How do I heal her?"

No answer came this time. Instead, an image of a hand appeared inside his head. It looked very much like his mother's, and it was beckoning for him to take it.

For the first time since he'd started down this path, Adrian hesitated. He trusted the Blackwood with his life—he'd buried his heart in it, after all—but this was different. The pieces of himself he'd offered paid only for getting the Blackwood's attention and asking his question. He'd known the healing would take more, but the beckoning hand in his head was very clear. The forest did not want a price. It wanted him to give it control.

That was a lot to ask. The Blackwood was a great and ancient force of nature. Adrian had never heard of it betraying a witch, but the forest's idea of helping didn't always line up with the conventional definition. For all Adrian knew, the Blackwood would teach Bex the incredible value of life by turning her into a mayfly.

"I want to *heal* her," he said again as he looked around at the silent crowd of animals, plants, and insects. "As in repair the damage to her present physical body. How can that be done, and what will it cost?"

He was already braced for the worst, but the beckoning hand in his head didn't go away. It just kept curling its fingers, its meaning crystal clear. There would be no trade. If Adrian wanted to heal Bex, he would have to put himself in the Blackwood's hand.

"Don't do it," Boston whispered from his crouch by Adrian's knee. "You're tied to the forest by bones, flesh, and soul. It knows everything you do, including how badly you want to fix Bex. This is why doing magic while angry is a bad idea! If it takes you at your word as you are now—which it absolutely will, since you're a Witch of the Present—you could end up putting your entire future in the hands of an emotional snap decision."

"I don't think that's it," Adrian said, staring up at the towering hardwoods who'd bent down to him like willows. "I'm angry, but the forest isn't. Listen." He cupped his hands to his ears. "It's totally silent."

The forest was waiting, Adrian realized with a start. The hand in his mind wasn't demanding. It was patient, quiet. The Blackwood had heard his question and given its answer, and now it was waiting for him to trust. Adrian didn't know why it couldn't just tell him, but that was why he'd made the offering in the first place—because he didn't know what to do, but the Blackwood did. Nature was the oldest and greatest healer. Boston had even compared Bex to a fire-damaged tree. The same sort of tree the Blackwood regrew all the time. If she could be restored, the forest would do it, and all it asked in return was Adrian's trust. A very fair price, because if he couldn't trust his forest, then Adrian had no right to call himself a witch.

There was no worse fate than that, so Adrian reached out to place his mental hand in the Blackwood's outstretched palm. It closed around him with a rush that made him grin. He still had no idea what was going to happen, but he was excited to see. If nothing else, it was going to be a hell of a spell.

That was Adrian's last conscious thought before the Blackwood flooded into him.

It was the same magic he always worked with, only instead of being herbs in his hands or roots in his heart, the forest was in every part of him. Adrian surrendered to it fully, letting the Blackwood move him out of the stone circle and into the woods beyond. Even Boston got sucked in, his frightened huffs fading to the same silence as all the other animals' as the forest moved him up to trot beside his witch.

They worked without speaking, without food or rest. Sometimes, they even worked without seeing, for the tasks the forest set them to were the sort that mortal senses couldn't perceive. Adrian had no idea why his hands moved the way they did or touched what they touched, but he could feel the beautiful complexity of the magic they were building. Even their footsteps were part of it, his boot marks crossing over Boston's pawprints to form subtle patterns in the dirt that were themselves part of a larger tapestry as interwoven and multilayered as the forest itself.

As it got bigger and bigger, Adrian understood why the forest had needed him to give it control. There was simply no way a mortal mind could understand the intricacies of everything that needed to be done. He wasn't even trying to comprehend the spell anymore. He just held on, doing and giving whatever the forest needed until suddenly, just before sunset, he looked up and found himself standing in front of a gigantic unlit bonfire.

That was a surprise. Fires were strong magic, but Adrian had never used one to heal before. He'd never built a bonfire like this before either. It was made of the oldest, rottenest wood in his forest. Some of the logs still had moss on them, and all of it was wet. He was wondering if the pile would even burn when he heard footsteps crunching behind him.

"Is it finished?"

Adrian turned unsteadily and saw Bex. She was dressed in her usual baggy clothes with a fresh pair of sunglasses on her face. He was trying to figure out if she was still bleeding or if her T-shirt was just very black today when his magic-addled brain realized he hadn't answered her question.

"I think so," he said, reaching down to pick up Boston, who was panting in a daze on his feet.

Bex's frown deepened. "You *think* so?"

"Magic this big is never certain," Adrian explained, placing his familiar carefully in the leaves outside the stone circle. When he turned back to Bex, however, she was staring at the pile of logs like she wanted to tear them down.

"You didn't have to do this."

"No," Adrian insisted. "I really, really did."

"I can't accept it," Bex argued, turning on him with a furious glare he could see through her sunglasses. "I've watched you working on this all day. You wouldn't speak to us, wouldn't stop. It was like you were in a trance! I've never seen you do magic like that, not even when you were burying your heart." She shook her head. "It's too much, Adrian. I can't just let you—"

"I am not yours to let," he interrupted sharply. "My craft is my own. I'm the only one who gets to say what I can and can't do, and I say I've done the exact right amount."

Of that he was sure. He might not have understood the Blackwood's beautiful, multilayered magic, but he'd felt the rightness of it to his bones. Whatever happened when he lit that bonfire, it would be *exactly* what Bex needed.

The forest was still inside him even now, pushing him to finish. But while Adrian didn't have a doubt in his mind, his opinion wasn't the one that mattered. He'd asked the Blackwood to do it, but the spell was for Bex. She had to have the final say, so Adrian pushed his forest back just a little and held out his hand.

"Do you want to be healed?"

Bex heaved a long breath. "I said I'd let you try."

"It has to be a yes or no," Adrian insisted, speaking quickly before the Blackwood took him over again. "This is great magic. I can't promise any specific results, but I *can* promise that you won't be the same when it's done. Like all true change, it will be painful and terrifying, but I'll be with you every step of the way. If this is acceptable, take my hand, and we'll begin."

That was not how Adrian would have chosen to explain it, but the forest was pounding in his head, demanding the magic be finished. He wasn't sure he *could* stop if she said no, but for all the contempt she'd shown herself, Bex had never been a coward. She grabbed his fingers hard, making Adrian sigh in relief as he led her into the stone circle.

The bonfire blazed to life the moment they stepped inside. Not a spark or a flare but a full roaring inferno that looked like it had already been burning for hours. The heat pouring off the wet logs was blistering, but Adrian didn't stop until he was nearly in the flames, standing over a bed of water-smoothed rocks from the inlet that he didn't even remember gathering.

"Lie down," the forest in him commanded.

Bex nodded and pulled off her leather jacket, tossing it and her sunglasses to Iggs, who was crouching next to Boston just outside of the stone ring. She took off her boots next, kicking them to safety before lying down flat on the rocks.

They must have been very hot. Her T-shirt started to smoke immediately, but she didn't cry out. She didn't make any sound at all as Adrian knelt beside her and pressed his hands over her injured side.

Her shirt was soaked when he touched it, coating his fingers in warm, black blood, but that actually made things easier. The forest inside him was certain that demon blood was the final component, so Adrian pressed down harder, making Bex gasp as he gathered her inky blood into his fists and cast it into the fire.

Bex's sense of impending doom had been growing from the moment she finally hauled herself out of the bathtub and came outside to see Adrian building a bonfire.

The sight had stopped her cold. There was no way he could have known. She hadn't told him, Drox *wouldn't* tell him, and her demons were sworn on their names not to breathe a word.

It had to be a coincidence, she told herself. Witches danced around bonfires all the time. He probably did this for all his healings, but the doomed feeling didn't go away.

Too nervous even to climb into her favorite tree, Bex had spent the day on Adrian's porch, watching him stack rotting logs in a trance the same way she'd watch a car crash. Her demons had joined her one by one, their faces excited, because even though they knew, they didn't. No one but her and Drox knew the entirety of what she'd lost, and the hope on their faces hurt worse than her bleeding wound.

Those looks were what she feared most. Bex would happily burn to death, but she couldn't bear the thought of disappointing her demons. That was why she'd taken Adrian's hand even though he'd looked terrifying—wild-eyed and larger than life with all that giant magic whipping inside him. She hated that he'd put himself into that state for her sake, and she still didn't think this was going to work, but of all the things Bex couldn't be anymore, she absolutely refused to be a coward. She would never sink that far, so she'd taken the witch's hand and followed him into the fire.

And it *hurt*. The stones he made her lie down on burned like coals, and her wound had stabbed like the first time when he'd shoved his hands into it, but the fire that roared up when he burned her blood was the worst. Even Drox had felt it, and her sword never felt pain. He was on her finger right now, screaming like metal in the forge. Bex was screaming, too, writhing in agony as the flames covered her body, but they did not consume her. They lifted her, carving her out of the husk of her body and flinging her into the air like a spark.

When Bex opened her eyes again, she was standing in Paradise.

She'd never been here before in this life, but there was no way she wouldn't know her home. This wasn't the mockery of Gilgamesh's Hells or the cheap illusion from the Anchor Market. This was Paradise as it had been before the conquest. The Paradise of endless green fields and shining blue rivers that sparkled like a thousand stars. The Paradise that no longer existed.

Because she'd lost it.

"Rebexa."

Bex whirled around, splashing water up her jeans from the glowing river she hadn't realized she was standing in. And standing in it next to her was the most beautiful woman Bex had ever seen.

She was seven feet tall, straight as a temple statue with wings like those of the wise owl. Ten heavenly spears were strapped across her back, and there was a shining sword in her hand, but she was not dressed for battle. Her billowing silk robe glittered like the Milky Way in summer, and her shining, unbound hair was crowned with six proud, tall horns—the same horns that were on Bex's head when she bowed it low, falling to her knees in the river at the woman's feet.

"Heavenly Ishtar," she whispered into the glowing water. "May I be found worthy in your sight."

The words came out by rote. She couldn't remember saying them before, but Bex knew in the same way she knew how to swing her sword that she'd said them countless times. She was Ishtar's creation. She could never *not* know her. But when Bex lifted her head to see why her goddess remained silent, the feeling of impending doom crashed back down like a hammer.

"Oh, my child," Ishtar whispered, her sparkling eyes horrified as she reached down to touch Bex's skeletal shoulder. "What have they done to you?"

Bex dropped her head again in shame. Unfortunately, this only gave her a better view of the sword wound in her ribs, which was leaking black blood into the glowing river like a plume of pollution. The sight made her want to run and hide, but there was no hiding here. All souls were laid bare in Paradise, so Bex took a shuddering breath and told her mother the truth.

"They didn't do this," she whispered. "I did."

Heavenly Ishtar said nothing. She just reached out, laying her blessed hands on Bex's horns the same way Lys used to as she waited for her to explain.

"I wasted your gift of rebirth," Bex choked out. "I was prideful and stupid. I challenged a prince, and then I burned up everything you gave me so I could win."

"What did you win?" the goddess asked.

Bex's bony hands fisted in the river's rich, sparkling mud. "One soul," she confessed. "I only saved one soul, and he's not even free. We still live like fugitives, hiding and running, because I—"

Bex stopped, scrubbing the ashy tears off her face before raising it to confess the worst.

"I failed you," she said, voice cracking. "You made me your sword, you brought me back from the dead, but I've done nothing with the life you've given me. I have not saved your people. Your enemy still sits on your brother's throne with your sacred sword in his hands, and I've done nothing to stop him." She bent back down to the glittering water. "I am unworthy to be your daughter."

"You are not unworthy," Ishtar said, her voice as gentle as her rivers. "I never expected you to win the war that killed us all in one lifetime. That is why I gave you so many. One-hundred-and-ninety-nine times now, you have fallen into my river, and one-hundred-and-ninety-eight times, I have thrown you back. But not this time."

A stab of dread went through Bex's chest. "Why not this time?"

The goddess pressed her hands to Bex's cheeks, guiding her head back up with a smile. "Because you are not dead."

Bex blinked in confusion. How could she not be dead? This was Paradise, the afterlife. But even as Bex rejected the idea, she felt Adrian's hands on her wound. She felt the hot stones pressing into her back, the ash of the bonfire falling on her face, and she knew.

"Adrian sent me to you to be healed."

"The Blackwood sent you to me," Ishtar corrected. "You are a child of Paradise, a creation of death. No force in the living world can restore you, so the forest in its wisdom sent you here, but I cannot heal you."

"Why not?" Bex demanded.

The goddess gave her a stern look, and Bex bowed her head again at once. "Why can you not fix me?" she asked, politely this time. "Am I not yours?"

"You are my daughter, born of my own flesh," Ishtar assured her proudly. "But I cannot fix you because you are not broken. Your current condition is the result of your reincarnations, not damage."

"That can't be," Bex insisted, pressing a hand to her bleeding side. "It's my fault this happened! I should have run when I saw the prince like Lys taught me, but I didn't want to leave Iggs behind. In my arrogance, I thought I could win, but even with all your power, I wasn't good enough. I let the prince hit me, let him—"

The goddess silenced her with a scowl. "You are my child, a scion of the gods. Do you think a mere *prince* could have touched you if you were not already so weak?"

Bex frowned in confusion, and the great Ishtar sighed. "You were never meant to be this way," she murmured, reaching down to touch Bex's hollowed cheek. "Like all of Paradise, you were created perfect, and then *that man* came and ruined everything."

Ishtar's fingers clenched against Bex's skin, making her flinch, but the goddess was too angry to notice.

"You cannot die because you are my daughter," she went on, "yet you cannot live because Gilgamesh's greed destroyed our home. Trapped between life and death, you can do nothing but cycle endlessly, and with every reincarnation, the wheel grinds you smaller."

Her lovely hands slid down to touch the black ring that circled Bex's skeletal finger. "You are like a sword that has been sharpened too many times. What was once a strong blade is now a sliver, a shadow of its former glory. What is left of you cannot be repaired. It can only be remade."

"Then do it," Bex begged, grabbing her mother's hand. "I've been fighting all my life—all my *lives*—and getting nowhere. I'm sick of seeing my people enslaved and being too weak to stop it. I'm sick of *losing*. If you can change that, make me strong enough to face the princes, I'll do anything!"

"'Anything' might not be enough," Ishtar warned. "Gilgamesh killed the gods. He killed me. The only reason I'm still able to speak with you like this is because I am the goddess of death, and you are my child. Part of me will always live in you, but if you wish to defeat Gilgamesh and take back what he stole, it's not enough to be reborn. You must become *greater*."

"I'll do," Bex swore, pressing her forehead into her mother's hand. "I'll do whatever it takes, just tell me how."

Ishtar pulled her hand back to point over her daughter's shoulder. When Bex turned around to see why, she nearly fell into the river.

The rolling green hills behind her were gone, replaced by a wall of fire. Now that she'd seen it, Bex didn't know how she hadn't noticed sooner. Heat was pouring off the fire like a forge, scorching the riverbank and boiling the glowing water. The steam was already hot enough to scald Bex's skin when she turned back to her mother.

"What is that?"

"What I told you of," Ishtar replied, the fire gleaming in her starry eyes as she seized her daughter's shoulders. "Paradise is lost, Rebexa. Gilgamesh stole it the same way he stole my sword and my powers, but he never got you. You alone escaped, and now, thanks to that fire, you alone have a chance."

"How is *that* a chance?" Bex cried, looking over her shoulder in horror. "The fire's destroying everything!"

"There can be no rebirth without destruction," Ishtar said as she forced her daughter's head back around. "That is the fire of life, Rebexa. The lands of death are conquered, chained to the Eternal King's will, but the living world still turns with the cycles. If you would be greater, you must learn to turn with it. You must *burn*."

Bex shuddered at the sacred, beloved word. "How?"

"That is up to you," her mother said. "You were created to be a blade of death, but those flames come from a forest teeming with life. They're hot enough to burn anything, even you, but if I use them to remake you, you will no longer be a creature of Paradise. You will be alive, with all that that implies."

The way the goddess said that made Bex shiver. "What does that mean?"

"It means you will no longer be immortal," Ishtar said, running her fingers through her daughter's hair. "The flames of life belong to the cycles, not me. If you throw yourself into them, you will burn as brightly as the mortals do—but only once. After that, your soul will pass on just like every other, and I'll no longer be able to catch you."

"No," Bex said in a panic, looking down at the river, which was shrinking smaller by the second. "If I do that, the cycle of reincarnation will be broken!"

"Would that be so bad?" her mother asked, her sacred voice tired. "You are all that's left of my Paradise, Rebexa. For five thousand years, you have bravely fought and died for us, but I have no more power to give you. Even this river comes from the deathly water you drink. So long as you keep it flowing, I can keep sending you back, but you will continue to diminish with every reincarnation. Do you understand what I am telling you?"

Bex did. Before the fight in Limbo, Drox had warned her that she was weaker than her previous incarnations. He'd done his best to frame it as an obstacle to be overcome with training and dedication, but Bex knew the truth. She was the least of all her selves.

That was why she'd decided to take the risk and free Iggs. Even if she was the weakest Bex yet, she'd wanted her life to mean something. She'd wanted a victory, any victory, and when it had blown up in her face, she'd started collecting deathly water so the next Bex wouldn't have to feel like she did. It wasn't much, but it was the only thing she'd been able to think of to keep herself from becoming useless. Now her goddess was offering her the chance to be great again, and all it would cost her was everything.

"I don't know if I can do it," Bex whispered. "Even if they make me weaker every time, the reincarnations are our hope. So long as one daughter of Ishtar remains, Paradise can never truly be lost. I've messed up so many times in this life already. If I throw myself into that fire and mess up again, it's over. Forever."

"That's what it means to be alive, darling," her mother said with a smile. "Everything else in creation only gets one chance. That's what makes life so precious, but the decision must be yours."

She looked down at the tiny stream that was all that remained of her glowing river. "There's just enough water left to send you back. You can still be reborn whole and uninjured, but you will be the weakest you have ever been. Or, you can break the cycle and jump into the fire. There's more than enough here for me to reforge you completely, but once it is finished, you will be forever lost from my sight."

Her heavenly face curled in a sad smile as she let Bex go. "The choice is yours, Rebexa, but make it quickly. There isn't much time left."

Barely a puddle remained at their feet. The deathly water still glowed like a fragment of sky in the hot orange glare of the flames, precious, safe and sacred, but Bex already knew what she'd choose.

"I said I'd do anything to be strong again," she whispered, clenching her bony fists to hide how much they shook. "And you can't win a war with a weapon that's always getting weaker."

"I hoped you'd say that," her mother replied, leaning down to kiss her daughter on the forehead before lifting her sacred sword.

"Bravest of my daughters," she cried, her face like lightning as the fire whipped around her, "I give you all that I have left! Go with the blessing of Paradise, and set my people free!"

She brought her sword down as she finished, slicing Bex in half. The cut seared through every part of her, but Bex did not die. She ignited, glowing like an iron in the heart of a forge as Ishtar—goddess of life and death— wrapped the roaring flames of the living world around her.

"Sword of Ishtar," the goddess roared, the words striking Bex like a blacksmith's hammer, "I command you be reborn as you were on the first day of creation! Let nothing stand in your path until Gilgamesh's kingdom is burned to ash. Do this in Ishtar's name and your own"—her smile flickered in the fire as they were both consumed—"Rebexa the Bonfire, Queen of Wrath."

Her name was the final strike. When the goddess spoke it, the roaring flames let go, dropping Rebexa one last time out of the sacred land of her births and deaths into the world of the living.

Chapter 13

Adrian was drowning in magic.

Power rolled through him, but he did not control it. He was merely the funnel the Blackwood was using to pour what felt like every forest fire since the evolution of trees down into Bex. Adrian had no idea what the forest thought all that fire would do for her, but he couldn't have stopped it if he tried.

Should have listened to Boston, he thought as the magic scorched through him. It was a familiar's job to be the voice of reason, but as always, Adrian hadn't listened. He'd let pride and temper run him into magic that was bigger than he had any business messing with. The Blackwood would never betray him, but the forest also expected its witches to know their limits, something Adrian seemed to have critically miscalculated. If the flames got any hotter, the Spider wouldn't even have to find his forest. Adrian Blackwood would kill his own fool self.

Bex was the only reason he hadn't already. It was one thing to die for his own mistakes, but Adrian absolutely refused to take her down with him. He was the one who'd bragged that he could heal the unhealable. She'd trusted him to make that happen, so even though it felt like his soul was burning to a crisp, Adrian forced himself to hold on, clinging to the magic with every bit of strength his training had earned him.

Keep holding, he told himself as his arms began to shake. *Just keep—*

All at once, the torrent of fire raging through him shrank to a whisper. The bonfire he'd built snuffed out as well, the geyser of flame vanishing like a blown-out candle.

Adrian didn't know if that was a good sign or a bad one, but he could still feel Bex breathing beneath his fingers, so he finally allowed himself to let go, collapsing onto the ash-covered ground beside her. When he touched her arm to ask if the spell had worked, though, her skin was so hot it burned his fingers. That was the only warning Adrian got before Bex's body burst into flames.

He rolled out of the stone circle with a shout. Boston jumped on him at once, using his paws to put out the fires that had sprung up all over Adrian's clothing.

"*What did you do?*" the cat cried as he batted.

Adrian didn't know. The Blackwood had chosen this course, not him. Since it was older and wiser than all witches put together, that was usually a good thing, but sometimes the forest made decisions that were beyond human understanding, like setting the person it was supposed to be healing on fire. But when Adrian tried to run back in and put out Bex's flames, Lys grabbed his shoulder.

"No," the lust demon said, their voice awed. "This is good."

Adrian was about to ask what part of burning his patient to death could possibly be described as *good* when Bex sat up. He winced at the motion, bracing for the writhing and screaming that would undoubtedly follow, but Bex made no sound at all. She simply rose to her feet.

All the demons fell to their knees as she did. Iggs leaned so far over, his horns dug into the ground. Lys was curled in a ball with tears streaming down their androgynous face. Even Nemini had bent her head, her snakes bowing in reverence before Bex, who was burning brighter than Blackwood's bonfire ever had.

It didn't even look like she had a body anymore. Her shape was nothing but whipping fire and long dark horns above a thin black sword that was suddenly hovering where her hand should be. Adrian had never seen anything like it, but he could feel the burning magic the Blackwood had poured through him rolling off of her in waves. He was still trying to figure out what that meant when the flames Bex had turned into snuffed out as fast as the bonfire had, leaving a stranger behind.

Adrian blinked in the sudden darkness. The woman standing in the center of his blackened stone circle was short, like Bex. She had Bex's dark hair and fair skin, but everything else looked so different, it took Adrian several seconds to realize that this Bex was *healthy*.

Her body was no longer skeletal. Adrian could see that for certain, because she was naked as a newborn. She stood in the ashes of the bonfire like Aphrodite risen from the sea foam, a divine figure radiating vitality and power as surely as a fire radiated heat. There was no more gauntness, no more frailty. Her figure was filled out, her muscles standing strong beneath her soft skin as she squeezed the black sword that still smoked like a hot poker in her right fist, but the biggest change of all was her eyes.

When Adrian had first seen them in her bedroom, they'd glowed like banked coals. When Bex looked at him now, though, her gaze was as bright as the bonfire. For a breathless moment, all he could do was stare. Then Bex doubled over, curling into a shaking ball around her sword as her demons rushed in to help.

One hour later, Adrian still had no idea what had happened.

He had plenty of *theories*, but they all felt highly unlikely. He would have dearly loved to talk to someone about it, but the demons had grabbed the new Bex and vanished into their RV. He was a little surprised they hadn't already driven off and left him in the dust.

"You do know what this means, right?" Boston asked for what had to be the millionth time.

"No, I don't," Adrian said pointedly, pouring one of his bottled nights of sleep into the smallest of his copper kettles. "And neither do you. You're supposed to be the responsible one, so let's not indulge in wild conjecture."

"There's nothing wild about it," the cat insisted, his green eyes glowing with excitement as he leaped onto the shelf above the stove where Adrian kept his potholders. "You saw the demons kneel at her feet. Who else would they do that for except—"

A knock at the front door made them both jump. After a quick glance at each other, Boston hopped down while Adrian removed his kettle from the stovetop. He went to the door next, brushing the ash from his clothes and smoothing his hair before he grabbed the knob and pulled it open to see Bex standing on his porch.

Even though he'd witnessed her change with his own eyes, the sight was still a shock. She just looked so *different*, and yet so the same. It was still Bex's worried face, still her glowing eyes looking nervously through her lashes at him, just brighter. Lovelier.

Adrian sighed. She was *so* much prettier like this. It was seriously throwing him off.

"May I come in?" she asked.

Not trusting his voice to answer, Adrian stepped aside. Bex scuttled in at once, passing right under his nose, which was how he noticed that she no longer smelled like smoke. New Bex smelled like fire. Hot, crackling, forest-consuming fire. Adrian was still trying to decide if that was a good change or not when Bex turned around.

"Do you have somewhere we could sit and talk?" she asked, twisting her hands over her black shirt, which looked exactly like the one the bonfire had burned off her, except this one wasn't bloody. It was still baggy, which Adrian was fine with. Her new figure was a miracle all by itself, and he didn't need any more distractions right now.

Giving himself a shake, Adrian led Bex into the greenhouse, the only room in his cabin that had an actual chair since he did most of his work standing up. He motioned for her to take a seat while he perched on the edge of the tub, which was still full of the blood-stopping potion he'd submerged her in last night.

Boston leaped into his lap the moment Adrian was still, ears swiveling so as not to miss a word. This earned him a scowl from Bex, but Boston had worked as hard on this spell as anyone, and Adrian wasn't about to make him sit this out. Bex must have realized that, because she leaned back in the chair with a sigh.

"I owe you an explanation," she said, fiddling with her shiny new hair.

Now it was Adrian's turn to sigh. "I'd be lying if I said I wasn't curious, but you don't owe me anything. Healing you was my idea from start to finish. If anything, I owe *you* an apology. That was bigger magic than I had any business attempting on my own. I'm just glad I didn't hurt you."

"You definitely didn't hurt me," Bex said, fiddling faster. "My wound is gone like it never was, and I—"

She stopped. Then, to Adrian's horror, she slid off the chair and got down on her knees, bending over until her horns touched the slate-tiled floor at his feet.

"Please don't," he begged, grabbing her shoulders to pull her up, but it was useless. If old Bex had felt like a cement pole, this one was a mountain.

"I owe you more than my life," she said, keeping her head stubbornly down. "Through your fire, I have been born anew. In Ishtar's name and by my own, I swear on Paradise itself that I will not rest until I have repaid you."

"What is it with you and payment?" Adrian said testily, flopping back down on the tub since moving her was clearly impossible. "*Please* get off the floor. I thought you hated kneeling."

"There is pride in kneeling when it's deserved," she said, sitting up at last. "Though I did have to wait until we were alone. The others wouldn't tolerate me lowering my head to a human."

"Because of what you are," Adrian said, unable to hold back any longer. "You're her, aren't you? You're the ninth queen. The one from the statues."

Bex dropped her glowing eyes. "You mean the Coward Queen."

It wasn't a question. It also wasn't what Adrian had said, but he shut up and let her finish.

"I didn't run away, you know," she said, still sitting on the floor even though the chair was right there. "Gilgamesh was the one who named me 'Coward Queen,' but I never ran from that battle."

"Then how did you escape?" Adrian asked, falling over himself with curiosity. "If you're really one of the nine demon queens, then you were there when Gilgamesh killed the gods and conquered Paradise five thousand years ago! If you didn't run away, how are you still alive?"

"It's kind of complicated," Bex said, pulling her knees up in front of her. "Can I tell you a story?"

Adrian couldn't think of a single thing he'd like better. He slid off the tub to sit cross-legged on the floor beside her, keeping Boston in his lap so neither of them would miss a word.

"I don't actually remember what happened," Bex warned. "That was a hundred-and-ninety-eight lifetimes ago. The only reason I know any of this is because of Drox."

"Drox?"

"My sword," Bex explained, holding up her right hand to show him the large black ring on her third finger. "Since he doesn't die like I do, he still has all of his memories, and he was with me—the original me—the day Gilgamesh invaded the Riverlands."

"What do you mean 'the Riverlands'?" Boston asked. "I thought Gilgamesh invaded the Hells."

"There was no Heaven or Hell back then," Bex explained, lowering her hand. "All was Paradise. There were the upper lands, where Anu, king of the gods, lived with his court, and the lower lands, which we called the Riverlands. The lands of Ishtar."

Her voice quivered a little when she spoke the goddess's name, but Adrian didn't say a word.

"Gilgamesh killed out the upper lands first," she continued when she could speak again. "Anu was a wise and cultured king. He wasn't a war god like Ishtar, which was why Gilgamesh targeted him first. By the time we realized

230

we were under attack, Gilgamesh's army had burned Anu's white city to the ground. He stopped the rivers of death next. The Styx, the Acheron, the Lethe: he dammed them all and turned the Riverlands into a desert."

"Why would he do that?" Boston asked.

"Because the rivers were Ishtar's strength," Bex explained. "Humans think their souls are ferried to the lands of the dead in a boat when they die, but that's just their hubris. Their souls *are* the river."

Adrian jerked away in horror. "So the deathly waters, all the blue bottles in your room..."

She nodded. "Human souls. Why else do you think they glow?"

Adrian hadn't thought about it, and now he wished he didn't know.

"So you eat souls?" Boston asked, fascinated.

"Of course not," Bex said. "I don't actually eat anything. The water was just there to keep the river of Ishtar flowing inside me. She's the source of my strength, or at least she used to be."

Bex looked down at her new hands, which were still long and elegant but strong now instead of bony.

"I'm Ishtar's daughter," she said. "My sisters and I were created to protect and rule over her people, the ones who are now called demons. Our sacred duty was to cleanse the souls that flowed down the rivers so they could be reborn free of the sins of the past. I was charged with stripping away their anger, which my people then devoured so that the world would not be poisoned. That's why I'm the Queen of Wrath."

"The kick demons," Adrian said, suddenly understanding. "They're your people."

"What's left of them," Bex said bitterly. "When Gilgamesh came to the Riverlands, we fought him with everything we had. Without her rivers, though, Ishtar was weakened, and our armies had no food. He killed the Queen of Pride first, which was how Gilgamesh learned that slaying a queen leaves her demons nameless and lost in the void left by her death. Most pride demons died on the spot. Others went mad, and the few that recovered were never the same."

Adrian frowned. He'd never heard of a pride demon, but then he wouldn't have if they'd all been...

"Nemini," he said suddenly, snapping his fingers. "You're talking about Nemini."

Bex nodded. "She is very old. I don't actually know when she joined me, but it must have been several reincarnations ago. I know she was already here when I got Lys, but I'm not sure about before." She sighed. "I don't know why she travels with me, to be honest, but I worry it's because she feels sorry for me."

"Why would Nemini feel sorry for you?"

"Because my demons fared even worse," Bex said in the bitterest voice Adrian had ever heard. "Gilgamesh came to the Riverlands for conquest and slaves. He killed the Queen of Pride, my sister, thinking that would give him dominion over her people, but demons lose their names when their queen dies. Nameless demons can't be controlled, so Gilgamesh started capturing queens instead. He has all my sisters locked up in his Hells. That's why human warlocks are able to command demons. It was never Gilgamesh's magic. It's *stolen*, the corrupted power of the queens."

"But he never captured you," Adrian said excitedly. "*That's* why you were able to name Iggs and why the wrath demons were damned to Limbo. Gilgamesh can't command them without you!"

"Don't say that like it's a good thing," Bex grumbled. "You've seen the kick demons. I left them in the worst Hell of all. I've actually considered surrendering to Gilgamesh if he'd agree to let them out, but then I'd only be rescuing them into normal slavery. Even if he said he'd set them free for real, though, I couldn't do it."

"Why not?" Boston asked.

Bex reached up to touch her horns. "Because I'm the last free queen. No matter how many times Gilgamesh killed me, I always came back to fight again. That's what gave my people hope even though I never actually won anything. So long as I was out there fighting, there was still a chance that things could change."

"I see," Adrian said cautiously. "But why are you speaking in past tense?"

"Because that's not how it is anymore," Bex replied, looking at him with her bright new eyes. "Your bonfire broke my endless cycle of reincarnation. This is now my last life, and—"

"Your last life?" Adrian cried, grabbing his frazzled hair. "No, no, *no*, this is all wrong! I asked the forest to *heal* you, not to—"

"It did heal me," Bex insisted. "Did you listen to nothing I just said? I've been fighting Gilgamesh for *five thousand years*. Do you have any idea how frustrating it is to grow up hearing fifty centuries' worth of stories of how you've been losing the same battle over and over? But hey, maybe this is the life where you finally get it right? Except I never do! I've been trying and failing to kill Gilgamesh from the moment he set foot in Paradise."

"I thought the Queen of Pride was the first to fight him," Boston said.

Bex dropped her burning eyes. "She was the first to die, but not the first to attack. When we noticed the rivers were running dry, I went upstream to investigate and caught Gilgamesh's army damming the waters. I flew into a rage and went to strike the king down as punishment, but he swatted me like a fly. If I hadn't landed in the lake he'd made from our dammed-up rivers, I would have been obliterated just like the Queen of Pride eventually was. The only reason my soul didn't shatter was because Ishtar's water was there to catch me."

She folded her fingers over her black ring. "I had my first reincarnation that same day. If Drox hadn't been on my finger, I wouldn't have even known who I was. He's the one who told me all of this, but by the time I was old enough to do anything about it, the war in Paradise had been over for years, and I couldn't get back."

Bex covered her face with her hands. "I failed. Failed my people, failed my goddess, failed myself. My only hope was the reincarnations. I thought if I could just keep trying, I'd find a way to fix things eventually, but I never did. Gilgamesh just kept getting stronger and stronger, while I got weaker and weaker."

She stopped, grinding her palms into her eyes like she was trying to keep Adrian from seeing her cry.

"I hated it," she whispered. "Can you imagine what it's like? Fighting the same battle for five thousand years and never winning? I'm pretty sure Ishtar made me forget every life on purpose, because if she didn't, I'd go insane. I'm not sure I didn't sometimes. It all felt so hopeless, but I couldn't stop. If I gave up, that'd be the same as telling my entire race they were doomed to be slaves forever, so I just

234

kept pretending. I sucked it up, put on a brave face, and told everyone things would be better in my next life, even though I knew they wouldn't. I thought I'd have to keep lying forever, but then you happened."

Adrian jumped when Bex dropped her hands, staring at him with a determined expression he'd never seen on her face before.

"You did it," she said, clenching her shaking fists. "You said you would fix me, and you *did it*. Thanks to your fire, Ishtar was able to reforge my powers back to what they were before Gilgamesh invaded. I had to give up my reincarnations to do it, but I'm Rebexa the Bonfire again! Everything is different now, and it's all thanks to you."

"What about you, though?" Adrian asked nervously. "Your body is obviously better, but what about your soul? If your reincarnations are gone, what happens when you die?"

"I just die," Bex said with a shrug. "I know I should probably be more upset about that, but honestly, I'm too excited to care. This is what I've been working toward my entire life! Only now, instead of collecting deathly water so the next Bex can have a shot, *I* get to do it. I get to *live*!" She closed her eyes as she sucked in a huge breath. "You have no idea how happy that makes me."

"I think I'm starting to," Adrian said, setting Boston aside so he could stand up. "If you're happy with the outcome, that's good enough for me, but what are you going to do now?"

"What I've always wanted to," Bex replied, rising to her feet as well. "I'm getting back into the fight. I've already talked to my demons, and we're all in agreement. I'd rather have one last life of glory than a thousand more years of failure, so I'm taking this new power and going to war with Gilgamesh."

"Oh," Adrian said with a quiet swallow.

"You don't have to join us," she assured him quickly. "I meant what I said earlier. Forget the goblin contract. We're going to stay and help you fight whatever you need to fight until I've paid you back for what you did today. When your enemies are defeated and your forest is strong enough to protect you on its own, my demons and I will start rounding up allies to take the fight to Heaven."

She looked deadly serious, but Adrian didn't know what to say. Having an actual demon queen on his team for the fight against the Spider was a great development, but Bex's plan to take Gilgamesh head-on was insane. Even the Blackwood didn't defy the Eternal King directly, and reborn or not, Bex was only one person. A person who could die for real now.

There were so many reasons why this plan wouldn't work, but Bex didn't look in the mood to listen to any of them, and Adrian didn't want to be the one who stomped on her joy. Those were all problems for the future, anyway. Doom could always come tomorrow, but Adrian was a Witch of the Present, and right now, the present was looking pretty miraculous.

"So what kind of powers did you get back?" he asked. "If you're Ishtar's daughter, that makes you a demigod, right?"

Bex's cheeks darkened. "I don't know if I'd say *demigod*."

"What other name is there for the child of the gods?" Adrian asked. "Ishtar was a war goddess, right? That means you must be pretty incredible, so what are we working with? Can you cause warlocks to spontaneously combust on sight now?"

"I... don't know, actually," Bex confessed, rubbing the back of her head. "I don't have any memories from my time in Paradise, and Drox has never taught me to use powers I don't have, so—"

She stopped, scowling at her ring, which was suddenly shaking on her finger like a rattlesnake's tail.

"What's he saying?" Adrian asked.

"Nothing that bears repeating," Bex grumbled. "Let's just go with 'Drox is aware of the problem, and now I have a training schedule.'"

"That's a great idea!"

She scowled at him for agreeing, and Adrian raised his hands. "What? Training your amazing new powers sounds like a fantastic use of your time. It'll certainly put us in a better position against the Spider if you're the fully empowered Queen of Wrath again."

"Oh, *definitely*," Bex said, cracking her knuckles. "You have no idea how long I've been waiting to cut loose against a jerk-lock like him."

Adrian chuckled. "Given how your memories work, I'm pretty sure you have no idea how long you've been waiting to cut loose either."

She laughed, making him jump. Not because the sound was so loud, but because he'd never heard Bex laugh before. It lit up her face and showed off her teeth, which Adrian just now realized were fanged like Iggs's. Her sharp points weren't nearly as prominent, but he'd never noticed them before. Adrian wasn't sure if that was because they were part of her new changes or if this was just the first chance he'd had to see her teeth, but he liked them. He liked everything about this new, happy Bex very much indeed.

"Come on," he said, waving for her to follow him back into the house. "Let me go drink my night of sleep, and then I'll make you a fireproof place where you can—"

A loud gurgling noise cut him off. The smile vanished off Bex's face when she heard it, leaving her blank with horror as she stared down at her body. "What in the Hells was that?"

"It sounded like your stomach," Adrian said, struggling not to laugh. "Bex, are you hungry?"

"Of course not. I already told you I don't eat."

Her stomach rumbled again as she finished, and Adrian lost his fight.

"It's not funny!" Bex snapped as his shoulders began to shake.

"Sorry, sorry," said Adrian, who wasn't actually sorry in the slightest. "But there's nothing to be embarrassed about. Being hungry is a totally natural feeling for people who only have one life."

"Ishtar did warn me I'd no longer be a creature of death," she muttered, staring down at her body. "But I've never been hungry before. I don't even know what I eat."

"I could make you some experiments," Adrian offered.

"You don't mind?"

"Not at all," he assured her as he walked back into his workshop. "I love feeding people, and this is an unprecedented opportunity. I mean, how many times does a demon queen from the land of the dead come back to life? Will you eat anger like Iggs, or do you need physical food like a human?"

"I have no idea," Bex said, looking utterly lost as she followed him to the kitchen table.

"Well, all of this was done with magic from the Blackwood, so why don't we start with fruits of the forest?" Adrian suggested, pushing a bowl of blackberries he'd foraged yesterday at her.

Bex eyed the lumpy black shapes like he'd passed her a bowl of bugs. The Blackwood's berries did have more styles—the poky little hairs left over from the blossom stage—than the commercial varieties, but they were the perfect blend of sweet and sour. Something Bex discovered for herself when she popped one into her mouth.

"Holy Ishtar," she said, her glowing eyes flying wide. "Those are *delicious*."

"Glad to hear you approve," Adrian replied as he set the kettle containing his night of sleep back on the stove. "I guess that answers the 'what do you eat?' question."

Bex was too busy devouring berries to comment. She started on his bowl of apples next, eating those more slowly as she watched Adrian open the stove grate to add another log.

"Can I ask you one more question about your spell?"

"Shoot," he said.

Bex set down the apple she'd been systematically biting into quarters. "Why didn't your fire make me taller?"

"What?"

"Why aren't I taller?" she repeated, waving a hand at her radiantly healthy, but still five-foot-two, body. "The food thing I get. I was reforged in the fires of life, and living things have to eat, but according to Drox, I used to be over six feet tall. I've never been more than five and a half feet in this life, and burning myself up to beat the prince took off another four inches. I want to know why those didn't come back. Everything else did."

Adrian frowned, considering the question.

"I suppose it's because the Blackwood didn't think it was important," he said at last. "Most things in nature don't change unless they have to. If the forest left you at that height, it must have decided that you being short wasn't enough of a problem to invest in fixing."

"Not enough of a problem?" Bex cried, holding out her arms. "I lost a foot of reach! Have you seen how tall war demons get?"

"Doesn't seem to have held you back so far," he pointed out, looking down at his kettle to hide his smirk. "And small flames do burn hotter."

Bex rolled her eyes with a disgusted sound, biting another quarter off her apple as she waited for Adrian to finish heating up his sleep.

Chapter 14

"**F**ound him."

It was about time. A full week had passed since the Spider had sent Trinaeous after the demoness mercenary with the overgrown horns. He'd felt his slave's binding shatter a few hours later, though not Trin's death, which was disappointing. War demons were usually so loyal.

"Pull over."

Salsit, his green-eyed envy demon, pulled the armored sedan onto the gravel of a derelict train yard. They were still technically inside Seattle, though a hideous portion of it down by the airport. The Spider wasn't sure why Trinaeous would run to such an ugly place, but Salsit was never wrong. Envy demons were the best trackers when it came to runaways, because deep down, even a loyal slave like Salsit envied those who were free.

"He's hiding in the blue shipping container," Salsit reported, his eyes flashing neon green beneath the crown of his curving sand-colored horns. "Shall I drag him before you, master?"

"No," the Spider said, opening his door and stepping out into the bright afternoon sunshine. "He might still have some bite left, and I don't want to waste time waiting for you to regenerate. I will deal with this."

Salsit bowed his head at once, keeping his eyes respectfully lowered as the Spider walked across the filthy gravel toward the shipping container his slave had indicated. Had the yard been empty, he would have commanded the demon to come out. But the Spider didn't wish to do this in view of the human workers who were already gawking at his car, so he stepped inside the metal box that reeked of garbage and demon blood to confront the giant figure huddled at the back.

"Trinaeous."

The war demon shrank in terror when the Spider said his name. As well he should, given his betrayal.

"Why did you not come back?"

"I knew you would send me to the Hells," Trinaeous whispered, clutching his four sapling-thin arms around his body.

The Spider arched a thin eyebrow. He hadn't thought that Bex demon was anything special when he'd seen her, but if his war demon was having to regrow *all* his arms, she must have had something up her sleeve. Still.

"The Hells are the only suitable place for a war demon who loses to a little girl," the Spider said, shifting his dress shoes to avoid the dried blood that covered the floor of the shipping container like paint. "But leniency can still be shown to those who prove their loyalty, especially if they come back with information. You knew that, so why run? Why ensure the worst possible outcome?"

The demon didn't reply. Just lowered his black eyes, which was answer enough. Even for war demons, the lure of freedom was too tempting.

"You should have run farther," the Spider advised, reaching down to touch the empty place on his index finger where Trinaeous's binding should have been. "But you may yet buy yourself some mercy. Tell me which of the local cabal's traitors freed you, and I will send you to the war demons' Hell."

Despite their loyalty to Gilgamesh, war demons were still demons and thus had their own Hell. Theirs was the least unpleasant of the nine but still hellish enough to make the big demon shake.

"Please, master," he begged, bowing his head until his flat horns bashed against the shipping container's floor. "Not there. Don't send me—"

"Then you'd better get talking," the Spider interrupted, crossing his arms over his chest. "Who removed your slave band? Was it the Seattle cabal's leader? The one who churlishly refused to help me?"

"It... it was not a warlock," Trinaeous said, speaking each word like it was being dragged out of him with pliers. "It was... it was the demon. The female with the large horns."

The Spider went still. "How is it possible that a demoness freed you?"

"She had a sword," Trinaeous said, looking away. "It gave her incredible strength, and when she touched it to my neck, my slave band vanished, and I was set free."

The warlock's eyes widened in shock. Then his thin face fell into a scowl, his black-marked fingers tapping rapidly against the suit sleeves covering his crossed arms.

"I see," he said at last. "Have you told anyone else about this?"

"No, master."

"Good," the Spider said, reaching into his jacket pocket. When his hand came out again, he was holding a small white disk the size of a quarter. It glowed like a drop of moonlight in his palm, lighting up the entire shipping container before the warlock popped it into his mouth. The quintessence dissolved instantly when he ground it between his teeth, flooding him with the pure power of the Eternal King's authority as the Spider raised his left hand.

"*Trinaeous*," he said, the word shaking the ground even though the Spider's voice was no louder than before. "I command you by your name to forget this conversation, and you are banished to the lowest level of the Hells. Rot there in anguish for…" He paused, weighing the benefits of burying what he'd just heard versus the cost of losing such a well-grown war demon. "Fifty years," he decided. "After that, you may seek another warlock's service, but you are never to speak of your time with me or anything that happened therein for the rest of your life."

"No!" the demon cried, his black eyes growing wild as he lunged at his old master. "I did as you said! You can't just send me to—"

But it was too late. The chains of the damned queens were already lashed around the war demon's body, dragging him through the hole that had opened in the shipping container's floor. The last the Spider saw of Trinaeous, he was drowning in the black waters of the lowest pit. Then the floor closed over him, and he was gone.

The Spider nodded and turned around, stepping out of the shipping container into the bright daylight… where he nearly walked straight into a worker wearing a reflective vest and a bright yellow hardhat.

"Hey!" the rough-looking human shouted, looking the Spider up and down with his scaled eyes. "What are you doing here? This is a worksite, jackass!"

"I was just leaving," the Spider said in the voice that made demons quiver. It did the same to this man, sending him scuttling back across the dusty gravel as the Spider returned to his still-running car.

"Drive," he ordered the moment he was inside. "And hear nothing. That's an order by your name, Salsit."

"Yes, master," his demon said, putting in a pair of earbuds with one hand while his other steered the car out of the train yard.

When he was satisfied that the combination of magic and blaring music would keep his demon deaf, the Spider opened the pull-down panel in the middle of the sedan's leather back seat. The compartment was supposed to be used for sliding skis and other large objects into the trunk, but this car had been modified. When the Spider opened the panel, it led to a metal safe spelled by a sorcerer to open only to his willing hand.

It opened for him now, revealing a gilded box bound with gold chains and sealed with the mark of the Eternal King. The protections unlocked beneath the Spider's tattooed fingers, the lid opening for him without so much as a click. And nestled within the white velvet interior, almost invisible in the car's low light, was a delicate glass bell.

It shone with the same moonlight glow as quintessence but made no sound when the Spider picked it up. He did so with enormous care, plucking the instrument from its velvet nook as delicately as a jeweler. The bell looked like a soap bubble between his fingers, the glass so thin that he could feel the pressure of his own grip through the handle. Shaking such a treasure felt like a sin, but not as great a sin as holding back what Trinaeous had just told him, so the Spider flicked his wrist, ringing the glass bell as delicately as he could.

No matter how many times he did this, the sound still surprised him. The tiny glass ornament looked like it would shatter before it jingled, but it rang as deep and golden as a temple bell. The noise reverberated through the car like an earthquake, nearly causing Salsit to rear-end the truck in front of them, but the Spider had no attention to spare for his demon. His eyes were focused on the figure that was suddenly sitting in the back seat beside him. The tall, beautiful, woman-shaped creature made of ivory and gold.

"Princess," the Spider murmured, bowing low in his seat.

"This had better be important," she said, her inhuman voice as high and light as her glass bell should have been. "My divine prince, ever may his glory bless us, has no patience for those who waste his time."

The Spider kept his head down, studiously avoiding the hard, metallic gaze of her etched golden eyes. "I assure you, this is of great importance to His Majesty and all the Eternal Kingdom. Seven days ago, my war demon was defeated by a demoness with tall horns wielding a sword that was capable of cutting his slave band."

The air in the car seemed to tighten as he spoke, but the princess's voice was as bright as ever when she replied.

"That is simply not possible," she informed him, tapping holes in the leather seat with the knife-sharp nails of her left hand. "The threat you're implying was killed in Limbo seven years ago. Unless your demon was defeated by a child, you must be mistaken."

"With the greatest of respect, my princess, there is no mistake," the Spider said. "I saw her myself. I should have recognized what she was sooner, but she looked very different from the reports, and as you said, I was not expecting her to return so soon. Once I realized my mistake, I bound the war demon to silence, banished him back to the Hells, and contacted you immediately."

"You always were a devoted servant," the princess said, moving her tapping to the door's mahogany inset, which instantly started to chip. "But this is a complicated matter. Let me consult with my prince."

246

The words had scarcely left her ivory-lipped mouth when the princess fell still, her carved body slumping against the car door like the doll it resembled. For several heartbeats, the Spider was alone. Then the princess sat back up with a jolt, turning to face him with the bored, haughty expression he'd learned to recognize as royal interest.

"His Highness the Celestial Prince, son of the Great King, Gilgamesh, wishes to convey his gratitude for bringing this incident to his attention," she intoned with great ceremony. "His Exalted Majesty also delivers unto you the following mandate: you are to continue your efforts to recover the runaway Blackwood and return him to our control, but you are also now ordered to locate and eliminate the renegade demoness and her sword."

She leaned closer. "I don't have to tell you that the utmost of discretion is expected in both of these efforts. The Blackwood boy is a matter of course, but if rumors were to spread that a certain enemy of Heaven was back before her appointed time, that would not be looked upon with favor."

"I shall say nothing," the Spider promised. "How would His Majesty prefer me to proceed?"

"Quickly," the princess said. "And thoroughly. The demoness you may kill as soon as possible. The Blackwood, of course, must be captured alive, but all damage up to the killing blow is acceptable in your prince's divine sight."

"I live only to serve His Majesty's will," the Spider replied reverently. Then his eyes flicked up. "But if this demoness is truly what she seems, it will be difficult for me to execute these orders alone. If the Celestial Prince wishes his servant success, I humbly ask that he grant me dominion over the local warlock cabal so that I may have

247

access to the resources necessary to ensure that Heaven's Will is done."

The princess looked upon him with an approving smile. "You're so good at this," she said, tapping her hand against the top of the Spider's head like a puppet pretending to pet a dog. "Faithful servant, you have earned much favor in my prince's sight. He has already foreseen your request in his wisdom, and bid me give you this."

The princess held out her right hand, which, unlike her left, was covered by a white glove. The Spider held out both of his hands in return, cupping his palms to receive the ring she dropped into them. It was made of gold and astonishingly heavy, as wide as the Spider's knuckle and stamped with the lion of Gilgamesh, the mark of divine authority.

"You do me great honor," the Spider said humbly, closing his tattooed fingers over the priceless gift.

"My prince has great faith in your abilities," the princess answered, patting him again. "The eyes of Heaven are ever upon you, warlock. Do not disappoint us."

"May I perish if I do," the Spider said.

That must have been the right answer, because the princess flashed him a sharp-toothed smile and vanished, leaving the car with the same deep ringing as when she'd entered.

The Spider kept bowing for five more breaths. When he was certain Heaven's attention had moved on, he raised his head with a grin. He slid the heavy ring onto his finger next, taking a moment to appreciate the weight of it, how it shone like a blessing even in the dim light of the tinted windows. Mortal eyes did not often get to witness a holy relic, but benefits like this were why he endured all the bowing and scraping. With this ring, his word was now the word of Heaven itself, and the Spider intended to leverage that power to the fullest.

Still smiling, he reached forward and tapped Salsit on the shoulder. When the demon took his earphones out, the Spider ordered him to drive to the Seattle cabal's main office.

A new order was about to be imposed in town.

Bex, restored Queen of Wrath, stood in the center of the fireproof gravel circle Adrian had made for her. She was perched on one foot, balanced on top of a narrow metal pole five feet off the ground with her other leg dangling in the air beside her and her black sword held out in front. For one long moment, she stood as still as a statue, the warm wind blowing through her sweaty, tied-up hair. Then, all at once, she swung, turning her torso to sweep her sword in a perfect arc. The black blade whistled as it cut the air, but when the tip reached the end of the arc and paused dramatically, nothing happened.

No, no, no, no, no! Drox roared in her mind. *How many times do I have to tell you? You don't "light" on fire. You are fire! You are Rebexa the Bonfire, the flaming sword of Ishtar! You have to—*

"I know," Bex snapped, shaking the sword to make it shut up as she rebalanced on the pole. "I'm trying."

You're not trying at all, her sword snapped back. *"Trying" implies effort and attempts to improve. You're just swinging me around like you always do!*

"How else am I supposed to swing you?" she yelled. "I'm doing my best, okay? It's not like I have an ignition button!"

You don't need one! You think this fleshy weakness is your true self? You used to live *as fire! I've told you countless times—*

"Hearing isn't the same as doing," Bex grumbled. "You might remember five thousand years of history—"

I remember all since the golden age of the gods.

"—but I only remember twenty-four," she finished. "Less than that if you take out all the years I was too young to do anything but drool. Cut me some slack!"

I will do no such thing, Drox said in an iron voice. *You are a queen of Paradise! It is your duty to be strong, the infallible light of your people. A queen does not ask for "slack." Now, return to first position.*

Bex balanced on one foot and raised her sword with a glower.

Loosen your grip.

She wiggled her fingers, and Drox's voice grew lulling. *Remember, Rebexa: wrath is not rage. Rage is a slathering beast. Wrath has purpose, gravity. Draw upon your wrath. Let it feed you. Picture your enemies being consumed by the fire of your righteous fury, then swing.*

Bex closed her eyes, remembering the power she'd felt inside the bonfire Adrian had built for her. She imagined using that power to burn the Spider's smug face into dust, and then she swung. A beautiful slash, perfectly balanced, her black sword moving like an extension of her arm.

Nothing happened.

"Damn it!" Bex roared, swinging her sword down so fiercely that she knocked herself off the pole. She hit the rocks hard, bruising her shoulder. Her restored body healed the damage instantly, but nothing stopped the sting of failure. The *bitter* sting, because she'd thought she was done with this. The whole point of giving up her reincarnations was so that she could finally stop failing. Everything was supposed to be good now, so why couldn't she do it?

You will, Drox said, his voice surprisingly comforting as he rested his weight in her palm. *You've been a shadow of yourself for a long, long time, but this is what you were born to do. You're only having trouble because so much was returned to you at once, but no matter how many lives you cycled through or how small they ground you down, you never stopped being the Bonfire of Wrath. Remember what you did to the prince in Limbo.*

"That doesn't count," Bex muttered.

It counts the most, Drox argued. *You have burned in this life before, my queen. Briefly, devastatingly, but for one glorious moment, you were everything that you have ever been.*

Her sword was wrong. Nothing about what Bex had done seven years ago was glorious. Even at the time, she'd known it was a dumb idea, but then Drox had pumped her up with all that "infallible light of your people" crap, and she'd just snapped. She'd told Adrian she'd gone into Limbo to free a kick demon, but the truth wasn't nearly so noble. Bex had been looking for a fight, a chance to hit back at all the humiliations she'd suffered, and like all flights of pride, it had ended with a crash.

She'd barely finished cutting the gray off Iggs before the prince had appeared and nearly destroyed her in one hit. It was only when Bex went flying that she'd realized how badly she'd messed up. The prince was even stronger than she'd imagined, but if she let him kill her, she'd die at seventeen with nothing to show for it. Nothing to show for Lys, who'd given up everything to raise her for the *third time.*

Disappointing Lys was the one thought teenage Bex hadn't been able to stand, so she'd thrown herself at the prince with everything she had. Absolutely everything, apparently, because she recalled very little of what happened next. Iggs had told her later that she'd been amazing—a roaring firestorm big enough to fill Limbo's gray sky—but all Bex remembered was burning. When Drox had assessed the damage after, he'd determined she'd lost the equivalent of five centuries off her soul.

Half a millennium of potential reincarnations, burned in three minutes.

It still stung. All that sacrifice, all that loss, and it hadn't even mattered. She'd freed Iggs, sure, but the prince she'd killed had been right back on his feet and hunting her a few days later. Bex didn't know if Gilgamesh had replaced him or simply ordered him back from the ashes, but it didn't make a difference. The day Bex saw him through the window of the motel room where Lys was treating her new skeletal body was the day she'd learned she couldn't win.

Nothing had been the same after that. She'd stopped drinking her water, stopped keeping herself up. There just didn't seem to be a point. She couldn't beat anything as a skeleton who went down like a leaf the second anything touched her wound, so Bex had come up with the deathly-water plan and kicked the can down the road to her next reincarnation. She'd kept her team together and aimed at a goal because she still couldn't stand the thought of letting them down, but in truth, Bex had felt like a dead demon walking for seven years. She wasn't a queen anymore. She was a corpse. A cut-off head that was still biting because it knew nothing else.

But then, like a miracle, all of that had changed. Thanks to one witch's unexpected stubbornness, everything

252

she'd lost had come roaring back: her strength, her hope, her chance to fix things. Every wish, every secret prayer Bex had uttered in the dark was suddenly right here, right under her fingertips, except she couldn't *make it work.*

It will come, Drox promised. *A bonfire can't help but burn. You just have to get out of its way. Now take your stance and try again.*

Bex nodded, pushing her new body off the rocks. She was about to climb back up on the pole when she heard someone calling her name.

When she looked over her shoulder, she saw a construction worker running toward her from across the forest clearing. He was thick-bodied and muscular, wearing a bright yellow hard hat and a reflective work vest with several train-company logos printed across it. He'd just gotten close enough for Bex to see the scales in his eyes when his body suddenly shifted, and then Lys was standing in front of her, their lovely face pulled into a serious scowl. One that got decidedly less serious as they got closer to Bex.

"Look at *you!*" the lust demon cried. "You're finally wearing the clothes I got you!"

"Only because my stuff doesn't fit anymore," Bex said, looking self-consciously at her skintight eggplant-purple leggings and matching midriff-baring tank top.

The workout set was demure compared to some of the other stuff Lys had given her, but it still showed more skin than Bex was comfortable with, especially now that she had something to keep covered besides bones. She wouldn't have worn these clothes outside her room normally, but the restoration had added thirty pounds to her frame. That was too much for even Bex's shapeless wardrobe to handle without pinching, especially when Drox kept making her twist her body into weird positions.

She'd chosen the workout gear because it was stretchy, but the gleam in Lys's eyes was giving her serious second thoughts.

"Don't make that face," the lust demon scolded, walking around Bex in a circle. "You look marvelous, but I knew you would. Purple was always your color."

"Stop it," Bex ordered, turning her sword back into a ring so she could cross her arms over her chest without stabbing anything. "What did you find?"

Lys looked grossly disappointed by the subject change, but matters must have been serious, because they began their report with no more teasing.

"Nothing we weren't expecting," they said, brushing the dust off the pantsuit they'd changed into. "The demon was right where you left him. I tried to get him to go lick his wounds somewhere less obvious, but you know how war demons are. They always have to make a fight out of *everything*. Anyway, Mr. Brilliant Strategist was convinced that his warlock wouldn't be able to find him without the binding, so his 'plan'"—Lys curled their elegant fingers into exaggerated air quotes—"was to hide in a box, which, *shocker*, didn't work. The Spider found him an hour ago and damned him to the lowest of the Hells."

Bex winced in sympathy. "Well," she said, striving for the silver lining, "if he got damned, that must mean he didn't talk."

Lys shook their head. "Oh no, he sang like a choir of canaries. Told his slaver the whole thrilling story, and then the Spider damned him anyway because warlocks are scum."

Now Bex winced in fear. "That's it, then," she said, slumping against her training pole. "They know I'm here."

"Most definitely," Lys agreed. "If we don't have every warlock on the West Coast coming down on us by the weekend, I'll eat your horns."

A pronouncement like that was normally their signal to bail. Of course, if things had still been normal, they would have driven away from Seattle the moment Bex confessed to freeing a demon. There'd been nothing else they could do back then. Now, though, things were different.

"We'll just have to be ready," Bex said, looking up at the dense forest canopy that no longer let in even a scrap of daylight.

Adrian had done a lot more with his week than she had. While Bex had been falling off poles and yelling at her sword, he'd turned his little tract of woodland into the densest, darkest forest she'd ever seen.

The trees weren't sequoias, so their trunks weren't car-sized, but they still towered impressively, and they grew so *thick*. Except for the clearing at the top of the hill, the forest was as dark as twilight even at high noon. Mist drifted between the mossy trunks at all times, and the ground was a treacherous maze of wet, waist-high roots, giant slippery fungus, and pools of leaf-covered water deep enough to swallow Iggs.

"Blackwood, indeed," Lys muttered, fingering the wooden charm Adrian had given all the demons so his new forest wouldn't eat them. "I swear I saw a barghest on my way over."

"Adrian said stuff might move in," Bex replied. "Blackwood groves are much more magical than the forests around them. All that power wakes things up and lures them over."

"I hope it lures something nasty with a taste for warlock," Lys said, rubbing their hands together as they turned to cast an approving look at the witch himself.

As he'd been practically every minute since he'd arrived in Seattle, Adrian was hard at work. He was on his porch this afternoon, making what appeared to be dozens of scarecrows out of dried branches and pumpkins from his garden. Bex didn't know why he needed so many. The local crows loved perching on his house, but they avoided his garden like the plague. They wouldn't even fly over it, choosing to go far around instead, as if they were afraid the leafy greens and giant squashes might eat *them*.

"Oooh, I can feel his lust for vengeance from here," Lys said with a shiver. "He might act all helpful and polite, but that witch has a delicious vicious streak." They licked their lips. "If he wasn't off-limits, I'd eat him right down to his hat."

"The no-eating-clients rule is still in effect," Bex warned.

"That's not what I was referring to," Lys said, turning back to her with the sly look Bex had learned to fear. "I'm leaving *that* dish on the table as a courtesy to you."

"There's nothing to be courteous about," Bex insisted, horrified to feel her face growing warm.

Lys rolled their eyes to the canopy. "*Please*, who do you think you're talking to? Witches of the Flesh have more control over these things than your average human, but I'd have to be a little baby succubus not to pick up that our Mr. Witch finds you *quite* attractive now that you're out of your husk stage."

Bex jumped like she'd been bitten, her face heating to roughly the surface of the sun while Lys cracked up beside her.

"Oh, oh, look at *yoooooou*!" they cried, flinging their arms around her. "How are you still this innocent?"

"It certainly wasn't with any help from you!" Bex said hotly. "And keep your voice down! He'll hear you."

Adrian was already looking at them quizzically. Bex waved at him before going back to shoving Lys, who was still hugging her like she was one of those giant stuffed carnival prizes.

"Would you *stop it*?"

"Never," Lys vowed, but they did let Bex go, though not without pinching her cheeks one last time. "You are too precious for words, baby queen."

"Just get back out there and figure out what we're in for," Bex ordered, pulling herself straight in a last-ditch effort to salvage some of her dignity. "I want to know how many warlocks to expect and when they'll arrive. The more information we can gather ahead of time, the better our chances of avoiding a disaster."

"Yes, Your Majesty," Lys replied in a singsong voice, blowing her a kiss before sauntering back into the woods. Bex was still glaring at their back to make sure they actually left when a man's voice spoke practically in her ear.

"What was that about?"

Bex jumped a foot in the air. She whirled when she landed, quashing the instinct to draw her sword just in time as she came around to see Adrian standing right beside her, looking as curious as his cat.

"Nothing," she said, furious that he could still sneak up on her even though her hearing was better than it had ever been. She was about to tell him she needed to get back to practice when she thought better of it.

"Actually, there is something. I've got bad news."

Adrian arched a dark eyebrow. "It didn't look like bad news."

"That's just Lys," Bex muttered, turning to glare at the patch of forest her demon had just disappeared into so Adrian wouldn't see her blushing like an idiot.

"The Spider's figured out who I am," she said. "I just sent Lys to determine how big a problem that's going to be, but we should probably get ready for a crowd."

She glanced back at Adrian nervously, bracing for anger, but he just shrugged.

"That was always the plan," he said, looking down at the long pieces of dried grass his quick, confident fingers were working into a six-plait braid. "The Spider never does anything by halves. I'm surprised he hasn't descended on us with an army already, though that's likely because the Seattle cabal is being the opposite of helpful." He smirked. "The only thing warlocks hate more than us is each other."

"I'm pretty sure that's about to change," Bex warned. "How much more time do you need to get ready?"

"Ideally, all of it," Adrian replied, continuing to braid even as he gazed up at the canopy of towering oaks, firs, and hemlocks. "Forests are infinitely expanding webs of complexity. By placing my heart at the center, I've tied myself to every leaf and twig, but even with a witch's help, growth takes time. I'm quite pleased with our progress so far, though. Obviously, I'd prefer more time, but even when they're young, Blackwoods have teeth."

That was certainly true. Even in the safety of the clearing, Bex could feel the menace radiating from the forest's shadows. She looked away with a shiver to find Adrian smiling at her.

"Here," he said, handing her the grass, which he'd finished braiding while her head was turned.

"What's this?" Bex asked, turning the smooth plait over in her fingers.

"A protection charm," he told her proudly, taking the braid back. He took her hand next and turned it over, tying the woven grass around her wrist to form a bracelet.

"Thanks," she said, dropping her eyes. "But you already made me a charm."

She pointed at the carved wooden disk he'd hung around her neck three days ago. It was identical to the one Lys had been wearing, but Adrian shook his head.

"Those were to keep you from getting lost," he explained, pulling Bex's hand closer to his chest as he showed her the four strands of his own dark hair that he'd woven into the end of the grass braid. "This one marks you as part of my body so the curses I'm about to put in don't target you." His gray-blue eyes grew deadly serious. "Do *not* take it off."

"Not planning on it," Bex said, pulling her hand out of his before her face could get any hotter. "What kind of curses are you working on?"

"Very unpleasant ones," Adrian promised as he pulled a fresh batch of grass out of his endless pockets to start on the next braid. "Let's just say those warlocks are about to learn why you don't force your way into a witch's home."

He tilted his head toward the RV, which was now parked at a steep angle thanks to the giant roots that had grown up under its tires. "I'll be making one of these for each of you. Please tell everyone not to leave the clearing without them."

"I'll spread the word," Bex said, hopping back up on her pole. "Thanks for being so on the ball. I've got to get back to practice if I'm going to be any good. Let me know if you need something else."

"Will do," Adrian said, turning back toward the pile of scarecrows on his porch. Bex was congratulating herself on a smooth, professional escape when he added, "Lys was right, by the way."

Bex looked down so fast, she nearly fell onto the gravel again. "What?"

"The purple," he clarified, pointing at her legging-covered calf, which, since she was standing on the pole, was at the same level as his head. "It's a great color on you."

"Thanks," Bex muttered, her brain scrambling to figure out just how much Adrian had overheard as he gave her a final smile and strolled back across the clearing.

Chapter 15

Adrian was on his knees in front of his heart tree, focusing as hard as he could on the iron nail he was painstakingly burying point-up in the ground. Beside him sat a box of fifty more, hopefully the last. A dozen more empty boxes were already piled on his porch, a testament to how long he'd been at this.

"You're overdoing it," Boston observed from his perch on Adrian's back. "Only twenty of these will trigger at most, and it's going to take forever to dig up all the duds when this is over. You're just making more work for yourself."

"Being thorough now is how I ensure I get the luxury of doing work later," Adrian said as he picked another nail out of the box. "And if anything's worth overdoing, it's our last line of defense."

His familiar sighed and hopped down to grab one of the little straw dolls he and Adrian had spent all of yesterday putting together. Boston brought the effigy over in his teeth, and Adrian dutifully stabbed the next iron nail straight through its stomach. When the nail was in, he buried the stabbed doll next to the nail he'd just finished and moved on, repeating the pattern of nail, doll, nail, doll until the ground surrounding his heart tree was covered in little graves.

"That is a *lot* of curses," Boston said when they were finally finished.

"Can't take down war demons the size of the Spider's with a charm," Adrian said, stretching out on the ground to rest his aching back.

It'd been three days since Lys had brought the news that the Spider would be coming loaded for demon queen, and ten since Bex's bonfire. Adrian had worked nonstop through all of them, but the last forty-eight hours had been the most exhausting by far. He was contemplating drinking another night of sleep, even though he'd already had two today, when Boston hopped onto his chest.

"Are you sure about this?"

Adrian chuckled. "Little late for that, don't you think?"

"It's never too late to change your mind," the cat said quietly, looking over his shoulder at the field of dirt mounds they'd just buried. "This isn't good witchcraft, Adrian. You've laid down too many curses. That's not healthy for your forest, or for you."

"I know," Adrian said grimly. "But it's necessary. This is what I came out here to do. If I'd wanted to play it safe, I would have stayed at home."

"Would that have been so bad?" Boston asked. "You loved the Blackwood."

"I still love it," Adrian said, petting his familiar's back. "I'll always love it. It was being trapped that I hated."

He sighed, looking up at the towering spire of his heart tree. "We were all trapped there because of me. The Spider's warlocks attacked my sisters, blocked us from making new groves, kept us locked up like sheep in a pen."

"And I'm as angry about that as you are," Boston assured him. "But there's only so much we can do, and I worry you're getting dragged in over your head."

He flicked his ears toward the demons' RV. The last time Adrian had looked over there, Bex had been practicing her sword like always. But that was two boxes of nails ago, and she must have finished, because she was back in her old position on top of the Winnebago's roof, playing her guitar.

"I have great sympathy for the demons' plight," Boston murmured as Adrian watched her. "And I *like* Bex. She's a good person, but this isn't what we signed up for. We were supposed to have a month to prepare for a fight against a single cabal far from their home turf. But it's barely been three weeks, and now that the Coward Queen's involved, it's looking more and more like we're about to be besieged by every warlock in the Pacific Northwest."

"It can't be helped," Adrian said.

"Yes, it can," Boston argued, digging his claws into his witch's coat. "You hired those demons so they could fight *your* battles, not so you could fight theirs. They're the ones going to war with Gilgamesh, not us." He lashed his tail. "You're a witch of your word, and I respect that, but this is a bad position, and I don't like how deep you're digging in."

Adrian sank flatter against the ground. As usual, his familiar had a point. They *were* in a bad position. He hadn't had enough time. His forest wasn't ready, so he'd made up the difference with curses. *Lots* of curses, but that decision came with its own cost.

He'd always taken comfort in the fairness of witchcraft, but that knife cut in both directions. Just as giving more got you more, taking from the magic always came back to bite you. Literally, in the case of curses. Whereas growing a forest also grew the witch, curses took their price out of the caster, and there was no telling how high the bill would be until it came due.

It was a reckless, dangerous way to do magic, but it was the best Adrian could manage on such short notice, and he didn't mind paying. Unlike Boston, he didn't blame Bex for their current situation. Her presence might have exacerbated things, but it was always going to come to this. The Spider had earned his name by never moving in until his prey was trapped. His attacks were always overwhelming, but Adrian was actually glad this first fight was shaping up to be huge. If the famous Spider went all-out and lost, maybe the cabals would *finally* leave him alone.

"I can do it," Adrian said, as much for himself as his familiar. "I am my mother's son, and she's the most curse-happy witch in the Blackwood. It won't be fun, but the demons will be doing the actual fighting. All I have to do is not die to my own magic."

"That's not funny," Boston said, bumping his head against Adrian's chin. "You really could die from this, you know."

"Death is the price of living," Adrian replied, but he gave his familiar a pet. "Thank you for worrying about me, Boston, but my mind is made up. Things might not be unfolding as we planned, but this is still what I came to Seattle to do, and I mean to see it through. Now let me up. I still have to put defenses on the beach."

Boston hopped off his chest with a sigh. Adrian gave the cat another pet for his patience and sent him inside to find their book on kelp forests. Neither of them had worked with sea plants before, but the side of the Blackwood that touched the saltwater inlet was woefully under-defended, and kelp seemed like a thriving, vigorous sort of plant. Adrian had always gotten along well with those, and it would be nice to have something watching his back in the water. He was lying on the ground, thinking about how he could convince the giant kelp stalks to grow themselves into a net, when he heard the crunch of Bex's footsteps.

"Are you okay?"

Adrian opened his eyes to see her standing over him. To his great disappointment, she was back in her usual baggy black. Adrian wore the color professionally and because it reminded him of home, but he preferred her in something brighter, especially since she'd told him she only wore black to hide her blood. Every time he saw her in it now, Adrian had to fight the urge to check for wounds, but Bex's fiery eyes were bright when she pulled off her sunglasses. She mostly looked worried about him.

"I'm fine," he assured her, pushing into a sitting position. "Just tired. Curses really take it out of me, and I've been doing them nonstop."

"I saw," Bex said, looking more concerned than ever as she offered her hands to help him to his feet. "Your forest has been getting darker every day."

Adrian blinked in surprise. Most non-witches didn't notice changes like that, but Bex had always been perceptive, and the woods were looking *very* dark.

"It is called 'black magic' for a reason," he said, grabbing her hands.

"Will it go back?" she asked as she lifted him easily off the ground.

"Of course," Adrian said, wobbling from the rapid ascent. "I'd have to be a truly evil witch to cut off sunlight from the undergrowth forever. This is only temporary. Once the warlocks get it through their skulls that I'm more trouble than I'm worth, I'll clean all this out and get my forest looking bright again."

He'd been hoping to make her smile, but Bex's face was graver than ever.

"We'll beat them," she promised, giving him a deadly serious look. "I said I'd repay you, and I keep my word. I don't intend to let anything get past us, but if a runner does make it through, don't use your curses. Just say my name, and I'll take care of it."

"That's good to know," Adrian said, leaning over to collect his empty nail box. "But I didn't dig all these holes not to use them. You've already got a job, and I can take care of myself, but I promise I'll yell if the water gets too hot."

Bex didn't look convinced, and Adrian couldn't blame her. He'd seen himself in the mirror. He looked like death warmed over. Not even bottled sleep could pick him up from this many curses, but Lys had reported this morning that warlocks were already poking around Bainbridge. It was only a matter of time before they closed in, and Adrian was determined to make every minute count. That didn't mean he was going to suffer Bex looking at him like he was a kitten who needed to be rescued from a gutter, though, so he decided to change the subject.

"What was the song you were playing earlier?" he asked, forcing himself to look alert as he gathered the empty cardboard nail boxes off his porch and dumped them in his composting bin. "I didn't recognize it."

"I don't either," Bex confessed, glancing at the guitar she'd left leaning against the RV. "It's another one of those things my fingers just know, though Drox is telling me it's Greek and originally meant to be played on the lyre." Her face pulled into a scowl. "Apparently, I was butchering it."

"I thought it sounded lovely," Adrian said. "Can you wear your sword all the time now that you're restored?"

She shook her head. "I could always wear it. I just didn't because my ring is a pretty big giveaway for anyone who knows what I am. Also, Drox is obnoxious."

"Obnoxious in what way?" Adrian asked, taking a seat on the edge of his porch to hide how badly his legs were wobbling.

"Every way," Bex said, rolling her eyes as she plopped down beside him. "Unlike me, Drox remembers everything that's ever happened to us along with commentary about how I could have done it all better. It's not exactly a fun mental soundtrack."

Adrian chuckled. "I can see how sharing your head with a hypercritical father figure would get annoying."

"It's more self-criticism, really," Bex said, wrinkling her nose. "Drox isn't a parent. He's part of me, except unlike my leg or my head or my life, I can't lose my sword. Even if my ring sank to the bottom of the ocean, I could always call it back. This also means I'm the only one who can wield my weapon, which has definitely been useful over the centuries." Her lips quirked into a self-deprecating smile. "Or so I've been told."

"I think it's extraordinary," Adrian said, staring at Drox in new awe. "Your ring has a firsthand account of five thousand years of history!"

"Don't get too excited," Bex warned. "Drox's memory might be perfect, but he's still a sword, which means he only remembers sword stuff."

Adrian frowned. "Sword stuff?"

"Stabbing, positioning, battle tactics, how so-and-so felt to cut, that kind of thing," she explained. "The only reason he knew the song I was playing just now is because the original lyrics were about a duel. If it doesn't have to do with fighting or the war with Gilgamesh, Drox doesn't care. I've never even gotten him to tell me if I had a lover or children in a past life. The most he'll say is that none of my reincarnations has ever made it past thirty-five, a failing Drox attributes to my sloppy footwork."

Adrian would never call any of Bex's confident, lightning-fast movements "sloppy," but he supposed ancient living weapons held things to a different standard. He was trying to think of an unsolved historical mystery he could ask about that would fit within Drox's limited scope when Bex spoke again.

"So, what about you?" she asked, tucking her dark hair behind her ear. "Did you have to deal with any hypercritical, hovering parents?"

That was so wrong that Adrian burst out laughing. "Quite the opposite," he said when he could speak again. "I've never met my father, and my mother's a big believer in letting children discover the world for themselves, sometimes to a dangerous degree. I have it on good authority that I was nearly eaten by a dragon when I was three."

Bex's glowing eyes went huge. "The Blackwood has *dragons*?"

"Ninety percent of the world's remaining population," Adrian told her proudly. "It's not normally an issue since Blackwood witches are smart enough to stay away from their roosts, but I was what my sisters called a 'roamer.' Fortunately, my aunt Muriel can see the future and was there to snatch me out of the dragon's mouth, or we wouldn't be having this conversation."

Bex shook her head. "Sounds like some family."

"We were quite feral," Adrian agreed. "But everything worked out in the—"

He froze, snapping his mouth shut as he listened to the crows cawing in the distance. Alarm calls were coming from the northeast, where the ferry dock was. Boston came barreling out of the house a second later, his fur standing on end.

"Looks like they're here," Adrian said. "Are you ready?"

There was no need to ask. By the time he turned back to Bex, she was on her feet with her black sword in her hands. He expected her to take off after that, but she turned around and offered her hand to help Adrian off the porch instead. When he took it, she squeezed his palm hard.

"We've got the front," she said, her eyes burning like her bonfire. "Remember what I said. If you get in trouble—"

"I'll call," Adrian promised, squeezing her hand in return.

Bex nodded and lifted him to his feet. Literally picked Adrian up off the porch like he was made of paper and set him on his heels. She held on a few seconds to make sure he was steady before turning to run for the RV. Iggs and Nemini were already out in front and dressed for combat in the same black that Bex wore. Lys joined them a second later, running down the RV's metal steps to grab Bex's guitar and place it safely inside while Bex gave orders in a tight, quiet voice. The others nodded, and then they were gone, vanishing into the woods like smoke.

Adrian could feel them moving through the trees if he concentrated, but he didn't need to. He trusted the demons to do their job, and he was too busy running for his own position, his feet flying across the dug-up ground toward his heart tree.

"The crows say there's a convoy on the road," Boston reported as Adrian joined him beneath the low, needle-laden branches. "I wish you were better at divination. It'd be nice to know what we're in for."

269

"Knowing wouldn't change what's coming," Adrian said, lying down beside the fir tree's massive trunk. "We've done the best we could with the time we had. We'll just have to hope it's enough."

"Hoping isn't a plan," Boston pointed out nervously.

"No, the plan's the plan," Adrian replied, taking off his pointed hat and setting it on the ground beside him. "And speaking of plans, it's time for ours. I'm going under. You stay there and watch my back. Don't leave me, whatever happens, and don't let me go too deep."

"I won't let you get lost," his familiar promised, lying down on Adrian's chest. "Be careful."

Adrian nodded, closing his eyes to let the world recede. When he could feel the earth turning beneath him and the weight of his cat like a boulder on his ribs, he pressed his back even harder to the needle-covered ground and breathed deep, sucking the smell of resin, dirt, and evergreen into his lungs until he was filled with forest.

A line of fifteen black SUVs rolled down the cracked country road that had once run between two sunny forests. Now, though, only one side of the road was sunlit. The other rose like a black cliff, a foreboding wall of trees so dark and dense, the air itself was chilled, beading the black SUVs with wet mist as they parked in the forest's mossy shadow. The vehicles opened their doors a second later, vomiting demons onto the roadside.

They came out in a swarm of horns, tails, hooves, and wings. Not one was bothering to hide their true nature. If any scale-eyed humans had been present, the whole convoy would have been kicked, but the Spider had already paid off the local police to block the area, leaving no witnesses to see the horned crowd arranging themselves obediently in the ditch.

Their masters emerged more slowly, fifty warlocks scraped up from all over Washington, Vancouver, and Oregon. Together, they represented five different cabals, all of whom hated each other. But those petty differences crumpled under the weight of Gilgamesh's golden ring, leaving the warlocks surly but silent as they moved to stand beside their demons.

When they were all finally in position, a sour-faced man in a much nicer suit than anyone else got out of the car at the convoy's head. Judging by the set of his small, wet mouth, he would have much rather been anywhere else, but orders were orders, and there was money to be made. His pockets were already stuffed with quintessence, payment just for showing up with even more promised upon success. Not too shabby for grabbing one runaway witch.

"All right, assholes," he bellowed at the milling warlocks. "The quicker we do this, the quicker we get paid, so stick to your groups and remember the brief." He pointed at the trees looming over them like the fangs of a giant beast. "This is a witch's wood. It will try to kill you at every opportunity, but that's why they're here."

He moved his finger to the last SUV in the convoy, where a knot of sorcerers looking extremely out of place in their business casual attire were standing as far from the army of demons as possible.

"It's their job to take care of the trees," the head warlock announced. "You just focus on finding the target." His wet mouth curved into a grin. "Remember the payout: ten million in cash and fifty pounds of quintessence to the man who brings Adrian Blackwood out alive. Now let's get in there and bag us a witch!"

That was enough to make the warlocks cheer. They might all hate being out here, especially with each other, but ten million was a lot of money, and fifty pounds of quintessence was unheard-of. You could buy an army of demons for that much, but the payout wasn't just there for the warlocks. It was also for the greed demons. Now that Blackwood's head was worth a fortune, they'd be able to track him anywhere, even through his moving forest.

Damn lot of money to waste on a runaway apprentice, but no one who flashed the Lion of Gilgamesh was cheap, and the Spider's plan was definitely working. The frog-faced greed demons were already flapping into the black trees, forcing their warlocks to scramble up the hill after them.

The sorcerers waited until all the warlocks were in the woods before beginning their spells. Part of their patience came from practicality: you couldn't close a trap before the bait was inside. Mostly, though, it was a matter of security. A sorcerer was only as valuable as his spells, and unlike their idiot masters, plenty of demons still spoke Sumerian. If one of those slaves overheard the sorcerers' words, their trade secrets could be compromised, and so they waited, standing patiently by their SUV until all the warlocks, including the ass appointed to lead this fiasco, disappeared into the forest.

"All right, let's get this over with," announced the youngest-looking one, who appeared to be in his thirties but was actually approaching ninety-one. This feat was enabled by his mastery of the Ninety-Nine Verses of Unending Youth, the learning of which was why the other two, who looked closer to their proper ages of sixty and fifty-five respectively, were serving as his assistants tonight.

"We'll start with the barrier," the leader announced in a bored, dry voice. "Rutger, if you would."

One of the sorcerers behind him nodded and drew a velvet pouch out of the pocket of his khakis. He retrieved two coins of quintessence from the sack and popped them into his mouth, breathing deep to draw in the power before throwing out his hand.

"O vault of disbelief," he said in Ancient Sumerian, the tongue of the Eternal King, from whose mouth all sorcery flowed. "Paint now the arc of sky with thy mysteries. A veil of forgetting, a hole in sight, let no vision pass thy threshold. No sound shall pierce thy silence, no scent cross thy boundary. In the name of Gilgamesh, King of All Heavens and Hells, let my words be manifest." Light sprang from his palm as the quintessence coalesced. *"Barrier of the Unknown!"*

When he spoke the final trigger, the light in his hand exploded outward, bathing the dark forest in brilliant white. Within seconds, the entire southern tip of the island was covered in a glowing dome that only the unscaled could detect. Normal, blind humans would see nothing, hear nothing, and smell nothing. They could still walk through the wall of shimmering light, but they should have no reason to. No matter what happened inside, the outside world would perceive nothing. That was important, because otherwise the next spell on the docket would have drawn every EMS responder in the state.

"Right," the head sorcerer said, crouching down on the pavement to roll out a map of Bainbridge with the witch's forest marked in green. "We'll make the walls of fire here, here, and here." He dragged his finger to make three lines across the Blackwood's southern, eastern, and western borders. "Our goal is to drive the witch toward the warlocks, not burn the entire island, so mind your pronunciation and keep the flames under control."

"Are you sure we *can* burn it?" one of the others asked, glancing over his shoulder at the wall of black trees the warlocks had vanished into. "Looks pretty wet in there."

"There's nothing the fires of Heaven cannot burn," the head sorcerer said with utter conviction. "Five coins of quintessence should do the trick."

"Better make it six," said one of his assistants. "The Coward Queen is famously resistant to—"

"*Shhhh!*" the head sorcerer hissed, slamming his hand over the man's mouth. "Not so loud, you dolt! The Spider gave us that information in strictest confidence. Not even the other warlocks know she's back yet, and if we don't want to get sent to the Hells ourselves, we'll keep it that way."

The other sorcerers exchanged nervous looks. "But—"

"No buts!" their leader snapped. "The Spider already said he'd take care of her, so shut your mouths and get your quintessence ready."

The other two sorcerers reached into their pockets. When they'd pulled out the appropriate amount, the leader nodded and raised his own handful of glowing coins.

"We speak the spell together on three," he said, hovering the fistful of magic under his chin. "One, two, th—"

"Gentlemen."

The sorcerer nearly dropped the magic he'd been about to shove into his mouth. He lowered his quintessence at once and whirled around to see the Spider standing not five feet away.

"Favored Voice of Heaven," the head sorcerer said, popping to his feet so he could bow properly. "What are you doing here?"

"What are *you* doing?" the Spider replied, leaning forward to eye the map at the sorcerers' feet. "Cartography?"

"We were performing the final calibrations for the burning of the witch's forest," the sorcerer said nervously. "As detailed in *your* plan, sir." His frown deepened. "Why aren't you in position?"

"I saw the barrier go off and decided to check on you three first," the Spider said, strolling forward alone, which seemed odd. The Spider never appeared without his demons.

"Does that spell require tending?"

"No, sir," replied Rutger, ever eager to show off. "*Barrier of the Unknown* is one of the fortress verses, and I cast it with the full stanza. It will stand by itself until morning."

"Or longer, should you desire," the head sorcerer added, glancing again at the empty street behind the Spider. "Forgive my impertinence, sir, but where are your war demons?"

"Where I told them to be," the Spider replied darkly, coming even closer. "Show me again where you're starting the fires."

The sorcerers exchanged a look. Everything about this situation was very strange, but one did not argue with the Voice of Heaven, so they did as they were told, crouching over the map to place their fingers where the walls of fire would appear. The lead sorcerer had just lifted his head to ask the Spider if he was satisfied when he felt the knife enter his back.

The blade slid cleanly between the fourth and fifth ribs to pierce his heart. It happened so quickly, the sorcerer couldn't do more than gasp. He gasped again when the knife slid back out, letting in a rush of shockingly cold air. He'd just fallen to the ground when his assistant collapsed beside him, also stabbed in the back. The third sorcerer went down to a cut throat, spraying blood all over the other two. The dying leader was still trying to figure out what had happened when a pair of delicate hands—neither of which had the golden Lion of Gilgamesh on its fingers—turned him over and began rummaging through his pockets.

"Damn, damn, damn," Lys muttered, digging through the still-twitching humans' clothing for a phone, a contact list, something *useful*. Like all sorcerers, though, these idiots had nothing on them but quintessence, which meant Lys now had a problem.

Shaking their head, they wiped their bloody hands on the sorcerers' ugly sports jackets and reached up to tap the radio bud in their ear.

"Bex?"

"That was fast," the queen said, her voice tinny over the tiny speaker. "How'd it go?"

"Good and bad," Lys reported, rolling the dead men's bodies off the map. "I found the sorcerers no problem. You were right—they *were* planning to torch the place. I took them out before they started any fires, but I did let them get off a barrier spell. I thought it'd be useful with how loud Iggs can get."

"Sounding awesome so far. What's the bad part?"

"They were surprised to see me," Lys said, looking at the black forest across the street. "Apparently, the Spider's supposed to be in some kind of special position."

"What special position?"

"I don't know. I couldn't exactly ask them where I was supposed to be, could I?" Lys turned to glance down the row of parked SUVs. "I didn't see him go in with the main charge, but other than that, I've got nothing."

"Damn," Bex muttered. "We'll keep our eyes peeled in here. You continue checking the perimeter. He's got to be somewhere."

"On it," Lys said, releasing the talk button to end the call. Their body shifted as they lowered their hand, shaping itself into a copy of one of the warlocks who had just gone into the Blackwood. When the form was perfect, Lys took a moment to toss the dead sorcerers into the ditch before setting off along the forest's edge to look for a spider.

Back in the Blackwood, perched in the branches of a shaggy tree that made her impossible to see from the ground, Bex released the button on the earbud radio she'd used to talk to Lys and reached down one branch to tap Iggs on the shoulder.

"Lys says the Spider's MIA," she whispered.

"I bet he wussed," Iggs whispered back. "Warlocks are all cowards. He's probably relaxing at a wine bar in town while his goons do the dirty work."

"Maybe," Bex said, but she didn't believe it. "How's the invasion going?"

Rather than answer, Iggs leaned to the side, letting the scene below speak for itself.

Despite the bright afternoon sunlight shining on the canopy, Adrian's Blackwood was darker than Bex had ever seen it, challenging even her normally excellent night vision. The warlocks were easy to spot by their flashlights, as were the gleaming bronze war demons who never left their masters' sides. The toad-like greed demons were harder to detect, and she couldn't see the fear demons at all, which was why Bex *hated* fighting fear demons. You never saw the scaly bastards until their claws were in your back.

"They're pretty spread out," Iggs whispered, shifting on his branch. "Give the signal?"

Now seemed as good a time as any, so Bex leaned back and rapped her knuckles quietly on the tree's scaly trunk. The first time her hand landed, all she felt was bark. On the second knock, the trunk yielded to her like flesh, almost as if she were pressing her fist into a man's work-roughened palm. That was all the warning she got before a host of twinkling lights flared up in the dark.

"Looks like Adrian got your signal," Iggs said, his voice quivering with anticipation. "Here we go."

Bex leaned forward, practically hanging upside down from her branch like a bat as she watched the forest shift into action.

So far, the Blackwood hadn't done anything but be dark and creepy. This was by design. Even a witch's wood couldn't separate people who were clinging together in fear, so Adrian had instructed Bex to play it coy, letting the warlocks' confidence and greed spread them out far enough for the trees to separate them.

If they'd been normal visitors, they would have stayed like that, suddenly alone and lost for hours before eventually stumbling out of the forest at the same place where they'd entered. The warlocks got no such kindness. When the black trees shifted now, it was to draw them deeper, tempting them with the little fires that burned so cheerfully in the dark.

The greed demons especially were drawn like moths. They scrambled forward, fluttering over roots on their stubby wings, not even noticing when their warlocks vanished behind them down unseen holes or into the branches of a tree. By the time the greed demons reached the light their instincts were so sure was Adrian Blackwood, they were alone, facing not their target, but a scarecrow with a carved, merrily burning pumpkin head that had Adrian's blood smeared inside. That was all they got to see before the scarecrow lurched forward, wrapping the greed demon in a smothering embrace before pulling it under the loamy ground.

"Wow," Iggs said as the closest scarecrow dragged a screaming demon into the earth. "That is so much creepier in person than Adrian made it sound."

"It's working, though," Bex said, looking out at the dark forest where flaming scarecrows were snuffing out one by one. "That takes care of the greed demons."

"Are you *sure* the witch isn't killing them?" Iggs whispered nervously. "Because that was very horror-movie."

"Positive," Bex whispered back. "They might look like squashed toads, but greed demons are the toughest of all of us. Lust fades, and wrath burns itself out, but greed is forever." She nodded at the scarecrow they'd just watched sink a demon into the ground. "Adrian's just holding them still for a bit. Once this is over, I'll dig them out and cut off their slave bands. For now, though, let's focus on the ones that can still bite us."

There were plenty left. Despite being one of the most populous demon species, not many warlocks kept greed demons. This meant there were still lots of enemies even after the scarecrows did their job. Adrian's curses were also going off nonstop as warlocks fell into them, filling the forest with screams that made their remaining targets extra cautious.

The ever-changing forest kept the invaders from seeing one another even with their flashlights, but nothing could separate a warlock from his demons if they were determined to stick together, and some of these bastards had shown up with armies. One man who'd already made it to the foot of Adrian's hill was surrounded by no fewer than five black-scaled fear demons. Not particularly large ones, but you didn't have to be big when you could walk up any surface, made no sound, and had claws like scythes.

"That one's getting pretty close to base," Iggs whispered. "Should we take him out?"

Bex shook her head and pressed a finger to her lips before pointing it at an oak tree just up the hill. The big one the warlock with the fear demons was about to walk under. The one Nemini was sitting in.

As if she'd been waiting for Bex's signal, the snake-haired void demon chose that moment to jump, dropping fifty feet to the ground like she was just stepping off a curb. She landed behind the warlock without a sound, and then the man collapsed like a cut rope. He didn't even get to scream. Bex's eyebrows were still rising in appreciation when the warlock's pack of fear demons turned and pounced on Nemini as one, knocking her to the ground.

"Poor brainwashed bastards," Iggs said, shaking his head. "They have no idea what they just jumped on."

"Nope," Bex said proudly, waiting until the count of five before reaching up to press the call button on her ear bud. "We saw that takedown," she whispered when the mic clicked on. "You okay?"

"As okay as anyone can be with the inescapable knowledge of their own demise," a flat voice replied from above her.

Bex barely stopped her jump in time. That was much better than Iggs, who actually fell out of the tree. He caught himself at the last second, snagging a branch with his leg just before he landed on an unsuspecting warlock's head.

"Don't *do* that!" he hissed as he climbed back up, glaring murder at Nemini, who was sitting casually in the tiny branches at the tree's crown. "How'd you get over here so fast, anyway?"

"Nothing is everywhere," Nemini replied with a shrug, her yellow eyes shining like a predator's in the dark.

"What did you do to that warlock?" Bex asked, both to distract Iggs from his anger and to satisfy her own curiosity. "I've seen you drop guys quick before, but he went out like a switch."

It was probably her imagination, but Bex would've sworn Nemini's blank face looked pleased. "He had a very high opinion of himself," the void demon said in her usual monotone. "The longer the fall, the harder the splat."

Bex grinned. "Good job."

"What about the fear demons?" Iggs asked, his good mood returning with the suffering of their enemies. "How bad did you get them?"

"Not at all, actually," Nemini said, tilting her head. "They ran away on their own as soon as they realized their warlock wouldn't be getting back up."

Good for them, Bex thought. She just wished more of the demons would follow suit.

Now that they'd realized how dangerous the holes in the ground could be, several war demons were working to haul warlocks out of the pits. Adrian's traps weren't giving them up easily, but things could go south quickly if the enemy got their feet back under them.

"Time to roll out the big guns," Bex said, pulling out her sword, which was vibrating in anticipation. "Nemini, you're on runners. I'll get the warlocks. Iggs, you take the war demons."

"With pleasure," he said, his red eyes glowing as brightly as Bex's in the dark. "It's clobbering time!"

Considering how carried away he could get when he went big, Bex did not appreciate the reference. This was her plan, though. They were way past the time for second-guessing, so she just got out of her wrath demon's way, hopping to a different tree entirely as Iggs launched himself at the nearest war demon.

The shiny bronze bastard didn't know what hit him. One minute, he was trailing behind his warlock like a guard dog. The next, a full-sized, fire-engine-red Iggs was swinging him *into* his warlock, knocking them both into the nearest tree so hard, the towering oak began to tilt.

It righted itself a second later. Bex could almost feel Adrian's hands tucking the roots back into the ground as the tree steadied itself just in time for her to land on the lowest branch. She fell into a crouch immediately, her glowing eyes narrowing as she surveyed what was now a very different scene.

All throughout the dark forest, warlocks and their demons were turning toward Iggs. Even the moving trees couldn't hide something that big and loud. Iggs was as huge as he'd been in Limbo, bellowing at the top of his lungs for the warlocks to come and get it. A month ago, that would have terrified her, but as she watched Iggs meet a charging war demon with a fist the size of a mini fridge, all Bex felt was righteous fury.

They were no longer hiding, no longer losing. That was *her* wrath demon smashing war demon traitors like pie plates while Gilgamesh's slavers backed away in fear.

Straight into her.

With a roar of her own, Bex dropped onto the warlock who'd taken shelter behind her tree, separating the human's head from his body in a single clean stroke. She took the next one out just as efficiently, then the next, then the next. They didn't even see her coming. They were too busy staring at—or running away from—Iggs to notice the black sword flying in behind them. By the time they felt the cut, it was too late. Their heads were already gone, and so was Bex, moving through the dark forest like a vengeful, smoky shadow. Every warlock she touched, she killed. Every demon she touched, she freed, shouting their names in a burning voice that scorched her throat.

Some ran when she cut them loose. Some cried. A few fought, bellowing in rage at Bex for making them look like defectors.

Bex bellowed right back, screaming in their faces with five millennia of pent-up fury. She didn't care if she made them look bad in front of their slavers. She would never kill one of her own, but she had no mercy for demons who danced for the warlocks' favor while the rest of their people languished in the Hells. She had no mercy at all.

Nice to see you acting like yourself again, Drox said, his blade moving like smoke in her hands as she cut down a warlock who'd been trying to crawl out of one of Adrian's pits, which appeared to be full of spiders. *Welcome back, Queen of Wrath.*

It was good to *be* back. Bex couldn't actually remember being queen, but she felt it in every move: the strength, the anger, the *purpose.* She was no longer numbly stumbling forward, chasing an impossible chance. She *was* the chance. She *was* the impossible, and she was going to *win.*

She fell on the next warlock with a cry that echoed to the Heavens. With Ishtar as her witness, she would tear it all down. Limbo, the warlocks, the sorcerers and the Anchors and the Heavenly City and everything else that held up Gilgamesh's throne. She would set everybody free: her wrath demons, all demons, Adrian and the Blackwood too. She would have it all or die trying. That was what this life—her last life—was for, and Bex threw herself into it with a vengeance, cutting down every warlock she saw while Iggs's roars shook the forest like an erupting volcano.

And all around her, unnoticed in the hail of vengeance, the Blackwood began to groan.

Chapter 16

Adrian was holding on by a hair.

Boston had been right as usual. There were too many curses, and they were all coming due at once. Adrian had been as careful as he could be—spreading the traps out evenly, keeping the parameters concise, using his trees to balance the load—but all the mitigation in the world couldn't change that his forest was carpeted in malicious magic. No single curse was a problem by itself, but every one bit like a viper when triggered, taking a piece out of Adrian in the process, and he was rapidly running out of pieces to give.

If he hadn't been so sure it was going to kill him, Adrian would have been proud. This might just be the greatest number of simultaneous curses any Blackwood had ever weathered. The only reasons he hadn't already gone down screaming were because he refused to leave his young forest to bear the curses alone, and because he couldn't pry his eyes off of Bex.

It was one thing to hear she was the daughter of a goddess, but actually watching her cut down warlocks like grass through the many eyes of his forest felt like witnessing divine wrath made manifest. She'd already sliced through half of the army that had driven up the road. Iggs was still buried in war demons who liked the fight too much to stop even when their masters lost their heads, but the rest of his forest was rapidly emptying out.

That didn't stop Bex. When she ran out of easy targets, she started digging for more, hauling the screaming warlocks out of Adrian's curses. He'd buried a huge variety—again, trying to spread the load since different curses bit in different ways—but whether she was sticking her hands into pits of spiders or stinging nettles, biting ants or hallucinogenic mushrooms, Bex didn't hesitate. She yanked her victims out like turnips, cutting off their heads and leaving their bodies to the trees, who ate them greedily.

Too greedily. Blood-fed trees turned predatory and started producing curses of their own in time. If Adrian survived this battle, he was going to have to spend weeks weaning them back onto more wholesome food. Right now, though, their deaths felt like blessings, because every warlock Bex hauled out of the ground was one less curse that was biting him. Adrian was starting to think he might actually make it through this when he felt Boston pawing at his head.

He didn't want to answer, which was proof that he should. It wasn't as extreme as when he'd let the Blackwood take him over completely, but sinking into the forest was still dangerous. It was too easy to forget that you were human down here, too easy to get so tangled in the visions that you couldn't find your way out.

Adrian hadn't thought he'd been under long enough for that, but no one ever did, which was why witches had familiars. They were the levelheaded voices, the ones who pulled you back. Adrian was dutifully obeying his when something cold, glassy, and flat smacked against his cheek, almost like he'd been slapped with a smart phone.

"It *is* a phone," Boston hissed, shoving the device harder against Adrian's face. "Lys has been calling you nonstop. They say it's an emergency."

An emergency was what would happen if Adrian took his attention away from the curses. There were still plenty of live warlocks thrashing in his traps, more than enough to kill him if Adrian didn't manage the bites precisely. But Lys wouldn't have called if it wasn't important, so Adrian nodded, keeping his hands and a good eighty percent of his attention on the roots wrapped around his body while he lifted his head just enough for Boston to press the phone against his ear.

"What's the emergency?"

"*The Spider's coming up the hill right now!*" The lust demon's voice was frantic and breathless, as if they were running. "I tried radioing Bex, but she's not answering. You have to get out of there!"

That really was impossible. If Adrian left his heart tree now, the full brunt of the curses would fall on his young forest, and the trees would rip themselves apart. He could never do that, not to his Blackwood, but he couldn't let the Spider catch him on his back either.

"Which direction is he coming from?" Adrian asked, sitting up under the branches.

"The inlet," said Lys as the sound of running got faster. "The frontal assault was a decoy. The Spider and his demons are coming from the water!"

Adrian froze. He'd been so distracted by the curses and Bex's spellbinding slaughter that he hadn't even noticed the footsteps coming up the hill from behind. Stupid mistake, because Lys was right. The Spider was practically in the clearing already, which meant Adrian needed to stand up.

"You can't," Boston said when he started to move. "You'll kill your forest, which will kill your *heart*."

"Not if I don't break the connection," Adrian panted, reaching out to his cat with hands so wrapped in roots, it looked like he was wearing potholders. "I'm the one the Spider wants. I have to face him, but you're connected to me just like I'm connected to the trees. You can stay hidden under the branches and be my bridge. I'll handle the Spider."

Boston's green eyes went huge, as well they should. What Adrian was suggesting was incredibly dangerous. But just when he was sure his familiar was going to balk, Boston reached out and hooked the roots with his claws.

"I'll hold them with my life," he promised as the forest's tendril slithered off Adrian to wrap around him. "Don't you dare let that warlock beat you."

"Never," Adrian swore, giving his brave cat a final pet before he turned to climb out from under his heart tree.

It was slow going. The bites from the curses made every movement painful, and the lingering connection to the roots made it hard to tell which parts were his body and which belonged to the trees. But Boston was taking over both with his usual efficiency. By the time Adrian made it to the edge of the fir tree's shelter, the disoriented feeling was gone, and the curse pain, though still dreadful, was at least throbbing evenly across his body. That was a lot better than he'd expected, leaving him clearheaded as he pushed through the final branches to see what he was in for.

War demons seemed to be the answer. The Spider kept every kind of slave he could get his hands on, but he was a stickler for using the right tool for the job. He would never go to war with any other kind, though this seemed excessive, even for him.

"Did you bring every war demon in the Hells?" Adrian asked, looking at the shining ring of four-armed bronze giants that was rapidly surrounding his heart tree. "I suppose this means you're not here to talk."

"If you could be talked into a reasonable course of action, things wouldn't have progressed to this deplorable state," a dry, familiar voice replied as the Spider stepped out from behind the largest of his escorts.

"Stand down, boy. It's over."

"Are you sure?" Adrian asked, tilting his head toward the screams that were still echoing out of his black forest. "It sounds like you're the one who's losing warlocks."

"An anticipated cost," the Spider said dismissively. "The local cabals performed exactly as I hoped. Their deaths kept your bloodthirsty demons occupied and kept you from noticing me until I had you surrounded." His thin lips pulled into a superior smile. "We're actually running ahead of schedule, so I'm going to give you one last chance. Surrender, and I won't burn your forest to the ground."

"How about this instead?" Adrian said as the trees surrounding his clearing began to lean inward. "I'll give *you* one last chance to give up your obsession with forcing me into your cabal and leave this place in peace before I kill you and every warlock you were arrogant enough to send into my Blackwood."

Given how many warlocks the Spider had lost already, Adrian thought that'd be enough to at least make the old man pause, but the Spider just waved his hand. Adrian's first thought was that he was flicking the threat away, which would be typical of the arrogant old stick, but then he saw something flash between the Spider's tattooed fingers. That was all he was able to make out before a shimmering object flew straight at him.

There was no time to dodge it. Not that Adrian could have dodged with Boston right behind him, but he wasn't too worried. The Spider had spoken no sorcery, and the ground around the heart tree was thick with curses that would knock any weapon off course before it could touch him. Adrian was still waiting for them to go off when the shining object plunged into his chest.

He looked down in confusion to see a dagger sticking out of his shirt. The weapon was buried to the hilt in his left pectoral, but it didn't hurt at all. There wasn't even any blood. It looked like he'd been stabbed by a hologram, because now that he was staring at it, Adrian could see that the knife wasn't actually shining. It was transparent: a ghostly white image of a dagger rather than an actual physical object. He was about to ask what in the Hells was going on when the Spider, who'd never been able to resist a good gloat, explained.

"It's a curse," he said, looking insufferably pleased with himself. "A real one made by sorcerers using quintessence, not one of those witchcraft hack jobs that bite the hand that wields them. You feel nothing right now, but that blade is plunged into your heart. Fail to do as I say, and it will become solid molecule by molecule until you really are bleeding out on the ground. Now." He flashed Adrian that cruel smirk again. "Shall we revisit that surrender?"

"Don't bother," Adrian said, crossing his arms through the transparent knife in his chest. "It's a clever curse, but it's not going to work against me."

The Spider clearly didn't want to dignify that with a response. But he was a methodical man who couldn't stand for any of his statements to be challenged, and in the end, he bit.

"Why not?"

Now it was Adrian's turn to smirk. "Because that's not where my heart is."

The confusion was still passing over the Spider's thin face when Adrian stomped on the ground, waking the nails he'd buried this morning. The curse was supposed to be triggered by aggression, but iron was stubborn and clearly did not consider a ghost dagger that couldn't be felt a real attack. Fortunately, Adrian had worked with iron before and knew to build himself a manual trigger. One stomp was all it took to send a hail of four-inch nails flying at the Spider's face. His war demons covered him immediately, but Adrian had another reason for choosing iron despite its stubbornness.

It stabbed right through bronze.

The iron nails bit into the war demons like a hail of teeth. They twisted as they hit, wiggling from side to side to widen the holes before the demons smashed them away. That *did* count as an attack, and the cursed nails circled back around with a vengeance, flying at the war demons guarding the Spider like a swarm of angry bees.

"*Subdue him!*" the warlock roared at the war demons who weren't being nailed.

They obeyed at once, marching into the circle of turned-up dirt the nails had come out of, which triggered the other half of the curses.

The moment their cloven hooves touched the ground inside the circle Adrian had made around his tree, iron spikes shot through the demon's armored stomachs. They looked like giant versions of the same nails pecking at the Spider's guards, because that was exactly what they were. When they'd stepped onto the cursed ground, the war demons had tied themselves to the straw dolls Adrian had buried earlier—the ones with iron nails stabbed through their torsos. Now that they were linked, the demons couldn't move any more than the dolls could. If they struggled, stepped forward, or did anything other than turn and flee, the giant nails would get bigger and bigger until they eventually ripped the demons in half.

Adrian hoped it wouldn't come to that. He'd promised Bex he wouldn't kill any of her people, but the nails wouldn't grow unless the war demons kept up the attack. Something they were already having trouble with since the nails through their guts automatically resized themselves to match their victims' giant bodies.

That was a lot of iron even for a war demon, and it was slowing them down hard. None of the demons the Spider ordered to grab him had made it more than five feet toward his heart tree yet. If adding another two dozen curses on top of the ones he was already carrying hadn't hurt so damn much, Adrian would have cheered.

"Be careful!" Boston hissed from inside the tree. "You're getting very close."

Adrian was well aware. The bite of all those new curses on top of the old ones hurt like nothing ever had. The pain was so bad, Adrian didn't even notice when the transparent dagger in his chest began to grow solid. Apparently, the Spider was making good on his threat. The blade was too short to do serious damage, especially since it was stabbing into an empty hollow, but it was still a spike of metal in his chest, and its handle remained insubstantial, which meant Adrian couldn't pull it out.

"Not so invulnerable after all," the Spider said, leaning out from under the shelter of his war demons—who were still swatting at the flying nails—to show Adrian a whole spread of transparent daggers. "I had the sorcerers make me a set. One for each organ, and all enchanted not to miss." He selected one of the glowing curses with a smile. "I wonder, have you misplaced your lungs as well?"

He flicked his hand, and the glowing dagger flew like a spark, zigzagging around the nailed-down demons to sink into Adrian's chest. The spectral blade didn't stop at the hilt this time. It flew straight through his shirt, skin, and muscle to land inside his right lung.

Once again, there was no pain. If Adrian hadn't seen the knife go in, he wouldn't have known it was there. The Spider hadn't activated the curse yet, but he was clearly about to. Either that, or he was getting ready to throw the rest, which was a far more serious threat. As a Witch of the Flesh, Adrian could manage one lost lung with minimal difficulty, but if he let the Spider take out both, or—Blackwood help him—his *brain*, it was over.

"I thought you wanted me alive?" he yelled, stalling for time so he could think. "My Blackwood blood's no good if you dump it all over the ground."

"I'm not worried about killing you," the Spider said, tossing another transparent knife into Adrian's abdomen. Kidney or liver, Adrian wasn't sure which. "If witches were so easily dispatched, my last two centuries would have been a lot easier. Those knives are merely precautions. They'll all go away the moment you stop being stubborn. Keep pushing me, though, and you won't like where you end up. I've been given permission to be *very* rough if you continue to be disobedient."

He turned his hand as he spoke, and Adrian went still. The Spider had a golden ring on his finger. He'd never seen one in person, but given how cocky his old master was acting—and how many warlocks he'd been able to pull together—Adrian was certain he was looking at a seal of Gilgamesh.

That was an unwelcome discovery. He'd known the Spider was a favored servant, but those rings were the most serious of serious business. The Eternal King would never hand one out just to help the Spider catch an errant Blackwood, which meant it had to be for Bex.

Adrian clenched his fists. He still thought Bex's plan to fight Gilgamesh was a pipe dream, but there was no way in the Hells he was letting the Spider rack up brownie points by killing her. If Bex could fight an entire forest full of warlocks for his sake, Adrian could face this one for her, especially since he'd already planned to kill the bastard. The Spider was the top warlock on the entire East Coast, the rock-star leader of the New England cabal. If Adrian defeated him, there was no one bigger they could send. Even more importantly, the Spider was the one obsessed with making Blackwoods into warlocks. If he died fighting one, the rest of his cabal might lose their stomach for the practice, and maybe the Blackwood could finally stop losing its children.

That was as good a hill to die on as Adrian could ask. He was arguably past his limit already, definitely too far for what he was thinking, but if he could win this fight, he might just win everything. That felt like a prize worthy of throwing the dice for, so Adrian reached into his coat and pulled out his ace.

It looked like a dried wasp. The insect was as long as his hand, its black body papery and delicate. Its yellowed wings looked like they'd fall apart at the slightest bump, but they shivered to life when Adrian breathed over them, blowing the wasp like a kiss at the Spider's face.

The old man didn't even see it coming. He already thought he'd won, tossing his knives from behind the shelter of his war demons like this whole thing was a demonstration he'd arranged to teach Adrian a lesson in futility. He was still smirking when the wasp flew around his defenders like a homing missile to sting him in the neck.

The Spider screamed when it struck. Not an angry scream or a surprised one, but a true bellow of pain. Adrian felt it, too, slapping his hand against his own neck as he dropped to his knees.

The karma wasp wasn't like his other curses. It was a spell of his own invention, an insect made of malice that would sting its victim once for every time they'd hurt another. Unfortunately, throwing the karma wasp at someone was itself an act of bad karma, which meant he couldn't use the spell without taking a sting himself. That normally wasn't a problem since Adrian had built up resistances to every poison he used, but he'd never thrown his wasp while he was this weak before, and the venom was hitting him like a truck.

He still couldn't bring himself to regret it. The karma wasp was one of his greatest achievements, and it was at its best against someone like the Spider: a remorseless slaver with centuries of abuses. It took Adrian a good twenty seconds to fight the poison back enough to raise his head, but the curse was still stinging his old master relentlessly. The Spider was writhing in agony, shrieking at his demons to kill the insect, kill Adrian, kill everything, but his words were growing less and less intelligible.

Despite his own churning nausea, Adrian grinned. His karma wasp wasn't a pretty curse, but it was an extremely satisfying one. Already, the Spider's face was swollen and purple from lack of oxygen. His hands were puffed up like balloons as they clawed at his useless throat, desperate for the air that couldn't make it past the swollen tissues.

The sight made Adrian smile. He wasn't typically a vengeful witch, but this was the man who'd dragged him from his home and beaten him when he refused to learn the warlocks' disgusting magic. The leader of the cabal that had threatened and coerced the Blackwood for centuries. He could rot in the same Hells he damned his demons to.

It took the Spider ten minutes to finish dying. He cursed Adrian the whole way down, activating the knife in his lung and attempting to throw more, but his swollen fingers couldn't pick up the glowing curses he'd dropped all over the ground, and his demons weren't helping. Now that the Spider couldn't speak to command them, they'd ceased moving toward Adrian or attempting to defend the old man. They simply stood wherever they'd happened to be when he'd fallen, silently watching their master die.

When the warlock's body finally stopped twitching, the demon army the Spider had brought with him stepped out of Adrian's circle of curses. He let them go gladly, calling back his swarm of flying nails. The demons tied to the dolls had already freed themselves when they retreated, since Adrian's pinning curse only nailed those who were trying to move toward him. Victims were always free to run, and run they did, fleeing down the hill without a word or a look back at the bloated corpse lying on the ground.

Adrian stared at it in a trance. The body was already starting to turn black from the wasp's poison, but it was still undeniably the Spider, the monster who'd terrorized his entire family. And he was dead, because of Adrian.

The surge of joy that followed that thought blew the pain of the curses, poison, and knives away. He threw his arms up with a whoop, laughing so hard that his punctured lung started to spasm.

That brought the pain right back, but Adrian was too happy to care. He'd done it. The crazy plan he'd been cooking up since he was a teenager had actually *worked*! He'd just killed one of the most powerful warlocks in the

Americas with a forest that was less than a month old. And a lot of demonic help, admittedly, but still... he'd *won*! There was no one the cabals could throw at him who was worse than the Spider. Anything else would be a walk in the woods after this, which meant he was free. *He was free*! He was—

"*Adrian!*"

Adrian stopped bouncing with joy long enough to look back at his cat, who was so wrapped up in the forest's roots that he looked like a ball of brown yarn.

"I know this is an exciting time," Boston said as he wiggled his worried face out of the mass of plants. "But you are still under the effects of over a hundred curses and have several internal injuries. If you want to survive to enjoy your new warlock-free life, you need to come back in here right now and let the forest heal you."

That was a very good idea. The thrill of victory was still making him lightheaded, but Adrian was coming down enough now to realize the feeling might actually be due to blood loss. He was bleeding quite a lot inside and out, and the wasp's poison still burned in his veins. If he'd been a normal human, he would have been in real trouble, but Adrian was a witch in his wood. Just as his forest had helped him bear the curses, it would help him get through this. He just had to do as Boston said and lie down under his tree. He was struggling to do so without falling on his face when a loud, beautiful sound rolled over the clearing.

The noise was so out of place, it took Adrian's endorphin-drunk brain several seconds to recognize it as a bell. A great golden *gong* was echoing through the air, bouncing off his trees like sunlight turned to sound. It made him want to weep, it was so lovely, but when Adrian turned to see where the beautiful sound was coming from, his labored breathing stopped short.

A woman was standing above the Spider's bloated corpse. She looked like an ivory statue come to life. Her hair was carved in waves around her beautiful face, which sported two inhuman eyes made from interlocking rings of hammered gold. She was dressed like ancient royalty in an ivory gown that had been carved to fall in gold-trimmed folds all the way to her delicate golden-sandal-wrapped feet. The only part of her that wasn't ivory or gold was the white silk glove covering her right hand.

If she hadn't been moving, Adrian would have thought she actually was a statue. But while her jerky motions reminded him of a puppet, she was definitely moving under her own power as she reached down and ripped the golden seal of Gilgamesh off the Spider's swollen finger.

"Is this your doing?"

Adrian jumped, his bloody chest heaving. The woman's voice had the same beautiful ringing sound as before, but higher and lighter. Tinkling, as if her bell were made from glass. It was so mesmerizing, so *strange*, that Adrian didn't realize the woman was speaking to him until she stepped forward.

"Did you do this?" the stranger demanded, pointing at the Spider's corpse. "Answer the question."

Dread began to pool in Adrian's stomach. The pain and poison made it difficult to think, but while he'd never seen one with his own eyes, he was growing more and more certain that the ivory woman was a princess. *Gilgamesh's* princess. One of the Eternal King's personal weapons, and she was staring right at him.

"I have no time for disobedience," the princess said, her lovely face pulling into an ugly sneer. "The Spider was a favored servant of the Celestial Princes, ever may their glory shine. Did you or did you not kill him?"

Adrian didn't answer. He just slipped his hand into his jacket. His best curse was already used, but he couldn't have taken another sting from the karma wasp even if he'd had an extra, and he didn't want to kill the princess. She was a direct servant of Gilgamesh. Attacking her was the same as attacking the Eternal King himself. Adrian couldn't take a risk like that, not when he'd just gotten free, but he wasn't sure what else to do.

He needed more time—needed to think—so he sank his hand into the pocket where he kept his sap traps. The princess would be mad about being stuck like a bug in amber, but at least it'd buy him breathing room to come up with a plan. That was good enough for now, but Adrian hadn't even gotten the sticky, fly-shaped trap out of his coat when the princess shot forward.

She moved as fast as Bex. Adrian didn't even have time to shout a warning before her golden-sandaled feet slammed into his circle of curses. Sure enough, the nailed dolls activated, but unlike the Spider's war demons, the princess didn't get stuck. She dodged each spike, and when the flying nails came after her, she dodged them, too, swatting the bits of iron out of the air so fast and hard that they shattered. By the time she got to Adrian a heartbeat later, his entire circle was exhausted, leaving him defenseless as she grabbed his arm and wrenched it behind his back.

"I'll take your silence as an admission of guilt," she said in her high, delicate voice as she bent his arm toward the breaking point. "An attack on a Celestial Prince's servant is the same as an attack on Heaven itself. For your crime against perfection, you shall now be..."

She trailed off, bending Adrian's head back with her free hand to get a look at his face.

"Wait," she said, the rings of her golden irises turning like focusing camera lenses. "I know you. You're the witch the Spider was tasked with bringing to heel. Agatha's son."

Adrian's stomach dropped at his mother's name. He had no idea why a princess of Gilgamesh would know who he was, but her face had flipped from deadly to smiling, which was much, much worse.

"Today is your blessed day, mortal," she announced, easing the arm she'd been about to break back down until she was merely pinning it behind Adrian's back. "Normally, I would kill you for robbing my divine prince of one of his favored servants, but you are fortunate enough to have captured Heaven's interest, so I'll be taking you back with me instead." She flashed him another brilliant smile. "Be of joy, witch! Today is the day you go to Heaven."

She clearly expected Adrian to fall over in thanks at this announcement, but he'd already dug his feet into the ground. His forest rushed up to meet him, wrapping the princess in roots as it tried to drag her away.

If both Blackwoods hadn't been through so much in the last hour, the attack might have worked. It definitely caught her by surprise, but the princess wasn't just as fast as Bex. She was also apparently as strong as her, effortlessly ripping the roots to pieces with her bare hands.

Their pain echoed through the forest into Adrian until he screamed. The princess arched a perfect white eyebrow at the sound, and then she hauled back and punched him across the jaw. The blow made his ears ring and blackened his vision. When he came back to himself a second later, the princess was carrying him under her arm like a sack.

That sent him into a true panic. Not over her threat to drag him to Heaven—as scary as that prospect was, it was still far away, a worry for the future. Adrian was petrified *right now* because his feet weren't touching the ground, which meant he was no longer in direct contact with his forest.

He started thrashing in the princess's arms like an animal, desperate to get any portion of his body back to the earth before he lost the connection for good. Forget Heaven. If he lost control, all the curses he'd been managing would start to cascade, causing his whole forest to collapse. He *had* to get free, but his battered body was so weak, and the princess was so strong.

Adrian tried anyway, his thoughts going red with fury as he pushed against the iron clamp of her white arm. It wasn't fair. This was supposed to be *his* victory, but the princess was already lifting her free hand toward the sky. And as he felt the hard white crackle of quintessence closing in around them, Adrian realized it was now or never.

"*Bex!*" he screamed, lurching against the princess's grip. "*Rebexa!*"

Just like on the ferry, her name came out of him like a thunderclap. Adrian was amazed he'd been able to speak it at all, given how weak he was. He wasn't sure if Bex could hear him out in the forest, but the princess certainly did. She stopped cold, the blinding white quintessence magic fading as she looked down at Adrian in surprise.

"How do you know that name?"

The question was still on her lips when Bex's fist slammed into the side of the princess's skull.

Adrian didn't even see where she came from. One second, the clearing was empty. The next, Bex was right on top of them, her fist plowing into the princess's cheek like a piston. The shock loosened the princess's grip, allowing Bex to snatch Adrian out of her arms before the white woman went flying. Bex set Adrian down a second later, her burning eyes flashing with terror as she took in his condition.

"Why didn't you call me sooner?" she demanded, pressing her pale hands frantically over Adrian's bleeding chest.

That certainly would have been the wiser decision, but Adrian shook his head. He'd wanted to win on his own. The whole point of doing this was to show the warlocks that they couldn't beat him. *Him*, Adrian Blackwood, not the Queen of Wrath. He'd been doing just fine, too, until the princess had come down and ruined it. That was more than Adrian had breath to explain, though, so he stuck to the important bits.

"*Tree*," he gasped, tilting his lolling head toward his heart tree.

Bex got the message. She picked up his wounded body and gently moved him under the fir tree's boughs. She was still getting him arranged when the princess she'd sent flying leaped back into the clearing.

Bex let go of Adrian at once, leaving him to wiggle the rest of the way on his own as she transformed her ring back into a smoking sword. When her weapon was in her hands, she stepped out of the branches to face the white woman, who was staring at Bex as if she'd seen a ghost.

"It really is you," the princess said, her golden eyes so wide that Adrian could see the balls moving inside her ivory skull. "You're still alive."

She stared in shock for another second, then gave herself a shake. It looked more like a vibration, but when it was over, the princess's haughtiness was back, leaving her looking more like a monster than ever.

"I can't believe you survived," she said, sneering down her nose at the much shorter demon. "After what happened in Limbo, most of us thought you'd finally crawled off and died for good."

"Happy to disappoint," Bex said, raising her smoking sword.

"It won't be a disappointment for long," the princess promised, pointing a gloved finger at Adrian. "Your death is preordained, but he has earned Heaven's interest. Step away from the witch, and my divine prince might yet show mercy."

"I'm not here for mercy," Bex told her, setting her boots more firmly in the turned-up dirt left by the broken curses. "And Adrian Blackwood is under my protection."

"Then you shall be removed," the princess said, getting down on her knees.

For a crazy second, Adrian thought she was kneeling to Bex like the other demons had. Then the overwhelming quintessence magic he'd felt earlier came down like a hammer. It landed on the clearing with a crash of bells and a flash of light so blindingly bright, Adrian was still blinking the spots out of his eyes when the thing the princess had actually been kneeling to stepped forward.

It looked like a golden statue. Then it reached down to pet the kneeling princess on the head like a dog, and Adrian saw it was a man. A tall, broad-shouldered man dressed from head to toe in shining golden armor made from thousands of overlapping scales stamped with sorcerous cuneiform. Given how the princess looked, Adrian was expecting another ivory monster, but when the man pushed up the visor of his crown-like helmet, the face he revealed was shockingly human.

He had olive skin just like Adrian's, and his brown hair was thick and curly, crowding in around his high cheekbones like embellishments on a gilded frame. His handsome features were oddly familiar, probably because he resembled the statues of Gilgamesh that dominated every Anchor Market, because there was no doubt in Adrian's mind that this was a Celestial Prince. One of the enforcers of Heaven's divine will. Gilgamesh's son.

Adrian scowled under his tree. He'd been taught to fear the Celestial Princes for as long as he could remember. Even his mother spoke of them only in whispers. After all that buildup, he'd expected something divinely horrible, but the prince looked almost...normal. Take away his golden armor and the ivory princess fawning at his feet, and he could have been just another cocky young man, at least until you got to his eyes.

That was where the illusion of normalcy ended. If the princess's eyes were spinning balls of overlapping gold, the prince's eyes were silver mirrors. They reflected everything they looked at: the gloomy green of the forest, the red of Adrian's blood, and, finally, the smoking black of Bex's sword, where they narrowed.

"Princess," he said, making Bex jump. Adrian jumped too. Again, the prince's body might have looked human, but his voice, like his eyes, was nothing of the sort. If the princess sounded like a tinkling glass bell, the prince was an iron one, his words ringing out like sword strikes as he looked over the bloody clearing.

"Why is my Spider dead?" he demanded, glaring at the kneeling woman in disgust. "And why is there still a battle going on? What do you think your job is?"

"To serve only you, my divine prince," the princess replied, pressing her face into the dirt between his golden boots. "I would never have called you to this filthy place if I did not believe it worthy of your attention, but these criminals who killed your servant are the ones the Spider spoke of."

"Ah," the prince said, his furious scowl transforming into a smirk as he spotted Adrian bleeding under the tree. "The runaway Blackwood boy. He's so dirty I hardly recognized him."

He took a step forward, but Bex got in his way, pointing her sword at the prince's golden chest.

He stepped, smile fading. "You again," he said, giving Adrian a view of Bex's deadly scowl in his mirrored eyes as looked her up and down. "The Spider said you were back. I almost didn't believe him. It normally takes you at least a decade and a half to crawl back up after we stomp you down, but I suppose I shouldn't be surprised." His reflective eyes narrowed. "You always were a resilient little cockroach."

"I could say the same for you," Bex replied in the coldest voice Adrian had ever heard. "I normally have a hard time telling you golden pricks apart, but I remember your face." She moved her sword closer. "You're the prince I killed in Limbo."

"A temporary inconvenience," the prince snarled. "And one that shall *not* be repeated. The only reason you had a chance back then is because Limbo is a cold hell filled with unruly demons, but this is civilized land. There's no help for you this time, Coward Queen. The Eternal King's radiance shines on Earth as brightly as it does in Heaven, and it shall burn you to ash."

"Not if I burn you first," Bex said, gripping her smoking sword.

The prince said nothing. He just held out his hand to the kneeling princess. She took it with a worshipful smile, clutching his golden gauntlet with the white-gloved fingers of her right hand.

Vaguely, in the back of his mind, that struck Adrian as odd. He'd assumed the princess was left-handed, since that was the hand she'd done everything with, including nearly breaking his arm. But when the prince grabbed her fingers, the princess's delicate glove vanished like frost in the sun, and Adrian saw it.

The rest of her body might have been an ivory statue, but the princess's right hand was flesh and blood. It looked like it had been cut off of a completely different woman, one with dark skin and long, calloused fingers, one of which was wearing a large ring so glossy and black, the prince's golden light seemed to slide right off it.

It looked like a shinier, less worn-out version of Bex's ring. Adrian must not have been the only one who thought so, because the moment Bex's glowing eyes saw the princess's bare hand, her expression went from watchful caution to a mask of pure rage.

"*No!*" she screamed, shaking the ground as she launched herself at the kneeling princess. "*Don't you touch her!*"

But it was too late. The moment the prince tightened his golden hand around the princess's fleshy one, her kneeling body vanished, leaving the prince holding a pure white sword. It was broader than Drox, with a thick, curved blade that stopped Bex's charge like a wall, though not for long. The first attack had barely failed before Bex swung again, smoke pouring off her body as she spun around to sweep her sword into the prince's back.

As fast as she was, though, the prince was even faster. He blocked her easily, stopping Bex's sword with one hand while grabbing her with the other. Black blood splattered to the ground as his fingers bit into her shoulder, and then he threw her away with the force of a cannon shot. She was inches from crashing into Adrian's heart tree when she suddenly righted herself and kicked off it instead, launching back at the prince with a scream of fury.

The prince stopped that attack as easily as the others, but Bex just kept coming, flying at him over and over like a streak of black lightning. Her strikes were so fast and deadly and *beautiful* that Adrian was almost fooled into missing the fact that they weren't working. She wasn't on fire, and the prince was blocking everything she threw at him.

There was no way Bex could win like that. He had to help her, get her the fire or magic or whatever she needed to turn back into the burning queen he'd seen inside the bonfire. He was patting his bloody pockets to see what he had left when something snagged the collar of his coat.

Adrian looked up in surprise to see Boston's claws dragging him farther under his heart tree. His familiar was in his biggest form, making him look like a jaguar with the coat of a housecat, but his eyes were the same determined green as he hauled his witch toward the spot where his heart was buried.

"What are you doing?" Adrian hissed, digging his fingers into the needle-covered ground. "I can't go under now! I have to help Bex! She's—"

"The only thing you have to do is *be still*," Boston snarled, letting go of Adrian's coat. "You're bleeding, poisoned, and riddled with curses. The only reason you're still conscious is because your adrenalin is pumping through the roof, but you are absolutely going to die in the next few minutes if you don't stop and let your forest help you."

That was good sense as usual, but Adrian shook his head. "I can't," he pleaded, struggling to sit up. "Bex came to help me, and she's fighting them alone. I can't just—"

"Bex is a demon queen," Boston growled as he shoved his witch back down with a paw the size of a dinner plate. "She can take care of herself, but you are absolutely going to die like an *idiot* if you go out there again, and I'm not just talking about your wounds. That's a *Celestial Prince*, Adrian!"

"I know!" he cried. "That's why I have to—"

"No, you don't know," the familiar snapped as he dug his paws into the dirt and started burying Adrian in the ground. "You're high on endorphins and running on instinct, because if you were thinking at all clearly, you'd know this is an impossible situation. Helping Bex now will put us in direct defiance of Gilgamesh. Even the Old Wives of the Blackwood don't rebel against Heaven!"

"I know," Adrian said, pushing weakly against the dirt the cat was piling over his chest. "But Boston, she's going to *die.*"

"But you won't," Boston said, his green eyes stricken. "I'm sorry, Adrian."

He shoved a pile of dirt over Adrian's head. The forest's roots came up with it, wrapping around his body like terrified arms to yank him into the ground.

It was their fear that finally made Adrian stop struggling. He hadn't realized just how bad things had gotten until he was back in the cradle of the Blackwood's perception. His young forest was shuddering like a dying breath. Thanks to Bex and her demons, most of the warlocks were dead, but the curses had still taken their toll, and the princess had done more damage to his heart tree's roots than he'd realized when she'd ripped free.

Add his own injuries to the mix, and both Blackwoods were dangerously close to falling through death's door. If Adrian was going to save anyone, he had to pull them back from the brink, but he had nothing left to pull with. Every reserve he'd prepared had already been depleted. For the first time since he'd arrived in Seattle, his hands were completely empty, so Adrian reached for the only power he had left.

Clutching his shuddering forest to his chest, he flung his mind out desperately, picturing the hand that had beckoned to him when he'd asked the Blackwood to heal Bex. He envisioned every detail of that moment—the silence, the animals, the sting of the still-healing cut on his arm—until they felt as real as his own battered body. He had no neatly portioned sacrifices to offer this time, no pretty words. Just the fear of death and the desperate will to survive. Fortunately for him, those instincts were the strongest call. Just like before, he felt the weight of the Great Blackwood's attention as it settled on his tiny forest and even tinier life.

As it landed on top of him, Adrian felt for the first time what a minuscule portion he was of the greater whole.

309

He and his Blackwood together were but a single blade of grass, a hair-thin thread in the endless tapestry that was the Great Forest. This overwhelming smallness came with a strong dose of censure. The Great Blackwood was angry with him. He'd hurt his young forest, risked the web of lives placed in his care for his own benefit. It was not good witchcraft.

Adrian couldn't even speak to apologize. Boston had buried him too deeply. If he opened his mouth like this, all he'd get was dirt, but there was no need for words. The truth was in his heart, which had been buried here since the beginning.

Without hesitation, Adrian offered it up again. The same sacrifice twice bought nothing, so he asked the roots to rip his heart open. He helped them do it, reaching through their connection to tear the organ apart.

It hurt even more than when he'd dug his heart out the first time, but Adrian embraced the feeling. Pain like this was the essence of the present, the essence of his magic, and he used its power to paint a picture with his lifeblood so that the Great Blackwood could see the world as he did. See how much was at stake. Why he'd laid those curses despite knowing what they would do. Why he'd done this.

To be free.

Those words were the beats of his still-spasming heart. All he'd ever wanted was to be a witch. His earliest memory was seeing his mother at her cauldron. Even back then, he'd felt the power of her magic, its warmth and beauty. He'd wanted to feel that, too. To work his own magic and make his own miracles, but he was always being dragged away.

The warlocks, the princes, Gilgamesh himself—they were always trying to keep him from the most beautiful thing in the world. They'd hunted him, and so he'd fought back. Surely the Great Blackwood understood?

The forest did. It didn't speak in words, but Adrian got the clear image of a fox gnawing off its own leg to escape a trap. That pitiable act often resulted in the fox's death, but Adrian was not a fox, and he was not the only one who was trapped. All of the Blackwood's witches had been cornered, and cornered creatures fought back. Such was nature's way, but the Great Forest did not leave its witches to fight alone. The Blackwood did not approve of Adrian's methods, but it understood his heart. His sacrifice was accepted, and as he gave, so did he get.

All these feelings were still flowing through Adrian's head like a torrent when the roots pressed his heart back together. The organ was still ripped open, but the forest made up the difference, patching the torn flesh with fungal nets and tiny rootlings. His heart could never be dug up now. It—and he—was bound to this forest forever.

Adrian wouldn't have had it any other way. He threw himself into the magic with a laugh of pure joy. This was what he'd fought for. All his life, he'd been told that the heart of a witch was the forest and the heart of the forest was a witch, but he'd never understood, never known how *literally* true that was until this moment. This beautiful, never-to-be-repeated heartbeat of the present when he was his forest and his forest was him, and they were both wholly and truly Adrian Blackwood.

His forest's joy echoed his own. The curses were still biting, but Adrian and his woods were too big to feel them now. They were part of the larger Blackwood now in a way they hadn't been before, and the turning of that great cycle was already casting off the damage of the battle like a shed skin. *All* the damage, including Adrian's, regrowing his ruptured cells just as trees regrew their leaves, leaving him haler and healthier than he'd ever been. He felt like a green shoot surging toward the sunlight, but as he lifted his hands to dig himself back to the surface, something caught his neck. Something hard, crushing, and cold as the grave.

"Stop."

Adrian jolted. If he hadn't trained so hard not to, he would have opened his eyes and likely gotten a root through his cornea. Fortunately, the forest's magic was in every part of him now, flooding his brain with its own senses until the darkness behind his closed eyes became a low, circular cavern.

It looked like the inside of the Celtic burial mounds the Blackwood witches still used for their dead. A disturbing image since he was lying in the pit at the center where the corpse should be, but not the worst. The *worst* thing Adrian saw was the old woman standing over him.

Her cave-pale skin was as wrinkled as a crone's, and her thick braided hair was bone-white. Her gnarled hands clutched a staff carved into the same raven as Bran, only hers wasn't a broomstick, and it wasn't made of wood. This raven was carved from a single piece of time-bleached bone, the handle of a scythe, whose curved blunt end was pressed hard into the soft flesh of Adrian's throat.

"Hello, nephew."

"Aunt Lydia," Adrian said, swallowing against the press of her scythe. "What are you doing here?"

"Saving your life," the old witch replied coldly, glaring down at him with furious blue eyes that looked just like his mother's. "Boston called out through the roots in a panic. He said you were half-dead and fighting a prince.

Naturally, I came as fast as I could, but when I arrived, what did I find? *You* looking hale as a spring colt with your heart stitched into the Blackwood's taproots."

She paused like she expected him to apologize. When Adrian didn't, she lifted her scythe from his neck with a curse.

"What do you think you're doing?" the old witch demanded, scowling at Adrian like he was an apprentice caught with his hand in the hexes. "You make your sapling forest rotten with curses, and then, when the Great Blackwood repairs the damage from the inevitable consequences of your shortsighted decisions, you decide to waste your miracle by going back for more?"

"That's not what happened," Adrian argued, sitting up in his grave. "The warlocks attacked, so I fought back. Thanks to the Blackwood, I'm *still* fighting back." He fisted his hands in the dirt. "I did use curses, but this is what I left the forest to do, Aunt, and the Blackwood is on my side."

"Of course it's your side," Aunt Lydia snapped. "You couldn't be a witch if it wasn't. But the Blackwood makes decisions with its heart, not its head. That's what we're for. We're supposed to be the forest's protectors, not the ones shoving it into danger."

Adrian shook his head. "We can't defend forever."

"Of course we can," Lydia said. "What do you think we've been doing for the past several thousand years?"

Adrian was opening his mouth to keep arguing when Aunt Lydia's scythe swooped in front of his nose.

"No," the old witch said in a grave-cold voice. "No more back talk. This experiment of yours is over."

"But—"

The scythe got closer. "I did not watch my sister beg on her knees for your life to stand back and let you throw it away."

"I'm not throwing anything away," Adrian said angrily, shoving the scythe out of his face. "I'm fighting back, because I believe a mother shouldn't have to beg for her child's life. You say you've defended the Blackwood for thousands of years, but you give Gilgamesh whatever he wants! That's not defending. That's capitulating."

Aunt Lydia narrowed her piercing eyes. "We sacrifice for the good of the forest."

"You sacrificed *me*!" Adrian roared, chest heaving. He hadn't even realized how angry he was until the words burst out, ripping through him with twelve years of repressed fury.

"Ever since the Blackwood moved to the New World, you've been giving up our boy children to the warlocks," he snarled. "We were your bribery, the price you paid to buy their *permission* so our magic could keep existing, but are we not part of the forest, too? How can you say you're defending the Blackwood when you're selling its children to Gilgamesh?"

"Adrian," Lydia said in a warning voice, but he didn't heed it.

"It's wrong, Aunt," he said as he pushed to his feet, "and you know it. The only reason I wasn't forced to grow up a warlock is because my mother didn't think like you. She fought for me!"

"And put the entire Blackwood under siege in the process."

"How is that her fault?" Adrian demanded. "You think I don't notice how many Blackwood witches—my *sisters*—said I should be thrown back to appease them? At least my mother believed in me."

"Your mother loves you," Aunt Lydia corrected bitterly. "She's done many stupid things for love."

"I don't count twelve years of apprenticeship as stupid," Adrian said in a deadly voice. "My mother didn't fight for my life so I could spend it hiding behind trees. She taught me to be a witch, just like you, but unlike you, I'm done appeasing."

Lydia stared at him for a long moment, her blue eyes shining like witchlights in the dark tomb. Then she leaned on her scythe, sighing like the old woman she was.

"You think you're the first to say those words? Do you know how many brave witches I've watched break themselves against the fist of Gilgamesh?" She shook her gray head. "Countless. *Countless* sisters have stood where you are now and told me they were done, and every single one of them died. So many lost, and all for nothing." Her eyes flicked back to him like icy blue knives. "What makes you think you're better?"

"Not better," Adrian said. "Different."

His face broke into a smile as he reached out to touch the hands she'd wrapped around her scythe. "It's different this time, Aunt. The Queen of Wrath is back, and she's on our side! With the help of her and her demons, my forest and I fought the Spider and all his warlocks, and we *won*. The Blackwood's greatest enemy is dead! You can't say that's for nothing."

"But what of the prince?" his aunt challenged, flicking her eyes pointedly at the tomb's root-filled ceiling. "I can feel him up there through your forest. He has the power of Heaven on his side. You can't hope to—"

"I can absolutely hope to," Adrian interrupted. "Bex has killed princes before. She'll kill this one too, I know it."

"And what about the next prince?" Lydia demanded. "Or the prince after that? One victory doesn't win a war, Adrian. A king like Gilgamesh cannot tolerate defiance, and unlike you, his resources are infinite. It doesn't matter how many of his weapons you break. He always has more, and eventually, they will kill you."

"So I should just lie down and do the job for him?" Adrian yelled. "There's no obvious way to win, so I shouldn't even try? Is that what you're saying?"

"I'm saying you should survive," Aunt Lydia argued, letting go of her scythe at last to grip his hand. "That's what Blackwoods do. We dig in. We endure. We regrow. Even if we are felled, we grow back from our severed stumps. That is the power of the forest, *our* power." She patted his fingers. "A witch of the Blackwood should understand that."

"Oh, I understand," Adrian said, removing his hand from hers. "I just don't agree. Just because we can grow back doesn't mean we should wait passively while they cut us down. The Blackwood is more than trees. It's also the cornered animal who fights for its life, the mother bird who fakes injury to draw predators away from its nest, the snake that still bites even after its head is severed. The forest taught me that when it *gave me back my heart,* and I will not ignore its lessons to satisfy your fear."

"Fear is the product of experience," the old witch growled, straightening back to her full height as she lifted her scythe again. "And I was not offering you a choice. You made a good stand, Adrian. Better than I expected, but the time for heroics is over."

Adrian took a step back, but his aunt's hand shot out, grabbing his shoulder like a bony hook.

"No," she said, gripping him hard. "No more defiance. Your mother isn't the only one who loves you. I also refuse to lose any more of my family to Gilgamesh, which means you're coming home."

"I won't," Adrian said, fighting against her hold. "I *can't*. My heart is bound here!"

"Heart trees can be replanted," Lydia reminded him. "That's how we moved the Blackwood to the Americas, and your tree is much smaller than—"

"I'm not moving my tree!" Adrian cried, fighting harder. "I didn't do all of this to just give up!"

"You're not giving up," his aunt said, her voice growing gentle even as her fingers dug into his shoulder. "You're doing what you must to keep living, just like the rest of us. There's no shame in that. You did your best, child, but it's time to go."

"I'm not a child," Adrian said, ripping his coat to break out of her hold at last. "And I'm not running."

"That's not your decision to make."

Adrian froze. Lydia's voice was the coldest it had been yet, because with those words, she was no longer speaking to him as his aunt. The woman he faced now was the Old Wife of the Bones, Witch of the Past, Eldest of the Three, and she was done being patient.

"Adrian Blackwood," she said, pointing her scythe at his chest, "by your vows to the Blackwood coven, I order you to cease all action and return to the central grove. You will cut your ties with the Coward Queen and her doomed crusade, and you are forbidden from setting foot outside of your mother's forest until we can convince the Eternal King that you were an ignorant child who had no idea whom he was helping."

The whole tomb was shaking by the time she finished. If this had happened two months ago, that would have been the end, but Adrian was no longer an apprentice. He was a witch in his own right, standing in his own forest, and he would not be dictated to.

"I will do no such thing," he said, planting his feet on the grave's dirt floor, which was suddenly full of roots. "My vows were sworn to the Blackwood, not to you. This is *my* forest grown from *my* heart, and I will not abandon it."

"Don't do this, Adrian," the Old Wife warned, gripping her scythe. "Don't challenge me."

"Then stop forcing me to!" Adrian cried, reaching out to her one last time. "Can't you see what's happening? You've become so obsessed with protecting the Blackwood that you've ended up doing Gilgamesh's work for him. The Eternal King doesn't have to crush us. We've crushed ourselves, hiding like mice under our roots and giving him whatever he asks. Of course he hasn't bothered to conquer us. We act like his servants already!"

"You think I don't realize that?" Lydia hissed. "I'm the Witch of the Past. I know exactly how far we've fallen, and I hate it more than you ever could. I've felt everything you're feeling, but unlike you, I don't have the luxury of engaging in false hope."

"What part of it is false?" Adrian demanded. "The Blackwood's the one who restored the Queen of Wrath. If our forest is strong enough to bring back the daughter of a goddess, why can't we fight? We're the force of nature, not Gilgamesh!"

"You only say that because you grew up in the shelter of the forest," Lydia snarled. "A shelter *we* sacrificed to make for you! You have no idea what Gilgamesh is capable of. There's a reason no one has rebelled against him in five thousand years."

"That doesn't mean we shouldn't try," Adrian said, lifting his chin. "All my life, you've taught me about the cycles, but the first rule of every cycle is that nothing stands forever, not even the Eternal King. The Blackwood knows that. That's why it's helping me. That's why it restored Bex. It wants this to end. *I* want it to end!"

Just like his anger before, Adrian didn't realize how true those words were until he said them. He'd thought Bex was crazy when she'd told him she was going to war with Gilgamesh, but now he understood. They'd *always* been at war. Gilgamesh was the reason all of this was happening. It didn't matter how many warlocks Adrian killed or how big his forest became. He would *never* be free so long as Gilgamesh was king. None of them would—not his coven, not the demons, nobody—and if fixing that wasn't worth his life, Adrian didn't know what was.

"I'm not leaving," he said fiercely. "I refuse your summons and your logic. It's not hopeless, because this isn't like all those times in the past. It's now." He planted his feet on the roots of his forest, which now filled the entire tomb. "This is *my* time, Lydia. My present to make into the future *I* want, and you will not take it from me."

The fury was still flashing in his aunt's eyes when Adrian slammed his forest into her. He did it as hard as he could, because the Old Wife of the Bones was the toughest of all of them. Her roots ran deeper than any others in the Blackwood, but as far as her reach extended, this was not her grove. It was *his* Blackwood, *his* land, and Adrian shoved her out of it, slamming the door of his magic on her so hard, he felt the impact all the way to the tops of his trees.

The echo made him wince. Aunt Lydia would be furious when she landed, but Adrian couldn't let her stop him, nor was he mad that she'd tried. She was the Witch of the Past. It was her duty to remember and warn, but the present existed to *do*, so Adrian did, lifting his hands so that the roots of the forest—*his* forest—could pull him back to the surface.

Chapter 17

Bex couldn't remember being so angry in her life. She knew she must have hit this level at least once before when she'd fought the prince in Limbo, but she couldn't remember. Now, though, Bex didn't know if she'd ever be able to erase the image of the princess's hand—her sister's beautiful, familiar hand stapled to that *thing*—from her mind.

She'd known it the instant she saw it. There'd been no other details, like which sister she was, or what she'd looked like, or what her name had been, but Bex had known to her bones that that hand belonged to a daughter of Ishtar just like her. It had been cut off, *stolen,* and stuck on that fawning ivory doll so this undeserving man could wield a queen's sword. They'd turned a Blade of Ishtar into a Blade of Gilgamesh, turned a goddess's divine weapon against her own people, and so long as Bex had a breath in her body, she was going to make them *pay.*

"Look at you," the prince sneered, barely moving his sword as he deflected her wild strikes. "Charging like an animal. No skill, no thought, no tactics." He shook his head with a tsk. "It's no wonder your kind are slaves."

She flew at him with a scream, swinging her black blade at his head, his armor, anything she could reach, but she couldn't touch him. The prince moved as fast as thought, his white sword like a wall no matter where she struck.

Rebexa, stop! Drox yelled. *He's baiting you. Calm down.*

Bex didn't want to calm down. All her life, she'd been swallowing this fury. Her body might not be on fire, but her mind was consumed with it, which made no sense. Why wasn't she burning? Wasn't this what she was made for? To be the Queen of Wrath?

Wrath is the poison the great Ishtar created you to cleanse, Drox told her patiently. *It's what you were made to burn, not to be, and unless you stop drowning yourself in it, you will lose.*

Easy for him to say. Drox was the true immortal. He actually remembered all this crap, but Bex had never felt more lost in her life. This battle was supposed to be her big comeback, the chance she'd traded all her future lives for, but she hadn't managed so much as a candle flame since she'd stepped out of the bonfire. What was the point of all that sacrifice if her stupid magic wouldn't work when she needed it to? Now this damn prince was going to kill all of them, and the vaunted Queen of Wrath couldn't do a damn thing.

"To the Hells with this," Bex snarled, jumping back to buy herself some room as she lifted her sword in front of her face. "*Drox!* Name me! If I can't get the fire going on my own, then we'll have to force it to—"

No, her sword snarled, nearly twisting out of her hand. *No shortcuts, not this time. You're the one who decided to risk everything on one last life. You will become a queen capable of winning that gamble, or you will die.*

Bex stared at her blade in shock, and then she swung it at the prince with a roar that shook the ground. Damn him, damn him, *damn him!* Drox was *her* sword! He supposed to help her, not—

I am *helping you,* Drox said coldly, settling hard into her palm. *Blades are forged in fire, Rebexa.*

Bex would *love* some fire. Any fire, because she couldn't do this again. Her body was stronger than she could ever remember it being, but her hits still bounced off

322

the prince's guard like pebbles off a mountain. She kept swinging anyway, but the grief was already climbing up from her guts to latch around her throat.

She was losing. Adrian's miracle, the loss of her reincarnations—it hadn't changed anything. She was still too weak to win. Her lungs were already heaving, and the prince hadn't even attacked her yet. He was just standing there, blocking and smirking like a damn—

Quick as a whip, the prince smacked the top of her sword hand, knocking Drox from her fingers. He let go of his own weapon and grabbed Bex's throat next, using his superior height—the same damn height the stupid forest magic hadn't thought she needed—to dangle her in front of him like a snared rabbit.

"Is that all you've got?" he asked, his handsome face disappointed. "The famous Coward Queen, nothing but a flailing child." He tilted his head. "What happened to the monster I fought in Limbo? At least that was a battle worthy of Heaven's attention. This farce barely merits the trip down."

He flashed her a smile, his mirror eyes reflecting her own choking face as he threw her to the ground. She landed hard on her back with a gasp, but when she called her dropped sword back to her hand to take a swing at him, the prince's golden boot landed on her wrist. He stomped his other boot on her neck a second later, crushing her windpipe as he leaned over her with a smirk.

"This is the point where you surrender," he told her in a conspiratorial whisper.

Bex couldn't speak with his boot on her throat, so she bared her fangs instead.

The prince laughed at the sight. "None of that," he chided, pressing down harder. "The time for defiance is over. There's nowhere left to run, so act like a queen for once in your miserable existence, and bow before your king. Give up your name and your sword just like your sisters did, and your wrath demons shall finally be brought out of exile to take their place among my father's slaves."

The anger that roared up inside Bex then was like nothing she'd ever felt. She didn't care about the boot on her neck. She didn't care that she'd already lost. She would *die* before she surrendered to this filth. All of them would. Her people were in Limbo because even after she'd fallen, not a single wrath demon had bowed to Gilgamesh. She would not be the first. She would die here on her back before she gave anything to that thieving, murdering, *fake* of a king.

The resolve was still clenching like a fist inside her when Bex felt something spark. It wasn't her anger—*that* had been roaring full blast for a while now—but at some point in the last few seconds, the direction had changed. All this time, in her training and in her fight with the prince, Bex had been furious over what she couldn't do: couldn't burn, couldn't change, couldn't win. She'd been drowning in it just like Drox had said, but all that impotent fury wasn't getting her anywhere. It was just a sloshing ocean, a swamp dragging her down, but the moment she'd dug in and said she *wouldn't,* all that anger had gone somewhere new, somewhere useful. It fed into her like a fuel into a furnace, and as it hit, fire flared up inside her bright as the sun.

Now you see, Drox said as the flames overwhelmed her. *Rage is useless, a knife with no handle that's as likely to cut yourself as the enemy, but wrath is directed. It has choice, intention. Rage is a poison, but wrath is a sword.* Your *sword.*

"You could have told me earlier," Bex whispered.

I did tell you, Drox said irritably as his blade started to smoke in her pinned hand. *Though I don't know why I bothered. You never were one to learn anything until you tripped over it for yourself.*

If the situation had been any less deadly, Bex would have laughed. Great Ishtar, what an idiot she was. Even the prince had called her out on it. She *had* been flailing like a child, a blind mass of anger lashing out in all directions. No wonder she couldn't hit anything. But if Bex took that same rage and gave it purpose—reached beyond the petty swamp of *her* shame, *her* loss, how *she* couldn't win—everything changed. Fury was no longer the forest she was lost in. It was the fuel for her fire, and with so much kindling built up inside her, all it took was a spark.

The prince must have seen it happening. He barely leaped off her in time before the bonfire Bex had been chasing for the past ten days roared back up like it had never left. Bex roared with it, breathing the fire hotter as the towering flames consumed her. They burned away her tiredness, burned away her fear. Burned away everything that was not the Bonfire of Wrath.

Excellent, Drox said in a satisfied voice. *Now, we may begin.*

Bex responded by swinging her sword in a smoking arc. The flames were so high and bright that she could no longer see her own body. It must have looked terrifying, because the prince—who hadn't done anything except sneer and block before this point—fell into a defensive crouch. He'd barely gotten his sword into position before Rebexa launched straight at him.

This wasn't like her wild charges earlier. She flew at him like a flaming arrow, straight and precise with her thin black sword already positioned to slide beneath the prince's guard. Even with his divine speed, he was barely fast enough to block her. His white sword caught her black one

325

by a razor's edge, sliding the strike to the side rather than stopping it cold. The burning queen smiled at his fear and tried another angle, leaping straight up and over his blade for a chop at the top of his skull.

The prince wasn't ready for such a high strike from a shorter opponent, but his sword was. The white blade moved in his hands of its own accord, flying up to protect its prince's head.

The raw fury at seeing her sister's hand forced to guard her slaver's son nearly knocked Bex out of the flames. But every second she spent burning gave her more control. She caught the slip in time and focused her wrath for another swing, this time at the prince's legs.

It was a good strike, but the prince was getting the hang of her new speed now, and he'd committed himself fully to defense. Bex was faster than he was in this form, but the prince was still taller, and his sword was wider, heavier, and determined to keep him safe. Together, they formed a wall that she and Drox couldn't break no matter where they struck.

After the tenth failed strike, Bex backed off with a glare. She needed to trick the prince into giving her an opening. The easiest way would be to bait him into an attack, but that only worked if Bex was fast enough to hit him and get out again before she got stabbed. A pretty big gamble since her speed only beat the prince's by a hair, but she wasn't getting anywhere like this.

There was nothing for it but to try, so Bex surged forward, swinging wildly at the prince just like she had at the beginning. She made sure to leave her sides open as bait, but though the golden bastard blocked every attack with room to spare, he never struck back. Even when Bex gave him a clear shot at her torso, he did nothing but defend, letting his sword do all the work while his body stayed perfectly still, almost as if he were afraid to move.

He was waiting for her to get tired, Bex realized with a jolt. While she darted around looking for an opening, he was conserving his energy, waiting for her to exhaust herself so he could butcher her at his leisure.

Once she realized what he was planning, Bex switched tactics. She didn't stop attacking, but she did stop moving around so much, fighting the prince head-on instead of circling for an opening. His defense was even more solid from the front, but nothing Bex did got through anyway, so she gave up trying to slip past his guard and just focused on keeping him busy.

While his mirrored eyes were on her sword, Bex focused on her newfound control. If she was the bonfire and anger was her fuel, then she should be able to reduce her burn by calming herself down. That was a lot easier now that she was making progress, so Bex pulled the logs of her fury off one by one, lowering her bonfire little by little until her flames were barely higher than her skin.

She slowed her swings at the same time, letting her arms drag as if her sword were growing heavy. It was difficult going—Bex had never been much of an actress, and holding back went against wrath's nature—but she wanted this badly enough that she forced herself to swallow it, squeezing her anger and playing at exhaustion until, at last, the prince took the bait.

He switched his style without warning, turning his white sword mid-block to slide over Drox for a stab at Bex's neck. She dodged out of the way in a flash, switching her own sword to one hand while she poured the anger she'd been keeping at bay into the other. The result was an eruption of white-hot flames in her empty palm, which was already flying at the prince's now-unguarded torso. She curled her hand into a fist at the last second, slamming her full-burn strength into his armored stomach.

The combination of force and heat threw the prince across the clearing. He would have slammed straight through a cluster of oaks on the other side if Bex hadn't gotten there first. As satisfying as it would have been to watch the prince crash, she wasn't about to let this bastard hurt Adrian's trees. She snagged his metal boot at the last second, digging her heels into the dirt to whirl the prince around and slam him into the ground instead.

He landed hard enough to make a crater. It didn't look like she'd broken any big bones, but something must have cracked, because the prince rolled over and started coughing up a white substance. For a moment, Bex was smug that she'd made the fancy golden prince barf. She was about to kick him in the face to add injury to insult when she realized the white stuff wasn't coming from his stomach.

It was his *blood*.

The chill that went through Bex then almost snuffed her fire. She'd always heard the Celestial Princes were Gilgamesh's actual children. That was why they were treated like miniature kings, but this prince didn't bleed like a human. The glowing white stuff dripping from his mouth and various other spots beneath his dented armor was liquid *quintessence*. He was bleeding pure magic, leaking it all over the ground. It had just started to form a shimmering pool around his knees when the prince gripped his sword and rasped, "Return me."

The blade obeyed at once, spinning in his hand like a spool winding up thread. His quintessence blood followed the motion, flowing back up into his body like a waterfall in reverse, and as it returned, the prince's injuries vanished. All of them.

Color returned to his face. His ragged breaths grew smooth and easy again. Even his dented armor popped back into shape. When it was over, the only evidence left that Bex had touched him was the crater on the ground. She was still staring in horror when the prince began to laugh.

"I never get tired of seeing that look," he said, squinting at her face. "Though your flames do make it difficult. I suppose that's why you're called the Bonfire of Wrath."

He paused to let her answer. When she didn't, the prince shrugged and moved on.

"I look forward to adding your fire to our collection. Ishtar's daughters all have such useful powers. Take mine, for instance."

"She's not yours," Bex snarled as her flames whipped higher. "You have no right to that sword, you *thief*!"

"I have every right," the prince replied, holding up his blade. "The right of conquest, the right of superior strength, the divine right of Heaven. By all these rights and more, this is my sword, a Blade of Gilgamesh, though you might remember it belonging to one who was once called the Queen of Greed."

Bex froze, waiting for the name to trigger a face, a memory, anything. As ever, though, all she got was a blank.

"Greed is a fine sin," the prince drawled on, ignoring her. "Her sword tolerates nothing to be stolen, not even life. You could dice me to pieces, and my beautiful princess would put me right back together without losing a drop of—"

"*Shut up!*" Bex roared, flying at him with her own sword. "Don't you dare speak about my sister like she's yours, you filthy—"

She cut off with a pained gasp when the prince lunged forward, turning Bex's own enraged charge against her as he stabbed his white sword into her stomach. He would have run her through if Bex hadn't turned at the last second, sliding her body along the blade instead of into it. The save still earned her a huge gash across her middle as she staggered sideways, painting the dirt with black blood that instantly started to boil from her heat.

If the prince was upset that he hadn't killed her, he didn't let it show. He just stepped back into his defensive position and motioned for her to come at him again.

Bex wasn't falling for the same trick twice. She was mad enough he'd baited her into such a dumb charge the first time. Her whole body was pulsing from the wound in her stomach, which wasn't knitting back together even though she'd shrugged off every other injury since Adrian's bonfire had let her go. The cut should have been closing before her eyes, but her skin hung open beneath her dancing flames, the boiling black blood gushing down her legs in a very familiar fashion.

Bex didn't know why she'd expected anything else. This new wound was much bigger than her old one, but it came from the exact same source. Even if it had once been her sister's, the prince's sword was a Blade of Gilgamesh now, and wounds from those never healed. That put Bex at an extreme disadvantage, because while she was bleeding out faster than her blood could boil away, the prince didn't even look winded from putting himself back together.

You can't let him hit you again, Drox warned. Very unnecessarily, Bex felt. *You have to finish this quickly, wound him in a way his sword can't repair.*

"I'm open to suggestions," she muttered, pressing one hand against her stomach to keep her wound together while gripping her sword with the other.

Take off his head?

Too obvious. Also dangerous, because the prince was as tall as Adrian. Swinging up as far as she needed to cut his neck would leave Bex's entire body open. A pointless risk since she was pretty sure the prince's sword would just rewind his head right back into place.

No beheadings, then, but she had to do *something*. Thanks to Adrian's healing fire, she was strong enough now that the wound in her stomach wasn't killing her immediately, but she could feel herself getting weaker with every pint of blood she lost. If she didn't act fast, the prince wouldn't need to hit her again. He could just sit there and keep blocking until she bled to death.

That seemed to be his plan, actually. But when Bex looked down to gauge how much time she had left, the steam rising from her wound as her fire boiled her blood away gave her an idea.

That could work, Drox said as he read the plan from her mind. *But it risks much.*

"No risk, no reward," Bex said, positioning her feet.

Indeed, the sword replied with a bloodthirsty chuckle. *Just make sure you don't miss.*

Bex didn't even let herself think about it as she darted forward. The prince raised his sword to block as usual, but Bex didn't strike him with her weapon. Just before her black blade would have landed, she pulled Drox

331

back into his ring and grabbed the prince's sword with her bare hands.

The white blade cut deep into her palms. It would have cut clean through them, but Bex moved with the strike, following the prince's angle as he tried to slice down. When she'd followed the sword to its lowest point and the blow had been thoroughly spoiled, Bex pulled down with her left hand and let go with her right, reaching over the prince's sword to tap her fingers against his stomach just above his golden belt.

There was no strength in the hit this time. She wasn't trying to punch the prince across the clearing again. All Bex cared about was getting inside his guard. The second her hand was in position, she transformed her ring back into a sword, shooting the black blade out like a spear to skewer the prince straight through his intestines.

His gasp of pain made her grin. Even if you could put yourself back together, gut wounds *hurt*. From the stricken look on his face, the prince definitely felt it. He was already swinging his sword back up to cut her off, but he couldn't get a good angle. The moment he'd moved his weapon, Bex had snuggled even closer, wrapping her left arm around the prince's back to lock their bodies together like lovers as she burst into white-hot flames.

The intensity of the heat surprised even her. She'd poured all the righteous anger she had into this, focusing on his callousness toward her stolen sister, on how he'd ordered her to surrender so his father could turn her demons into slaves. There was so much she hated about this man, but rather than letting the wrongs overwhelm her, Bex took each one and threw it onto the fire of her wrath.

The result was a focused fury that burned like a cutting torch. The prince screamed in her embrace, dropping his sword in a desperate attempt to pry Bex off of him, but every part of her was a blast furnace now, and he couldn't get a grip. Her heat melted his golden armor like butter wherever they touched, but her real target—the real victory—was his blood.

Pressed up against his chest, Bex could *hear* the prince's quintessence boiling inside his chest. It hissed and popped inside his veins, leaving him screaming while his sword tried desperately to heal him. It'd turned back into its female form the moment he dropped it, but though the Princess of Gilgamesh was as strong as a tank, she was no more heatproof than her prince. Less so, actually, because she was carved from ivory. Where the prince's golden armor melted and his flesh cooked, her body shattered, the beautiful carvings blackening and splitting like bones in a blast furnace.

She still fought to the very end. Sobbing and wailing, the princess tried to pry Bex off with her splinters. The prince's armor was a river of molten gold by this point, but Bex didn't dare let go. She just kept burning, pushing hotter and hotter until nothing was left but ashes, slagged gold, blackened ivory, and a woman's dark-skinned hand, lying untouched on the ground.

Bex dived for it at once. For a beautiful moment, she felt her sister's warm, living skin against her burning fingertips. But just as she was about to snatch the hand into her own, a blast of sound crashed into the clearing like a meteor.

It was a bell. A great golden bell ringing loud enough to make her ears bleed. The sound waves went through her like punches, knocking her sister's hand out of her grasp. Bex was scrambling back to it when another hand appeared.

It came out of nowhere, materializing from of the sound itself. It was large and masculine with dark, golden-tanned skin. Each of the strong, thick fingers was decorated with golden rings, but it was clearly a warrior's hand, thick-calloused and crisscrossed with fine white scars from a life of battle. It reached unhurriedly through air, plucking the queen's hand from the ashes like a jeweler picking up a delicate piece of filigree. It vanished immediately after, disappearing as suddenly as it had arrived to leave Bex grasping at nothing.

"*No!*" she screamed, pawing frantically at the blackened dirt, but it was too late. Her sister's hand was gone, and though her enemies were burned to crisps around her, all Bex felt was loss.

Why are you so upset? Drox asked. *You knew he had them.*

Not like this. Bex had seen the queens kneeling in Gilgamesh's Anchor statues, but she'd always assumed he kept them bound in chains or locked in cells, something she could rescue them from. She knew she must have seen the truth the first time she'd killed the prince in Limbo, but Bex couldn't remember anything from the end of that fight, and she was starting to worry this was why. What had that mad king *done* to her sisters? And how could Bex possibly rescue them from it when she couldn't even save one hand?

The wave of hopelessness that followed that thought was almost enough to snuff her out. Back when Bex had done crazy things like plan attacks on Heaven, her first objective had always been to free the other queens. Not only were they her family, the queens were how Gilgamesh controlled his slave population. Without them, warlocks couldn't name or control their demons, not to mention every queen she freed would be as strong as Bex herself.

Probably stronger, since they hadn't been ground down by constant reincarnations.

That was what she'd always assumed, anyway. Now, though, Bex had no idea. Even if she made it back to Paradise, Gilgamesh had cut her sisters to pieces. Could she find them all? Put them back together? And if so, would their minds still be intact? The princess she'd fought hadn't sounded sane, but was she still the Queen of Greed or just an empty doll made to hold a sword?

Bex didn't know, and that terrified her. She'd always been so sure that if she could just get to her sisters, they could win. They would kill Gilgamesh, restore the rivers of Ishtar, free their people, and set everything right. Even when she'd had no hope of it ever happening, at least she'd known what to do. In the heady hour after Adrian had restored her fire, she'd really thought they had a chance, but now...

Now...

Bex collapsed into the ashes, scattering the shattered bones and slagged gold. She'd been so naive. How had she ever thought she could beat something as big as Heaven? It'd taken her hottest fire just to burn one prince, and he wouldn't even stay dead. There'd always be another and another and *another*, but she only had one life left in her. There was no way Bex could collect all the parts of her sisters against odds like that. It was impossible. Even with her restored fire, she would never—

Her downward spiral stumbled to a halt as the ground beneath her face began to change. Bex jerked herself up, scrambling back to her still-flaming knees as the blasted-out crater she'd been lying in suddenly filled with a carpet of bright green grass and tiny purple flowers.

It was all like that. All around the torn-up clearing where she'd fought the prince, the trees were growing taller, their roots spreading like streams through the soil. Bright new leaves replaced dull old ones, turning what had been a dim, gloomy forest into a riot of green-dappled sunlight.

Bex sat back on her heels in amazement. When she'd gone out to stop the warlocks an hour ago, the Blackwood had been as dark and forbidding as its name. Now, it looked like an entirely different forest. The trees were bigger and brighter, their trunks covered in tufts of electric-green moss that glowed like jewels in the hazy sunlight. Pools that had been stagnant holes designed to suck men to their deaths were now clear ponds filled with frogs and salamanders. Mice hid among the knotted roots, birds called in the canopy, squirrels quarreled in the branches, and the drone of insects was everywhere.

She had no idea where the changes were coming from, but the forest was suddenly so full of life that Bex could feel it with every sense. Even the air tasted like water and loam, filling her lungs with soothing coolness. She was sucking in a deep breath just for the pleasure of it when a familiar voice called out behind her.

"You won!"

Bex whirled around, nearly losing her balance in the process. All the blood she'd lost must have made her loopy, because that was Adrian jogging toward the edge of her crater, and he looked just as changed as everything else.

He still looked like himself: same handsome smiling face, same bright blue-gray eyes, same curling dark hair under the same black hat. But while his clothing sported several alarmingly bloody new holes, the olive skin beneath was whole and positively glowing with health. Looking at him was like seeing all of summer condensed into a person.

It made Bex feel small and dirty by comparison, a sad little fire about to gutter out.

That thought made her even more depressed. She was about to apologize and slink away when Adrian crouched down beside her and reached out to touch her face.

"Don't!" she cried, jerking out of his reach. "I'll burn you."

"You won't burn me," he said with his usual absurd confidence, closing the distance to press his hand against her burning cheek. Bex squeezed her eyes shut as it happened, but Adrian didn't cry out in pain. He just brushed his thumb over the ridge of her cheekbone to wipe away the sizzling tears she hadn't realized she'd shed.

"How am I not hurting you?" she whispered in awe.

"Because you're the Bonfire of Wrath," Adrian replied with a grin. "I'm pretty sure that means you only burn things you're mad at."

Bex supposed that made sense, but... "How did you know that?"

"Because you're not burning the grass," he said, pointing at where her flaming knees were buried in a thick carpet of new, healthy growth.

"Even if I was wrong, I still would've done it," he continued with a wink. "A little burn would be nothing to make you stop crying."

Bex stared at him in bewilderment, then she lowered her head. "I'm sorry," she whispered, not caring if that was a word queens didn't say. "This was all my fault. They never would have sent a prince if I hadn't been here. It's my—"

"This was *not* your fault," Adrian told her sternly. "Not to ding your royal ego, but the princess came down because I killed the Spider. Not because of you."

"Oh," she said, blinking as she processed that. Then she shook her head. "It doesn't matter. I still killed him, which means you're going to take the blame. I said I'd defend you until your forest could stand on its own, but no one stands against the princes. It took the hottest fire I had just to burn that one, but he'll be back soon enough. They're just going to keep coming and coming, and I can't... I don't..."

She didn't know what to do. Bex was the queen, the one who was supposed to win the war and fix everything, but she no longer knew how. It all just felt so hopeless. She was already sinking back into her crater when Adrian wrapped his arms around her.

"It's okay," he whispered, hugging her gently. "It's okay, Bex."

She froze at the contact, going stiff in his arms. Then, like a bursting dam, Bex collapsed against him, burying her face in Adrian's shoulder as she began to cry.

"How can you say that?" she sobbed, clinging to his coat. "Gilgamesh can't let anyone involved in the death of a prince get away. He's going to hunt you forever now."

"I think that was inevitable," Adrian said quietly.

"I'm supposed to be paying you back," Bex went on. "I'm supposed to be fixing things, but I barely won that fight. If the princes ever show up in pairs, I won't be enough to stop them." She started crying harder. "How am I supposed to take back all of Paradise if I can't fight the enemy unless they come at me one at a time?"

"I don't know," Adrian said, squeezing her tighter. "But we'll figure it out."

Bex pressed her face into his coat.. "How can you be so sure?"

"Because they threw their worst at us today, and we still won," he said, pushing her off him so that she could see his grin. "We *won*, Bex! Heaven threw a killing blow at us today, and it *didn't work*. The warlocks didn't drag me away. They didn't destroy my forest. And when a prince came down to finish the job, you burned him to ash. All the armies of Gilgamesh could fall on our heads tomorrow, and it wouldn't change the fact that we did what was supposed to be impossible. We stood up against the Eternal King today, and if we did it once, we can do it again."

"Are you out of your mind?" Bex cried, pointing at the crater they were crouching in. "You didn't see how close that fight was! If I'd been just a little bit slower, I'd be dead right now. For *real* dead."

"But you aren't," Adrian told her proudly. "You beat that prince, and when the next one shows up, you'll do even better, because I'll be there to help."

She stared at him in confusion. "Why would you do that?"

"Because I'm joining your fight," he said, sitting back on his heels with a purposeful look.

"Demons aren't the only ones Gilgamesh has stepped on. My coven used to be part of a rich druidic tradition that spanned all of Europe. Now the Blackwoods are the only groves left. The warlocks do his dirty work, but Gilgamesh is the real reason witches are afraid to come out of the forest. He's wiped out every other magical tradition and does everything he can to stop new ones from forming. This world is rich with magic, but every human on the planet is born with scales in their eyes that keep them from seeing it *because of him*." His fingers curled into fists on his knees. "He's hurt all of us, Bex, and I'm done rolling over for it."

"I get that," she said. "Believe me, I do, but..." She lowered her head. "He's so *strong*."

"So are we," Adrian said, ducking down to look at her. "So are *you*. Gilgamesh might be a king now, but he was a man once."

"A man who killed the gods."

"Exactly!" Adrian agreed with a grin. "If an ancient human could conquer all of Paradise using Bronze Age weaponry, surely we've got a chance."

Bex heaved a long sigh, which for some reason only made Adrian's smile bigger.

"I know it sounds crazy," he admitted, sitting up again. "I thought you were crazy, too, when you said you were going to fight him, but you were right. You were *right*, Bex. I know that now, so it doesn't matter if Gilgamesh puts me on his prince-killer wanted list, because from here on out, I'm fighting with you. Whatever he throws next, we'll beat it together. You don't have to fight him alone."

Bex locked her eyes on the thick grass growing around her burning legs. She was still heartbroken over her sisters, and she had no idea how they were going to kill a king who never left his Heavenly fortress and could knock her over with a bell, but when Adrian said they could do it with that smile on his face, Bex believed him. She couldn't *not* believe him, because he'd been right, too.

They *had* won.

Now that Adrian had pulled her out of her literal pit of despair, Bex could hear Iggs and the others out in the woods, rounding up the last of the demons who hadn't run when their warlocks died. No one sounded injured, Adrian's forest was beautiful and sunny again, there were no armies of Heaven falling out of the sky to crush them. They were all just... alive. They were *alive*.

She started laughing then, grabbing Adrian's arm for support as everything they'd accomplished started hitting her all at once. Forget the prince. They'd just killed every warlock in the Pacific Northwest! None of *those* assholes would be coming back, which made this her most successful slave-freeing run ever. For the first time in her life, she'd scored a lasting victory, and she hadn't had to burn anything irreplaceable to do it!

That was the headiest thought of all. She'd killed a prince, and her life wasn't ruined. That brought her prince-kill count for this life up to two, a damn impressive number for divine monsters no one was supposed to be able to touch. It was still a far cry from taking on the armies of Heaven, but if Bex kept training and getting better at using her bonfire, maybe Adrian's idea wasn't so crazy. Maybe they *could* keep winning. Maybe this was the start of something—

All those dizzying hopes became actual dizziness as the whole world began to spin. *Oh yeah*, Bex thought as Adrian steadied her. Still bleeding. Pretty badly, if Adrian's horrified expression was anything to go by.

"I didn't realize you were so injured," he said, his voice shifting into serious doctor mode as he started digging through his pockets. "We've got to get that bleeding under control. Put your flames out, and we'll get you back into the medicinal bath. That should keep you stable until—"

"No," Bex said.

Adrian's head whipped back up. "Why not?"

She crossed her arms over her chest, face flaming brighter than ever. "Because if I put my flames out, I'll be naked, and unlike the rest of you, I still care about that."

He looked at her like she was crazy, and Bex dropped her eyes before she died of embarrassment.

"Just let me go up to my room for a shirt or something," she grumbled, struggling to stand. "I've made it this far. I won't bleed to death in the next five—"

Her voice cut off as Adrian shot to his feet and turned around. He took off his coat next, passing it behind his back to her without looking.

Bex took it with a sheepish expression. Nothing she'd done so far had singed him, but she still breathed a sigh of relief when the black fabric didn't burst into flames as she wrapped it around her body. Maybe in time she could learn not to burn off her own clothes when she ignited. For now, though, Bex was perfectly happy to let her flames die out as she snuggled into Adrian's coat. She was still enjoying the amazing smell—seriously, everything the man owned smelled like an expensive tea shop—when Adrian scooped her into his arms and started running through the thick new grass toward his house, yelling at Boston to get the water going.

Chapter 18

On the other side of the country, in a beautiful forest where night had already fallen, a teenage girl with pale skin, dark hair, and bright blue eyes crouched in the moss beneath an ancient tree, watching moths.

It was one of her favorite activities. Moths' flights were so chaotic, and unlike butterflies, they were *fast*. No matter how closely she watched, the girl could never guess which direction their frantically fluttering wings would take them, which was a real treat for her. Most things were so predictable she have could set a clock by them. The grave by her feet, for example, would be bursting open in three... two... one...

A pale, gnarled hand shot up through the freshly turned dirt. A second hand followed a moment later, this one clutching the long, carved-bone handle of a scythe. The hand dropped the scythe as soon as it was out, freeing both palms to press into the mossy ground as Lydia Blackwood, Old Wife of the Bones, levered her body out of the earth.

She sat up in her grave with a gasp that turned into a choke as she began coughing out mouthfuls of dirt. Never taking her eyes off the moths, the teenage girl handed her the towel she'd brought along for exactly this purpose. Lydia snatched it at once and began wiping the rich, loamy soil out of her eyes with a furious scowl.

"You could have dug me out."

"I could have," the girl admitted, her eyes locked on the furiously fluttering wings of a hawk moth. "But I knew you'd be in a foul mood, so I decided to let you take it out on the dirt instead of me."

Lydia stopped scrubbing the towel over her face. "You knew he'd refuse to come home?"

The girl turned away from the moths just long enough to give the old witch a scathing look, and Lydia went back to cleaning her face with a sigh.

"If you already knew how this would end, why did you let me waste my time?" she grumbled, sticking the corner of the towel into her mouth to get the dirt off her teeth. "Does he survive the prince, at least? Or did I just abandon our nephew to his death?"

"He's fine," the girl said, her expression growing sad as the last of the moths flew away. "Agatha's children are resilient."

"Try pigheaded."

"The Blackwood loves him," the girl reminded her. "Always has. That's why Agatha let him come back."

"That means absolutely nothing," Lydia snapped as she hauled the rest of her bony old body out of the ground. "The Blackwood loves everyone who spreads its seeds, and Agatha's always been soft when it comes to her children."

"But I am not," the girl said, rising to her feet. "Don't forget, I also voted to let Adrian return."

Her young face curled into a smile at Lydia's cutting look. "It was a calculated risk. One that's already paying off if he was able to kick *you* out of his forest."

"Adrian's prowess as a witch was never in question," Lydia grumbled, her wrinkled face growing worried. "But I fear for him, Muriel, and for us. I recognize these events. This is the path you warned us about when we first agreed to move our trees to the New World. The one you said you didn't want to take."

"I don't want it," the Witch of the Future admitted, her narrow shoulders sagging. "But the world doesn't care what I want, and we're running out of options." She looked up at the moonlight shining through the forest's canopy. "The Blackwood grows smaller. The warlocks have done much damage in their greed. Damage they could not have inflicted if the Eternal King did not permit it."

She looked back at her older sister. "Gilgamesh's patience with us grows thin. When it runs out, he will do to our coven what he did to all the others."

"He won't," Lydia said, gripping her scythe. "He *can't*. He needs us."

"He sits upon the throne of the gods," Muriel reminded her. "Every year, his control over the cycles strengthens. Soon, he will want for nothing. We must act before that happens, or there won't be much use for a Witch of the Future."

"And Adrian's the one you chose?" Lydia asked skeptically.

"You grow the seeds you're given," Muriel replied with a shrug. "But he's always been a clever boy. I'm sure he'll figure it out."

Lydia arched a pale, wispy eyebrow. "Is that what the future shows you, or are you just saying what you hope?"

The girl smiled cryptically as she grabbed Lydia's hands, pulling her oldest sister deeper into the forest.

Bex did fall asleep in the bath this time.

Technically, she was asleep before she got in. Adrian and Boston were still dumping herbs into the soapstone tub when she passed out right there in the greenhouse chair, though not from blood loss. Once Adrian got a proper bandage on her wound, she'd started regenerating blood like crazy. It was the fire that had burned her out.

She hadn't realized how exhausting all that anger was until it stopped. Maybe wrath *was* a poison, because now that her flames were gone, Bex felt like she'd been on a week-long bender. Everything hurt and *nothing* worked, leaving her uncoordinated and punch-drunk as Adrian scrambled to get her into the tub.

She woke up several times during the night but always drifted right back off. She was just so tired, and the water was so *nice*. The warmth and the sweet smell of the numbing herbs sucked the pain right out of her, leaving her feeling weightless and clean when she finally opened her eyes to see the morning light falling through the dappled leaves above the greenhouse's glass roof. She was enjoying the unexpected beauty of the silver steam wafting through the sunlight when she realized Adrian was sleeping in the chair beside her.

Bex went still, holding her breath. She'd never seen him asleep before. She didn't think he'd slept since he'd arrived in Seattle, actually. Bottled nights must not have been good for everything, though, because he looked as exhausted as she'd been. He was slumped over in his chair with his head resting against an enormous potted fiddle-leaf fig and Boston snoring in his lap. They'd clearly been watching over her all night. Bex waited to feel guilty about that, but all she felt was grateful and cared for.

That was enough to send a blush all the way to her toes. She ducked deeper into the water to hide it, which was when she realized her body didn't just feel painless. It felt *amazing*, even better than the first time she'd stepped out of the bonfire, and her wound didn't hurt at—

She jerked, splashing the water as her hands went to her stomach, but there was nothing to feel. The giant gash the prince had put across her abdomen was gone. At least, she assumed it was gone. Bex couldn't actually see her stomach because this bath was much more opaque than the last one.

She didn't know if that was medical necessity or a practical measure to keep her from dying of embarrassment again, but Bex was very grateful for it, especially since the blue-green water was so beautiful. It glowed when she moved her hands through it, the ripples sparkling like stars. She was dripping some off her fingers just to watch it twinkle when she heard Adrian moving.

"Hi," she said when he opened his eyes.

"Hi yourself," he replied with a yawn, rolling his shoulders to stretch out the kinks. "How are you feeling?"

"Incredible," Bex told him, shaking her horns to knock the condensation off before it could drip into her hair, which he'd once again braided into a coil on top of her head.

She was going to have to ask him how he did that sometime. For now, though, Bex sat up as much as she could without exposing herself and bowed her head.

"Thank you for healing me," she said respectfully, keeping her horns down until she heard him start to squirm. "This makes twice you've saved my life, but how did you heal the cut from the Blade of Gilgamesh without putting me back into the fire?"

"Experience," Adrian said, petting his cat with a proud look on his exhausted face. "Spells are always easier the second time you do them, and I had a bit of extra help."

He nodded at the empty bottles scattered all over the floor. Very familiar empty bottles, Bex realized as her glowing eyes shot wide.

"You used my deathly water?"

She hadn't meant to sound so accusatory. Adrian had healed the unhealable twice now. The least she could do was pitch in, but she'd been fighting to collect that water drop by drop for so long. Dumping it into a bathtub, even a magical healing one, just felt wrong.

"We only used five bottles," Adrian assured her. "It was Iggs's idea, actually. I was planning to build another bonfire, but he said you used to bathe in the rivers to heal after battle. Since you're still a daughter of Ishtar, we figured it was worth a shot."

Bex blinked. She didn't remember bathing in any healing rivers, of course, but she hadn't considered that Iggs might. He never talked about it, but all the wrath demons trapped in Limbo were the original ones captured during the war. It made sense, then, that Iggs would remember the time before Gilgamesh came. He might even have known Bex back when she'd been an actual queen, which was weird to think about, though it would explain why Iggs had always been so quick to bow.

"Well," she said, stowing those questions for later, "I'm just glad it worked. I've got tons of water now that I don't have to save up for my next life anymore, which is lucky, since I'm probably going to be taking a lot more hits now."

She expected Adrian to scowl at that, but he just nodded. "How long do you think we have before they attack again?"

"I'm surprised they haven't already," Bex answered honestly. "It's nice to know Gilgamesh can't pull princes out of his hat, but I don't think he'll let us rest for long." She bit her lip. "Are you *really* sure you want to—"

"Yes," Adrian said, moving a yawning Boston to the floor. When his legs were free, he slid off the chair and crouched beside the tub.

"I meant every word I said yesterday," he told her in a solemn voice. "The only reason I wasn't all-in from the beginning is because I didn't realize how big this was. I thought my troubles ended with the warlocks, but that's like thinking you've rid your house of termites because you've killed the ones you can see. This whole world is rotten with Gilgamesh. I don't know if I can fix that, but I'll be damned if I don't try."

Bex looked down at the water. "You're more likely to be damned if you *do* try."

"Good thing my soul already belongs to the Blackwood, then," he said with a laugh.

She was about to tell him this wasn't something to joke about when Adrian stuck out his hand, wiggling his fingers until Bex gave him hers.

"I know exactly how serious this is," he said, squeezing her palm tight. "I saw the aftermath of your fight with the prince, and it doesn't change a thing. You're the only person I've ever met who's been willing to fight back against Gilgamesh, so I'm with you, Bex." He squeezed even tighter. "I'm with you to the end."

It was on the tip of her tongue to say it'd be a short trip, but the words wouldn't come, because when Adrian looked at her like that—like he honestly believed they could win—Bex believed it, too.

"Guess I'd better get out of my stew pot, then," she said, freeing her hand before he noticed she was shaking. "Is there a towel?"

349

"On the stool beside the stove," Adrian said, rising to his feet with another stretch. "Lys brought you some clothes as well. I'm going to go warm up a night of sleep. The healing wasn't bad, but I forgot how hard that chair is on my back."

"Thanks for sitting up with me," Bex said.

He gave her a warm smile. "Anytime."

Bex sank back into the tub, counting on the hot water to explain why she was so flushed. When she heard Adrian moving things around in the other room, she stood up and toweled off, making sure she was dry enough not to drip all over the floor before stepping out of the tub to grab the stack of folded clothes.

Considering who'd picked them, Bex was braced for something scandalous, but Lys had stuck to Bex's usual uniform of baggy black T-shirt, shapeless black jeans, black sports bra, and black underwear sold by the twelve-pack. It was the same outfit she'd been wearing since her first fight with the prince in Limbo: cheap, easily replaceable clothing that concealed her boniness and didn't show blood. Each piece was a solid, practical choice, but as she held the clothes in her hands, all Bex could think was how much she hated them.

She didn't want be someone who dressed like she was already dead anymore. That was probably why her fire burned these clothes and not Adrian's, because deep down, she'd been furious. Not at the clothes themselves, but at what they represented: the surrender, the waste, a whole life just written off. *That* was what Bex hated, and it was just starting to occur to her that she didn't have to put up with it anymore.

In losing her immortality, she'd gotten back her life. Not some future version of herself who'd do better, but *this* life. She could buy clothes she actually liked, spend money on things other than bare necessities, because Bex was no longer scavenging a ruined existence. She was just...alive. And until Gilgamesh found a way to crush that out of her, Bex decided right here, right now, that she was going to make the most of it.

Feeling better than she could ever remember, Bex threw her on her ugly clothes for the last time and jogged through Adrian's house into the clearing. She'd intended to find her crew and have a serious talk about what came next, but when she got outside, a whole scene was waiting.

Thanks to whatever Adrian had done during her fight with the prince, the clearing in front of his house was now a charming meadow carpeted in grass and dotted with flowers. It was also *full* of demons. Lys and Iggs were over by the RV while Nemini sat on the roof, not even pretending to read as she kept an eye on the crowd of strangers. Iggs waved when he saw Bex coming. Bex was about to wave back when she spotted the pile in the grass at her wrath demon's feet.

"Holy crap," she said, hurrying over for a better look.

Iggs was standing in front of a heap of wallets as tall as his knees. There were car keys in there as well, also smart phones, designer watches, diamond tie pins, money clips full of cash, and an entire five-gallon bucket of quintessence that Lys was swinging from their fingers like a hunting trophy.

"What's all this?" Bex asked.

"Loot," Iggs answered smugly. "While you were inside having your spa treatment, the rest of us cleaned up the forest and searched the bodies. This is our take."

Bex gaped at the pile on the grass. "All of *this* came from the warlocks?"

"Even bad warlocks are rich," Lys said, patting their bucket of quintessence.

Bex nodded, still in shock. It was finally starting to dawn on her just how *many* warlocks they'd eliminated. "What did you do with all the bodies?"

"Adrian has a composting system," Iggs said casually. "The trees were eating some, but apparently that's not good forest management, so he made the roots cough them up, and then we gave what was left to the pigs."

She blinked in confusion. "Since when does Adrian have pigs?"

"They're not *his* pigs," Iggs explained. "He borrowed them from a farm up the island."

"In the middle of the night?"

"I don't know if the farmers in question *realize* their pigs were borrowed," Iggs admitted. "But it's fine. He's going to give them back."

"Well, I think it's very efficient," Lys said blithely. "Cleans up the whole mess at very little inconvenience to ourselves. He really is the best client we've ever had."

Iggs grinned. "Not a client anymore. Adrian told me he's joining on legit. You know what that means, right?" He rubbed his big hands together. "We finally have a cook!"

"Why are you excited about that?" Bex asked. "You don't eat food. What's he going to do, simmer your gamer rage?"

"Just because I don't technically need to eat doesn't mean pasta isn't life," Iggs argued. "And *you* eat food now. Someone has to make that, and Adrian knows how. He also comes with a hidden base, medical skills, and a *cat*! Seriously, we are making out like bandits here."

Bex couldn't fault that logic, so she ceded the field to Iggs and turned around to study the silent crowd of demons watching them from the clearing's other side.

She'd assumed they were the freed victims of Adrian's traps. Now that she was actually looking, though, Bex realized there were a lot more demons here than the traps accounted for. They were all different kinds, too, including several non-combat demons she was certain hadn't been in the mix yesterday.

"Where did the non-coms come from?" she whispered to Lys.

"Same place as everyone else," Lys whispered back. "The warlocks weren't going to risk their house slaves on a raid, but then they died and left those demons alone. The demons didn't know what to do, so they called the other slaves, and eventually everyone ended up here."

"Why here?"

"Because that's where you are," Lys said, flicking their eyes to Bex's horns. "They're waiting for you to tell them what to do."

Because she was a queen.

"Right," Bex said, taking a deep breath. "Here we go."

Lys gave her a reassuring squeeze and stepped back, falling into line beside Iggs as Bex walked toward the crowd.

It was pretty intimidating. Bex had known who she was and what was expected of her since before she could remember, but she had almost no experience with normal queen stuff, like public speaking. That suddenly felt much scarier than fighting a prince. Gilgamesh's sons just wanted her to die, but these demons were looking at Bex like Lys did, like she was their golden ticket out of the Hells. That was a lot of pressure, but some part of Bex must have still remembered how to do this, because her feet walked her right up to the front of the crowd before her brain could chicken out.

The mass of demons backed away as she got closer. Some bowed their heads, but most just stared, which made sense. Unlike her wrath demons, who'd been damned to an eternity in Limbo, the other queens' subjects still lived, loved, and died as normal. Like Lys, they'd been born into the Hells with Gilgamesh as their only king. The Coward Queen was a legend to them, and not always a good one. She was still a queen, though, a figure from the mythical time before they were all slaves. That seemed to be enough to buy Bex a listen, so she stepped up on a stump, trying to channel Adrian-levels of optimism as she raised her voice over the insect drone and bird calls that filled the new, sunny Blackwood.

"Free demons," she said, "you know me as the Coward Queen, but that is not my name. I am Bex, Queen of Wrath, and I did not run away. I was the first to attack Gilgamesh when he arrived in our lands, but my rage got the better of me, and I was defeated. Unlike the late Queen of Pride, however, Gilgamesh did not destroy me, and I was reincarnated in the living world through the grace of Ishtar. By the time I was old enough to rejoin the battle, Paradise was lost, but it will not remain that way."

She took a deep breath, raising her horned head high. This was what she'd been preparing for, the goal of all her lives. Drox must have felt it, too, because her sword transformed before she could give the signal, appearing in her hand like a smoking brand.

"The time to strike back is now," she said, lifting the black blade over her head. "For fifty centuries, my demons and I have been waging war. I know you've heard rumors of a band of free demons killing warlocks. That was us. We've been fighting Gilgamesh since the beginning, but I was weakened by my deaths and couldn't fight like I needed to. Like *you* needed me to. Now, though, things are different."

She gripped her sword and concentrated, all too aware that this was the same part of the clearing where she'd been failing to ignite all week. Her practice pole was just a few feet to her left, covered in blooming vines. But Bex was as different as the forest was now, and when she fed her wrath into the bonfire this time—the same fury that had burned inside her from the moment Lys first taught her what a slave was—the flames roared up in answer, breaking over her like the dawn.

The crowd of demons stepped back with a gasp. Bex could see the light of her fire dancing over their terrified faces, but the grass at her feet stayed green and supple. Her clothes weren't catching, either, probably because she'd already decided to get rid of them. The sight was still a huge confidence boost, though, and it sent a smile over her face as she raised her sword even higher.

"Thanks to our ally, Adrian of the Blackwood, I have been reborn in my full power," she announced, looking over the silent crowd as her bonfire roared. "I am the Sword of Ishtar once more. *Your* sword, and I swear to you here and now, I will be Gilgamesh's death."

"That's impossible," said a long-faced sorrow demon standing in the front row. "He's the Eternal King. He killed the *gods*."

"He's still human," Bex reminded them. "Humans are mortal, and mortals die. The Celestial Princes were also supposed to be undefeatable, but I killed one and broke his sword just yesterday. If the Eternal King was actually as divine as he claims to be, I should have been destroyed in a pillar of holy fire, yet here I stand, because Gilgamesh *isn't* actually divine or eternal. He's just a king, and no king rules forever."

"But he never leaves Heaven!" cried someone in the back. "He has whole armies up there!"

"Armies that can't leave," Bex reminded them with a grin. "With the exception of the princes, the denizens of Heaven are so bloated on quintessence that they can no longer set foot outside the Anchor Markets. Gilgamesh's only forces here on Earth are warlocks, sorcerers, and princes, and we've already proven we can kill those just fine. With that in mind, here's what we're going to do."

She turned and pointed her smoking sword at the pile of wallets, cash, and keys.

"I want each of you to come up here and claim your warlocks' stuff. I'm giving you their cars, their money, everything. Once you've taken what's yours, I'll cut your slave bands, and you'll be free to go wherever you like. I suggest staying in the greater Seattle area because we've already cleared out all the warlocks here, but it's up to you. The only place you can't be is here with me. I'm the one Gilgamesh will be targeting, and I don't want any of you in the line of fire."

"Why won't you let us stay?" demanded a fear demon, who looked like a pale young woman with fair hair and two wickedly sharp black horns that curved above her head like sickles in her human form. "We want to fight, too! Do you have any idea what they did to us?"

"I do," Bex said. "And there *will* be a time to fight, just not yet. I need you all to take this money and go to ground. Dig in deep, build up your resources, and make a safe refuge for all the other demons I'm about to free. We're just a few right now, but we'll grow with every victory. I need you to help me build on those successes so that when the time comes, Gilgamesh won't be facing a slave rebellion. He'll be facing an equipped and organized army just like the one he used when he conquered Paradise."

A huge round of whispering kicked up at this, and then the only war demon in the clearing, a rare female, stepped forward.

"What if you *don't* win?" she asked, her black eyes shining like obsidian in the roaring light of Bex's fire. "Everyone's here because you're a queen, but we had nine queens once, and Gilgamesh crushed them all. I stayed because I wanted to hear how this time would be different, but killing a prince doesn't win a war. If we do what you say and go off on our own, the warlocks will just hunt us down again, but loyalty is rewarded. If we go back with information about you, maybe we won't be punished."

"And maybe you will," Bex said darkly, sweeping her burning eyes over the crowd. "Let me be absolutely clear. I could order each and every one of you by your names never to mention what happened in this forest. That would be the smart, strategic decision, but I'm not going to do it, because I'm *not like them*. I said you were free to go wherever you wished, and I mean it. If you want to run back to your slavers, I won't stop you, but understand this: if you go willingly back to our enemy, then I will treat you like an enemy, demon or no."

A shiver rippled through the crowd, and Bex took a breath before continuing in a gentler voice.

"I know going free is a risk. Gilgamesh's slave catchers have gotten very good at their job over the eons, but you're not normal runaway demons. You're going to have all the same funds and equipment your warlocks did, and you're going to have me. What I've got planned is going to keep Gilgamesh's forces so busy, they won't have time to worry about where you've gone. And when it's over, when I *win*, there won't be any slave catchers, because *we* will control Paradise, and everyone will be free."

The crowd was quiet when she finished. Bex couldn't tell if it was a hopeful silence or a disbelieving one, but either way, she was committed.

"That's my offer," she said, snuffing out her fire as she lowered her sword. "If you still want to run back to the Hells, you're free to go. Everyone else, form a line to claim your warlock's items. I'll cut your slave bands when you're ready to leave."

The crowd started whispering again the second she finished. Bex left them to it, walking back over to Lys, who was smirking so wide that Bex could see their tiny fangs.

"Nice speech," they whispered as she joined them next to the pile of wallets. "But are you really going to start killing demons who go back to Gilgamesh?"

"No," Bex said quietly, brushing the ash off her shoulder. "But they don't know that, do they?"

Lys chuckled, but Iggs was fuming.

"Well, I don't see why you just gave away our loot," he grumped. "I get that we can't send them out naked, but did you have to give them all our stuff?"

"Yes," Bex said, waving her hand at the wallets and phones and everything else. "The warlocks earned this through their demons' labor. It belongs to them if it belongs to anyone."

"Yeah, but we stole it!"

"Think of it as the price of change," Bex cajoled, lowering her voice. "And this stuff's going to do us a lot more good in their hands than it would in ours. A normal escaped demon has nothing, which makes them easy prey.

We're sending this crowd out with wheels, money, and clean necks. Even if Gilgamesh comes down tomorrow to personally murder us, it'll take the warlocks years to hunt down all the demons we'll set free today. Trust me, we're getting a great return on our investment."

Iggs clearly didn't see it that way, but he accepted her logic with no more grousing, stepping forward to herd the approaching crowd into an orderly line as Bex and Lys got to work figuring out whose stuff was whose.

It took all day to get everyone sorted. Removing the slave bands proved to be the trickiest part, because while the vast majority of demons were happy to be freed, none of them wanted to lose the actual markings. Bex understood why. Clean necks were a spotlight for summoning trouble. Even she painted on fake slave marks when she didn't want to attract attention, which none of these demons did.

She wasn't sure how to do it, though, so Bex, Drox, and a lust demon volunteer sat down to do some fiddling. After a lot of fire and some very close cutting, Bex figured out a way of slicing part of the band instead of burning off the whole thing. This ruined the warlocks' ability to read the demon's name but left the tattoo intact so the demons could still masquerade as bound if they wanted. It wouldn't save them from being re-enslaved later if a warlock learned their name through other means, but discovering a demon's name outside of the Hells was nearly impossible if the demon kept their mouth shut, so Bex deemed it good enough.

When the last demon had been freed and escorted through the Blackwood to the road outside, which no longer had a single SUV parked on its shoulder, Bex stumbled back into the clearing and flopped down next to Adrian, who was sitting on his porch, eating a bowl of pasta.

"Here," he said, handing her a bowl of her own.

"What is it?" Bex asked warily. Not that Adrian's cooking was ever bad, but this whole eating thing was new to her, and she still wasn't entirely sold.

"Penne in marinara," he replied with a grin. "The pasta's nothing special, but the sauce is amazing."

Bex frowned at it for a second, then she picked up her fork and popped a piece of red-coated pasta into her mouth.

"Wow," she said when she'd finished chewing. "That *is* amazing."

"Isn't it?" Adrian said excitedly. "It's from the batch we made right before I left home. The taste will be more complex later in the summer, but the first harvest is always the sweetest." He took another bite and sighed in bliss. "Sauce this good is dangerous. Seriously, I had to cut Iggs off when I caught him drinking a jar in my pantry."

Bex chuckled at the image, chasing the pasta tubes around with her fork for a while as she and Adrian ate in silence.

"That was quite the queenly affair, by the way," he said a few minutes later. "I particularly liked the fire. Very dramatic touch, and you didn't burn your clothes this time!"

"I do figure stuff out eventually," Bex replied with a smile. "I'm just glad I got through everyone in one day. I wasn't sure if I was going to make it toward the end. Even when they're willing, naming demons who haven't bowed to me is exhausting."

"Is that why I was able to say your name so easily when the princess was dragging me away?" Adrian asked curiously. "Because of the time you bowed to me in the greenhouse?"

"I'm sure that helped," Bex said. "But even if I lower my head, my name isn't something just anyone can say. Good thing, too, or I'd really be in trouble." She frowned, thinking. "I think it happened because I told you to call me."

Adrian chuckled. "Thanks for volunteering, then. If you hadn't come running to my rescue, I'm not sure where I'd be right now."

Bex didn't, either, and that bothered her. She was too tired to think about it right now, though, so she ate a few more bites of pasta and set her bowl aside, lying back on the porch to let her aching body relax into the cool, smooth-sanded wooden floorboards.

"I hope we don't get attacked tomorrow," she said, staring up at the beams that supported the porch's roof. "I'd like to sleep in for once. I also want to go shopping."

"Shopping for what?"

"I don't know yet," Bex replied as a smile spread over her face. "Guess I'll figure it out when I get there."

"I need some stuff, too," Adrian said, pulling out his phone to check one of his thousand lists. "Now that I'm settling in permanently, there's a lot of improvements I want to make to the house. Mind if I tag along?"

Bex's smile grew wider in the dark.

"Wouldn't miss it for the world."

Epilogue

In the highest palace of the High Heavens, in a shining tower far above the clouds, a lonely princess waited for her prince.

Only Gilgamesh's golden automatons were allowed to wait with her, for a single princess was a volatile, destructive creature. She howled as she waited, hurling potted plants off the soaring balconies. She sobbed and she cursed, begging the ever-watching golden eye above the door for any information, anything at all. When no answer came, she flew into a rage, tearing gouges in the walls with her dagger-sharp nails. She'd nearly torn the room to shreds when the golden door finally opened, and the Crown Princess stepped inside.

Like all princesses, she was beautiful: as white and gold as the light of Heaven itself save for her hideous hand, which she kept safely hidden under a glove. Unlike the rest of her sisters, however, the Crown Princess had one mirrored silver eye in addition to the usual golden one. It was a gift from the Crown Prince and a mark of her authority, it was also useful for displaying her disgust as she gazed down at the sobbing girl on the floor.

"Get up."

"*No!*" the princess wailed, beating her hands against the polished floor until the marble cracked. "Where is he? Where is my prince?"

"He's no longer yours to cry over," the Crown Princess told her testily. "The Crown Prince, ever may his wisdom guide us, has declared that your fool will not be restored."

The princess stared at her, uncomprehending. Then she launched herself at the Crown Princess with a shriek.

"*No!*" she screamed, clawing at the taller woman's mismatched eyes. "You will not take him from me! You're just *jealous*! You want all the princes for yourself, you—"

She shrieked again as the Crown Princess backhanded her across the room.

"Cease your wailing, selfish creature," the Crown Princess snarled as her sister crashed through the stone wall. "Your failure of a prince brought this upon himself! This is the second time he's died to the Coward Queen. He is unworthy of the glory of Gilgamesh, and so are you. If I had my way, you'd be in the foundry undergoing a full refurbishment to correct your obvious personality flaws. Fortunately for you, the Crown Prince is an angel of patience and mercy, and he has decreed that you shall be given a new prince."

The princess stopped pulling herself out of the wreckage long enough to scoff. "A new prince? From where?"

"One is being decanted from storage as we speak," the Crown Princess informed her haughtily. "Old princes are famously unstable, but that should make you two peas in a pod."

The princess glowered.

"More importantly, he's strong," the Crown Princess continued. "A proven killer from the purges, which is good, since all your sword can do is *heal*."

"It doesn't matter how good he is," the princess said, turning up her nose. "My prince was the love of my life. I will accept no others!"

"You will take whatever the Eternal King gives you," the Crown Princess told her in a deadly voice.

She would have said more, but at that moment, the golden doors opened, and the prince walked in.

It was obvious from first glance that he was an old one. He had the same olive skin and thick, dark hair as all the princes, but he was much shorter than his newer brothers, and his handsome face was ruined by scars. He had a wild, confused look in his silver eyes, a side effect, no doubt, from his time in the Sleep. Gilgamesh took much from his sons after they were retired from service, but this one didn't look *too* degraded. Not that it mattered.

"I won't have him!" the princess declared, stomping her feet. "I want *my* prince!"

"You'll do as you are told," the Crown Princess snarled, her silver eye gleaming, "*Talia.*"

At the sound of her name, the princess went as still as the ivory statue she resembled. Once she was docile, the Crown Princess took her hands and led her over to the prince, who was starting to look very alarmed.

"Celestial Highness," she said, bowing before him. "Welcome back. Your return is a blessing we are all privileged to receive. To celebrate the great joy of your presence amongst us once again, your great and holy father, ever may his wisdom guide us, has given you a princess."

She pushed the still-catatonic Talia forward, plucking the girl's glove off at the last second to press her bare hand into the prince's.

"This is your prince now, Talia," she said, squeezing her sister's shoulders. "He is your reason for living, the light of your life, Heaven made flesh. From this moment forward, your heart beats only for him, and every breath you take shall be in his service."

"I see," Talia whispered, clutching the prince's scarred hand in her trembling one. "My prince, my love, my only love." She fell to her knees, tears streaming down her white face as she pressed her lips against his blessed fingers. "Thank you, sister. Thank you for giving me back my heart."

"You're welcome," the Crown Princess said, patting her on the head. "Now take your prince to the rehabilitation chamber. He has slumbered for many years and will be confused. I expect you to take good care of him until he is ready to complete the task your previous prince failed."

"Speak not of him," the princess begged, staring up at her new prince with adoration. "He was a failure, unworthy of Heaven. There is but one love in my heart now, and he stands in front of me."

She rose to her feet again, smiling at her confused prince as she guided him into the hall. "Come, my beloved majesty. Let's get you back to your glorious self."

The mirror-eyed man followed where she led, stumbling and cursing in a forgotten language as the Crown Princess closed the doors behind him.

Thank you for reading!

Thanks for giving *Hell For Hire* a try!

If you enjoyed Bex and Adrian's story, I hope you'll consider leaving a review. Reviews, good or bad, are vital to every author's career, and I would be extremely grateful if you'd take a moment to write one for me.

The second book in the series is already written and coming out later this year. If you want to be the first to know when it's ready, sign up for my over at rachelaaron.net! List members always get first dibs on anything I put out, and I only email when I've got something new, so there's zero spam. Signing up is free and easy, so come on over and join the fun!

Again, thank you so, *so* much for being my reader. There would be no books without you. Thank you from the bottom of my heart, and I'll see you in the next book!

Yours sincerely,
Rachel Aaron

Want More Books?

Hell for Hire is only the latest addition to the Rachel Aaron menagerie. I have plenty more titles of all sorts for you to enjoy, including five finished series!

Keep paging forward to see my top picks for new readers or visit rachelaaron.net for the full list, and, as always, thank you for reading!

Fortune's Pawn

(written as Rachel Bach)

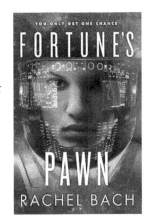

A propulsive space opera perfect for fans of *Firefly* and *Killjoys*!

"Devi is hands-down one of the best sci-fi heroines I've read in a long time." - **RT Book Reviews**

Devi Morris isn't your average mercenary. She has plans. Big ones. And a ton of ambition. It's a combination that's going to get her killed one day—but not just yet.

That is, until she just gets a job on a tiny trade ship with a nasty reputation for surprises. *The Glorious Fool* isn't misnamed: it likes to get into trouble, so much so that one year of security work under its captain is equal to five years everywhere else. With odds like that, Devi knows she's found the perfect way to get the jump on the next part of her Plan. But the Fool doesn't give up its secrets without a fight, and one year on this ship might be more than even Devi can handle.

Powered armor and kissing, what more could you want?

Nice Dragons Finish Last

"Super fun, fast-paced urban fantasy full of heart, and plenty of magic, charm and humor to spare, this self-published gem was one of my favorite discoveries this year!" - **The Midnight Garden**

"A deliriously smart and funny beginning to a new urban fantasy series about dragons in the ruins of Detroit...inventive, uproariously clever, and completely un-put-down-able!" - **SF Signal**

As the smallest dragon in the Heartstriker clan, Julius survives by a simple code: stay quiet, don't cause trouble, and keep out of the way of bigger dragons. But this meek behavior doesn't cut it in a family of ambitious predators, and his mother, Bethesda the Heartstriker, has finally reached the end of her patience.

Now, sealed in human form and banished to the DFZ--a vertical metropolis built on the ruins of Old Detroit--Julius has one month to prove to his mother that he can be a ruthless dragon or lose his true shape forever. But in a city of modern mages and vengeful spirits where dragons are seen as monsters to be exterminated, he's going to need some serious help to survive this test.

He just hopes humans are more trustworthy than dragons.

The first and most popular DFZ series, complete at 5 books.

Minimum Wage Magic

"A catchy title, a plucky protagonist and a maximum effort by the author, honestly readers can't ask for more in the urban fantasy genre."- **Fantasy Book Critic**

The DFZ, the metropolis formerly known as Detroit, is the world's most magical city with a population of nine million and zero public safety laws. That's a lot of mages, cybernetically enhanced chrome heads, and mythical beasties who die, get into debt, and otherwise fail to pay their rent. When they can't pay their bills, their stuff gets sold to the highest bidder to cover the tab.

That's when they call me. My name is Opal Yong-ae, and I'm a Cleaner: a freelance mage with an art history degree who's employed by the DFZ to sort through the mountains of magical junk people leave behind. It's not a pretty job, or a safe one--there's a reason I wear bite-proof gloves--but when you're deep in debt in a lawless city where gods are real, dragons are traffic hazards, and buildings move around on their own, you don't get to be picky about where your money comes from. You just have to make it work, even when the only thing of value in your latest repossessed apartment is the dead body of the mage who used to live there.

A fun, standalone adventure set in the always-wild DFZ, complete at 3 books.

About the Author

Rachel Aaron is the author of twenty-plus novels both self-published and through Orbit Books. When she's not holed up in her writing cave, she lives a nerdy, bookish life in Colorado with her perpetual-motion son, long-suffering husband, and mountains of books. To learn more about Rachel and read samples of all her work, visit rachelaaron.net!

Cover Illustration by *Luisa Preissler*
Cover Design by *Rachel Aaron*
Editing provided by *Red Adept Editing*

As ever, this book would not be as good without my beta reader Linda Hall, the keenest typo-hunter of all time.

Printed in the USA
CPSIA information can be obtained
at www.ICGtesting.com
LVHW042259301124
798033LV00024B/274